1095

MOTHER
GLASGOW

As in *Jamesie's People* and *Incomers*, the first two books of this Gorbals Trilogy, most of the places and many of the events in this book are based on historical fact. While there were people like those in *Mother Glasgow*, all of the characters depicted are of the author's creation and bear no similarity to people living today.

MOTHER GLASGOW

JOHN BURROWES

MAINSTREAM
PUBLISHING

Distributed by
Trafalgar Square
North Pomfret, Vermont 05053

In memory of Wee Meg, 1893–1986,
the Mother Glasgow who made
all this possible.

First published in Great Britain in 1991 by
MAINSTREAM PUBLISHING COMPANY
(EDINBURGH) LTD
7 Albany Street
Edinburgh EH1 3UG

ISBN 1 85158 402 1 (paper)

A catalogue record for this book is available from the
British Library

Typeset in 11/12 Linotron Baskerville by CentraCet
Printed in Great Britain by Billings & Sons, Worcester

CONTENTS

CONTENTS

Mother Glasgow

In the second city of the empire,
Mother Glasgow watches all her weans,
Trying hard to feed her little starlings,
Unconciously she clips their little wings.

(Quoted with grateful acknowledgment
        to songwriter Michael Marra)

CHAPTER I

FEAR

FEAR WAS SOMETHING FRANKIE BURNS AND Sonny Riley knew about. They didn't know it the way other people did, those who understood that courage was the taste of blood, fear the threat of a rusty knife. For fear only happened to other people. Maybe it was that something they would experience if they thought they had cancer, or TB, and knew they were about to die. Perhaps they had been absent when the rules of life were being explained, or some constitutional quotient had freaked and escaped their genes. The only encounter Burns and Riley had with fear was seeing it in others. And when they saw it they revelled in it just as the great Baxter did when he mesmerised the opposition on the football pitch, or like the legendary Benny, the greatest boxer of them all, when another opponent departed the conscious world and two raised fists proclaimed his genius.

But Frankie Burns and Sonny Riley were not of the nobility which was truly exempt from fear. They were fearless but they weren't brave. Bravery was when you knew the livid loneliness of fear and knowingly conquered it. Neither had ever had to do that. Their psyche shortfall couldn't comprehend courage.

That was why Burns had had to suppress the derision

he felt when his Brigade Commander in Malaya congratu-
lated him for his 'devotion to duty ... outstanding gal-
lantry ... distinguished conduct' and pinned on his
Military Medal. Defending his platoon the way he had
under attack, and getting the chance to shoot dead four
they had termed terrorists, was for Burns a dux prize not a
bravery medal. And that was why the shooting hadn't
stopped when his two years in the jungle finished.

There were plenty of people, including the London twins,
who would pay Frankie Burns to do his shooting, or others
who would request, as they pressed the brown envelope
into his hands, 'Just give him a fright, Frankie.'

He never had to defend the fact that he lived by the
wages of fear, for no one ever asked. But if they had he
would have said that it was his luck, just as it was that of
the tennis or the golf champion. That was the way he felt
about getting paid for something he enjoyed.

Sonny Riley had fought in a different kind of jungle but
he had watched the same kind of fear. Burns enjoyed the
fear he gave as a professional, Riley relied on it like a life
support. Fear made Burns a living. Fear was what Riley
lived for.

Burns was from Calton on the north bank of the river
that had mothered Glasgow, Riley was from the Gorbals.
They knew of but didn't know each other, the way that
sportsmen would know those who were and who weren't
their rivals. But that made no difference to Frankie Burns
the night Bert Steed phoned him in London. Burns the
professional never asked why. Only who? And how much?
The sum had been right – an amount that would take a
tradesman half a year to earn. He smiled to himself as he
pondered the name, like a prizefighter would have done
when told an opponent was someone he considered needed
more than a boxing lesson.

'And it's the full message?' he inquired casually, repeating the phraseology Steed had used.

'That's right,' Steed had replied. 'What about an advance?'

'Like a deposit, you mean?'

'Aye.'

'Come off it, Bert. I'm your old army china. Think Frankie Burns forgets the night you helped me out in that scrap we had with the Navy boys in Kuala Lumpur ... and all the other nights we had in old KL? But some expenses wouldn't go amiss. After that it's COD. And, Bert, the "C" stands for cash. Okay?'

'No problem.'

'When do you have in mind?'

'Whenever it suits you. The person who, eh, requested the order asked me to wait till they'd left the country. She's been away about a month now so anytime you can make it'll be fine.'

'She ...! You mean Sonny Riley can't handle his woman problems?'

'Frankie ... it's no' anything like that. It's ...'

'Hold it, Bert. I'm not the jury. Questions aren't my game. I was just surprised, that's all.'

No one had been more surprised than Bert Steed when his boss, Star Nelson, had asked him to arrange Sonny Riley's execution. Bert, the best of her public house managers before becoming her senior executive, knew Star as a close friend. And the Star Nelson he knew was about justice and honesty. Whatever the decision, she would always say, it had to be based on truth and propriety. Others could scorn the system, but she never did. They could have a philosophy that came off the back of a lorry if they liked, but Star would never follow the mob. Even when Sonny Riley had been freed in the great Tallyman trial that had shocked the city and had then murdered her husband's close friend, again with impunity, it was her instinct that justice should prevail. But the justice they kept saying was the finest there was hadn't been just ... had it?

If people like Riley could flout the system, it must be seen that it was being more intent on protecting the accused than the innocent.

Star Nelson had no remedy for a society whose very justice seemed threatened by the way it was being manipulated by lawyers and others. That was beyond her. But the removal of Sonny Riley, the terror of Glasgow's South Side, wasn't. She knew about Frankie Burns, as did others who knew how that stratum of Glasgow society worked. A guarantee didn't come with the justice you bought from the lawyers. But one did when you paid for what you were buying from Frankie Burns. He was lawyer, counsel, judge . . . and executioner.

After the train left Motherwell on the final leg of its long run up from London, Frankie Burns, Guardsman tall and ruggedly handsome and knowing it, smoothed his hair with a big comb, sweeping his long black mane round to the rear to meet in a precise DA, a strange tonsorial art form which placed as much importance on your exits as your entrances.

He smiled into the dirty mirror of the carriage's cramped toilet as he glued on the bushy theatrical moustache, pressing it to his upper lip before neatly combing it into place. It was the dramatic change in his features which made him want to laugh out loud. 'One minute it's Dana Andrews and the next . . . Christ, I'm Joe Stalin,' he thought, and grinned even more.

He had figured there would be a Special Branch 'Busy' hanging about, as there usually was around Platform One where the trains came in from London and the South. Frankie used to infuriate them with a cheeky nod of recognition when he saw them near the ticket gates. But that was when he was on more innocuous visits, merely administering a 'fright' or acting as bodyguard to someone anticipating a 'fright' . . . or worse! But when he was on a rarer kind of mission north, like this one, he didn't want it publicised that Frankie Burns was in town. They had terrible habits, these people they called 'Busies'. They asked questions.

The carriage lurched and jerked as its bogies screeched in protest at negotiating the final right-hand curve from the main line into the gloomy and begrimed cavern of Central Station.

The Central Station in the early Sixties was never the best place to arrive in Glasgow. It was a black and sepia cathedral, an advertisement for everything that was foul about the Industrial Revolution. It jolted you into the monochrome reality of the big city that lay outside, ravaged by such high-intensity smoke pollution that it had garmented the pink and honey freestone of its glorious Victorian splendour in a sullen and sombre pitch pallor. It was a city dressed for its own funeral.

The Special Branch man was there, as Burns had expected, instantly betrayed by the same questioning face and the flitting, filtering eyes as the others. He didn't see, or pretended he didn't see Burns, who had observed him with diverted glances.

It took only two days for Frankie Burns to decide on a time and a place.

Bert Steed had given him what he knew about Riley's routine. He moved around a lot during the day, mainly in his Tallyman operation which, incredibly, was flourishing more than ever despite the sensational trial and the fact that the newspapers had devoted countless pages to the sordid saga of horrendous brutality and the scope of moneylending racketeers in the city. It made people think again about the city they loved and would defend with the protest that such events only happened in a dark and murky past. There it was in black and white for them in the morning and evening editions. Their beloved home-town was as dark and murky as ever it had been.

The gangster Sonny Riley had spread his network of fear and domination by extending into and conquering the gangs of Govan, the dockside and shipyard suburb a couple of miles west along the Clyde from the Gorbals. That made him the undisputed leader south of the river, and one of just three who ruled all the organised forces operating outwith the law in the city.

Had they resided in London or the cities of the New World, Riley and his confrères would have been men of style, even gaining a perverted respectability. The twins, the London twins for whom Frankie Burns had worked, were like that, being hailed as 'friends' by those in show business, by some who were in Westminster and even by the occasional nobleman. But there was no such acknowl-edgment for those who qualified as dignitaries in the world of Glasgow hard men, except the respect of fear from those among whom they lived in the squalor of what was the lot of the ordinary working man. They wished for nothing better and if there was an excuse to be made for that, it would be that they knew nothing better.

Riley's days were predictable. He would visit a group of pubs in Govan Road between Neptune Street and Har-mony Row, where he moved with the authority of an Arabian potentate conducting his majlis. He would decree the punishment to be doled out to recalcitrants of his suzerainty or to those miserable unfortunates who could not raise the four shillings interest it cost them each week for the borrowed pound which bought them their fortified wine, the cheapest merchandisable commodity that could bring some delight to their wretched existence.

At night he could be found near his home in Crown Street in the Gorbals. Home for the man who was the potential king of the Glasgow underworld was a meagre room-and-kitchen flat, one flight up, first door on the left, in a long tenement building, uniformly built like the majority of Gorbals tenements, of blond Giffnock stone, three storeys high, and as with most of them, now suffering from an acute form of advanced senility due to the climate, the pollution and the greedy landlords whose financial commitment to their properties was strictly one-way and based on one of the simplest of principles – greed.

The Gorbals, like its houses, was dying fast. But some of the old style of life still existed. Within a short distance of Riley's house there were over a hundred pubs, 'shops' as they were known, carved from the lower quarters of the serried tenement buildings in which a township of 40,000 souls lived in an acreage approximately that of a modest Ayrshire dairy farm. That was the Gorbals. It mattered little whether the drinking 'shops' were humbly known by the names of their proprietors, like Milligan's, Morrison's, Elder's, Webster's, Quinn's and Lorimer's, or by a flight of the fanciful, like The Why Not, The Bible Class, The Glue Pot or The Splash. They were places to be endured rather than enjoyed: stark and functional academies of the morose where the libation was the only liberation from the engulfing dourness.

Paddy McClafferty's pub, the Old Judge in Lawmoor Street, was Sonny Riley's regular evening haunt, as it had been that of his father before him. Just as Steed had said, he could be found there most nights, but his presence was guaranteed on Thursdays and Fridays.

Because he was known to many of them, Frankie had to take precautions. There was no question of him going into any of the Gorbals' scores of pubs where staring eyes demanded passports of anyone they considered a stranger be fully stamped with a Who, Why, What and From Where. But with a two-day growth, an ill-fitting suit topped with a grubby unbuttoned raincoat and a stained cap, all purchased that day in the Briggait market, Frankie Burns sunk into the near anonymity of the average inhabitant in the bustling south-side suburb.

On the evening of the day after he arrived, a miserably wet November Thursday, Frankie Burns, standing in the dark, outside the Old Judge, observing the comings and goings, made his first sighting of Riley. It was easy to stand unnoticed in one of the dilapidated tenements' entry ways, or closes as they were known – mean, narrow slits carved into the buildings, like letterboxes for humans. They were handy shelters from the rain, or waiting places. Young couples made love in the rear sections of them. Others used them as urinals.

Riley had come out of the pub with a group of people. They had stood together talking loudly while Burns had held his breath and closed his eyes for an orgasmic second at the onrush of that peculiar and thrilling excitement he always experienced in moments like this. He had felt it often in the jungle, the real jungle in Malaya, during that time referred to as 'The Emergency' when the Iban trackers, men they had brought all the way from Borneo and who frequently accompanied their patrols, would suddenly freeze and indicate there was 'enemy' in the vicinity. It was that same sensation experienced by the big-game hunters, when they came upon their first spoor of some prized beast they were after. And there he was, Frankie Burns's very own prized beast, standing only a few yards away and laughing in that distinctive way of his which was more an announcement than an expression of enjoyment.

Riley had been pointed out to him once before when they had been in the same pub. He had that familiar face of someone he didn't quite know but had seen often before in dance and snooker halls and pubs where men of their sort mixed. And despite all the other noises in the busy room, he heard, and was always to remember, Riley's laugh. It was a raucous, challenging cackle that turned heads but defied anyone to ask 'What're you laughing at?'; a laugh that said, 'Look at me, but meddle at your peril.'

There was a woman with Riley and when the group split up she had gone with him, her tight skirt restricting her steps, forcing her to semi-trot as she walked beside him hanging on to an arm. Steed had been right about that guarantee of him being there on a Thursday night. It would be the same, therefore, the following night.

It had been a long wait but it was worth it, for Burns was able to establish that, in the poorly lit streets, there was no problem in following the couple unobserved to Riley's house in Crown Street. He was also able to establish exactly where that house was. The thought crossed his mind that this would be as good a time as any to do what he had to do to this man. But, no, he would wait till the following night for that would give him a chance to study an escape route from Riley's house. That was a much more professional thing to do.

The best way, he was to discover after the couple went into the house, would be out the rear of the building into that area they called the back court, where they housed the refuse bins in brick shelters. These rear yards were divided by high, metal railings which once were topped with vicious spikes, but because of the shortage of metal during the war, these had been removed, making the railings easy to scale. However, there would be no need for scaling – big gaps in the railings made it possible to run unhindered through to the adjoining back court of the houses in Hospital Street, and from there it was only a short walk to Main Street which led to the bridge across the Clyde and into the city. Then he could retrieve his good clothes which he had left in a case at the left luggage office in the Central Station, where he could also get a quick bath, change, revert to his 'Stalin' look, then relax with a drink on the train south.

As with the Guards, it was training, preparation and planning which this game was all about and he now had his plan formulated in his mind. All it required was for Riley to comply with his usual Friday night routine, just as he had this Thursday night.

Burns stayed that night as he had the previous night in a rooming house for men in Lawmoor Street only a few hundred yards from the Old Judge. It was one of the places they knew in Glasgow as a 'model', a shortened term for model lodging house, a title that was more of a lie than a euphemism. There was nowhere more anonymous to live than in a model. In a society which created its drop-outs and then cast them aside, the models were the only refuge. There were few cities anywhere which had a bigger army of men who, for one reason or another, but mainly because of alcohol, had become discarded from the mainstream of normal life. At the entrance of the Lawmoor Street model there was a crudely scrawled sign which obviously wasn't to be taken seriously as the first wording announced 'No drunks admitted'. Thereafter were the prices, one shilling and ninepence for a dormitory bed and two shillings and sixpence for a 'room'. The use of that word was a real joke. The 'rooms' were in a dormitory which had been divided into rows of eight by four foot cubicles made of three-ply board. The furniture was a bed, a chair and a wall hook. The regulars called them 'coffins wi' doors'.

The jungle had been great training for staying in a place like the Lawmoor Street model. The 'modellers' were in the main harmless enough when you saw them during the day, their world being a fuzz created by the weird concoctions they drank of methylated spirits, metal and shoe polishes, colognes and fortified wine made in England from tankered grape ferment spiked with cheap raw spirits. But it was at night that their real worlds emerged, when the agonies of sobriety and dereliction convulsed in pitiful eruptions of nightmares and fantasies. They would vent the height of their feelings with bouts of fearful oaths and epithets amidst the stench, the God-awful stench of urine and vomit. But dedication was the code of the good soldier, the officers would say in the Guards, and besides, didn't such privations always heighten the thrill and the achievement of his work?

A mangy mongrel lifted its leg at the tenement entrance where Frankie Burns stood, the rancid smell of its hot, steamy piss contributing to the putrid mix that was the mark of so many of these close entries. He gave a shiver of disgust at the familiar smells he remembered of the old Glasgow he knew, a rank and raw ragout of blocked drains, overflowing communal toilets, the stench of urine fighting for supremacy with the omnipresent Glasgow tenement malodour of the stale pig and mutton fat they rendered from animal guts and called lard and used for their favourite fried meals. The stinking confusion caught the back of his throat. He had expected it to be like that in the model but he had forgotten that the ordinary people of the old suburbs like the Gorbals still endured life in a fashion of another age. It brought everything back to him of the Glasgow he had once loved but now loathed because he had discovered a better life away from it. He hated it for its poverty, its harshness and, despite the fact he was as hard and as feared as any one of them, he hated it for the fact you had to constantly demonstrate that hardness to gain respect.

It was Friday evening and Burns had returned to the same Lawmoor Street close. It was all so unbelievably predictable. He had been standing there from early on, diagonally across from the Old Judge, and had seen Riley go in, once more in the company of a woman, although a different one from the night before. It would be the same routine when the ten o'clock closing hour was announced. There would be the strident bells and barmen's harsh cries of 'time' in a scenario which had more to do with a penitentiary slop-out than a public house empty-out.

They milled about after they had been cleared from the pub, friends looking for friends, others standing around talking. His attention had been diverted momentarily when there had been a slight skirmish between two men. But then there was always that. Riley and his crowd were standing beneath the same street lamp as the previous night. There were more of them this time, eight men and six women and more coming out of the pub to join them. He could hear them asking if such and such a person was with them and there were louder shouts, women's names that rang out in the night like distress calls ... 'Haw Mag'ret', 'Hey Ina', 'C'mon Sadie'. They were the noisiest of all the groups that had come out of the Old Judge.

Two policemen walked past, then stopped at the far corner of the street, as though discussing whether or not to break up the noisy crowd, now about twenty-strong, standing with Riley. Some groups of this sort were easy to disperse but the sight of Riley and certain others around him indicated this wasn't one of them and after another look in their direction the policemen continued on their beat. Someone in the crowd made a remark and Burns could hear Riley's laughter once more. 'Enjoy yourself, Sonny boy,' Burns thought to himself. 'You haven't many more laughs left.'

After a few more minutes, when it appeared they had all gathered, they moved off together, northwards along Lawmoor Street towards the wide thoroughfare of Caledonia Road. That was in the direction of Riley's house, although they could still be heading anywhere. Normally it would be the men who would carry the heavy bags of alcohol they bought from the pub, but tonight it seemed that the women had been given the task, which puzzled Frankie Burns. Perhaps it was a 'hens' night'. Whatever, it didn't look as promising as it had the previous night; Riley and his

woman stayed with the others as they turned left into
Caledonia Road. At least they were still heading in the
rough direction of Riley's house but wherever they were
destined, it certainly looked like they had a party in mind.
Just as well he had bought himself two big screwtop bottles
of ale. They would soothe away some of the time it looked
like he would have to spend waiting for Riley to be parted
from the mob he was with.

What if the party's in Riley's house? he thought. Shit!
That'd really complicate things. Or would it? He rehearsed
a scenario for that eventuality. He would wait till they were
all gone, and then go up to the house. There would be no
real problem in that, except that it would mean a longer
wait. The woman would be there, of course, but like Riley
she would be half-cut and getting ready to drop her
knickers. All she would remember was some manky bastard
coming to the door. 'And the next thing I knew was that
poor Sonny was lying deid. It was terrible so it was.' Burns
smiled. Of course, when it came to the bit he would have
to find some ruse to get Riley to the door. But Frankie was
good at extemporising and he had a facility with accents
and voices that had always been successfully persuasive on
such occasions in the past.

It started to look more promising as he followed them
along Cu iberland Street in the direction of Crown Street,
walking about fifty yards behind, on the other side of the
road. They stopped at one of the tenement entrances and
three of the women left the group. That was a surprise.
What, weren't they invited to the party or were they off to
another one? Whatever, they were a noisy bunch of scruff,
he thought to himself as the women departed, two of the
men shouting loud sexual innuendoes at them. But there
was a good side to the noise, because when they were noisy
like that they wouldn't be thinking of the anonymous man
trailing behind them and watching every move they made.

When they came to the junction with Camden Street,

four of the women, one of them carrying a bag of booze, parted company from them, again with the same loud and suggestive farewells. What was happening? Frankie wondered. Was it not a party night after all? And why weren't any of the men carrying booze? That seemed strange. Nevertheless, it was encouraging that they were diminishing in numbers, although Riley was still in the company of all the men who had left the pub with him.

They continued walking again, this time down a block's length of Camden Street towards Cumberland Street. They stopped at the crossroads. Two more women shouted their farewells and the remainder of the group carried on, turning left into Cumberland Street. All of the women had now left, except the one who clung tightly to Riley. Would she also leave the men or was she going home with him? The good news was that they were still heading in the direction of Riley's house and since the women with the booze had all left, there was certainly not going to be a party. All he needed now was for Riley to part company from the men – and being with the woman, the chances of that looked good.

It was just after he had passed the well-known pub called The Moy, which had been given a hideous art-deco face-lift of vitriolite and glass brick, and while he was deeply engrossed in the climaxing moves of his stalk, that two men approached walking in the opposite direction. He had been concentrating so much on the group he was following that he hadn't noticed them until they were almost upon him. You had to be sharp at making assessments of men you met late at night on the streets and few were sharper at that practice than Frankie Burns. A glance was enough for these two. They weren't harmless modellers. They were up a notch, maybe two, from that level, which put them in the bracket of gadgies or tappers, the kind that squatted in the derelict houses which the Gorbals now had. Spot on, he thought as he heard their gruff and rough voices, not the

kind you would associate with samaritans. He had pur-
posely walked wide of them but one of them blocked his
route, holding his hands with that feigned look of friendship
as he appealed in a voice that was having great difficulty
in not sounding aggressive, 'Got a fag, pal?'

He had been just a schoolboy when he had first heard
that old Glasgow no-win question. If you had the fag for
which they asked, they would get you as you reached for
your pockets and if you had none they would get you just
for the spite of it.

'Fuck off,' rasped Burns, angrily. He detested parasites
like this.

'Oh, smart bastard . . .' The two of them closed on him.
It was over in a flash. The big heavy screwtop bottle had
exploded in a fountain of sticky beer and blood when Burns
crashed it down on the bald skull of the nearest of the two.
Still clutching the broken-off neck of the bottle, Burns
turned quickly as the other man came at him. It wasn't his
style, but this was war and with a short but powerful nine-
inch jab he pushed the jagged weapon hard into the face of
his attacker, who fell blinded beside his concussed mate.

Frankie cursed his luck at being waylaid at such a vital
moment and when he looked round for the group he could
see them standing together about a hundred yards away at
the far corner of the intersection of Cumberland Street with
Crown Street, one of the main thoroughfares of the Gorbals. They were obviously unaware that anything had
happened and, if they were, it was of no interest to them.
A one-minute skirmish between three men on a Gorbals
pavement! Sunday School stuff, that.

He hurried to make up the distance he had lost, stopping
to turn into the second-last tenement entrance before the
junction, where he could stand unseen and observe as the
group stood talking together in a small circle.

'Hey! Piss off, Jimmy!' said a man's voice in frustration
as much as in anger. He turned quickly and through the

dim and flickering gaslight of the close he could make out the rounded shape of a woman's bare bottom, a hand on each cheek heaving it rhythmically towards the man whose face he could now see. 'Gies a fuckin' break, Jimmy!' Burns smiled and quickly darted out of the close. There was another one not many yards from the junction and he headed for it.

The woman was still with Riley and as she was now the only one in the group his guess was that they would soon break up as he would be anxious to get her to his home, or somewhere, for whatever he had planned for her. Wherever, it would be a lot more comfortable than that couple in the close.

Although the pubs had long since emptied, the street was still busy, with people heading for the nearby Deep Sea fish and chip shop, coming from their houses to get one of the morning papers the vendor was loudly shouting about, or coming off the buses from a night out in the city. Riley was in good spirits judging by the number of times he threw his head back in laughter at something.

Just as the group started to break up, a policeman approached Burns's close. He was checking, as they did in that part of the Gorbals, that the padlocks and doors of the various shops and premises were secure. Across the road he could see his mate, torch in hand, performing the same routine for the businesses on that side. If Burns was seen standing suspiciously where he was, there would certainly be questions and once they got a look at his dress it would be difficult to give them answers. He would have to act fast. Quickly he drew his cigarettes and a lighter from his pocket, then strode purposefully out from the building, stopping briefly and in full view of the policeman to light his cigarette, a signal he hoped would be read as 'here's a man with nothing to hide'. Then he resumed a brisk step again to hurry past the policeman with a greeting in the broadest Cockney he could muster, 'Lovely night, guv.'

The policeman stopped, gave him a quizzical stare, but made no reply. Frankie sighed with relief that it had worked. Then he devilishly pondered on the sight the cop would see if he checked the next close, plus the very different surprise of the two casualties awaiting him further along the road.

He was in the open now and committed to walking in the direction of the group he had been following so meticulously. The newspaper vendor was still bawling 'S'Press an' Reh . . . Kid', and he headed towards him. Although he was now in full view of Riley and his pals, he wasn't concerned as none of them would have recognised him the way he was and, anyway, there were other people milling around the vendor, some stopping after they had got their papers to study the rear pages for the news that was of most importance to them, the winners and the losers of that night's dog race meetings. He did likewise and it was then that he saw the final act of his hunt develop. He could hear their shouts this time as they parted, the men, with the exception of Riley, walking off together, Riley and his woman heading in the opposite direction towards his house.

Why, he asked himself, had he been so concerned earlier on? It was all going to work out beautifully, just as he had originally thought. But he would have to move fast – he wanted to be as near as he could to Riley when he turned into his tenement entry. The thick crêpe-soled shoes he was wearing meant he could run silently to catch up without even the hint of a telltale sound. He slowed to a walk again when he got to within ten yards of Riley, near enough to hear him talking and to be enveloped in the wake of cheap perfume from the woman he could now see had long blonde hair. She seemed much younger than her companion.

As he reached for the inside pocket of his jacket to retrieve the blue-steel Browning pistol, Burns wondered what might be on Riley's mind at that precise moment. Such thoughts had always intrigued him, for whatever thoughts they were, they would be Riley's last impressions on earth. At that point he felt a close and curious empathy with the man who was to be his next victim. He, and only he, knew that Riley had only minutes of his life left. He, and only he, was in charge of that man's destiny. What an awesome power a weapon such as a gun could give a man.

Riley and the woman turned into the dark entrance of the building and as they did so Burns observed his prey give the briefest of glances in both directions of the street, like some wily animal might as it slunk into its den.

They had gone up the first flight of stairs, disappearing out of sight at the half-landing when Burns entered the close. He sprinted soundlessly along the passageway then quickly ran up the first flight of stairs, halting on the last step before the half-landing to cock the Browning. The door to Riley's house was on the left at the top of the first floor and he could hear him turning the key of what sounded like a heavy mortice lock. Just one more step, then a turn to his right and Riley would be there before him at the top of the stairs, a mere twelve feet away. He felt elated at that point, for not only was he achieving yet another mission but for the first time since becoming a hired killer he was also performing a community service. Like everyone else he had read all about the great Tallyman case and he had thought then that Glasgow would be a much better place without people like Sonny Riley. This city had enough parasites. But when he turned that landing corner and raised his gun to take aim there would be one parasite less. Frankie Burns felt good about that.

CHAPTER 2

IN EXILE

THE SHOTS THAT SHOOK A CITY WERE TO reverberate around the world. For years to come people would remember precisely where they were on that fateful day in November 1963. Star Nelson would certainly never forget. She was in the lounge of the weatherboard bungalow she had rented in Elwood Street, Bendigo, in the State of Victoria, Australia.

She still wasn't used to Australian commercial radio at the time. It was like a whole new medium after having been accustomed to the authoritative World Service of the BBC. There seemed to be a different station at every point on the dial, all with their frenetic and seemingly endless advertisements. And because of that non-stop flippancy, she suspected that perhaps the devastating announcement she heard on the first newscast early that Saturday morning, 23 November 1963, on the station they called 3BO, wasn't true after all.

'God, it just can't be,' she had thought.

Not long afterwards, in more sombre and less frenzied tones, it was repeated on the 8 a.m. national news of the Australian Broadcasting Commission. 'It has just been announced,' said the broadcaster gravely, 'that John F. Kennedy, the President of the United States of America, died at 6 a.m. Australian Eastern Time in the Parkland Memorial Hospital in Dallas, Texas. The President had been rushed there after being shot and fatally wounded at 12.30 p.m. local time on Friday.

'The President was on a motorcade in downtown Dallas when the shots rang out. It is not known at this stage how many gunmen were involved and no arrests have so far been reported. We are still awaiting full details but it has been confirmed that the FBI have launched the biggest murder hunt in American history. We will be giving you further bulletins as we receive them throughout the day.'

Star bent over to pick up her little son James, happily playing with some fluffy toys in his basket pram, and hugged him to her in a reflex action of comfort and protection. The death of a husband was something she knew very much about.

Star Nelson still couldn't believe she was in Australia. But then it was still difficult for her to accept all that had happened to her life in the past two years. Not even in the wildest of her dreams, the most far-fetched realms of her imagination, could she have foreseen the events that were to so dramatically unfold in such quick succession. And as for her being where she was, in the land they called the Lucky Country, that would have been not only unbelievable, but unthinkable.

Star Nelson was of Glasgow as much as the tree that never grew, the bird that never flew. Her father, Jamesie, had been one of the legendary characters in the years after World War One; albeit he was a street fighter, but fighters in a place like Glasgow had a far better prospect of being hailed as legend than most. Star Nelson had been a fighter herself, but of another kind. Where Jamesie had out-fought his rivals, she had out-thought hers in her battle to escape the grinding poverty of the Gorbals.

As she held her young son to her, she nudged his face softly with her own and as he giggled in response she wondered for a moment whether this was a dream she was living. Another news bulletin came over the radio, but it was just a sound in the background to her as she paced up and down with her son in her arms, then gazed out at the uniquely rich blue of the Australian sky and thought about the days it seemed had been only yesterday.

It had been a bright blue sky too, the fresh and light blue of a Scottish sky, on the day when she had married her one and only lover, Russell. When you said his name like that no one asked any questions or raised an eyebrow. But Russell was an anglicised form of his real name. That was Rasool. Rasool Jehan, to give him his full name.

Rasool Jehan was from the Punjab in Pakistan. He was one of the sub-continent's light-skinned northerners whose home had been near the Kashmir border. There was an importance in Glasgow then, and probably still would be for many years to come, in such tones of skin colour, for she remembered how any time she announced that she was engaged and going to marry her man from Pakistan they would say quite openly, 'But he's not . . . you know?', and then stop at that and say nothing further. What they meant was that he was all right because he wasn't too dark or, heaven forbid, black, *but* . . . They didn't whisper any longer if you married an Italian, even a Jew. But to marry a Pakistani in Glasgow in the year 1960!

God! Hadn't her Russell been through enough without the whisperers? How many of them had been brought up in a wealthy family and then, in a day and a night, had their parents slain before their very eyes and every earthly possession destroyed at the same time? How many of them had had to trek, penniless and without food, for miles to another country in order to live in peace? How many of them had uprooted themselves even further and gone across the seas in order to seek their fortune . . . and had made it?

It had all happened to her husband. He had lost everything during that bloody time in 1947 when the death knell of the British Raj and the birth pangs of the newly independent dominions of Pakistan and India were to spark the worst violence the sub-continent had known – the Partition Riots. Thereafter, he had joined the millions who took part in history's greatest-ever migration, as Hindu fled from Muslim, Muslim from Hindu, in that period when their respective religions could only demonstrate that they were about hatred and not above love.

Like many others, Rasool's flight was to end in Scotland. And just like the woman who was to be his wife, he too was a battler. He was to begin life in his new homeland like many of his countrymen, as a pedlar, 'going with the case', as they would call it. From that he had progressed to owning a small food store, then another, and yet another until he had a chain of retail outlets under the umbrella of a parent company called Russell Enterprises, with sufficient capital to invest in a wider variety of businesses.

She smiled fondly to herself as she remembered that episode of her life when she had first encountered these new traders from the East. It was in the days of what they called the 'butter war' in Glasgow. In order to attract customers, some Pakistani shops were selling cheap butter, in an early version of the loss-leader tactics which the giant supermarkets were to adopt in later years. She had a small chain of shops and had gone to war with rival Pakistanis who somehow managed to sell their butter cheaper than she did. It had gone to such extreme lengths that she discovered one rival Pakistani buying his butter . . . from her shops. He would then, in turn, sell it for a halfpenny or a penny cheaper, thereby restricting his losses to only that amount per pound, whereas had he been buying from a wholesaler he would have incurred substantially greater losses. But Star was not to be outdone and when she discovered his trick she had posed as an official and confronted him about the way he was buying his butter. The man had been so fearful of any investigations over his dubious butter-buying methods that the trading war swiftly ended.

Star had grown to admire these adventurous Punjabi traders who had come to settle in Scotland, mostly in Glasgow. 'Why shouldn't we be like them?' she used to argue with her Uncle Sammy, Sammy Nelson, her guardian and brother of the father she had lost as a baby. He would infuriate her, of course, when he referred to them as 'darkies'. But Sammy was as much old Gorbals as old rascal and she knew he meant no harm in the expression.

'It's the same with everyone that comes here,' Sammy would state. 'They all get on. And we just sit back and watch them . . . and moan at them.'

'Well, you won't catch me moaning,' she had said. 'I'm going to show them that we can do even better.'

She had. Her attitude was that if they could have drive, zest and enthusiasm then why couldn't she? What did it matter if their forefathers were among the most vigorous traders in Asia? She was as good as the ones who had come here . . . and she would damn well show them.

It was because of that that she had met Russell, her husband-to-be. Her business, established with the help of her Uncle Sammy had by that time developed into a chain of licensed grocers. And her lifestyle had changed dramatically from that of a poor Gorbals girl whose home had been a broom-cupboard of a house, a single-end in a tumble-down and decaying tenement building in the Gorbals, to that of a confident, successful, and beautiful young businesswoman living in a spacious and graceful villa in Pollokshields, a suburb of stone mansions, and one of the most affluent places in the country. At a party in one such house there, Star had been introduced to Russell as a business rival. She fell in love with her handsome Prince Charming from the East. There was no glass slipper, and there were no ugly sisters. But the pair certainly seemed destined to live happily ever after.

Of course, her Uncle Sammy had been shocked at the thought of the girl he regarded as his own daughter marrying a Pakistani. But his opposition was short-lived; he had immediately taken to the man for whom his niece had fallen and after their marriage in Glasgow he had even accepted, although with considerable reluctance, the further and greater shock when they announced they were going off to live in Pakistan, where Russell wanted to consolidate the considerable business interests he had also established there, and Sammy gave them his full blessing when they left for the East.

'It won't be for ever, Sammy,' Star had consoled him. 'I love you too much . . . I love Glasgow too much to stay abroad for long. But I must go with my husband. You understand, don't you, Sammy?' And he did. For Sammy would understand anything that Star wanted. Anyway, just as she had said, he would be busy running the latest aspect of their joint business enterprise, the highly successful chain of lounge bars which she had pioneered and built up from meagre beginnings.

'You'll be so busy, Sammy, you won't even miss me for a minute,' she had told him. 'And when you're not busy with the business you'll be spending your time writing me long letters to let me know everything that's happening.'

The main news bulletin had now come on and she was back in the present once more. This time there were more details of the sensational assassination. They still didn't have the identity of the gunman or gunmen, although they were already beginning to speculate about conspiracy theories, just like they had when Lincoln had been shot.

There was also an item about Mrs Kennedy and how she had been in the car with the President and had witnessed the whole tragic event. How horrible, Star thought, that must have been for her. And there was particular feeling in her thoughts at that moment. For like Jackie Kennedy, she was newly widowed. Her husband had not gone in such a dramatic fashion, but she would never forget the shock it had been when he had died and how alone in the world she had felt; a stranger in a very foreign and very strange land. How fragile, she thought, the thread of life was. There was the President, probably one of the most famous men in the world, and a mysterious gunman ends it all with the pull of the trigger. Star's husband hadn't gone like that, yet it had seemed as untimely and as quick.

He had come home from the office that night complaining of a severe headache and of tiredness. But he had scoffed at her concern and refused to phone for a doctor. 'Don't worry,' he had assured her. 'I've just been working too hard. I'll have a little nap and be a completely new man when I get up.'

She would never forget that night. It was just after the month of the Ramadan fast, which had been such a new experience for her. Russell had gone to work that day, a Saturday – in Pakistan, the equivalent of a British Monday, being the first working day after their holy day. It had been unusual for him to complain about being tired, so instead of having dinner he had gone to bed. His last words were that she was not to forget to waken him later when they would have a meal together. But when she had gone through to his room just three hours later he was lying dead, having suffered a massive brain tumour. They buried him the following morning in a little cemetery where only small rough boulders without an inscription marked the fact a grave was there.

Everything had been such a shock to her ... the suddenness of his death, the way they had taken him away so early the following morning wrapped merely in a plain white shroud, barring her way when she had wanted to accompany them to the graveyard. The impact on her of the abrupt ending to his life had been compounded by the almost instantaneous burial.

She had felt she was living a nightmare and that strange men in weird and exotic clothing had come and forcibly taken her husband from her without showing her where they were going with him. He had been there in life with her one day, dead and buried with barely an earthly trace of him the following.

It had been only a year since they had left Glasgow for Pakistan, an affluent young couple with such a promising life ahead of them. Now everything had gone. Even the considerable wealth that he had generated in his life was not to be hers for, and again by Muslim tradition, it had to be shared among the family, and an amazing number of beneficiaries had come forward, cousins and yet more cousins and their families. By the time they had got what their laws decreed, Star was left with a meagre amount to bring up her little son. She could never have afforded him the kind of education in Pakistan she would have wished and without the influence of a father she decided she would have to leave. But to go where?

Little James had gone to sleep now and she adjusted the mosquito net around his cot. At least the ones in this part of Australia didn't carry malaria like they did in the Punjab. But they still gave a nasty bite and the young child had just that week suffered two bad nights' sleep because of the itchy bites he had on his legs.

She was able now to listen more intently to the special programmes on the radio about the world-shattering news from Dallas. They were looking at every aspect of the late President's life. There was one programme on the Cuban crisis and how he had stood up to the Russians over the sending of missiles to Havana. There was another on his well-publicised trips around Europe, including the one with his famous speech in Berlin. There were other programmes on his life story, on the Kennedys and on his beautiful wife Jackie. Each hour brought up some new aspect of one of the most sensational assassinations of the century. There was also a feature programme on the friends of the Kennedys and on how the President had relied on a small inner-circle of lifelong associates as his closest advisers and confidants. 'Where would he have been without these people?' the announcer relating the story had said.

Star thought that very same thing. For where would she have been without her lifelong friend Ella Brady when Russell had died? Despite the support they would have offered her and wished her to have, Russell's family were alien to her. Their ways were not her ways, nor ever would have been. But Ella Brady's were. Ella had been Star's closest and longest friend. They had gone to the Camden Street School together in the Gorbals. And when she had returned to live there after the years she had spent as a wartime evacuee in the country, it had been Ella who had found her work in Gordon's clothing factory as a trainee machinist.

They had kept up a regular correspondence when, with her husband Bill and their two young daughters, Ella had migrated under the Government's Assisted Passages scheme to Australia. Their letters had become even more regular when Star had gone to Pakistan and it had been to Ella that she had opened her heart about the crisis in her life following the death of her husband. She remembered the terrible plight she had been in when she had written that letter.

My dear Ella,

I have the most terrible news. My darling Russell died two nights ago of a brain tumour. He was buried, literally, within hours. It has been the most terrible shock to me for everything happened so quickly. It was as though they snatched him from me. As is the custom here, there's not even a decent resting place for him, in the sense, that is, that we might think of one at home. Oh, dear Ella, it has been awful. I feel my whole world has come to an end. Of course I should be returning straight home with young James to Sammy . . . but, Ella, something has happened to him. He hasn't written for nearly a year, not even a reply to the news that I was pregnant and that he would be a 'grandfather'. It took me weeks to get a phone call through and when I did there were new owners living in our house in Pollokshields. They had no information about Sammy. I fear the worst for him. I have never felt like this in my life. Thank God for little James, he is such a comfort to me.

Ella had replied immediately.

Dearest Star,

Oh how I feel for you, my dear. I wish I could put down on paper some words of true comfort but what can one say that soothes at a time like this? You must be terribly, terribly lonely. About your Uncle Sammy, Star. I had a letter this week from May McKinlay. Remember she worked in your lounge bar? She said there are new owners and that Sammy has gone off to America. Does that make sense? But at least he appears to be all right. As for you, Star dear, you must get away from Pakistan as soon as you can and be with your own people. We would love to have you here. Bill inquired at the shipping office. There's a monthly sailing from

Karachi to Melbourne and it only takes about ten days. You could be here as quick as you would be going home. Accommodation is plentiful and anyway we have a spare room you can have till you get a place of your own. The weather is just magnificent. Australia is such a relaxing place and the change will help you get over things until you decide about the future. Don't think twice about it, Star. Write and tell us you'll be coming. We all love you.

It had been the news from another friend which made Star's mind up about her future. The letter was from Bert Steed and had arrived within a week of the invitation from Ella to go to Australia. It read:

Dear Star,
  I should have written this letter a long, long time ago. I only write now because of recent developments. Obviously I cannot spell everything out in a letter but know that you will understand all that I write here.
  I went ahead and arranged what you requested and it was due to take place one month after you and Russell left for Pakistan. He came up from London and was pleased to take on the work for he said it would benefit Glasgow. But then on the night he had it all planned, everything went wrong. Heaven only knows what happened as he was a very methodical and careful planner about things like this. As you can imagine, it has had a devastating effect on us all. Your Uncle Sammy had to go to America because of it and I am now living and working in England. Sammy, by the way, went to Kearny, New Jersey. You will obviously be interested in the cutting from the newspaper I am enclosing. I know you will understand and forgive me taking so long to write.

The story from the newspaper had been headed '*MALAYA HERO FOUND STABBED*' and went on:

Former Scots Guardsman Frank Burns who was decorated with the Military Medal for his bravery on active service in Malaya was found stabbed to death in the early hours of yesterday morning. His body was discovered by cleansing department workers as they were collecting refuse from the rear of houses in Hospital Street, Gorbals. Police believe that Burns, originally from the Calton but who had been living in London, was the victim of a gang feud. It is understood that a number of men may have been involved in his death. A senior detective revealed that he could not recall a murder in which the victim had been so badly mutilated. No arrests have been made so far but inquiries are continuing.

Star was never to tell her friend Ella this aspect of the chapter of events which had occurred in her life. That was between her and Bert Steed and not another living soul; not even her Uncle Sammy had known. But it was certainly the deciding factor that late summer's day in 1963. She had gone to the P&O agent's office in Sialkot to arrange tickets for her and her young son to sail to Melbourne.

'And when do you wish to return, madam?' the clerk had politely inquired.

'Oh . . . just single tickets, please,' Star had replied. 'We won't be returning.'

CHAPTER 3

DOWN UNDER

AUSTRALIA WAS A WORLD AWAY FROM ANY-where, thought Star, cradling James to her as their ship left the stormy waters of the Southern Ocean and the treacherous Bass Strait to sail through the narrow gap they called the Rip and into the more placid waters of Port Phillip Bay. The chill southerly wind, the grey, threatening skies and the distant hills looming reminded her of the Firth of Clyde and of Scotland. Less than two weeks ago when she had left Karachi it had been late summer, with stifling temperatures well into the hundreds every day. Now, just these few days later, it was into late winter. Another season, another climate . . . another world.

There was pandemonium when the ship edged slowly in towards Station Pier at Port Melbourne. Before leaving the Mediterranean and calling at Karachi, the ship had picked up hundreds of migrants at Kalamata in southern Greece. The big liner had anchored in the deep water off the small town and the emigrants had struggled on board laden with their possessions in bulging, battered cases, and cardboard boxes full of oranges, cheeses and sausages. For some reason they were under the illusion that they would have to feed themselves until reaching their destination in the Southern Hemisphere.

Many of them were young single women and that was the principal reason for the pandemonium at the pier. They were proxy wives, sent for, as was the custom of the Greek exiles, on the basis of a photograph or the recommendation of their family. And before the ship had a chance to tie up, the young husbands-to-be were in a near riot with police and customs men as they scrambled and fought to shin up the first of the mooring ropes, while others made spectacular and perilous leaps from the quayside to grab the ship's rails, in order to clamber on board and search for the real-life version of the photograph they held aloft.

There were hundreds of others too, from Sicily and southern Italy, and they were fighting on the dockside with the Greeks, never the best of friends, to be as near to the ship as they could. Exasperated police were battling to keep order, as were the customs men, endeavouring in vain to enforce Australia's strict food hygiene laws and prevent anyone in that mad and frenzied crowd from catching the salamis and the mortadellas and salciccia and other native specialities relatives had brought and were tossing from the ship.

From the big liner's rail, the women passengers were screaming in Italian, Greek, Turkish, Maltese and a panoply of patois in a bid to get the attention of someone they had recognised in the dockside mêlée.

Star had been standing on an upper deck looking for a sign of Ella but instead had been caught up in watching the near riot among the waiting men on the dock. A tall and lean returning Australian standing beside her took a quick look at the scramble and turned in her direction. 'Bloody dagoes,' he said in obvious disgust. 'Our bloody country's going to be overrun by the bastards and all the other bloody DPs they're bringing over. And they're calling them bloody New Australians now. Know what I'd do with the lot of them? Send the bastards packing.'

It was a memorable welcome to Australia.

*

'Here, slip this under your feet,' said Ella, pushing a long, heavy object towards Star. 'It's more than just an ordinary foot rest. They're a great idea,' she continued as she helped her friend settle into the train at Spencer Street Station for the journey north from Melbourne to Bendigo.

'Oh . . . it's warm,' said Star, surprised.

'It's made of lead and they heat them up in the winter then put them in the carriages to keep you warm.'

'That's funny. On the train we took south to Karachi they did the very opposite. There were big containers overhead in the carriages and they put ice in them . . . to keep you cool.'

'What a beaut idea,' said Ella.

'Beaut?' repeated Star, laughing. 'My, but you've certainly got the Aussie twang.'

'Too right,' said Ella, exaggerating her new-found accent. 'I did a crash course on it. Do you know, when we first arrived in Bendigo they couldn't make out a word we said. Really. I mean, we weren't all that broad . . . were we? Anyway, they just didn't understand what we were talking about. So it was either go through life like that or else try and speak the way they do. I don't want to speak exactly like them, but we've had to adapt so that's why I'm full of beauts . . . and too rights . . . and she'll be apples . . . and bloody hell and bastards too. But they're not really swear words here . . . bloody and bastards. You never hear eff, you know, but it's bloody and bastards all the time. Just an acceptable part of the language. No one even looks up when they're said. But they don't say them the way they do at home. You know, all that anger . . . that venom.'

The two women had warmly embraced when they had finally met up at the ship, Ella emotionally weeping at the occasion. Now in their mid-thirties, they were as different in appearance and style as they had always been. Star was slim, elegant and composed, her long auburn hair tied in a chic broad red ribbon, Ella matronly and fussing after her old friend like an older sister.

'You've always meant a lot to me, Star, but now you mean much much more,' she had said. 'Just seeing someone from home . . . and talking to them . . . and holding them . . . oh my God, you've no idea the thrill this gives me.'

'No Glasgow people where you are, then?'

'Haven't met any. It's such a huge country. Unbelievably huge. Well, for instance, it's winter here just now. But if you go up north the sun would be splitting the stones. And because we're such a big country you don't find large groups of Scots in any particular place.'

'You said because "we're" such a big country, there, Ella. Like it was *your* country.'

'Well, it's been nearly eight years now. I suppose in a sense we do think of it as our country. Scotland's home, where we were brought up, the greatest wee country with the greatest people in the world. But I think I'd say that about Australia too, and with a lot more conviction, if I'd been born here. This place is *really* something special. Anyway, I'm sure you'll like Bendigo. It's only about a hundred miles to the north but it's on the other side of what they call the Great Dividing Range of mountains and that makes a lot of difference to the climate. In the winter we don't get cold, grey days like this. Much more blue skies. You'll love it.'

Life in Bendigo, the old Australian gold town, was easy to take. Just over a hundred years ago it had been a lonely country creek with little to be seen apart from the abundant and unique wildlife of the island continent and the sheep the settlers who they called squatters and graziers had brought with them. Then the news went round the world. They were discovering gold nuggets the size of turnips.

There was a picture of one miner standing beside his huge
find and it was as big as the leg of a bullock. It was another
Klondyke and they poured in, more than 100,000 of them,
from America and Europe. Big sailing ships lay deserted in
the harbours of Sydney, Melbourne and Adelaide, their
crews abandoning them to join in the rush. The prospectors
walked all the way from Melbourne pushing wheelbarrows
that carried a few tools and their meagre possessions. Such
was the word about the size of the nuggets, Chinese even
deserted the diggings in California, in the land they had
named Old Gold Hill, to try their luck in the Bendigo
fields, in the land they were to call New Gold Hill.

The gold had all but gone now, what remained being too
expensive to mine. But all the old names were still there:
Sailors' Gully and Jackass Flat, Diamond Hill and Golden
Gully, Kangaroo Flat and California Gully, Peg Leg Gully,
Eaglehawk and Golden Square. The gold rush capital was
now a pleasant pastoral town about the size of Ayr or
Kilmarnock and they proudly called it a city because it
had a cathedral.

But the men who had come and taken the gold had left
their mark and in the bush country around the town you
could still see the ravages of the 100,000 diggers – the
scarred and pockmarked acres, the abandoned minework-
ings, their poppetheads standing like spindly tombstones
as if commemorating a pestilence that had come and gone.
It was called the progress of man.

Bendigo evoked many memories for Star of the years she
had spent as a wartime evacuee in the hill farm called
Glenmulloch, near Kirkconnel, at the head of the beautiful
valley of the Nith in Dumfriesshire. Bendigo, of course, was
much bigger than Kirkconnel but there was the same
relaxed country air about the place, the same rural people
with none of the urban hardness or edge of the city
dwellers. In the mornings when a distant cockerel welcomed the first light and then another took up its boastful

43

song, Bendigo and Kirkconnel seemed very close. That more than anything would bring back those happy, carefree days on the high Dumfriesshire moorlands. It was always the cockerel at the farm called Neviston, a huge and proud wyandotte, that announced the reveille first, then the one at nearby Samsiston would take up the call, followed by the ones at Hillhead, Knowehead, The Hall, and then, finally, their own, all declaring themselves kings of their own little castles.

It seemed an eternity ago, in another time. In another world. It was now 1963 and all forms of modern progress were changing life in the workplace and in the home. And yet, just twenty years previously, when she had lived at Glenmulloch, Wullie Cameron, its jovial farmer, would joke as they were working together in the fields . . . 'Robbie Burns would hae ken't this life,' for on these lonely farms little had changed since the poet's days. There had been no gas or electricity or sewerage, and a pair of loyal Clydesdale horses together with the muscle and sweat of the farmer, his wife, and his worker, Wull Andrews, provided all the energy that made the farm work. They had been hard days for a young girl from the Gorbals but the contrast between life in the hills and at home – a cramped single room in a stinking slum tenement in the Gorbals – was to have a lasting effect on her. Like most of the other children of the Gorbals she had never seen a sheep or a cow, a field of hay or corn even, and despite all its ardours, she had fallen very much in love with her new, albeit temporary, life at Glenmulloch.

Star couldn't figure out the strange warbling sounds when she awakened that first morning in the large spare bedroom of Ella's house in Golden Square, the southern suburb of Bendigo. When she peered through the venetian blinds she was amazed to see the side lawn covered in white frost.

'I can't believe it . . . it's freezing,' she said when Ella came in with a tray.

'It's like that in winter here in Bendigo. But, wait till you see, by lunchtime it'll be warmer than a summer's day at home. The weather's really fabulous, Star.'

'What was that peculiar warbling sound? It's been going all morning. Was it these possum things or something?'

Ella laughed. 'Stone the crows, mate . . . as they say. But that's just what it was . . . crows. Only they don't call them crows here, they call them magpies because they're black and white. And they make that lovely chattering sound in the mornings. You've got to watch them, though, when they're nesting in the springtime. They get quite vicious and they'll go for you, even if you just happen to pass by a tree they're in.'

They picnicked with the children later that day in Rosalind Park, just off the main street, Pall Mall, in the centre of town. As Ella had said, the winter weather was mild and the children happily played endless games on the manicured lawns of the park while the two women reminisced about their own childhood and their lives in the Gorbals. Star had been anxious to hear about Australia and encouraged Ella to talk about life in her new country.

'You must love it here, Ella. It's just beautiful and so peaceful. So different from Glasgow . . . from Scotland.'

'Yes, we do love it. Bill has a super job as a mechanic in Hanro, the clothing factory. And there's good prospects. People move around a lot more in their jobs. They're not as content with doing the one thing for life as we are and at the slightest opportunity they're up and off to something completely different.'

'D'you get on well with them . . . the Australians?'

'Oh yes. No problems. They're good sorts, as they say. I've only been called a Pom once. A Scotch Pom, actually. It was a silly old besom who called me it when I used to work in the baker's shop in Hargreaves Street. But she was a bitch.

45

'They do have a thing about foreigners, but you've just got to accept it, I s'ppose, though it's a bit ironic when you think that just over a hundred years ago the only people who weren't foreigners here were the Aborigines. But like everyone else they've got minuses and plusses. The minuses include that attitude about foreigners. But being Scots we seem to be exempt from it. Two or three of them have even said "salt of the earth" to me when they've heard my accent. That makes you feel a bit special. But if you're English you're a Pom or a Pommie Bastard. And if you're anything else you're a New Australian. They brought that term out to get them to stop calling everyone who arrived a DP.'

'What . . . a Displaced Person?'

'Yes. Lots of them came here after the war and the tag stuck to everyone. It wasn't so much being called a DP. It was the way that they said it. New Australian sounds fine when you say it like that, but when they say it there's an attitude in their voice. And, of course, if you're any way dark, you're a dago. That's their worst minus, I suppose.

'And, of course, there's the isolation. When I first came out in the mid-fifties, Bill and I went downtown that first Saturday to do our shopping. You've got to get everything done by mid-day on Saturdays for the shops all close then and it's dead – and I really mean dead – until the Monday. I was wearing slacks. It was like a scene out of the movies. I couldn't believe it. Women were stopping beside me and pointing me out . . . and actually laughing in my face.

'We discovered later just why – they'd never seen a woman wearing slacks before. Can you believe that? But it was the way they treated me . . . the humiliation. It was like what they did to those collaborators in France after the war. Pointing them out publicly in the street. But all I'd been doing was wearing something that was totally strange to them. I ran home crying my eyes out and wanted to go back to Glasgow the very next day.

'Anyway, we talked it over and stuck it out. In fact, we had no option. When you come here under the ten-pound scheme you have to surrender your passport to the Government for two years and if you want it back before then you have to refund the passage money out. We couldn't have afforded one return ticket between us, let alone return fares for all the family.

'But friends explained to us later why people acted the way they did that day I wore my slacks. It's because they're so cut off and have been since the days of the first settlers. Remember, everyone and everything that comes here is by ship and that takes a month. They're saying now that in ten years or so more and more will be flown in, but that's just talk at the moment. It's a bit easier now, but at first we couldn't even phone home. It was a bit like the Wild West, I s'ppose . . . you still got the occasional family from the country coming into town in their horse and buggies – you can see tying posts for them outside some buildings. They had these ancient cars . . . Bill said they were T-model Fords. Cars last forever, you see, because the air is so dry and nothing rusts.

'But it's not all minuses living here, Star. There's lots of plusses. They're outgoing and if you're not introduced they introduce themselves right away. And resourceful! There's none of this waiting around until "they" do it . . . you know, like we're always saying at home, "That's terrible, 'they' should fix this, 'they' should do that." Here they just do it. They've got to be really stuck here before they'll call in a tradesman.

'And most young kids who get married here build their own homes. They'll perhaps get a builder to put up a frame for them, then after that they roll up their sleeves and finish it off.

'They can be a rough and ready lot but they're not coarse like some of the ones you and I know at home. Yes, I love it, Star.'

Ella's eyes filled up as she said that. 'I do . . . I really do love it here. But, oh, Star . . . it's not home. Oh God, how I long for home at times. How I long for the feel and the comfort of the people I know best around me. It's not rational – is it? – to be like this. Look at this beautiful park, the colourful birds, those lovely palm trees, that blue sky, this gorgeous warm day, sunshine in the middle of winter, our lovely house, the healthy way our girls look with their lovely tans . . . everything. But, Star . . . it's not home. Why do I miss it all so much? When you think of the horrible weather, the black tenements, the dowdiness. What is it makes me feel like this, Star?'

'Mother Glasgow, I suppose. That's what she's like to us all. Like an old mother. Doesn't matter that she's ugly, got warts, is bad tempered, needs her face washed. She's old mother to us all. Old Mother Glasgow.

'Before Russell died, I thought living in that part of the Punjab where we were was like being in paradise. Every morning from my bedroom window I could see the distant hills of Kashmir and the Karakorums. I've never seen a sight like that in my life. I had every conceivable comfort you could imagine. Our house had an entire staff running it – one person to look after little James, another for the cooking, two who tended the garden. We even had our own watchman who sat by our gate all day. We had the most affluent of lifestyles. Yet, I used to think of her . . . old Mother Glasgow. And I pined for her too, Ella. I missed her terribly. I suppose she has that effect on us all. We're her children and she never lets you forget it. That's one of the reasons why I've only come here for a few months. Once I feel like taking on the world again, I'll be leaving and going back to Glasgow.'

CHAPTER 4

BODGIES AND WIDGIES

AUSTRALIA WAS TO BE EVERYTHING HER friend Ella said it would be. Star had been devastated by the death of her husband, much more than she ever feared. It had been her firm belief when she left Pakistan that she would never recover from the shock. Her whole life seemed in ruins. After all those years in which she had emerged from one of the most deprived households in the Gorbals to progress by the sheer strength of personality, an intuitive determination and a great gift of enterprise to a position of some wealth and certainly great security, all seemed lost. Thankfully she had little James, her lifeline to the future. Perhaps a few months in Australia together with friends would restore her to her old self.

The time spent with Ella, Bill and their children in the peaceful country town of Bendigo and the experience of life in this new land was to be even more of a tonic to her than she had imagined it would, although from time to time she would be taken aback by the Australians' acute xenophobia and their breathtaking frankness. Lats, Balts, Dagoes, Spics, Poms, DPs . . . everyone had a pejorative without care if they were even ethnically correct in usage. What did it matter? – they were all bloody New Australians anyway, except the Boongs. They were just bloody Boongs. They didn't care about calling you a Pom to your face and when Star had corrected one by saying she wasn't English in the hope that might make some difference, the reply had been 'Then you're a bloody Scotch Pom.'

She appreciated that they didn't really mean to hurt her feelings. It was just that they did. And there was no worse example of that than when she had first met her next-door neighbour at the house she leased for six months in Elwood Street, just round the corner from her friends Ella and Bill. She was big Martha, a strapping widow in her late fifties who had worked most of her life 'up in the mulga', as she termed the isolated backblocks of Northern Victoria where it bordered with New South Wales. She was a hardy and resourceful character, as mulga people all were, and despite being a woman of over fifteen stone, would think nothing of shinnying up a ladder to the roof of her house to carry out repairs that needed doing. She chopped all her own wood, showing that she could swing an axe with the best of men, and Star had gasped when she had seen her despatch one of the hens she kept at the back of her house by holding it on a block with one hand and lopping its head off with a hefty felling axe in the other.

'Well, that's the way we do it in the mulga,' she had replied when Star had queried her dubious slaughtering methods.

Martha was generally regarded in their own jargon as a 'good sort', which meant she was amiable, a good mixer and a good neighbour. All of which she was. But that wasn't the first impression Star had formed on the day they met. Martha had come forward to her in a typically Australian outgoing and friendly way, introducing herself with a cheery 'G'day. I'm yer neighbour Martha. Need any help, luv, just give me a shout.' Then she had looked admiringly at little James in his pram. 'Good little fellah, isn't he?' she said as he giggled when she tickled his chin. 'Touch of the Abo in him, luv?'

It was the first time that Star had heard the expression and she had quizzically repeated the word.

'Yeah, Abo. Aboriginals, luv. You don't have dark hair like he does.'

Hurt at the blatant way Martha had come out with it, Star had replied haughtily, 'That's right, I don't have dark hair like he does. It does take two to make a child.'

Yet, despite her insensitiveness, the woman Martha really was the good sort they all said she was and was a friendly and helpful neighbour.

Star envied the relaxed life these Australians in rural Victoria enjoyed, refreshingly free of the tensions and stresses so many other lands endured. Their men had gone off to fight in three wars on behalf of the land they still called the Mother Country but their own lucky continent never had a war fought on its own soil. Maybe that was why they were so easy-going and carefree. Not for them the agonies and pressures of other nationalities. Didn't one of Ella's own neighbours, just an ordinary bloke, as the Australians would have him, tell Star in all earnestness that the biggest problem he had in life was whether he should buy a new caravan or build a holiday home for the family?

If they had concerns, it seemed they were confined to the great passions of their life, their 'footy', as they knew their Australian Rules Football, and horse racing, both pursuits marking the indelible stamp of Ireland on their national character. And, of course, their love for cricket, which, whether they liked it or not, was the English portion of that character. There was also that great passion which was of their own creation . . . the weekend. And what zest they put into that! Their trades union movement had pioneered the eight-hour day and the five-day week and they made sure when they achieved their two-day weekend that it would be something to be revered and enjoyed.

Like the rest of them, Star looked forward to those

weekends in her Australian sojourn, joining Ella and the family when they picnicked and barbecued and swam in the boundless reservoirs in the rolling and ample surrounding countryside. They played out Huckleberry pursuits with the kids, like fishing for yabbies, the little freshwater crayfish, simply and easily caught by merely dangling in the water pieces of meat tied with string. If you found the right dam you could fill half a bucket in no time.

After hearing the news of the death of President Kennedy, Star had gone over to Ella's that Saturday at lunchtime and they sat together to share in some of the grief of the great tragedy. As the big H-aerial on top of their house indicated, Ella and Bill were one of the few to possess the latest medium to arrive in the town. The big tower recently erected on the Great Dividing Range brought television for the first time to Central Victoria.

The first pictures that were screened showed reactions from politicians, personalities and others around Australia, and were shown together with clips from old newsreels of the Kennedys. In succeeding days, when up-to-date film of the unfolding drama had arrived by plane from the States, they were to see all the familiar scenes of that tragic day in downtown Dallas and the processional solemnities of the funeral extravaganza demanded by the State on such occasions.

Star was glad that, unlike Mrs Kennedy, she had been spared the ordeal of a funeral and she reflected that perhaps that had been just as well. She marvelled at the courage and bravery of this beautiful American woman, so much in control, so aloof. What was there about these blue-bloods who could hold their composure like this on such occasions? Say what you like about them, there were qualities that had to be admired.

And was it not strange sitting in their very own home

watching such scenes because of the wonders of this amazing invention . . . just as in the near future they would be watching scenes of all nature of things, flooding in from all over the world. They would see people in the strangest forms of dress, even more strange and bizarre to the Australians than the slacks they had so boorishly ridiculed Ella for wearing, and the pictures would be beamed right there before them in their own living-rooms. Between that and the big jet aeroplanes that within a few years would replace the slow ships which brought them everything, Australia would never be the same again.

Over supper, Bill had mentioned that *Carmen Jones* was on at the cinema and how he would love to see it. 'You know I'm a big fan of Harry Belafonte and, know what? . . . Pearl Bailey is in it as well? Got a great write up in the *Advertiser*.'

'Why don't you go then?' said Ella. 'I don't mind you going off on your own.'

'No. I'd like you to see it. Anyway, you'd suspect I'd meet some little sheila.'

'That'll be right.'

'That's it settled,' said Star. 'After months of doing nothing, why haven't you asked me to babysit? Goodness, I'll be away in a couple of months and you won't have any handy babysitters after that. The nights are so balmy just now I can take the kids down to the park or else go to Angie's cafe . . . you know how much the girls love his sarsaparilla? And I'm just crazy for those chocolate milk-shakes he makes. Now that's something we can't get at home . . . milk-shakes like they make here. I'm not taking no for an answer. You're both going to see *Carmen Jones*.'

November nights were idyllic in Bendigo. In mid-summer even at night it could be oppressively warm, the temperature often lingering on in the nineties till late in the evening. But it wasn't like that this November night as Star and the children slowly walked towards the centre of town.

The evening air was filled with the fragrance of Bougain-villaea and jacaranda blossom and every now and then, as they passed someone's garden gate, there would be the exquisite bouquet from a daphne bush which overpowered all the other evening perfumes.

How lucky these Australians were in a place like Bendigo, she thought as she contrasted their lifestyles with people in Glasgow. Here they were, all with their gardens, some of them on huge plots, or blocks as they called them, at the rear of which many cultivated their own produce – tomatoes, peppers, shiny eggplant and their favourite, pumpkin. There would be trees heavy with juicy peaches, plums as big as apples and glossy, dark cherries. Everything growing in great profusion. Some of the houses weren't up to all that much, humble, weatherboard constructions which the Scottish climate would have devastated in a couple of weekends. But they were all detached and on their own piece of property and Australia had none of the problems of the Scottish climate. What was it Ella had said about the weather? They had counted ninety-three – or was it ninety-six? – consecutive weekends in which the sun had shone from morning till night. Then they had lost count as it seemed that just every weekend was that way.

There was a fire brigade practice going on at the small station they passed on their way to town and Susan, the eldest of Ella's girls, who seemed to know about such things, explained to Star that the firemen in the country were all amateurs and that running with firecarts and setting up the hoses, as they were doing now, was a big sport. 'Dad took us last year to the big carnival where they had their championships and it was really great,' she said. Young James, sitting up in his pram, loved the spectacle too – the men running in teams, their leader shouting loud instructions about their carts and equipment. Best of all for the children was the climax of each race when the firemen would shoot off big jets of water from their newly unreeled hoses.

Just after that a big group of racing cyclists who had been out on a training run had passed, their trim, white ankle socks highlighting deeply bronzed and muscular legs. They merged with other groups of athletes and sportsmen coming and going to their various venues. Star hadn't realised there was such activity at night from so many sportsmen and women.

The café to which they had gone was in the centre of the town's main commercial area. Star was surprised at how quiet it was. The girls were served their sarsaparilla, little James his ice cream and Star the favourite milk-shake known as a chocolate malted, and then they strolled towards home again, taking a different route, along the side of the delightful Rosalind Park. They had just crossed the wide Pall Mall thoroughfare when the loud bells of the Post Office clock, like a strident and off-key Big Ben, rang out the half-hour chimes for eight-thirty.

'We were told a story about the clock in our local history lessons at school,' said Susan eagerly. 'Did you know most of the chimes don't ring right through the night? You see, it's because a famous opera singer called Nellie something complained about them keeping her from sleeping, so they put them off for her and they haven't rung late at night since.'

'That would be Dame Nellie Melba. She was very famous,' said Star.

The loud and booming chimes seemed to accentuate the peacefulness of the night that followed as they walked slowly homewards by the side of the palm-fringed gardens. It was so much quieter now in contrast to the activity they had encountered earlier and the only people that seemed to be about were the group of mixed local youths she could see approaching them. They seemed the usual noisy and cheery bunch, casually dressed in their sloppy-joe shirts, shorts and tennis shoes. There were about fifteen of them, mainly boys. It was the one in the front, a boy of about sixteen or seventeen, who had made the remark.

'Nice pair of lungs you've got, Missus,' he said, eyeing Star and then whistling while the others laughed. The two girls, sensing something wasn't right, came in closer to Star as the rest of the group got nearer.

There was no one else around on the long stretch of broad pavement that ran along the park side. There wasn't even any traffic in the street and when she realised that, the first chill of fear flushed through Star.

Another of the youths, a bigger boy with staring eyes who had obviously been drinking, broke from the group to stand directly in Star's path. She changed course slightly to avoid him, and he did likewise to block her way again.

'How about a kiss then?' he said cockily, holding out his arms.

'Please,' said Star. 'Would you get out of my way?'

They laughed at that.

'Would you get out of my way?' mimicked one of the girls in a crude impersonation, then adding, 'She's a New Chum.'

'What kind of New Australian are you, luv?' said the youth who blocked her way.

One of the girls shouted, 'She's a Pom, Kevin.'

'A bloody Pom,' said one of the boys.

The tall one who had confronted Star now prevented her from walking and she said angrily, 'Get out of my way.'

'Oh la-di-da-di-dah,' mocked a boy from the crowd.

'Bloody drongo voice that,' said another.

The two girls were now clinging tightly to Star, Susan boldly shouting to the youths, 'Leave us alone.'

'Oh, so the Pom has an Australian daughter. Who's your daddy, luv?'

'Bloody dago by the looks of the one in the pram,' sneered one to the amusement of the others.

They had now surrounded Star and the children and the tall boy, the one who had stood directly in her path, began making obscene suggestions which brought mocking laughter from the gang.

'Go on then, Kevin,' said one of the girls. 'I bloody well dare you to kiss the Pom!'

'Get her to kiss yer arse, Kev,' urged one of the boys.

'Give's a kiss, luv, and we'll let you go.'

'Only if she gives all of us a kiss,' said another from the back of the group.

'Will you get out of my way!' demanded Star furiously.

'Poms don't tell Australians what to do,' retorted the tall youth, the smile gone now and facing Star so close she could smell the stale stink of his breath. 'You either give us a kiss or you're not going anywhere . . . understand me, Mrs Pom?'

Star controlled the panic she felt. She didn't want the children to get more frightened than they were. The younger of the two girls was already so fearful she had buried her face in Star's wide summer skirt. Because of the crowd around her, now shoving and pushing each other to be as close to the confrontation as possible, Star couldn't see whether or not there was anyone in the street, although she thought she heard a car somewhere in the distance. It seemed there was nowhere to turn.

'Oh God,' she said to herself as her thoughts spiralled in a crazy kaleidoscope of confusion, and when the pattern settled it was that awful, awful day again when she was just in her mid-teens, and the two boys, Andrew and Robbie Fordyce, twin sons of the wealthy laird of Glenmulloch and names ingrained on her mind forever, had tried to rape her. No other memory dominated her mind like that horrendous Martinmas Day when she had been lured into the big estate mansion, Lydeburn House, by the two public schoolboys. There was no worse terror than that which went through her mind in those final minutes before being sexually violated. Not even death was a worse prospect, for there was freedom with death. Rape was a life sentence; it became part of you, like some incurable disease; it haunted and tortured you forever and it was that thought above all others which was in her mind now, in the park, Ella's girls clinging to her, as the leering and half-stupefied youths cavorted around her.

'You'll be in serious trouble when they hear me scream,' she said loudly and angrily, her thoughts once more in the present.

The big youth sniggered in her face at that and some of the others laughed derisively.

'Got a right silly galah here,' came a voice.

'Only a dinkum Pom would say something like that.'

'Go on, Kev . . . Bloody well dare you, mate,' said another of the girls.

Star put a reassuring arm round the two girls as her mind raced through the options she might have. Should she reason with them? Plead with them perhaps? Scream like she had threatened? Try to run off? Feign abject terror and hope they might pity her? Shout for help? Persuade the females among them that for the children's sake they should be left alone?

'Go on, Kev,' the girl had shouted once more, and just as he bent forward to try and kiss Star there was the loud crash of a car driven at speed over the kerb and on to the pavement in front of them. Almost simultaneously there was another similar crashing noise behind them and the air was filled with the shouts of men, some of them in uniform, others in plain clothes, as the group who had been surrounding Star scattered in a variety of directions.

A young and strikingly handsome man in a lightweight suit and a smart brim hat came over to Star, asking her with obvious concern, 'Are you all right, Ma'am?' She assured him she was, emphasising that she just wanted to get away from that spot as quickly as she could and to get the children home.

'No . . . I'll have you run home. You've obviously been through enough tonight. The police station isn't far . . . let me get you a cup of tea.'

'Thanks . . . don't trouble. We'll be all right. But that was just awful . . . frightening . . . horrible. The kids were good, though . . . like me they were scared out of their minds. It was the shock of it all . . . I didn't think there were people like that here.'

'We have our problems,' said the man, introducing himself as Detective Sergeant Bob Cantrell of the Bendigo Police. 'And you're . . . Mrs?'

'Star Jehan.'

'Unusual name. Are you from Ireland?'

'Well, that makes a change from being called a Pom. No, I'm not Irish. I'm from Scotland.'

'Sorry, but I'm not good with accents. And I'm truly sorry about tonight. Like I said, we do have our problems. Our main ones at the moment are those bodgies and widgies.'

'Is that what that lot were?'

'That's right. Larrikins, every one of them. But real troublemakers. By the looks of it, we've got most of them though. On account of the evidence we have on this lot now, warrants were issued for their arrest earlier tonight. Some of them now face serious charges. Very serious charges. I hate to think what might have happened tonight had we not decided to round them up.'

Star took a deep breath and replied, 'So do I.'

CHAPTER 5

A BRIEF ENCOUNTER

ELLA AND BILL HAD BEEN JUST AS SHOCKED
when they heard the story after returning that night from
the cinema. The children had recovered from their fright and
Star had put the girls to bed, with James asleep in his pram.

Bill collected some of the big litre bottles of Melbourne
Bitter he kept in the fridge and they went outside to sit
together on the big divan on the back verandah of the
house. The evening was light with the moon and a brilliant
canopy of stars, that night featuring a bright milky way
which Bill said was the Southern Lights, the brilliant
phenomenon of the Southern Hemisphere's heavens.

'That's the first I've seen it. Isn't it just fabulous?' said
Star. 'In fact, I was thinking about how fabulous everything is tonight as I walked down to town with the children.
People here want for nothing. What a beautiful climate
they have. And each of them with their own houses . . . it
seems you just never see anyone wanting for anything.
None of the scenes like we have at home – the slums, the
dirt and decay and the stark aggression that we're so often
confronted with. Then that incident had to happen tonight.
I must say, it shattered a few of the illusions I had about
the place. God, it was really alarming. I shudder to think
what might have been had those police not turned up.'

'Look,' said Bill, 'everything really is beaut and easy-going for them as you say, Star. But it certainly isn't perfect. The boys at work tell some real hairy stories about what goes on below the surface in Bendigo. Touch of the old *Peyton Place* and that. There's one current story about midnight romps in the nude up at one of the dams, with all sorts of prominent people being involved. You know, these Christian wowser types they have here with all their do-goody talk? . . . seems they and a few randy sheilas had a right old-fashioned orgy to themselves. And it wasn't the first, the boys were saying.'

'What a right old gossip you are, Bill!' said Ella.

'But it's true,' he protested. 'I mean, there's just got to be something like that going on somewhere around here. It's human nature for society to be made up of all types. So why not here in Bendigo? I mean, you just can't get a place of this size being as nice and sweet and innocent as it looks. Okay, we never have to lock our doors, nothing ever gets nicked, but there is corruption and all types of sex scandals go on all the time. We're never confronted with them and none of them ever affect our lives so we don't worry. Then there's this fairly new thing with the bodgies and widgies, like poor Star copped tonight. I've come across them a couple of times when I've been downtown having a drink. Three of them tried to have a go at me one night when I was coming home from my mate Bruce's place. One was a real fat kid. Know what he did when I kicked him in the you-know-whats? He burst out crying like a baby. And the two bodgies with him ran for their lives.'

'Yes, I've seen groups of them occasionally too,' said Ella. 'They hang around one of the cafés in Hargreaves Street. They had that kind of look about them, I suppose, but it's so damned difficult to tell here for they're all well-fed and well-dressed. Everybody looks like they've just stepped out of the shower. You wouldn't think they would be capable of some of the things they say they have been doing. Martha, your neighbour, was telling me about them one day. She says that Australia has always had its share of larrikins, or hooligans, but the bodgie widgie thing is a new development. She blamed it all on the Yanks. Says that everything bad about the place has been brought in from the States.'

'Trust Martha. She would have to blame someone from outside of Australia for them. Does she have a name for them too?' Star asked.

'Americans, you mean? Come to think of it, they don't have a knocking name for the Yanks.'

'Well, they must be the only ones,' Star smiled. 'Getting back to tonight, though. I must say the detective in charge was really sympathetic. Went to great lengths to make sure we were okay, even persuaded me to go with him down to the police station for a cup of tea and then he drove us home.'

'Will you have to appear in court?'

'No . . . that's another thing. He was quite clear about that. He said if he put a complete report in, it would mean us all having to give full statements and that we would then be summonsed to give evidence in court. "Too much of an ordeal for you and the kids," he said. They had plenty on the ones they were out to catch tonight and he would have the others charged with being part of a disorderly mob. I thought that decent of him, to spare us having to go to court.'

'What did you say his name was?' asked Ella.

'Cantrell. Bob Cantrell.'

'Isn't he the one, Bill, there was a story about in the *Advertiser* because he had just arrived here from somewhere up the Bush a bit?'

'The one who said he saw himself as a bit of a crusader when it comes to law-breaking and that he would do his best to make a drastic cut in crime here?'

'That's right. I remember, for there was a picture of him

and I thought, coo, doesn't he look like a film star? Hey, Star? Maybe he took a fancy to you?' laughed Ella. 'Lucky old you if he did.'

'He looked a bit limp to me,' said Bill, at which the girls laughed and teased him for being jealous.

Two days later Star got the phone call from Bob Cantrell. 'Look,' he said, 'I've got some inquiries to make in your area and I was just wondering if you would be at home and if I could pop in.'

'By all means.'

She had been playing with James under the big sun awning that was in popular use, made by putting a custom-made covering over what Australians would say was their very own invention, the rotary clothes hoist. It was a hot afternoon and Star was in a two-piece swimsuit, over which she wore a pair of shorts. She had been splashing with James in the baby pool.

Cantrell had walked round the side of the house to the big rear garden and sat down on one of the lounge chairs under the sun canopy. 'Like your outfit,' he said, admiring her shapely figure. 'We should be allowed to wear shorts like they do up in Queensland, but no, it's got to be a suit, collar and tie, even when it gets stinking hot.'

'Some cool fruit juice, or a beer?' she asked.

'Didn't you know police are not supposed to drink on duty, Mrs Jehan?' he said in mock earnestness. Then he smiled broadly. 'Would love nothing better than a beer, Star. Tell me about your name?'

'For police files?'

'No . . . for Bob Cantrell's files.'

'Why . . . does Bob Cantrell keep files on ladies?'

'Only beautiful ones.'

'Now you're flirting.'

'Pardon me, but I didn't mean to come on like that. Now

you've made me feel like a bit of a Lothario. I'm not really, you know.'

'So, how can I help you about the other night?'

'No need. Everything's all fixed up about that. I said I wouldn't put you through the worry of having to go to court and that's the way it is. We've got plenty on the larrikins. There's one in particular I've been after for some time. I know he's committed at least two rapes and if there's anything makes me go spare about a bloke it's that. But I've got him now on an armed robbery charge and being in possession of drugs . . . and other charges. He'll get seven years at least. Bloody mongrels, these people. But I'll get them on the run in this town if it's the last thing I do. I don't know what it is about me, but I just can't stand people who try to walk over other people. That's why I'm a cop. I love my job. I love it every time I nail somebody. I don't mean petty thieves and the like, although I've got little time for them either. I mean thugs that use violence. They need a good dose of their own medicine.'

'I must admit that for a while the other night I had similar thoughts myself.'

'Don't you think that way all the time about them?'

'No, I don't actually. I tend to be a bit more philosophical about them. You know, think about the factors which make them the way they are, environment and the other influences in life which may affect them?'

'You mean environment can make a rapist?'

'Certain aspects of environment can.'

'Strewth, Star. I'm glad I'm not philosophical about them or else I wouldn't have the bastards behind bars.'

She was getting used to the way they used words loosely like that, although it still gave her a jolt, coming from such a thoroughly respectable-looking policeman. And, relaxing the way he was on the lounger with his hat off, he was even more ruggedly handsome than she remembered him that night in the park.

'So how then can I help the police?'

'There's no need.'

'So,' she paused briefly, 'it's not a police call?'

'No. I just wanted to speak to you.'

'Why? Because I told you the other night I had been widowed and that I wouldn't be in Australia for long?'

'Please, Star. Don't put it like that.'

'Then how should I put it?'

'Maybe you could say ... Do you want me to crack another bottle of beer?'

'Persuasive, aren't you!'

'Well?'

'All right. Would you, as the Australians say, like me to crack another bottle of beer?'

'How nice of you to ask, Star. Don't mind if I do.'

'I was downtown this morning and got some lovely crays from that Greek place in Mitchell Street. Would you like to stay for a bite?'

'Too right, mate. Or should I translate that?'

'No need. The Scotch Pom here is learning fast about you Australians.'

'Love your cute accent, Star.'

'I think you'll like the crays even better.'

There had been more visits from the good-looking and easy-going young Australian and they had gone on outings together to some local beauty spots, once for a picnic to the viewpoint park at One Tree Hill where on the summit there was a fire lookout with magnificent views over hundreds of square miles of the tranquil bushland, a eucalyptus forest that stretched to the far horizon and seemed of Amazonian dimensions.

Bob told Star he had never been out of Australia. He was a country boy from Echuca, a town on the Murray, further upstate, and although he said they were taught more about the history of England than that of Australia at school, he found great difficulty in trying to imagine what kind of place it was. 'I can only think about it from the movies I've seen, you know, *Lavender Hill Mob* and *The Belles of St Trinians*, that sort of thing. There was a Scottish picture once that they liked here about this bloke who came to the Olympics in Melbourne and his sheila kept shouting, "Come away, my wee Georgie."'

'My wee Geordie.'

'That's right . . . it was Geordie. So you know it! Well, that's what I think Scotland is like. All heather and hills and wee Georgies or Geordies or whatever you call them running about in their kilts, tossing big tree trunks up in the air. Is it really like that?'

'Bob, you're making me cringe. That was as much like Scotland as some of your films with Chips Rafferty are like Australia. I remember the first one I saw with him. It was *The Overlanders*.'

Bob laughed loudly. 'Hey, hold on, sport! That *was* dinkum Australia.'

Ella had taken her turn to babysit that night and Star had gone with Bob to a dinner dance at the Shamrock Hotel, the old Victorian building which graciously dominated Pall Mall.

'Why don't you stay in Australia, Star?' he had asked her, filling her glass with the black-red Coonawarra they had been drinking, then boasting, 'We're the best country in the world, you know. And I bet you don't get wine like that in Scotland! Look at the good friends you have here already, as well as your own mates, Ella and Bill . . . and you're going to have me hanging around as much as I can.'

'Bob . . . you're forgetting our agreement. No involvement, emotionally that is. I've loved Australia, much much more than I imagined. People who are born here should thank their lucky stars that they come from such a wonderful country. But I'm all booked up now to go home . . .

we're off on the *Fair Sky*, the little Italian liner, in just under a month's time. I've just got to go back.'

'Why?'

'It's too long a story. Too untellable a story.'

'He must be nice.'

'He . . . yes, there is a he. But not like you imagine. He happens to be a monster of a man. And my long and untellable story revolves round the fact that I have unfinished business with him that I have a duty to put right.'

'How can someone as beautiful as you be involved in such intrigue?'

'Oh, I know it sounds all so dark and mysterious. I don't mean it to be. It's just about something that I think I can do to bring to an end the activities of someone who has brought a lot of misery to an awful lot of people, including my very own family. I tried to sort it out once before but everything went wrong.'

'Sounds like you need the company of a good hitman.'

'Oh, God, Bob! If only you knew . . . If only you knew. Anyway, besides that I've got pressing family affairs that need tending to and I want my son to have a good Scottish education and background.'

'You don't really need to go into details. We've all got untellable tales in our lives.'

'Including yourself?'

'Yes, including myself,' he smiled.

'And is she nice?'

'If only she was. But it's not that kind of untellable tale.'

'What kind is it then?'

'An untellably untellable tale.'

'And no details?'

'No, luv. No details.'

Although it was billed as a dinner dance, it reminded Star of an old-fashioned sort of tea dance, the men in their best suits, the woman in brightly coloured floral dresses with stiff petticoats which flared their skirts, dancing to yesterday's music performed by a sextet of elderly musicians. But there were some quicksteps and foxtrots too and when Star and her new friend waltzed they danced closely, like two young lovers, and there were nudges and whispers from some of the wives who were there because Cantrell had become something of a personality in the town through his masterminding of his anti-crime drives and particularly through his appearances on local television when he urged viewers to co-operate more with the police.

'Is he the copper that wants us all to become police narks?' one of them asked.

'Same fellah.'

'Dancing a bit close to the sheila, isn't he? Don't know her. Is she a New Australian?'

'She's a Pom,' whispered another.

'Thought she might be.'

They had danced even closer later that night to soft music from one of the all-night radio stations playing in the lounge of the house Star had leased. It had been years since Star had been in the arms of a man like this. She felt safe with him as he was gentle and thoughtful and when they sat back together on the big sofa, he ran his hand over her long hair and a quiver ran through her of sheer bliss and ecstasy. She had never experienced a lover who aroused her so and she went uncontrollably with him as he pulled her slowly to his body and there was a long and passionate kiss during which they gently caressed then fondled and stroked and whispered over and over how much they each treasured these moments. And as he softly kissed her breasts Star closed her eyes in the utmost joy of that special sensation in which all the heartbreak and agony she had endured in the past year seemed to lift away from her and in its place was a warm and comforting feeling of absolute delight and enchantment. This unforgettable evening, she said slowly and softly into his ear, would be one that she would remember and cherish for the rest of her life.

Gently, but firmly, she removed his hand from her breasts as she got up from the sofa and in the dim light of a solitary fireside lamp, she gazed longingly down on the man who had brought so much happiness to her that night in Bendigo. And then she began slowly to unbutton her dress.

CHAPTER 6

FAREWELL MY LOVE

THE TELEPHONE HAD RUNG EARLY THAT MORN-
ing, as Star had just emerged from the shower. It was Ella.
She sounded anxious. 'Star . . . did you get the paper this
morning? The '*Tiser*?'

'No, the boy we've got is always late. Something in it I
should read?'

'My word there is. Listen, I'm just putting the girls out
to school, then I'll be right round.'

Her own newspaper boy had come before Ella had
arrived and Star was visibly shocked when she answered
the door. 'You've read it, then?' said Ella.

'Yes . . . and I just can't believe it. Then again, maybe I
can. He was determined to get these people. Too determined obviously.'

The sensational headline on that day's *Bendigo Advertiser*
told it all. It was the biggest headline she had seen on the
town's morning broadsheet. It read: '*CRIMEBUSTER
ARRESTED*.'

> Senior detectives from the police headquarters in Rus-
> sell Street, Melbourne, last night arrested one of Ben-
> digo's most well-known policemen. Detective Sergeant
> Bob Cantrell was taken to the State capital and is due

to appear in the city court this morning. It is understood he is being charged with a serious offence which involves the planting of evidence on suspects accused of a variety of crimes. The offences, it is said, occurred at various times in the last two years.

Sgt Cantrell came to Bendigo just over two years ago and made a marked effect on the reduction of crime, particularly among teenagers in the district. He was regarded as one of Bendigo's most respected policemen and had been a regular guest speaker at the local Rotary, Lions and Jaycees organisations as well as having addressed the congregations at the Wesley Church and St John's Presbyterian Church.

'Shocking, isn't it?' said Ella.

'Yes, shocking. But understandable. He felt so strongly about people who used violence. Not that it's excusable, but I'm sure that none of the people involved would have been innocent.'

'But, Star, you can't have policemen doing terrible things like that.'

'I know . . . I know, Ella. There's no question of condoning it. It's just that I understand why. Poor Bob! I do feel for him. He tried to tell me about it, but didn't . . . or couldn't. But then we all have untellable tales in our lives. Don't we? I'll need to go and see him before I go.'

'Goodness, Star, it just seems like yesterday when I met you from the ship at Melbourne. Now you're almost set to go. I'm going to miss you. We're all going to miss you, especially the girls. They just love their Auntie Star . . . spoils them something terrible, so she does. Star . . . do you really need to? Go, that is.'

'I'm afraid so, Ella. You were so right about Australia and persuading me to come here. I've got over the death of Russell now and that terrible period I had, not knowing about Uncle Sammy and all that. And there were other things. I would have had a nervous breakdown if I hadn't come here. You and Bill have been just super. Bob was a help too. A great help. Now I'm on a level course again and ready to tackle all I have to back in Glasgow.'

Not the least of that, but something she had never mentioned to Ella, was her quest to solve the mystery of the death of Frankie Burns. Only one person could have been responsible for Burns's death and that was Sonny Riley. But how had it all come about? How would Riley have known that Burns was in Glasgow for the purpose of killing him? Whatever answer there was to that, one fact remained and that was that Riley was still a free man. He quite possibly was involved in some way with the mysterious flight of Sammy Nelson to America. Apart from her love of Glasgow, Star had these vital reasons for return.

After a tearful farewell from Ella, Bill and their girls, with promises that she would return to Bendigo at some time, Star left for Melbourne a day early in order to visit Bob Cantrell, still held in custody in the remand wing of the Pentridge Stockade, the State's main prison just off the Sydney Road, in Coburg, a northern suburb of the Victorian capital. It was an old, bluestone fortress of a building and although it wasn't begrimed with soot like Barlinnie, it reminded her of the kind of grim and foreboding place the Glasgow prison was.

Being an untried prisoner, Bob Cantrell was casually dressed in his own check summer shirt and slacks. 'Where's the baby?' he had asked when he took his seat at the other side of the wire grill which separated them.

'We're staying in the Australia Hotel overnight and they've got a crêche. We sail tomorrow, Bob.'

'God . . . so soon!'

'How are you bearing up?'

'I'll be all right. They'll just have to get me a little jail of my own somewhere, for the other prisoners don't like people like me.'

'Will you . . .?'

'Go down? Too right, Star. They've got me good and proper. I'm surprised you even came to see a person like me who does terrible things like that.'

'Bob . . . do you remember I told you I had an untellable tale?'

'Yes, and I said I had a more untellable one.'

'Well, mine was that I too had taken the law into my own hands and as a result a man died who shouldn't have. That's one of the reasons why I'm returning, Bob. The man who should have paid the penalty is still free. I want to see that they get him in some way, but within the law. That will be the only thing which will relieve my conscience.'

'That's quite a story, Star. I thought what I was doing would have been infallible. But it wasn't. I trusted an officer I shouldn't have trusted. They had him working on me to make a dossier on what I'd been doing. He made some job of it. Maybe there's a moral somewhere in our stories.' He paused at that for a few seconds. 'I'll tell you what that moral is, Star. Do it right . . . and don't get caught.'

'How long . . .?'

'Will I get? There was an officer done last year for something similar. He got five years. With luck that'll be the maximum I'll get.'

Star bowed her head.

'Hey, there. You're not going to weep for me. Wherever they send me I'm going with a beautiful memory of a beautiful woman.'

'I can't tell you how much you helped me, Bob. My life was at a very low ebb when we met. I said there was to be no emotional involvement . . . and it was difficult. Really difficult. But I had to keep it that way for my sake . . . for your sake. Australia was only ever to be a temporary thing for me. But that didn't stop me from enjoying the happiness and company you brought me. I'll never forget that. Never.'

He spoke slowly and softly. 'Star, darling, please don't say another word. I just want to remember you looking the way you are and those very last words you said to me there.' He rose slowly from his chair and leaned closer to the wire grill. 'Farewell, my love.' Then he turned and walked away with the prison guard.

CHAPTER 7

KEARNY

SAMMY NELSON HAD ARRANGED TO MEET HIS old friend Alex Mitchell at Graham's Bar. It was as familiar a name for a Scots bar as you could get, although it wasn't the famous landmark one at Glasgow Cross. But in many ways it might have been.

A drunk man approached clutching, with all the affection of an offspring, a big brown paper bag whose contents were betrayed by cheerful clinking sounds. The sounds emanating from the approaching drunk weren't so cheery. He was an aggressive-looking man and Sammy gave him plenty of room to pass.

'Was that an insult, a man passing me wide in the street like that? Does he think I'm drunk or something?' The mind that he had swapped for an alcoholic binge was on an expedition for confrontation. It was commanding challenges to be issued but as they went through the various stages of his befuddled thought process all that emerged were jumbled incoherencies. The man performed a stagger of a pirouette and Sammy walked on, the clinking bottles and the meaningless mutterings fading into the distance.

The town was new to him and, as he had time, he slowly took in all the sights of the pleasant and orderly main street. It was not the kind of place where he would have expected to come upon a drunk like that. There was a butcher called Stewart's with a sign in white scroll on the window declaring the availability of potted head, links, black pudding and sausage rolls; another called Cameron's, with more window writing, this time for tripe, bridies and steak pies. There was a shop called The Pipers' Cove with souvenirs and various tartan gewgaws and, in the window, a book bearing the sobering title, *Teach Yourself To Play The Great Highland Bagpipe*. At Molly's Café nearby a less sobering sign boasted: 'Scots Do It Better in the Kilt'. Then there was McKinnon's the bakers – 'pies and pastries our speciality' – and at a small war memorial he paused to read off the names . . . Dougan, McMillan, Green, Davidson, Deans, Turnbull and Reid. Just after that he saw the name Reid again . . . the local undertakers.

Not far along the road two particular shops made him stop in his tracks. One was called the Thistle, the other the Argyle and he stood outside to take in a deep breath of the pungent odour emanating from the latter. It was beautiful. They could say what they liked, thought Sammy, about the succulence of any food anywhere in the world but nothing, absolutely nothing, could compare with the sensational delights of a fish and chip shop.

The shop was crowded with people using the restaurant section for sit-in meals while others were leaving with big, steaming parcels to eat elsewhere. He remembered how, years ago, they used to sit at home with neither crockery or cutlery, just the big newspaper-wrapped pile, already vinegared and salted, before them on an uncovered table for that rare treat which was a chip tea.

He stood outside transfixed, as the aroma grew stronger, encircled him, blasted its hot evocative fumes all over him, eventually taking him prisoner as a whole flood of other memories was released.

He was a little boy again running about the Gorbals. The suburb was a metropolis which rarely slept. He could

see and feel and hear the very heart-throb of the place . . .
Fish Jean standing, all wrapped up against the cold, leather
apron on top of her coat, with her big barrow at the Stead
and Simpson's corner in Cumberland Street and her cries
of 'Loch Fie-yenn herr-renn' in contest with Harry the
fruitman at his barrow further up the street shouting his
'hon-nee peh-hers', mixing with the strident 'cookhouse
door' bugle blast of the ragman, who always had something
to give you, even though it was just a balloon, for whatever
you might have for him . . . the grind of iron-rimmed
wheels on cobbles as a lorry passed, pulled by a Clydesdale
as big as a mastodon, its crabbed-faced carter ready to flick
you on the behind with his whip should he catch you
getting a free hang-ride, a 'hudgie', at the rear . . . and the
roars and explosive thuds and piercing screeches of steam
whistles that went night and day from the big ironworks of
Dixon's Blazes, the awesome place threatening adults
would call 'the bad fire'.

. . . And Jamesie was there with him waiting for the right
moment to go into Bridie Travis's chip shop, that moment
as they lifted a fresh basket of newly cooked chips from the
sea of bubbling fat. It was then that you would get the best
of the scraps and other debris not good enough to be sold
as chips. They called them 'crispy crumbs'. Then Jamesie
would push him up to the counter to hand over the
ha'penny he clutched with the urchin knowledge that the
smaller the boy the bigger the bag. And the truth was,
there could be no greater delight than that ha'penny bag of
Bridie's crispy crumbs, at least not when you were five and
in the company of your brother and the whole world was a
big happy game.

'Excuse me, sir,' the man said politely. Sammy had been
blocking the entrance of the Argyle fish and chip shop and
he apologised before going on his way again. Not many
minutes later, at the corner of a block, he could see
Graham's Bar.

The whole of Sammy Nelson's world had gone wrong since the day his niece, Star, had left to live in Pakistan with her husband. She was much more to him than a niece. He and his family had taken her as their own daughter after her mother's death when the two of them had lived in the most basic of tenement accommodation, a one-roomed 'single-end' in one of the oldest and worst tenements in Florence Street.

It wasn't because of the sad parting of Star that things had gone wrong, although at times it did seem that way. When she had left Scotland, Sammy had been a man of some substance. In his day he had been one of the Gorbals' best-known entrepreneurs, attaining almost legendary status for his wartime exploits as the district's most sought-after black marketeer and illicit whisky manufacturer which, in that alcohol-deprived era, boosted both popularity and fame. There was then a period in which he was involved in the property market in the Gorbals, an episode which he preferred to think little about and most definitely say nothing of. A man could have his proud moments to look back on in life but there could be other times too when, if they were to be pondered upon, it was best to stay away from the shaving mirror.

But he had been, as he considered it, respectable since departing from property, first of all going into what he had thought of as 'showbusiness', through ownership of the Pantheon Cinema, which to the people of the Gorbals was as much an institution as a picture house.

As a young woman, Star had joined him in his business ventures, demonstrating remarkable flair and enterprise which took Sammy Nelson into new avenues in the drinks trade, this time legal and respectable. Their company pioneered the modern new lounge bars which were to revolutionise drinking habits in Glasgow in the late fifties. The Star Lounge Bar Group was to become one of the most successful of its kind and was a thriving business when Star married and made her farewell from Sammar, the handsome stone villa in which they stayed in Pollokshields.

Although she couldn't say when, there had been reassurances from Star that she and her husband Russell were not going off to live in the East forever, merely to consolidate his business activities there.

Sammy had missed the professional guidance of Star, but the blows that were to follow her leaving were to have a profound effect on his life. His second wife, Emma, had died and there was no one to whom he could turn when his problems began. Misfortune had been heaped upon misfortune and it was the culmination of these that had him walking along the main street of this strange town towards a destination called Graham's Bar and a man called Alex Mitchell.

CHAPTER 8

NEW YORK, NEW YORK

ALEX MITCHELL WAS THERE AS HE HAD PROM-
ised, sitting on one of the high wooden stools, a row of
which flanked the long bar, all of them occupied. Despite
the years since they had last met, there was instant
recognition when Sammy stepped into the bar-room, and
there was a prolonged pumping handshake with a flurry of
questions about families and friends and health and an
expression of sorrow over the loss of Emma.

'God, this is some town,' exclaimed Sammy, looking
round the traditional bar-room scene and the familiar faces,
none of which he knew, though he felt he did. 'I'm only
here about twenty-four hours, slept most of this morning
and have just had my first walk down the street there. And
I can't believe it. You wouldn't think for one minute that
you were not in Scotland. It's like,' he paused, searching
for an approximation, 'it's like Main Street . . . Rutherglen.
Not a bit like I imagined Main Street, Kearny, New Jersey,
would be. I didn't even realise it was so close to New York.
You can see the skyline down the road a bit.'

'Aye, and despite that you still get conductors shouting
"Paisley Cross" when the bus stops outside the door there
at the intersection,' said Mitchell before turning to indicate
some of the adornments on the bar gantry: a miscellany of

tartanry and various photographs of Scottish scenes, including a big group picture of the Scottish international football team and a signed portrait of the Rangers star Jim Baxter, some Scottish one-pound notes and a selection of printed slogans and notices. One read 'I'm Glad I'm Scots' and another claimed 'God Made The Scottish'.

Sammy shook his head in astonishment. 'Think they're trying to tell you something in here?'

'Right, before any more natter you'd better meet Big Hamish. He's the barman . . . and watch him serve. Look . . . three customers at the one time. Not like some of our boys at home. Big deal for them just to pour a pint.'

As Mitchell had said, the big barman was pouring a beer for one customer, filling a glass of spirits for another and taking an order for a third, keeping up the routine as he worked his way down the bar before catching Mitchell's eye.

'Hamish, come and meet Sammy here. Just arrived.'

'Hi there,' he said in an all-American way with a friendly smile and thrusting out a big welcoming fist. 'It's Hamish Dugald Cameron and we're from Inverness-shire . . . but that was my great-great-grandfather. From the Old Country then, Sammy?' adding, without waiting for a reply, 'Glasgow?'

Sammy nodded.

'Well, welcome to Kearny, New Jersey. When did you get into town?'

'Just arrived. Came on a flight yesterday. Still got some of that jeg lag carry on.'

'Where you staying?'

'Temporary accommodation in Davis Street. My pal Claney got me fixed up till he comes back from his holidays.'

'Claney? Don't know him.'

'Jim McLean,' broke in Mitchell.

'You call him that . . . Claney? So you're a friend of Jim!

Now he's some guy. Got a real neat sense of humour. In here a lot. What are you having? Say, don't suppose you know much about the history of Kearny? Be right with you . . .'

There was another flurry of activity from the affable big American as he joked and served customers, always in multiples, speeding up his dispensing process by helping himself to the little mounds of change each drinker kept in front of him on the bar.

'That the custom here?' inquired Sammy.

'Aye,' said Mitchell. 'And you can get up and go out to the toilet and nobody would think of touching a cent.'

'Bit different from the Moy or any of our old pubs.'

'Mind auld Bum Beaton . . . parasite bastard? Turn your back and he'd knock your pint.'

'Or swap his one of slops for your good one.'

Hamish was back again setting up their drink. 'So you wanna know something about the history of Kearny?'

Sammy had not indicated one way or another, but saw no harm in listening.

'Try and stop him,' joked Mitchell. 'If you're new to Kearny, Big Hamish makes sure you get the facts.'

It came classroom fashion and although he didn't have a script in front of him, it sounded like he did. Without interrupting his non-stop service at the bar, Hamish began his spiel. It was to be a captivating performance as he delivered one bit, then broke off, repeating orders customers had made, serving them and returning to pick up again at the precise point where he had left off, all without breaking his flow of speech.

'Just to begin with and to help you get the hang of just where Kearny is, we're in the Hudson County of New Jersey which is on the first ridge back from the Meadow-land Depression and between the Hackensack and Passaic Rivers and there's only Hoboken and Jersey City between us and Manhattan . . . three Scotch and five beers coming right up, and what's your order, sir? . . . The first settlers were the Dutch in 1668. The Passaic at the time was afforested with tall cedars but the Dutch had to cut them down because they were being used as cover and hiding places for the river pirates who proliferated at the time, among them being the infamous Scottish privateer Captain Kidd, hanged in 1701 . . . Was it that good-looking guy with the beard there who just ordered four bottles of Coors? . . . And there you go with the change from that hundred-dollar bill . . . Kearny here takes its name from one of our early military adventurers, General Philip Kearny, who went off to fight with Garibaldi in Italy and Napoleon III in Algeria. I know you're just itching to ask how come the Scottish connection began with our town, well I'll tell you. That began about 1870 when two men, Andrew Coats and George A. Clark, both from Paisley, which is near Glasgow, built thread mills in New Jersey. They were followed by Sir Mitchell Nairn from Kirkcaldy, and that sure is some word to get the hang of, who opened his Nairn Linoleum Corporation plant here in Kearny, the three mills instigating a big influx of workers from Scotland who have been followed over the years by friends and relatives who took up jobs in all other forms of industry in this area . . . And it's six Kreugers for the top of the bar there and don't forget that slogan, there's a lot more cheer with a Kreuger beer . . . And that connection is kept up to this very day in Kearny where we have a Scots-American Club, an Irish-American Club, an Ulster Club and an Antrim and Down Club . . . Who was it asked me there for four bourbons?'

Then, in something of a parting gesture, Hamish turned to Sammy and said, 'Wanna know something? Let anyone say one word against the Scots in this place and they're out that door before you can say son-of-a-bitch.'

Sammy was shaking his head at Hamish's cabaret. 'Your man is something else,' he said to Mitchell. 'He'd be a rare turn at the Empire. And this place . . . God, I don't know whether I'm at Gorbals Cross, Brig'ton Cross, or bloody Paisley Cross.'

Mitchell laughed. 'Well that picture up there of Baxter should remind you you're not at Holy Cross.'

And the pair of them laughed.

Alex Mitchell was now in his mid-forties. He had been a one-time employee of Sammy's, beginning as a barman, then as a manager before going to work as a representative for one of the big brewing companies. But they had more than an employee-employer relationship and would often meet together with Claney, Sammy's oldest and closest friend. It was Claney who had arranged for Mitchell to look after Sammy for the few days it would take him to return from a long motoring holiday to California.

'Claney was saying you've hit it right hard. How bad was it, Sammy?'

He paused for a while before replying. 'You saw me laughing there. Well, that's the first I've laughed, even smiled, since I don't know when. That's how bad it's been. At times I thought I was for the Clyde. I would be telling a lie if I said I had been completely cleaned out. But not far from it.'

Mitchell gave a soft whistle. 'God, Sammy. That sounds serious. Really serious. You were well set up. Big house in the 'Shields and all.'

'Aye. House in the 'Shields. The Daimler Conquest. First-class holidays to the Continent. Regular tables at the One-O-One and Ferrari's. Wanted for nothing. Now the lot has gone. My second wife died and I've even lost the lassie that I brought up as my daughter . . .'

'Star, you mean?'

'Aye. Married a Paki and went off to live in his country. I've nothing against the Pakis, but when they take your lassie away to their country with them! I've tried to write and tell her what's happened but couldn't even begin, there was so much to tell. Now I've lost contact. And that's worse than everything else that I lost.'

'So, how in hell did it all happen?'

'Oh, one thing just came crashing on top of another. Kind of situation you read that happens to other people but never yourself. The money all went because I got landed with this swindler. He was one of my managers and did I not have to go and make him my top man, senior manager of all the bars? He must have been waiting all his life for a chance like this. He teamed up with a bent stocktaker who had been a pal of his. The stocktaker kept giving me phoney reports while the pair of them soaked me rotten. First I knew about it was when the bank manager called me in.'

It had been Bert Steed, on the recommendation of Star before she left to live in Pakistan, who had followed the loyal and trusted Claney as the company manager for the Star Lounge Bars Group. The best pub managers weren't hired for their expertise of the trade. Nor for their ability to be diligent and hard-working. The best pub managers were hired if just one quality could be ascertained about them. Honesty. Because of the numbers they employed, the big groups, simply called 'the brewers', couldn't be as scrupulous in their choice of managers. They enforced security measures with such practices as the spot check, which would often result in that regular feature of the trade, the clean out. That would take place after the spot check revealed that manager and staff were all involved in the game of defrauding the company. In some establishments the game was like a pyramid. Delivery men would cheat staff and staff would be cheating the chargehand who would be cheating the manager who would be cheating the owners.

Claney and Steed were trusted implicitly. Sure, they would help themselves to their share of that great British pursuit . . . expenses. But they were legitimate – weren't they? – for everyone above the status of the shopfloor man had his perk or his expenses and it was universally acceptable. Sammy and Star both knew that. But they also knew it stopped there and should a member of their staff ever try to have his or her extra share in the company profits they would be dispensed with immediately.

Not many months after Star had left for the East, company manager Bert Steed disappeared. No money had been taken from the company – an immediate audit revealed that everything was intact. Steed's family had been vague about his disappearance, but confirmed that he was in good health and living somewhere in England. Other than that they would say nothing.

Sammy had then promoted the man he considered to be the most reliable bar manager in the company to the number one post as his senior executive, with the responsibility of handling the company finances.

The swindlers had been traced to southern Spain. Glasgow fraud squad detectives had told Sammy when they were called in to investigate the disappearance of his company funds. 'We're not surprised you or any other senior people in the company knew nothing because these two did it superbly,' the officer in charge told Sammy. 'They've milked you rotten. But what surprises us is that your bank said nothing.'

The pair had set up the perfect fraud. While the manager syphoned off the money, the stocktaker, a 'professional gentleman' from an established Glasgow company, supplied endless statements certifying that everything was in order.

To stave off brewers, supply companies, tobacco firms, and others who were threatening to foreclose, Sammy had to sell Sammar, his beautiful villa in Pollokshields. Even that didn't prove to be enough. His neglected company went into an irreversible decline and in order to salvage what little was left, he had put the company on the market for a quick sale. By the time the remaining debtors had been squared, there was little left. His old friend Claney was the only one to whom he could turn and when he wrote the immediate reply had been, 'Come on over till you get things sorted out.' Not long afterwards, Sammy Nelson was on his way.

Mitchell expressed his sympathy at Sammy's story of misfortune. However, there was a lot more to tell. Sammy was keeping that for Claney.

'What about yourself, Alex?' Sammy inquired, moving the subject away from himself. 'Don't suppose you'll get homesick with all this Scottish stuff that's around?'

'Homesick!' exclaimed Mitchell. 'That's the last thing I'd be here. I'll tell you my thoughts on Glasgow and Scotland. Glasgow is the greatest city in the greatest wee country that's going, because I come from there and don't let anybody say anything against the place. But as for going back there . . . you'd have to carry me screaming to the plane. This is the place for me. I've got virtually the same job I had with the brewers, only the company I work for is into all aspects of the service industry and I'm with their drinks division. Know how much I earn here? Eight times the wage I got at home. Eight times, Sammy . . . no kidding. And there's no snaffle from snooty-nosed bosses who think they're that good their own crap doesn't smell. I don't mean that about you when you were my boss – it's the ones at the brewers I'm referring to . . . shower of jumped-up wasters with the old school tie. I work about the same hours here, but you've got to perform a lot better than in Scotland. Same for the bosses. They've got to turn the goods in. But that's the way of it here. No one does you any favours. But you do your bit at work and you've got no problems. Sammy, it's no wonder they all go about here waving the flag. And I'm one of them. We've been here eight years now and you should see the set-up we've got. Smart house, good wage, a big Pontiac with an eight-

cylinder engine. Eight cylinders for Crissakes, Sammy!
That's the kind of thing they build at John Brown's! Wait
till you see the size of it, Sammy. When I got it at first Jean
asked if I needed a bus driver's licence for it. And the
lifestyle is good. As for the kids, well they just slotted in
and within a year they were all-American teenagers who
think their mother and father have got real crazy accents.

'I know I joked there about Baxter and Holy Cross, but
that's something else I like about here. None of your daft
bigotry. There's as many Tims in this bar and around the
Scottish and Irish Clubs we go to as there are Proddies.
And a dime to a dollar you'll never hear the bigotry stuff.
People seem to enjoy themselves more and behave themselves better with or without the drink.'

Sammy cut in. 'One of the first sights I saw today was a
drunk out there on the main street . . . and he was looking
for a dust-up as well.'

'Bet you anything you like he's here on a charter for his
holidays. Holidays! That reminds me. Got a phone call
from Claney last night. He's been in Hollywood. Went to
meet the stars, he says, and it turned out they all wanted
to meet him! He's still the same old bloke. Says he's asking
for you and he'll be back here soon.'

Hamish the barman was quick, as usual, to catch
Sammy's eye for an order and as he set up their drinks he
said, 'You'll know, of course, what President Woodrow
Wilson had to say about the Scots?' The question invited
no answer. 'Well, he said, "Every line of strength in
American history is a line coloured by Scottish blood."'

'Imagine that,' said Sammy, deadpan.

CHAPTER 9

SAMMY'S STORY

CLANEY, BECAUSE HE WAS CLANEY, WAS TO hear a lot more about Sammy's story than Alex Mitchell had been told. For there was a special closeness between the two old friends. Claney and Sammy were men of the Gorbals ... and the Calton ... and Brig'ton. Which meant, of course, they were men of the world.

Their friendship had been forged in a time when their city was one of great hardship that was now just a memory, a good one for the romantics and those whose only grasp of life was of that which was in the past, a bad memory for those who could remember it as it really was.

Over the years that friendship had been further bonded, as well as tried and tested to its utmost, in the dark days when an individual had terrorised them, their families and colleagues, two of whom were killed. Because of the mutual respect which existed between them and in honour of their friendship, they had, unknown to each other, set out to exterminate that man. Now, a generation on, his son was figuring in their lives.

Sammy told it like it was. As he had outlined to Mitchell, it all seemed to begin with the departure of Star to Pakistan. But he was sure that had only been a coincidence. First there had been the sensational murder of Frankie

Burns and, not long after, the disappearance of Bert Steed. Then events had taken on a new and sinister turn when Sammy had observed that Sonny Riley, the gangster son of Steven 'Snakey' Holden, the man that Claney and Sammy had both set out to kill, was seen on several occasions in the vicinity of Sammy's office and later near his home.

There had been no arrests for the murder of Frankie Burns but those in the know – and Sammy was certainly one of them – were aware of who had been responsible. The police knew too but there hadn't been the tiniest item of evidence produced to link Riley with Burns's horrific death. When questioned by the police he offered them at least six names who were willing to testify he wasn't even in Glasgow on the night of the murder – he had been at a party in Airdrie. At least, that's what they were willing to tell any court.

Sammy knew that Steed and Burns had been old friends and had served in the Army together in Malaya and that Steed's disappearance had most certainly something to do with Burns's death. But what? The two men were deeply engrossed in trying to figure that out the night that Claney returned from his touring holiday in California.

They had been more cheerful at first, when they had met earlier that day. 'Sammy, I don't believe it . . . you're looking a million dollars. Looking more like a wealthy bookie than ever.'

'Might look like a bookie, but you can forget the wealthy bit now,' Sammy had quipped back, before going on to joke that he looked the way he did because he was much younger than Claney.

'Who are you trying to kid? You and I are ages. We're in the final straight before coming up for the pension. Isn't that right?'

'Aye, but look at the way I'm running. Just a boy at heart,' said Sammy, adding, 'but tell you what, though. Never thought I'd see the day you dressed and looked like this.' He tugged the sleeve of the colourful beach shirt Claney had brought back from California. Together with his lightweight pants, white shoes and deep tan, it dramatically altered the image of the man he had known all his working days in and around the Gorbals. 'Christ, Claney, you're sitting there like Bob Hope in *The Road to Bali.*'

But they couldn't stay away for long from the subject of Sammy's downfall, the mystery of Burns and Steed and the behaviour of Sonny Riley.

'What was your barman's name ... the one that did you?'

'McGlinchey. Desi McGlinchey.'

'Wi' a stupid blink?'

'Aye, he had a kind of nervous twitch. Know him?'

'Aye. Remember him when he used to work in the Seven Ways at Brig'ton Cross. He was at the slops game. It would make him about a shilling a night. And I always said, Sammy, that anybody who's into the slops game is the same kind that would do their granny. Never fancied the bastard. And you get landed with him!'

'Aye. I was granny. But don't rub it in.'

'So what do you reckon Riley had against the Burns man?'

'I've thought of everything. Was he maybe getting ambitious and trying to show the London boys that he was a better hitman than Frankie? Quite a few I spoke to reckon that's what it was.'

'Or was Frankie doing an order for somebody on Riley?'

'Well, he certainly wasn't into doing his own "homers".'

'And about Bert Steed? Looks like there was a connection there ... maybe somebody was using Bert as a go-between to get Burns to knock off Riley.'

'That's the one that keeps coming back to me,' said Sammy. 'For if that was the case, and Riley thought it was the case, that could be why he started taking an interest in me.'

'I see what you mean . . . he thought that Steed, being your man, was acting as your agent to arrange for Burns to do him in. Makes a lot of sense, Sammy. You certainly did the right thing getting the hell out of it. We've just a wee jungle by comparison to this place, but by Christ it can be a right vicious wee jungle. No messing.'

'But I'm not staying away forever just because of that vicious swine. Not my style, Claney . . . you know that. Then Star's going to come back some day. They weren't going away forever. Although she's going to get one hell of a shock when she finds out everything that's happened.'

'Why don't you write to her?'

'Oh, I've tried and tried. How d'you write a letter like that? Dear Star . . . Your Uncle Sammy is a daft old bastard . . . and as soon as you left he lost every penny he ever had. Come on!'

'Are you totally cleaned out?'

'Comparatively . . . aye. Totally . . . no. I kept a few wee other accounts, you know . . . rainy-day jobs? And that was what financed me here. And there's enough left to see me out for the rest of my days in humble circumstances. But, Claney, I'm over sixty, and unless it's under a bus, I'm not due the wooden box for a long while yet so I don't fancy seeing out the rest of my days in humble circumstances, if you know what I mean. So if there's any of these big American opportunities come my way, I'll go right along with it.'

'You had a boy, didn't you?' Claney asked.

'Aye. John. Did well the boy. We put him through Hutchie Grammar and after that it was Uni, law degree, went on to be an advocate, married a judge's daughter and is one of the establishment lot in Edinburgh.'

'What did he have to say about it all?'

'Never told the lad. When he got into the law and went to Edinburgh he was into another world altogether. He would never have understood some of the tricks you and I

92

used to get up to and as for all this last carry-on, well, I just don't know what he'd have said. Probably have wanted to take somebody to court for it. You know what the legal brains are like? So I just phoned and told him I had sold up and was coming over here for a spell and he said, "I think that's just marvellous, Dad." Speaks very well, you know. No' scruff like you and me, Claney.'

They were still laughing at that when Big Hamish came to serve them. His banter came as a welcome relief to the grim world the two men had been discussing.

'You're about to get two of the finest-poured Guinness you've ever set your eyes on,' he said as he expertly poured then set down two tumblers with marshmallow heads covering the blackest of beers. 'Say, Sammy,' said Hamish, 'did you know that when they signed the Declaration of Independence on 4 July 1776, two Scots, one James Wilson and one John Wotherspoon, were signatories? Dollar says you didn't know that.'

He was off serving more customers before there was an answer.

It had been over four years since they last met and that gave Sammy and Claney a lot of catching up to do.

'Did Mitchell tell you about the wages and conditions here? Unbeatable. The kids told us when we came that we should just retire and take turns at living with them. They're all in New Jersey and doing real well. But not long after we arrived we heard about this little number. They wanted a couple to look after the local high school, supervise the cleaning agency that did it, organise and staff its commissary and the like. That was us. We don't bust a gut, the hours are a treat, there's good long breaks between semesters, and our bosses on the school committee couldn't be nicer. Great wee number! And like the rest we're paying up a pension plan so we're well covered for the future. Which reminds me, Sammy, make sure you get yourself a health insurance plan. If you meet that bus you were talking about they wouldn't even lift you if they thought you weren't fully paid up.'

There was a lot of reminiscing about the old days and the old characters and friends. Claney mentioned various people in Kearny that Sammy might recollect from their old haunts in Glasgow.

'You'll remember Charlie Donnelly and Hughie Boyle?'

'Two of the crowd that used to hang about at the foot of McNeil Street . . . never out of the Pig 'n Whistle?'

'Same pair. Never worked after the war and came out here about fifteen years ago. It was the old barman down at the Irish-American club that was telling me. When they got off the boat they hadn't a tosser between them. Arse hanging out their pants. It was the thing then that when the new ones arrived there would be a chip in for them and when they saw the state of these two, they made a special effort. They got the lot. Clothes, bedsheets, pots and pans. They didn't have a trade so somebody tells them . . . "Get into flowers." That's right. Flowers. It was a cheap way of getting into business. A couple of big grocery baskets and you were off. They set themselves up outside hospitals and the like, buying cheap and multiplying the price umpteen times. You should see them now! Run two of the biggest florists in the county, live in swanky big houses out Orange way. And that's two boys that didnae know a daisy from a dandelion before they came here.

'Tell you another one. Davie McQueen.'

'Wee Dainty Davie that used to come into the lounge bar in Ballater Street? Always had on polished brogue shoes and carried one of these wee combs the weans got in lucky bags to comb his moustache?'

'Aye, that was him on his way at night to knock off that big wife that lived at the bottom end of Florence Street.'

'Her man was a Teuchter from the islands and worked nightshift at the distillery?'

'That's the one. Well, he's another that's hit the big

league here. He's an interior designer – well, that's what he calls himself. Remember what he did at home?'

'Carpet fitter, wasn't it?'

'That's right. Well, when he came here he got himself a wee shop and sold carpets – seconds he was picking up at the mills. Then he starts giving customers the patter about getting the kind of carpet that suited their personality, their husband's personality, their kids' personality, and that kind of crap. They're suckers for that kind of stuff here. No' cynical bastards like us. So wee Davie now owns Mood Carpets Incorporated and makes a fortune. Know what he does at weekends? Has one of these big four-wheel-drive things and goes camping and shooting in the Ramapo Mountains away upstate where he bought ten acres. Shoots birds, deer and anything that moves. I met him one day in a saloon. You should have seen him! Big, thick tartan shirt, lumberjack boots, and draped with big hunting knives and ammo belts. Thinks he's fuckin' Davy Crockett! But he still combs his wee moustache and still does it on the side, this time with a wife that runs one of his two shops.'

'How about Johnny D'Alessandro? Did he come here or was he one of the lot that went to Chicago?'

'Johnny D. – you know him?'

'Behave yourself, Claney. We came out of the same close in Florence Street. Lived on the same landing. Born the same month. Tasted my first ever spaghetti in his house . . . and it was absolutely *rotten*. You see, Johnny's mother was a Donegal woman. Couldn't have told you the difference between spaghetti and confetti till she married his father. The old man was a labourer and had hardly any English and when he shows old Mary how to cook spaghetti he tells her, "Put da lotta spices in it." But the only spice Mary ever heard of was white pepper. And that was the nearest they ever got to Italian spaghetti. I went in for my tea one night and she serves up this big plate of the stuff. Jesus Christ, Claney. You've never tasted anything as hot and horrible in all your life. Burned the bloody mouth off me. Yet they lived on it, for the old man couldn't teach her anything else.'

'Well, the news is Johnny didn't go to Chicago. He's in New York. Doing very well too. Split up with his first wife after they came here. She got homesick, silly bitch. Johnny wouldn't go back. And he married a nice wee Italian lassie from Hoboken. He was in the drinks business, like Alex.'

'That's right. He used to work for Ambrosio's, the Italian licensed grocers in the Gallowgate.'

'I met him quite recently. He brought the wife down to the Scots-American club for a dance they had. He runs a couple of bars in New York. Come to think of it, Sammy, he might just be the very man for you to get in touch with. You know, see if he has any contacts who could fix you up with a job? You'd be good in the drinks trade here.'

'Might be a thought.'

'I can get his number down at the club. Want me to fix up a meeting with him?'

'I'm more interested in meeting up with Johnny again than I am about the job. God, the times we had as young boys. Are you for another one?'

CHAPTER 10

JOHNNY D.

HE WAS STANDING AT THE CORNER OF A BLOCK, dressed for open warfare. There was the big gun on his hip and a thick black belt draped with the kind of weaponry and gadgetry a man needed for his type of war. Some might have said he could have retaken the Alamo with the bullets he carried and that bunch of keys could surely get him into Fort Knox. There were also handcuffs, radio, torch and a stout baton, one smack from which would mean instant surrender or unconsciousness. He was a New York policeman.

He didn't even make eye contact when Sammy approached to speak to him, although his jaws kept working over whatever he had in his mouth, presumably a fistful of chewing gum. 'Excuse me, officer,' said Sammy, 'am I in the right direction to get the M15 bus for South Ferry?'

The mouth moved again, this time to utter a few contemptuous words. 'Go buy a fuckin' guide,' it spoke. The eyes looked in one direction up First Avenue, then the other, still without making contact. The body that owned the mouth turned and walked away.

Sammy Nelson stood shocked in disbelief at the policeman's retort. Claney had warned him the previous day about New York. 'Dress casual like you're an ordinary Joe,

none of your camel coat and gold watch stuff . . . Watch it
when you get down around the Bowery . . . Get the train
in and back again at peak times when there are lots of
people around . . . If a mugger comes at you with a knife
or gun, surrender! . . . Remember, all they think is, "Here
comes lunch."' But he hadn't said anything about policemen who behaved like this. And besides, so far he had seen
lots of well-dressed men and women walking around
relaxed and unconcerned. It obviously wasn't as bad a
place as he had made out. Just surprising, that's all. And
with policemen who had missed out on their community
relations classes.

He was on his way for a meeting with his old friend
Johnny D'Alessandro. 'Umberto's Sea Food House, Mulberry Street, Little Italy. Easy to find. Right next to
Chinatown. Be there for one o'clock.' The word had come
from Claney who had arranged their meeting.

Sammy had left Kearny early, as Claney had advised,
and travelled into the city with the morning commuters. A
bit different from the Cathcart Circle, he had thought, as
he stared in amazement at the proliferation of art-form
graffiti, then looked around the carriage packed with people
of more races than he had ever seen gathered in one place.
He had heard New York described as the big melting pot
and here he was right in the middle of it.

'You'll be there early so take in the sights,' Claney had
suggested. He did. He had strolled all the way down East
42nd Street from the legendary Grand Central Station,
past Lexington, then Third and Second Avenues, soaking
in the incredible scene of man-made, concrete Alps, noting
the Chrysler Building as his favourite, then crossed over
First Avenue to go down to the waterfront where he could
see the huge glass slab that had just been erected as the
headquarters of the United Nations.

After his encounter with the policeman he had taken a
bus some of the way, getting off in the Bowery, where

JOHNNY D.

Claney had warned him to take care. It was certainly different from the first part of his walk along the broad sidewalks and among the affluent people of Uptown Manhattan. Now he was in Downtown – in more ways than one, it appeared. It was like being back in the old Gorbals, the bad bit of the bad old Gorbals, the kind of place Hogarth would liked to have painted and into which L. S. Lowry would have put his people, only he would have had to make many of them brown and black and yellow.

He saw several groups of derelict men with lunar faces ravaged by daily flushing with alcohol and in clothes that indicated they had no others. Nothing like the Bowery Boys in that great series *The Dead End Kids*. They were funny people but there weren't many smiles among these guys.

The district was obviously the headquarters of the food service industry. You could get anything you wanted, it appeared, if you were in that line. There were companies for new and used dishes, bakery and pizza equipment, bar warehouse suppliers and fountain suppliers, a catering employment agency, a specialist in new and rebuilt meat slicers, another for restaurant equipment, all housed in a jumble of old buildings, some painted in gaudy colours, one a vivid red, and all of them latticed with fire escape ladders. That was something that *was* always in *The Dead End Kids'* movies, buildings with fire escape ladders.

A big Negro exploded from a bar and Sammy smartly crossed the road, for the man had obviously declared war on the world. He was shouting at the top of his voice about what he was going to do to the Germans. They weren't pleasant things. Fortunately he was facing the opposite direction as he blasted his venomous abuse. Sammy mused at the sign on the bar from which the man had made his sudden exit: 'Where Good Friends Meet'.

He took another short bus-ride and asked one of the passengers how he would know when they were at China-

99

town. The reply had been, 'When you see China people, buster.' He vowed there and then he would never ever ask another question in New York.

Sammy had never been to the East, but it had to be like this. As the man on the bus had said, it was the place where China people were. Countless thousands of them. Everything around them was Chinese. Even the telephone boxes were pagoda-shaped. He looked in wonderment at the restaurants whose outside windows were adorned with the carcasses of dyed-red birds, or were they animals and if they were, what sort?

Inside the windows, where diners would normally be sitting, there were men at heavy wooden tables preparing, chopping and slicing pieces of uncooked food which they passed to other men beside them with enormous bowl-shaped frying pans, steaming and spluttering. The cooks were shouting to the waiters who were shouting back. It was a scene the likes of which he had never seen in his life. All around were premises with strange Chinese names: the Kee Hong Bakery, Kan Man Products, the Loong Lau Restaurant, the Kam Hop Hing Coffee Shop and Mon Fung Grocery Company.

Then, just as he turned the corner from Mott Street into Grand Street, the names changed dramatically to other sounds. There was Di Paolo's dairy store with big sun-blinds advertising ricotta, mozzarella and latticini freschi. There was a scad of restaurants which included Florio's and Ruggero's and Cellini's and the one called the Puglia which was painted in the Italian national colours of green, white and red and had a five-storey tenement above it. There was no hiding the fact that he had found Little Italy.

Sammy was now savouring this American trip as he walked along Mulberry Street towards Umberto's Sea Food House. Why hadn't he thought of coming here for a vacation in the days when things had been going well for him in Glasgow? What a great chance this had been for catching up with all his old pals, like Alex Mitchell and Claney and a few others he had met around the Scottish clubs in Kearny. Now he was about to meet his very first childhood pal, Johnny D'Alessandro.

The suit was gaberdine, expensively cut. A hand-painted silk tie neatly emerged from the crisp shirt collar and the shoes were stylish Paolo Mecozzi moccasins.

'I don't believe it,' said Sammy, laughing enthusiastically as he held Johnny's arms after they had greeted each other. 'I came here to meet my old china Johnny D'Alessandro . . . and who do I get? Jesus, you're the double of Ezio Pinza.'

'Well, you're not going to get *One Enchanted Evening*. Sammy Nelson . . . you old son of a gun, you're looking just fantastic. And so young and fit looking!'

The accent was unmistakably Glasgow, although the glottal stop had been ironed out and many of the edges had been honed down. There were hints of tones that were more Bronx and Brooklyn than Glasgow and Gorbals.

Sammy joked back about him stealing some of his best lines.

'How long do you reckon it is since we last met?' Johnny then asked.

'Fifteen years? Well, that's what Claney and I reckoned last night when we were speaking about you.'

'Let me see. You were in the property business and, I think, talking about going into public houses . . .'

'And you had just moved up to that big Italian licensed grocer's in Renfew Street . . . the one with all the sacks of stuff as you went in the door.'

'God, that's right, Sammy. So that makes it sixteen years. How time flies. Claney tell you about my set up? Remarried. Lovely Italian girl. Much younger than me. Two kids. Own two bars and going after a third. Love New

York. Working myself damn hard. But it's paying off. We've got a good lifestyle. The kids go to the best schools and they'll have a good business to take over when this guy gets too old to run it. Say, but never heed all that. God, but it's great to see you again, Sammy. Remember the times we had as kids?'

'Like me beating you to be the first to climb our backcourt midden?'

'Yeah, but you only did it because your big brother Jamesie helped you . . . dirty cheat!'

'How about when we used to go about tying people's doors together with rope we stole from the stables in Cumberland Lane, then ringing their doorbells before running away?'

'But we got a fright when we did it to Opalkos the Poles and Greens the Jews and big fat Bernie Green came up and caught us . . .'

'Then falls down the stairs on his arse chasing us!'

'Remember that cheeky wee bugger from down the street that you said you wouldn't fight because he was too small? Then he lands you one on the nose . . .!'

'Aye . . . and he turns out to be Benny Lynch, world champion!'

'What about Nancy Bell?'

'Knickers Nancy. God, she was something else.'

'Did you . . .?'

'Aye . . . before you!'

'Where?'

'In the Cally Road cemetery.'

'Don't believe you.'

'Then they split us up from going to school together.'

'Boy, didn't we kick up blue murder for that.'

'Imagine preventing two wee pals from going to the same school because one's a Catholic and the other's a Protestant.'

'They call it apartheid in South Africa. Anyway, Sammy,

they don't do it here. No, sir. You go to a state school and
everybody is there. Anyway, we made up for it when you
and Jamesie let me be the only Catholic in your football
team.'

'And you helped me get into the St John's Boys Guild
Boxing Club by vouching I was a Catholic.'

'Then you had to go and louse it all up by calling Father
Fletcher . . . "Mister". They knew right away you were a
Protestant toe-rag!'

They laughed loudly at the memory of the incident.

'Happy days . . . eh, Sammy?'

'You're right, Johnny. Happy, happy, carefree days.'

'So how are things now, Sammy? Claney mentioned
you've hit a bad patch.'

'Could be worse . . . a lot worse. I've got my health and
despite my age I think a lot about the future.'

'Just like me, Sammy. Maybe I should be thinking about
retiring, but I never do. As a matter of fact, I've got a deal
going right now that's going to really involve me in a lot of
activity. And do you know, when I heard you were around
I thought right away . . . would you be interested? I've got
a proposition which I think you'll like.'

'Tell me more.'

'Sure. But let's eat first, Sammy. They do a great
spaghetti in here. It's done with a spicy sauce.'

'Spicy spaghetti! No. I think I'll pass.' Sammy smiled to
himself.

CHAPTER II

AN OFFER

SAMMY LOOKED UP STARTLED AND NODDED AT
his friend Johnny D'Alessandro as he wrapped another ball
of glistening red spaghetti round his fork. 'Get a look at
them, Johnny. Just behind you,' whispered Sammy.

He looked again at the two men sitting eating their meals
on high stools at the counter section of the restaurant. They
were both big and beefy, wearing black simulated alpaca
zip jerkins, below which and very clearly visible were the
objects causing Sammy Nelson's obvious concern.

'You mean their guns?'

'Right. Jesus, look at the size of them! Who . . . What
. . .?'

'It's okay. It's not a stick-up. There's a court-house near
here. I've seen these guys before. They're guards at the
court and don't wear police uniform. Don't worry about
the guns. You'll see plenty of them here in New York.
Hopefully all pointing in the other direction. They're gun-
crazy here. I was reading in the *Post* just before you came
in that they had a big drugs raid last night in the Bronx
and arrested forty men together with a pile of cocaine.
Know how many guns they had between them? Twenty-
two handguns, seven assault rifles and half a dozen
machine-guns. I mean, that's D-Day stuff, isn't it? And

there was another story in the same newspaper about a cop who caught some guy trying to steal a car. Stealing a car in New York, Sammy, is nothing. It's as big a deal as when you and I used to nick the toffee apples outside Lena's Fruitshop at Gorbals Cross. Anyway, when the guy sees the cop he runs away. No violence . . . nothing. Know what happens? The guy gets shot three times in the back. Okay, he shouldn't have been messing around with cars . . . but shot three times in the back, for Chrissakes! The NYPD were asked for a comment and their man said the shooting was amply justified under the law of the State.

'It's one hell of a town. But if you let your mind dwell on all these things that go on you'd never ride the trains, never walk the streets and you'd end up sitting in your room with a couple of howitzers waiting for some hood to come and mug you.

'I take some precautions, but I don't really bother with it. I've got an it-always-happens-to-the-other-guy attitude. Statistics show that in the biggest proportion of all shootings there's a relationship between the victim and the guy who pops the gun at him. Tell you something, Sammy – I reckon you still stand a bigger chance of getting in trouble back home just because you look at somebody the wrong way. You know that thing we have about eye contact? I've never had any experience of it here. But what are we talking about? I said I had a proposition.

'Sammy, I've got a deal I want to put to you. In simple terms it means – I need your help. Here's the story. Like I told you, I've got a couple of bars. One is on First Avenue near East 59th Street. Good area. Nice food stores and delis and restaurants. Lots of apartment blocks around and heaps of offices nearby. So the custom is good and with a bit of class. It's called Murphy's. A pub isn't a pub in New York unless you give it an Irish name. Walk around and you'll even see several with the same Irish name. When I first arrived I thought I was walking in circles coming to a

bar with the same name as one I had passed half an hour
ago. Anyway, if they like Irish names for their pubs, they
get them. My other bar is a lot different. It was the first
place I got and I've had it now for about eight years. It's
in the Bowery . . .'

'And you're going to tell me it's got a sign outside saying
"Where Good Friends Meet"?'

'The Bowery Belle . . . you know it?'

'Is that its name! I passed one this morning when I was
taking a walk. There was a bit of a commotion outside and
I happened to notice the sign about the good friends. So
you own that!'

'That's what started the ball rolling for me here. Before
that I was a salesman with Leone's, one of the big drink
distributors. Angela, my wife, is related to one of the
Leones and they helped get me started at the Bowery Belle.
It's a great little earner too. Okay, the guys who use it are
not the kind you'll meet at Sardi's or a Broadway first-
nighter, but they're human and they like to booze. And
they've got bucks to spend. Guys at home like them have
to resort to meths, brasso, boot polish and sticking milk in
the gas pipe. But here when you're at that level, you've got
enough bucks to get what you want. And in Bowery Belle's
we've got the best strong wines on the market. I've got
them all: Moonlight Express Fine Apple Wine, Thunder-
flier, Olde Irish "500" Malt Liquor, Wild Shamrock Liquor
and Huntzheimer's Grand Old Times Seltzer, twenty per
cent by volume alcohol. Now if that's what these guys
want, that's what these guys get. That's the name of the
game in New York. If the customer wants it, get it for
them.

'So, the proposition. I've got a problem. I'm after a new
place. It's going to be good, Sammy. Real classy. It's called
Fausto's. It's Uptown but a bit rundown which means I
can stretch it for the price and also turn it round to be a

number one spot. It'll be my star place. If I get it, it'll really set me up for life.'

'And the problem?'

'Life's not that simple here. There are a lot of people to, shall we say, arrange. Make deals with, that sort of thing. Know what I mean? And you've got to get everything like that fixed before you take over or open up. It takes a lot of time and effort. A lot of running about, a lot of seeing people. That's what I'm doing right now. But now I've hit this snag. I've got managers who look after Murphy's and the Belle, and I've got a guy called Bobby Ryan who supervises them. Well, he's just made himself a nice deal at the Plaza. That's big bucks stuff that I can't match. Now, normally I could take over for a few months or so, or longer, and do what he's doing. But not right now with all this running around trying to fix up my deal for Fausto's. So that's the score, Sammy. I need you. How about it? Be my head manager. You know what's wanted and it won't take you long to adapt to the different ways. Play the rules here, Sammy, and it's an okay town. But you've got to play it their way.'

Sammy was staggered at the offer, although he didn't reveal that. 'That's taken me by surprise,' he said. 'You know I wasn't figuring on taking on anything like that in New York. But you know, maybe I should get something to tide me over till I figure my future out.' He didn't want to push his feigned indifference too far in case D'Alessandro withdrew the deal. 'You'll give me a couple of days to think it over?'

D'Alessandro shook his head. 'Tomorrow. I've got to know by then because if you can't take it on, then I've got another couple of guys I want to see. I've really got to move fast on this. But I hope you can do it, Sammy. It'd mean a lot to me, having an old friend like you doing the job.'

*

When he saw Claney that night to report on his meeting with Johnny D'Alessandro, Sammy said he was overjoyed at the offer and that he would be phoning him the next day to accept.

As it was to turn out, the job was to be the very tonic which Sammy Nelson needed in his life. It restored all the old bounce and confidence which had vanished when his little business empire had collapsed in Glasgow, taking with it his luxurious home in Pollokshields. When he had come to New York his future had seemed so bleak and uncertain he couldn't even contemplate what it might bring. Now everything had changed; there was a future once more. And what pleased him more about that future was the fact that he had heard from Star again. She was back in Glasgow with her young son James and Sammy had written to say that once his friend Johnny D'Alessandro had secured his new business venture and didn't require him any longer he would be returning to Scotland: 'We'll show them once more, Star. We'll show them the real fighting spirit of the Nelsons.'

CHAPTER 12

BOWERY BELLE

EARLY ONE MORNING ABOUT A YEAR AFTER HE
had started work as the head manager at the Bowery Belle
and Murphy's, the telephone rang at Sammy's flat. The
woman was sobbing uncontrollably and all she could say
at first was 'Sammy . . . Oh, Sammy.' It took about a
minute for her to be composed enough to say her next
words. 'It's Johnny. Oh, Sammy . . . it's Johnny.'

It was Angela D'Alessandro, Johnny's wife. Sammy
soothed her, trying to find out what was wrong by prompt-
ing her. 'An accident, Angela? Has he been in an accident?'

'No, Sammy. He's in hospital . . . it's his heart.'

She began sobbing again but was able to slowly part
with most of the story. 'It happened early this morning . . .
he had just got up. All of a sudden he started taking pains
in his arm and then his chest and . . . then, oh Sammy . . .
he just collapsed. It was like he had died. The ambulance
came and rushed him to hospital.

'They suspect a heart attack. I went with the ambulance
to the hospital but they said I should go home again and
that they'd be in touch. I've been telephoning but all they'll
say is "No news yet, Mrs D'Alessandro." Oh, Sammy, will
he be all right?'

'Angela, take it easy, dear, and just tell me the name of the hospital and where it is and I'll go right there.'

'It was the Bellevue . . . First Avenue and 26th Street.'

'Know exactly where you are . . . pass there every morning on my way down to the Bowery from here. Didn't know it was a hospital, though.'

There were more calming words and reassurances that Johnny was a healthy man and that heart attacks weren't as bad nowadays as they used to be, and so on. It seemed to work, for she sounded much better when he said he would contact her from the Bellevue the moment he heard anything.

Sammy had moved to New York since accepting his old friend Johnny D'Alessandro's offer of supervising manager. To be nearer his work he had moved from Kearny to a rented studio flat in a small apartment block in East 58th Street on the East River side of First Avenue, in that part of New York they call Midtown Manhattan. If he ever got lost while out walking, as he often did in the first weeks there, he merely headed in the direction of the huge glass slab that was the United Nations building and which was near his flat.

Despite his age – he was sixty-two now – Sammy had adapted quickly to New York. It was his kind of town, full of character and characters. But then, maybe his appreci-ation of it had something to do with having served his apprenticeship for the game of life back in the Twenties and Thirties in a place called the Gorbals.

Sammy hadn't travelled much, but this city over-whelmed as he imagined no other place could. He knew its statistics were bad news. He had seen some of them and they were a nightmare. More shootings, more stabbings, more violence, more deaths, more crimes of any kind, than all of Britain put together. There were weird crazes and fads, the latest being attacking firemen. So many had been victims they had started keeping figures which revealed that in one year eleven firemen had been shot and on 571 occasions they had been abused, harassed, and attacked with missiles like cans filled with sand and petrol bombs. There was also a ten per cent increase in false alarm calls to derelict buildings, arranged for the exclusive purpose of attacking the unfortunate fire fighters.

A radio broadcast he had recently heard had revealed there were 10,000 heroin addicts and that 1,000 had died of overdoses . . . and that was just among pupils at New York Schools. That death toll figure was expected to rise the following year to 1,500. But Sammy had seen the kids at the Manhattan College and the School of Music and they all looked honest, wholesome young Americans. He had read too about the university professor who castigated New York by saying it had become the product of a chaotic society in which the emphasis was 'How do I get mine?' with utter disregard as to what the impact might be . . . the right to revert to the laws of the jungle. Yet it never seemed like that to him when he wandered around the Rockefeller Centre and the other new plazas they were creating in the city they weren't allowing to grow old. Nor did he ever see signs of those horrific statistics when he explored the most impressive Avenue of the Americas or when he walked about Manhattan, even down around the Bowery Belle Bar where he spent some part of each working day.

Learn the rules and stick with them, Johnny D'Alessandro had advised. And he did. So he didn't wander in the places they called the 'no go' areas – some policemen referred to them as the 'war zones' – places like Hunt's Point where sixteen people died violent deaths every day and where delivery men moved around like they were serving under General Patton making an armed raid.

New York could be heaven. New York could be hell. Sammy had learned the rules enough to keep on the right side of heaven and because he had done that the city had so far been a memorable experience, despite some of the events that had taken place at the bar he looked after.

As he had promised, Sammy phoned Angela as soon as he had news for her. It was everything she wanted to hear. 'He's going to be okay,' was Sammy's message. 'And that's no flannel for I've just seen him. He's looking a million dollars. And I've spoken to the doctor, or professor or whatever he was. You're right, it was a heart attack but they got him here in time for the sedation and the rest, whatever it is they do. He won't need an operation or anything like that. Just one thing, Angela. You're going to have him around the house with you for quite a while, for they did stress that he'll need lots of rest when he gets out, which will be in a day or two. Get a cab and come on over and see him for yourself.'

The work that Johnny had put into acquiring his new uptown bar, Fausto's, had caused his ill-health. At least that was the consensus when the three of them talked it over in the Bellevue later that week just before he was to be discharged. Johnny held Sammy's hand tightly while Angela sat on the bed gazing at her husband and stroking his other hand.

He looked relaxed and was smiling at Sammy. 'What a godsend you've been, Sammy. You arrived out of the blue just when I needed someone to help me. And you've run everything while I've been laid up like this. Angela and I talked things over last night, Sammy. She's insisting I go away for a month before I return to work. And so too, by the way, is the doc. So we're going down to Florida. It's springtime, not too warm down there. It's a quiet time of year and that's just what I need . . . quiet and rest.

'We're going to a little place called Lantana – Angela's folks have a property down there. It's not all that far from West Palm Beach, and well out of the way of the holiday crowds. There's a fabulous beach just at the back of the house and I can't wait to get on to it . . . lie there and do nothing.

'Setting up Fausto's took more out of me than I imagined. It was one heck of a runaround. Now all that's over and it's working like a clock. But I need your help, Sammy, for I can't do any of this without you. Can you run the operation for me for the month while I'm away? You've got Murphy's and Bowery Belle going like clockwork so it's just a case of keeping your eye on Fausto's. Pino has worked out to be a good and trustworthy guy there and I know you and he get along fine. He's from a recommended family and won't get up to any tricks. But it's always good to have another eye . . . you know what I'm talking about, Sammy. One thing . . . you'll have to organise the liquor supplies for all three bars. As you know I always did that through Leone's so just keep it going. Other than that, there should be no problems.'

Sammy was reassuring Johnny that everything would be all right and that he could handle all three bars when Angela cut in. 'I think you've spoken enough about business, darling. Remember what the doctor said. You've to rest. And I'm going to make sure you do just that.'

Running Johnny D'Alessandro's two New York bars had been a whole new challenge for Sammy Nelson. There were few similarities between that operation and the Star Lounge Bars in Glasgow. For a start there were the customers. New York customers weren't like Glasgow customers. If your shop or store, restaurant or bar didn't have the goods and didn't offer the service, there was one next door or across the road only too happy to give it. The New York customer was assertive. The Glasgow customer was passive. One would say, 'Do you have?' . . . the other, 'I want'. In business, as in so much of life in New York, there were the haves and the have-nots and to be a have-not was the biggest sin of all.

They were fickle customers at Murphy's, with its club atmosphere. There was the regular lunchtime crowd, many of whom returned in the evening before taking long commuting rides to the city's far-flung suburbs and over the boundary to New Jersey. Then there was the evening set, composed of those from the apartment blocks in the area around the pub. They were middle-class people from the professions, advertising, various media and lower-echelon executives from the banking world and multinational corporations.

Sammy was good for them for his accent was, as they would say, cute. And he had that very important and essential New York quality . . . he was different. This was a city that appreciated being different more than any other. Sammy was ready-made for his newly acquired set, and being Sammy it didn't take him long to latch on to that fact.

To their great amusement, he would parody his accent for them, varying it from guttural Gorbals to posh Pollok-shields, the subtleties of the variations so beyond them they thought one was what they called Gaelic and the other BBC faggot. It was all good fun and Sammy enjoyed the joke as much as them. But when the smiles were over and they asked for a bottle of Margaux there was no point replying, in even the most persuasive of tones, that the Pinot Noir in stock was even better. If it was Margaux they wanted it was Margaux they had to get. He had learned that lesson.

They were no less assertive at the Bowery Belle where he had to perform a different kind of psychology in order to win control of the place he had nicknamed 'Poosie Nancy's'.

Claney had laughed out loud at the name one evening Sammy had taken the night off to return to Kearny for a drink at Graham's Bar with him and Alex Mitchell. 'Tell you what,' Sammy had said, 'if Burns had seen this place it would have made The Great American Poem, but not "The Jolly Beggars" . . . "The Brawlin' Beggars". That's the Bowery Belle. Oh Jesus, here comes Mr-Know-Your-Scotland. Hello, Hamish. Bet you're just dying to tell me something I didn't know about Scotland . . . as well as set us up three Bells and three Guinness.'

'For you, Sammy, no problem. Did you know that such great Americans as Elizabeth Arden of perfume fame, Thomas Alva Edison, inventor of the light bulb, the Proctor of Proctor and Gamble, the big stores people, J. Willard Marriott of the Marriott Inns chain, and Brown of Brown-Forman distillers who make Kentucky bourbon are all from Scottish stock?'

'Imagine that,' replied Sammy, smiling then turning to Claney and Mitchell when Hamish went to serve other customers. 'I'd hate to come in when the bar was empty. You'd be stuck with the bugger for the night.'

Sammy regaled them with tales of the characters and some of the situations in which he had become involved at the Bowery Belle.

'I'll never forget my first showdown at the place. Remember Rose's Homes . . . you know, in Craignestock Street, the wee street near Templeton's carpet factory in Brig'ton. Well, that's the Bowery Belle's kind of clientèle. Difference is, our dossers had nothing to spend and bevvied all sorts of muck. But these guys down at the Bowery Belle seem to get the bucks okay. And you keep them sweet as long as you've got the brands of wine they like – twenty per cent alcohol stuff. They come in from all over the place, guys that have ridden the rods up from the South, from Chicago, from over in the West, Texans, moonshiners from Kentucky, Cajuns from Louisiana, up to make their fortune in the Big Apple and end up in some doss-house in Downtown Manhattan, boozing their days away at Bowery Belle's.

'Must tell you about one character. They call him Wild Man. Don't think anyone knows his right name. It's just Wild Man. Makes his money panhandling about the streets in Chinatown where there're loads of tourists. Just one look at the big bastard and you don't think of saying "Get lost" when he starts tapping you. Apparently he's been a lumberjack, a heavyweight boxing champ, a wrestler, and he was at Iwo Jima with the Marines. Get the picture! In the mornings he drinks two bottles of Thunderbird . . . and that's just to get him sort of started up. Once he gets going he switches to Good Old Times Seltzer.

'So, this day I was in checking on things and he's kicking up a stink because all they have is Sunshine Mountain Seltzer . . . think it's made by the Hatfields and the McCoys in hillbilly country. So Wild Man goes bananas. With one hand he grabs the manager by the neck and picks him up off his feet. So, what am I supposed to do . . . play at Wyatt Earp? I mean he could have picked me up and tossed me right out on the street with his two wee fingers. But I had to do something, 'cause there was my manager, face like a beetroot and choking to death.

'Anyway, I tell him the Sunshine stuff is good news and he bangs his other fist on the counter – I'm not kidding, you've never seen a bunch of Fyffe's like it. Then he lets fly with a mouthful the like of which I never knew existed. I mean, you and I know that when it comes to foul-mouthing it we've got a few champs back home. But this Wild Man . . . you should have heard him at me. "Why you short-assed, pig-fuckin', piss-ass'd, whore-mongering, mother-fuckin'" . . . and that's just the ones I remember – it went on and on. None of your plain wee effin' B's or C's with him.

'Meanwhile, the whole bar is hushed, all eyes on the action. So I says to him in dead broad Gorbals, "Hey, big man," – trying to act kind of tough, like – "d'you know, we haven't met? I know your name is Wild Man. But has no one told you my name?"

'And the big dumb bastard shakes his head in reply. So I says, "Well now, Wild Man. My name is Jesus. And I would like you to join in while we all sing . . . Oh what a friend we have in Jesus." Don't know what the hell made me think of it, but by Christ it worked. The whole place fell about and Wild Man dropped the manager and roared with laughter. He's been my best pal ever since. See, if anyone steps out of line now, Wild Man is down on them like a ton of bricks. I reckon I'm the safest guy in the Bowery. But, just as a guarantee, I always make sure we've got more than ample stock of Thunderbird . . . and Good Old Times Seltzer.'

They were still laughing loudly when Sammy called Hamish over. 'Set us up another round. And, Hamish, did you go on any haggis hunts when you visited Inverness?'

'Haggis hunts!'

'Aye, haggis hunts. Quite popular, especially in Inverness-shire. Bet you didn't know the haggis is unique only to the Highlands of Scotland? There's never been one found any other place either in Britain or the rest of the world.'

'Why, now I never did know that,' said Hamish seriously.

'There you go then, Hamish. Another one for your facts book. Include that in your speech at the next Rotary lunch.'

The three men looked at each other and laughed again as the barman went off to serve more customers.

Being involved in the drinks trade, Alex Mitchell was interested in the running of Johnny D'Alessandro's three New York bars. 'Is it different suppliers you use for each of them, or what?' he asked.

'No. The one. Leone's.'

'That must be a fair bill.'

'Aye, I got a surprise myself when I signed for it the other day. More than $60,000 for the month.'

Mitchell whistled softly. 'Wish I had a wee order like that. Know how much commission I would earn from that . . . more than 300 bucks.'

'Really?' said Sammy, surprised. 'Just one off?'

'No way. Every month.'

It was Sammy's turn to whistle. 'That's a lot of money. But could you supply that amount?'

'No problem. I do it all the time to other bars and outlets that I do business with. But most or nearly all of my business is renewals. I hardly get any new orders, especially ones that size.'

'What about the range? I mean it's not your ordinary stuff like you get in here. Fausto's, Murphy's and the Belle are three very different kettles of fish. Between the three of them there's everything on offer. At Fausto's we carry fifteen different Scotch Malts, ten champagnes and you name it, we've got it in wines. Murphy's is much the same, but with an emphasis on the top cask beers, and I've got to keep my boys at Bowery Belle's happy like I said . . . everything from Sunshine to moonshine.'

'Sammy, I work for Acme. They're one of the biggest in the trade on the entire East Coast. We carry the lot. No problem supplying you.'

'Tell you what I'll do. I'll get the full list and if you carry all the stock and can better Leone's price you might have yourself a deal . . . and 150 bucks a month commission.'

'I said 300.'

'And what about Sammy?'

Claney laughed at the two. 'I'm enjoying this,' he said. 'See watching a couple of Scotsmen on the make? Takes a bit of beating, I'm telling you.'

*

Two days later Alex came to see Sammy, working at the time in Murphy's Bar.

'Boy, do I have great news for you, Sammy? I've gone over that Leone list with a fine toothcomb. They're doing you rotten. Why, I can better that price by over two grand. And I would still be making my 300 smackers in commission.'

'Our 300,' corrected Sammy.

'All right . . . our 300. But what about the two grand you would be saving?'

'I wouldn't be saving a penny, Alex. It's Johnny D'Alessandro that'd be saving.'

'Aye, if you tell him.'

'I'll be telling him, Alex.'

'Okay, got the message, Sammy. Right, let's get down to business. What are the chances of switching?'

'Don't see why not. The Leone man is due on Friday, I'll tell him the party is over. How long would it take you to organise supplies?'

'No problem to Acme. Phone an order before 9 a.m. any weekday and it's in your cellar within twenty-four hours . . . anywhere in New York State or in New Jersey. We're no slouches.'

'There goes the real company boy,' Sammy smiled. 'Like a Guinness?'

'Not when I'm working. Anyway, I've got more orders to do. When can you confirm the order?'

'Let's say starting next week.'

The man from Leone was grim-faced when Sammy told him he didn't require their supplies any longer. 'Are you sure you know what you're doing?' he asked.

'What d'you mean?' Sammy came back. 'Think I'm an amateur at this game?'

'So who's going to supply you?'

'That's between me and the new boy . . . isn't it?'

'But just let me make the point again, Mr Nelson. Are you really sure you know all the implications in cancelling out with our company?'

'I've read the order contracts. There's no restrictions in the print. So I'm free to go to the guy who gives me the best price. That's the name of the game in New York . . . you should know that.'

'And you're aware of nothing else?'

'Like what?'

'Like . . . loyalty.'

'Don't make me laugh. Loyalty in New York! The King and the Queen and the President and God are all known by one name here. The dollar. That's the only thing you've got loyalty to in this town. And that's most certainly where my loyalty is.'

'So you really aren't aware of anything else?'

'Are you trying to tell me something?'

'Not really. I'm just trying to ascertain if you're aware, that's all.'

'Aware of what?'

'Oh . . . just let's call it loyalty and leave it at that. I'll report the fact you want to cancel to my office and they'll let you know.'

'Know what?'

'Let's just say, they'll let you know.'

There had never been any need for Johnny D'Alessandro to tell Sammy his reasons for dealing with Leone's. It figured that perhaps he used them because of the Italian connection but other than that Sammy had never given it a thought. But what Johnny D'Alessandro had never mentioned was that as part of his deal in establishing the bar he called Fausto's, he had been forced to use the Leone company for all his drink supplies.

Fausto's was in the area of Manhattan under the protection of the Petruccis, the elder of whom was one Salvatore

Petrucci, now in his seventies. He had come to New York as a babe in the arms of his parents, a poor family from Corleone in the mountains above Palermo in Sicily. Corleone – the name means 'lionheart' – was the holiest of holy places in Mafia history and Salvatore was now one of the five godfathers of Mafia families who operated numerous rackets in the state. They had various industries and supply agencies totally under their control. Among them were meat distribution, waste disposal, building materials and the fruit markets. Petrucci's line was in protection, drink supplies and drug running from South America. As part of his protection deal in the catering and drinks business, the price of the insurance policy was buying all supplies from his thriving alcohol trading company, Leone's. It acted as the upfront and legal division of his multifarious activities. And when you agreed to take a Leone order and all that went with it, there was no such word as 'cancellation'.

The following morning just after the staff had opened up Murphy's, two well-dressed men walked in, both of them wearing the snappy and fashionable narrow-brimmed soft hats called Borsalinos. One of them stood at the back of the room and had the habit of constantly adjusting his tie. The other walked slowly to the bar and inquired, 'Mr Nelson?'

'Well, what can I do for you?' said Sammy cheerfully, once he had ushered the two men into his back office. He thought they were either in to make a booking for one of the office functions which were regular affairs at Murphy's, or else were representatives offering some new service, like cleaning or fire precautions.

The man who kept adjusting his tie closed the door behind him and stood by it while the other, a handsome man with piercing brown eyes, took the seat in front of Sammy's desk. 'I just wanna confirm what you've done,' said the handsome one seated in front of Sammy. 'My

superiors tell me you wish to cancel your contract with
Leone's.'

That took Sammy by complete surprise. 'Leone's . . .
yes. Cancel . . . yes, that's right. But what's it to do with
you? And just who are you anyway?'

'Let's just say we act on behalf of the Leone Distribution
Agency, and our job is to speak to people who might be,
shall we say, a little unhappy with any aspect of the
company, and to persuade such people that it's not good
business to be unhappy with the company and that if they
want to insist on being that way with Leone's then we've
got a nice little parking lot arranged for them . . . at the
foot of the East River. Does that make it clear who we are?'

Sammy sat back, shocked. 'What the hell . . . What are
you doing in here threatening me?'

'Threaten,' said the man in front of his desk nonchalantly, looking at his fingernails. 'We don't threaten,
Mr Nelson. We're not boys like that. We make promises.
But we don't threaten. And I'll make you a promise right
here and now and that is if you don't call Leone's and get
that order reconstituted, I'll guarantee you that what I
said about the East River comes true!'

At that, he slowly reached into an inside pocket of his
jacket and pulled out an object which he thumped down
on the desk in front of Sammy. 'Being a man of the world,
Mr Nelson, you'll know what that is.'

Sammy looked at the small, shiny, snub-nosed gun lying
menacingly on the blotting pad of his desk.

'You could, of course, tell me, Mr Nelson, to go fuck a
duck. There's your chance right there in front of you. It's
fully loaded. Just pick it up and start poppin' it at us. Go
on, Mr Cancellation Nelson. Pick it up and let's see how
good you are at the funfair.'

The other man at the door wasn't fixing his collar any
more, and he was staring hard at Sammy and the gun.

Sammy looked at him and then at the gun. The thought of picking it up was the furthest thing from his mind.

Normally he was good in showdown situations like this. There was always an answer, even to the most delicate of situations. But this time he could think of no response. If ever anyone had him trapped, these two did. He knew it. They knew it.

Could I bluff them? he wondered. It was always the last resort. And this was a last resort situation. 'What if I say I can't cancel? That the company I have signed the new contract with are really big boys and would just hate it if I told them that a couple of well-dressed punks wanted me to take my business away from them?' he said.

The man at the door stiffened at the word punk and the faint smile on the other man's face vanished as he indicated the telephone. 'There's your message boy, Mr Wiseguy. Go on, let the other outfit know about these two punks. And tell them that this punk will spell out the message loud and clear to them just in case they don't believe you. Okay, Mr Smartass Nelson?'

A myriad of responses flushed through Sammy's mind. So what do you do when bluff is met by counterbluff? Keep on playing the game? But then these guys aren't playing games. Or are they? Maybe they're not really as tough as they make out. Big boys with a wee gun, that's all. Yeah, wide men wi' a shooter. God, Jamesie would have hunted the pair of them with his bare hands. I'm no Jamesie . . . but at least I can try.

'Listen, pal,' said Sammy, taking a new stance. The way he said that short three-letter word 'pal' spelled out just what that stance was. 'If you two are looking for trouble then I know the very boys who'll give it to you. And they're very very big boys,' said Sammy.

It was a brilliant portrayal of the tough-talking, no-nonsense, non-compromising dealer. But he could see in an instant that it didn't impress the man in front of him who was once more examining his fingernails.

'So you've got friends, Mr Nelson. We would just love to meet them, wouldn't we, Gino?' he said without looking round. The other man by the door made no acknowledgment.

The hand he had been so carefully examining then slowly stretched across the table to casually retrieve the revolver, picking it up as if in slow motion, and pointing it at Sammy's face before returning it to the inside of his jacket.

'Let's just get things clear before we leave, Mr Nelson. The Leone agent will be here as usual next week and you will make your usual order with him and tell him how sorry you were about wanting to cancel out. If for some reason that doesn't happen, then we'll be back in this room a week today at exactly the same time. Ciao, Mr Nelson.'

Nothing more was said and as he got up, the other man opened the door, allowing him to walk out ahead.

Claney had suggested meeting in the Scots-American Club in Kearny when Sammy phoned later that morning. 'It's imperative I see you and Alex tonight. But not at Graham's. I'm in no mood for the Scots encyclopaedia. Where's the Scots-American again? I get mixed up between it and the Irish-American and the Ulster Club. Oh yes, that's right, I should have remembered. Leave the main street at the fire station and go down to Highland Avenue.'

The two men were waiting for him in the club's St Andrew's lounge when he arrived at seven o'clock. It was obvious from his demeanour that something was wrong.

'Here, put that in you first,' said Claney, placing a glass of whisky in front of him. 'I've never known you as uptight as you were on the phone this morning, Sammy. What's happened? Problems?'

'Aye,' replied Sammy, shaking his head. 'Problems all right. And I need solutions. Badly. And quickly.'

He told the story as it had happened that morning. 'Okay, I've read about the Mafia. Al Capone and the mob and that sort of stuff. And I've seen all the pictures ... Edward G. Robinson, George Raft, Bogart and the rest. But that's the movies. I mean ... is it really like that? Bang, bang and you're dead. Okay, you guys, give him a concrete overcoat. Were these ones the real thing? Fixing me up with a place at the foot of the East River! I mean ... were they for real?'

Alex Mitchell nodded. 'Aye, Sammy, they're for real, as you say. We've come across this situation before with Leone's. It's owned by a guy called Petrucci and he's said to be one of the real Mr Bigs in the Mafia. He's very bad news, Sammy.'

'Jesus Christ, Alex ... you knew that things like this happen and you let me go ahead and cancel with them? Why the bloody hell didn't you warn me?'

'Because it's never happened to me. I've just heard about it. You tend not to believe these things till it's you that's affected.'

'Well, it's fucking well *me* that's affected. In a big way,' cut in Sammy. 'What am I going to do?'

'Sammy, when you deal with these guys, choice is the last thing you've got. Just you make sure when the Leone man pays his next call you make the usual order with him. No messing. And that'll be it. Your problem will be over.'

'How about your end of things?'

'I can fix that all right.'

'Tell you what, this is really sticking in my throat. I don't like having to submit to people like this. Makes me feel I want to do something to get my own back. The idea of just meekly bowing to them, letting them walk all over me, gets my dander up.'

'Sammy,' said Mitchell, 'don't even think about bucking

them. Not for one second. What you're up against is not just a couple of guys. It's a whole institution that has no respect for what you and I know as the rules of the game. The only law they know is their own. No one else's. And God help anyone who bucks their laws. That's why you've got no option, Sammy.'

'Christ, they were like two boys playing a role in the pictures, one of them sitting there looking at his nails like he was John Garfield. I was just waiting on him bringing the nail file out. If he had I'd have laughed in his face. And his china . . . standing at the door playing the dumbo bodyguard. Couple of bloody play-actors. How many times have you watched that scene? Good mind to bring Wild Man down from the Bowery to sort the pair of them out.'

'Sammy . . . for Christ sake stop it. These guys are no actors. They're the real McCoy, Sammy.'

Sammy gave a sardonic chuckle and Claney asked what was going through his mind. 'That'd be a good one for Hamish's book of Scottish facts,' said Sammy, still smiling. 'Who was the first Scot to end up in the East River as a result of sticking two fingers up at the Mafia?' Then, to dispel the alarmed look on Alex Mitchell's face, 'It's all right, Alex. Just joking . . . that's all. Just joking. Another Bells?'

CHAPTER 13

NAILED

HIS FRIENDS CLANEY AND ALEX MITCHELL HAD
said what they had to say. They were right. You didn't
buck the Mafia and get away with it. Sammy knew that
now. He had a week to decide whether or not to cancel his
order with Alex Mitchell's Acme Company and tell Leone's
to resume deliveries . . . or else! 'Or else what?' he had
thought.

Before going to work the following day, he had taken a
cab up to the top of East 59th Street to Central Park and
taken a walk along its miles of paths and avenues. It was
just what he wanted for there was a lot on his mind and he
had to come up with some kind of answer – an answer that
would satisfy Sammy Nelson.

He had gone for walks in Central Park before, particularly on a Sunday morning when it was busy with strollers
and others partaking in the new exercise and fitness craze
that was starting to sweep the country. It was always an
enjoyable place and parts of it would remind him of the
best of Glasgow parks; there was even a section in which
he could imagine he was in the Glasgow Green, his city's
oldest park, because of that rare combination of rural and
urban, trees and parkland and birds singing all within
earshot of the throb of the city.

The pending confrontation with the men from the Mafia worried him. He considered every aspect of it. With their dress and dramatics, it had been easy to think lightly of them but he knew he was deluding himself by doing that. These weren't the guys from the movies.

He cursed the irony of it all. He had left his own city partly because of a sinister threat of violence, and here he was, 3,000 miles away and just more than a year later, facing a similar predicament. Whoever could have foreseen that twist to his life?

He would have had a much better chance of doing something about the events that faced him in Glasgow. There he knew every aspect of the system; what could be done and what couldn't be done. Something could have been done about Sonny Riley. But this, as the New Yorkers were always saying, was a different ball-game. A different ball-game in a different ball park.

But, curse it, it was against every basic principle of his life to sit back and accept such a state of affairs. He just had to respond in some way. All right, he knew that Sammy Nelson couldn't just declare war on the Mafia. 'Sammy Nelson declares war on the Mafia,' he repeated to himself with an inward chuckle, at the same time dismissing the thought. Anyway, that would have implicated his friend Johnny D'Alessandro who had said his wife had 'a connection' to the Leones, although he didn't seem prepared to elaborate. He did wonder, though, what that connection was. Then he had thought, did that really matter?

His mind chased up one avenue, down another, went round in a circle in one direction, then tried it in another. He was in a mental maze from which he could find no way out . . . except to comply. But the more he considered it the more the detestation within him grew at the prospect of meekly caving in to these people without some kind of fight . . . without making them think you just can't go around standing on everyone like that.

He told himself again the story he had so often quoted about the world being full of tinpot bullies and dictators and unless you stood up to them it made your own existence meaningless. He remembered Hughie Scott, the bully in his class in the Gorbals. Big boy with a face like a pig . . . well, that's the way it looked to him when he was just ten years of age. Scott, because he had failed his exams and had been put back a class, was at that vital stage in his development where the rest of the class were just young boys and he was like a young man. He had a gruff masculine voice and was physically far superior, and nothing was easier or more satisfying to him than being the bully.

Because of Scott, Sammy had arranged with Johnny D'Alessandro to get smuggled into the St John's Boys Guild Boxing Club, and even when they discovered later he was a Protestant they had invited him back again. It was the dedication he had put into the lessons and coaching he had received there that had enabled him to revenge the bullying that Scott had made him endure by bloodying his nose one day in what he remembered as a classic school playground battle.

Then there had been Steven 'Snakey' Holden, father of Sonny Riley. He had been the worst-ever menace to his life, terrifying his first wife to an extent that had led to her complete nervous breakdown and eventual early death. Holden had also been responsible for the death of two of his closest associates. So Sammy had had to stand up to Holden too, by taking the only course that seemed available. The mission he had undertaken to exterminate Holden had only been thwarted because he had been beaten to the task by Claney, a man of many similar feelings to himself.

He realised Claney was taking a different stance now

over what he could do about these men from the Mafia. But that was for the simple reason there was no obvious option . . . or was there? For two hours of a beautiful spring morning in Central Park, that was the only thought which occupied Sammy Nelson's mind.

When he left the park by the big main gates at Fifth Avenue, where the men with the horse-drawn cabs stood, he crossed the road to the Plaza Hotel, the ritzy Plaza, the best-known and priciest hotel in New York. He wanted to speak to Bobby Ryan, the man he had replaced as Johnny D'Alessandro's senior manager, who was now an executive in the hotel. At Ryan's invitation he had been to speak to him several times in the past, Ryan obviously enjoying Sammy's company, hearing about the old customers at the Bowery Belle and catching up on the gossip from Murphy's.

Bobby Ryan shook his head several times when Sammy told him the story about the men from Leone's. 'Sammy, the fact you are Johnny's friend doesn't matter a cuss to these people,' he said before revealing some of the background to the history of D'Alessandro's connection with Leone's.

'Listen, maybe things are a bit more complicated than you realise. With Italians in New York, nothing is straightforward. Johnny's wife Angela is from a family called Sabbatini. Her father is Mario Sabbatini. His parents, Angela's grandparents, come from a town called Corleone in Sicily. Corleone is no ordinary town. It's the Mecca . . . the Medina . . . the Jerusalem of the Mafia. No place is more holy to them. Now old Petrucci, who owns Leone's, is also from Corleone. Once the two families were friends. But you know what friends can be like! I mean, I'm from Irish stock and you know what we can be like. But this lot! Anyway, it had been hoped that Angela would marry a Petrucci and seal the families closer together. Then Johnny appears and marries her and the families drew apart

instead. Then there was a feud. Someone was eliminated
. . . they said it was by accident. The next thing you know
the Petruccis and the Sabbatinis are enemies.

'When Johnny went after Fausto's he discovered that it's
in the area run by the Petrucci clan. So he went to them,
told them his family are out of Naples via Scotland and
have got nothing to do with the Sicilians and their problems. Old man Petrucci let him have the place, but on
the same terms as any outsider. Absolutely no favours.
He'd have to deal with Leone's for all his supplies. The
Sabbatinis tried to get Johnny to pull out of the deal but,
through Angela, Johnny convinced her old man that any
interference would cause them big financial trouble. So
for his daughter's sake old Sabbatini allowed Johnny to
continue his dealings with Petrucci and Leone's.

'Now the way Leone's would read it when you
bucked them is that Johnny had asked you to do it. Like
I said, nothing's simple when you're dealing with Italians
in New York. If you cancel that order I'll give you a
written guarantee right here and now that you're not only
signing your own death warrant, but that's the end of
Johnny's business. They'd probably take care of Johnny
too. Christ, Sammy, you could spark off a whole new
Mafia war. You're sitting on a time bomb. How many
days has it left to tick? Three, you say? Well, I wouldn't
even play around with that fuse. It might be a short
one.'

The two men from Leone's had said they would be back to
see him in a week's time, although the agent who came for
the orders would be back before then, on the Friday of that
week. It had been Tuesday when he had spoken to Bobby
Ryan at the Plaza. He agonised over the situation, not
recontacting Claney or Alex Mitchell because they would

only tell him the obvious and it was the obvious to which he was trying to find an alternative answer.

Events moved fast in the next few days, far faster than he thought he could handle. He had his mind set on a definite course and there was a lot of work to be done. There were a variety of calls to be made in the city and a lot of arrangements to be made prior to the visit of the man from Leone's.

Late on Friday afternoon, when he was checking affairs at the Bowery Belle, his manager came to the office to say the Leone rep had called. It was the same one as had warned him about cancelling his order and this time he had what Sammy considered a smug look about him. That look, as Sammy read it, was saying, 'I've come to see you crawl, mister.'

'Nice to see you again, Mr Nelson,' said the man, emphasising the Mister. 'So it will be business as usual I take it, Mister Nelson?'

'That's right, my friend. It's business as usual.'

The man started to write on the form uppermost on the clipboard he carried.

'Hey . . . wait a minute,' said Sammy. 'I said business as usual. But I didn't say with you. My business as usual is with the Acme Company. You can write *that* down on your little piece of paper if you want. And while you're at it, write something else down and give it to your two pals who came here to threaten me. You'll know them. Fingernails and Gino. Maybe you'll be seeing them. Give 'em the message . . . go fuck a duck. Got it? Now on your way, pal.'

Sammy smiled as the man, his face still flushed with anger, walked out of his office without saying anything further.

There were still two days remaining till the Monday morning deadline the two men from Leone's had given him to make up his mind. That gave him the time he needed to complete the remaining arrangements and to spend time tidying his office and having meetings with the staff; he wanted everything clarified and set straight. By the Sunday night he had achieved all he had planned to do. They could come any time now. He was prepared for them.

Just after midday, on schedule, as he had thought they would be, the big black sedan pulled up outside the bar and two well-dressed men got out, leaving a driver at the wheel. It was a repeat performance of their meeting the previous week. Both were in the same smart clothes. Fingernails wore a dark blue shirt and a light tie this time.

'That was bad news you gave our Mr Buontempi from Leone's last Friday,' said Fingernails, easing himself into the chair in front of Sammy's desk. Gino took up the same stance by the side of the door. 'Maybe you were just having some kind of joke with him?'

'About what?'

'About terminating your order with the company.'

'Look, let's get this perfectly clear,' said Sammy. 'I legitimately stopped my order with Leone's and I legitimately made a new one with the Acme Company. Are you telling me I can't do that?'

'Are you some kind of a dumb nut or something? How many times do we have to tell you? You have a deal with Leone's and there's no cancelling.'

'And if I insist on cancelling will you threaten me with the gun like you did last week?'

'Listen, mister. I don't think you know what's law here. Your boss pays protection money to our company and part of the deal is that he takes his booze order from Leone's. That's your insurance policy and you've just cancelled it. And when you cancel an insurance policy like that, you pay the penalty. There's plenty in New York can tell you what we do to people who play this kind of game with us. You ask if I'm going to threaten you with the gun like I did last week. No, mister. There's no threats this week. You've just signed your own death warrant and you're a dead man. A very dead man.'

Sammy sat impassively as Fingernails turned slowly to his mate and nodded casually. 'There's your very last chance,' he said, looking at the gun Gino was holding and pointing at Sammy. 'Don't say you weren't warned, you Limey screwball.'

It was just then that the door opened with the kind of force that an explosion might have created. But this explosion was two beefy detectives, guns in hand, who had been waiting outside. Gino turned the gun on them and as three quick shots rang out, Sammy ducked behind the desk listening to the bullets ricocheting round the room, praying their final destination wouldn't be somewhere inside him. There was a cry of agonised pain as a bullet smacked into Gino's shoulder and his revolver clattered loudly on the tiled floor. Then, for a few seconds, there was complete silence as everyone stilled. The detective who had returned the shot aimed at him, calmly walked up to the wounded Italian and despite the man's agony, kneed him, with all the force he could muster, squarely in the genitals. The Italian howled loudly as he jack-knifed with the excruciating pain, whereupon the policeman hit him three vicious blows with the barrel of his revolver.

With the shooting stopped, Sammy got up and watched in amazement as the two policemen left the agonised Italian sprawled on the floor and walked towards Fingernails, sitting in surrender, coolly and unemotionally viewing the sight of his wounded and beaten colleague. The two policemen then set about him with their handguns, one still using the barrel, the other hitting him repeatedly with the heavy butt on his head and upper body until he too fell to the floor, his nose smashed and blood pouring from deep gashes on his forehead.

'That's what's known as legitimate force in order to suppress a violent criminal who tried to shoot a member of the NYPD,' said one of the detectives to Sammy as he carefully wiped the blood from the barrel of his revolver with the handkerchief from Fingernails' jacket pocket before replacing the gun in his shoulder holster.

'Gino Baldini and Pino Cefalu,' said the other detective. 'Now isn't that a beautiful sight. What naughty, naughty boys you've been. Attempting to murder a policeman, resisting arrest, intimidation, threatening with a firearm, and according to police files there are warrants out for outstanding charges of attempted murder and causing grievous bodily harm plus other warrants by the Nevada State Police for offences committed in Las Vegas.

'All right you guys, everything by the book. If you can hear me, what I'm saying is that you're under no obligation to make any statement which may incriminate you and you've the right to call an attorney.'

Then he turned to Sammy and with a smile and a wink said, 'You see, Mr Nelson. We're a fair country and we even give hoods like this all the benefit of the law.' The detective bent down and handcuffed each of the semi-conscious men lying on the floor. He then helped Sammy off with his jacket so he could unbutton his shirt and extract the tape recorder that had been affixed to his body.

'That went real well, Mr Nelson. They said everything a court would just love to hear. It's taken us a long time to get these two. And if it hadn't been for your courage they'd have gone on for a long time yet.'

Claney and Alex Mitchell were wide-eyed and silent as the long story unfolded over the course of several rounds of drinks. 'Good God,' exclaimed Claney. 'That's the old Sammy Nelson stuff. Doing the Mafia . . . and getting away with it!'

'Yes . . . but not without what happened to poor old Johnny.'

Sammy had gone over the whole story in the fullest of detail with them. It had all begun, he told them, when he had considered going to the police the first time he was threatened by the pair from the Leone Company. But it hadn't been till after he had got the full story from Bobby Ryan that the way had been made clear and his mind made up to go through with it.

There had been a call to Murphy's later that day from Angela in Lantana, Florida. Johnny had suffered another heart attack and was in an oxygen tent in the intensive care unit in the hospital at Fort Lauderdale. When he finished work, at midnight that night, Sammy had called the number she had left.

'Mr D'Alessandro passed away this evening at 10.22. I'm very sorry,' said the sympathetic female voice at the hospital reception.

Then Sammy had started making the various arrangements. Because of the fear of a backlash on his friend Johnny D'Alessandro, he had been reluctant to go to the police. With Johnny's death that threat had been removed. There was just one vulnerable person left . . . himself.

He had spoken to the New York District Attorney's Office that week and had been told that if he signed an affidavit and that if the police could overhear any threats from the Leone men and make a tape recording of them, there would be sufficient evidence to proceed with a prosecution. The Assistant District Attorney to whom he had spoken said he reckoned he could get them at least five to ten years for this offence in conjunction with the other outstanding charges and their history of previous convictions.

'You have the sincere thanks of the New York Police Department,' the District Attorney had said, shaking Sammy's hand during his visit after the arrests.

Sammy paused, looking at Claney and Mitchell. 'It's rotten in a way how things have ended up, though. There's

Johnny gone and I was just getting used to this place. I think I fell in love with New York. And that certainly goes for Kearny too. But Star's back home now and we've some unfinished business there. You know what I mean! The District Attorney has cleared me to leave the country and, anyway, I think the Italian connection in New York will be out for some time as far as I'm concerned. Don't fancy any more trips to Little Italy. So it's back to Bonnie Scotland. Ach, it's always great to get home . . . isn't it? Dear old Glesca toun and all that.'

At that, he waved an airline ticket for a flight from New York to Prestwick later that week. 'The bad boys up in New York don't know my Kearny connection so I'm safe till I get the plane. I'm going to have a few days enjoying myself here with you guys and the rest of the boys around the clubs. Oh, and I must go and see Big Hamish and give him another fact for his book. The name of the first Scot to buck the Mafia . . . and get away with it.'

CHAPTER 14

REUNITED

AUSTRALIA WAS TECHNICOLOUR. GLASGOW
was black and white. New York was jazz – the loudest, the
brassiest and played by the biggest orchestra. Glasgow was
ragtime, but the quartet were All Stars. And when you had
bathed in that technicolour and been a part of that
orchestra's jazz, Glasgow took on a whole new and different
meaning. That was the way of it for Star and her Uncle
Sammy when they returned to live in the city of their birth
once more.

They had been away only a brief few years but it had
been an epoch. They had left when dancing was foxtrots
and quicksteps. They returned when it was the Twist. It
had been bebop when they departed. It was rock-'n-roll
when they came back. Lounge bars had been a drinkers'
novelty. Now they were a necessity. The war had seemed
like just yesterday when they had gone, now it was in the
dark and distant past. Then people had been happy with
mince, now they wanted moussaka, and it was better to
boast about Blankenberg and Benidorm than Blackpool.

The great rebuilding schemes of the Sixties which had
just been started when they left were now in full swing.
The Glasgow that was, was no more. What had started out
as redevelopment had become metamorphosis. Trans-

figuration became disfiguration. The new order was the planners' dream, the people's nightmare.

It had taken them hours that first day after Sammy had flown in from New York to catch up with what had happened to each of them in the years they had been parted. They had cried unashamedly when Sammy had emerged from the Arrivals Hall at Prestwick Airport. The great joy of being reunited had been double for Sammy as he held up Star's son James, the boy he thought of as his grandson, and said proudly, 'So this is our wee Jamesie!'

'James,' Star had reproved.

'Call him what you like, darling. He's wee Jamesie to me.' They left it at that.

Star had bought a two-room-and-kitchen flat just off Calder Street in Govanhill and it was to be Sammy's first home on his return.

'Some change, eh, Star?' he had said. 'When you think what we had . . . what we achieved. There you were out in cowboy country in Australia and me the New York kid with what they call "a smart pad".' He looked around the little apartment on the top floor of the red sandstone tenement block, the main lounge doubling as kitchen with cooker and wash basin. 'Different . . . eh?' shrugged Sammy. 'Tell you something, though, that was really brought home to me in New York. You can make money there all right but you've to be sharp and on the ball. You've really got to be up early in the morning to be ahead of that lot. The place is teeming with hustlers. Think up some new way of making money there and before you know it you've got rivals moving in on you with the same idea, trying to cut you out. Every man, woman and child is a hunter and they're out there in that big concrete jungle looking for the game that'll make them their million.

'It's not like that here. We're too easy-going. Everybody's content to get a job and make money for somebody else. Why, for God's sake? The way to make money is get other people to work for you . . . not for you to work for other people. And that's what makes it easy to make money here. If you're a hunter here you can get it all your own way. I learned that lesson away back in the days when I worked for Myer's. Know where I'd be now if I'd still been with them? I'd probably be in charge of a department . . . a floorwalker, but still earning sweeties.'

'And living in the likes of a red sandstone tenement just off Calder Street in Govanhill!' laughed Star.

'Don't rub it in, love. That's just irony, that's all. We'll not be here long . . . you wait and see. I've got plans and the first of them includes us getting a bigger place, with a garden for young Jamesie to run about.'

'Sammy . . . what's the rush? I don't mind it here. Goodness, you're just back. You should have seen the dump I rented until I got this place. I can start something myself and get a bigger place. I've got confidence too, you know.'

'Aye, but I'm the one that's in a hurry. In a few years time I might not feel like running about the way I'm ready to do now.'

'Sammy Nelson putting his feet up! I think that's a long way off, Sammy, even though you're . . . what is it now?'

'Never you heed.'

'Tell me about your plans, then.'

'Oh, nothing definite yet. Could be anything. But there's something out there just waiting for Sammy Nelson, I'll guarantee you that.'

It took them days to get fully acquainted with what had happened to each other during the years they had been separated. As the stories unfolded there had been moments of sadness and tears, hilarity, reminiscences of old friends and characters, and fascinating accounts of foreign parts, all overshadowed by Sammy's dramatic account of his encounter with the Mafia.

'Sammy . . . it could only happen to you! And to think you actually got away with it. My God, you're so lucky just to be sitting here. I don't know how on earth you even got away from New York!'

It was after they had got to know each other again that the subject of Frankie Burns and Sonny Riley had emerged. Star had gasped when told about Riley's sinister interest in her uncle before he had left for the States. She had listened intently to his convincing theories on why Riley had acted the way he had.

'No, Sammy,' Star had said. 'No, no, no. You're wrong. For I know why. God, I know . . . I know . . . I know.'

Sammy waited, intrigued.

'It was me he should have been out to get. Because I hired Frankie Burns to kill Sonny Riley. And Bert Steed was the go-between. That's obviously why he vanished – Riley must have found out the two of them had been in touch . . . I don't know how. After that he'd have assumed you were behind it. That was why he came after you following Frankie Burns being killed. All the time it should have been me he was looking for. God, Sammy, do you realise I could have been paying for your execution?'

'Paying?'

'Oh yes. Paying. I left an open cheque for Frankie to dispose of Riley. He was a mercenary, after all, and certainly wasn't out to do me a favour. That's how the man lived. I agonised over my decision, but in the end decided it was totally justifiable that Riley should be disposed of: our legal system had tried, but failed miserably. They had decreed that Riley should be tried for what he had done because they knew he was the culprit, but they let him slip through their fingers – that was their weakness. In the name of justice, I could see no reason why he should escape and that was my justification for taking up where the system had failed. That's why I took it upon myself to see that justice be done to Riley.

'But justice wasn't done . . . was it? And I don't know how much sleep I've lost over poor Frankie Burns going to his death because of my decision. I consoled myself to some extent by the way that Burns lived. He was a professional executioner and I suppose he must have come to terms with the fact that one day someone would want to do to him as he'd done to others.'

It was all too much for Sammy to take in and he sat back in his chair visibly shocked. 'Do you realise that makes you as big a target for that swine Riley as it does me? I haven't checked up yet where that monster is . . . maybe he's inside for all I know. Oh, to hell with him, Star,' he said, recovering from the impact of the news. 'We can't spend our lives worrying about that bam. Besides, he'll have made so many new enemies since he last saw us, we'll be real old hat.'

'I'm glad you see it that way, Sammy. We can't let our lives be ruled by him. But his time will come . . . and I'd love nothing better than having a hand in it in some way.'

'That's the Jamesie in you talking, Star.'

From the window of their flat they could see the tall spindly cranes at work on the new skyline rising in the Gorbals, creating the new high-rise blocks they called 'the multis'. The bulldozers had moved in on the uniform three-storey tenement blocks and were slowly erasing all evidence that there ever had been a place called the Gorbals.

In many areas of the city it was clear that what they were doing was in the name of redevelopment. In the Gorbals it had all the appearance of being in the name of revenge. Gorbals was their scapegoat and they blamed it for giving their city a bad name. They wanted it expunged from the map. They had become infected with the new science called Public Relations and its practitioners had told them that rid of its Gorbals, Glasgow would in the future have a good image – imagery was more important than citizenry. The new district which the politicians and the planners were creating would even have a new name. Everything that had ever been about the Gorbals would be no more.

'That's it, Star,' said Sammy pointing to the new meccano and lego skyline dominating the horizon to the north. 'There's our future.'

'What . . . in a multi-storey?'

'Not "in" a multi-storey, Star. "Out" of a multi-storey. Lots of multi-storeys. It's been in the newspapers. They're going up all over the place. In that new scheme near wee Carmunnock, in Drumchapel and a new place called Castlehouse. All over the place. Hundreds of other new houses as well. And when you've as many new houses as that, there'll be lots of new services needed. That's the way it is here. One gets it, they all want it. Remember the fashion for contemporary fireplaces? Then it was flush doors and fancy nameplates. There'll be new rages of all sorts once they move into their new houses. You mark my word. They'll be wanting something to make their new places look different – to tart them up in some way. And whatever it is, your man here'll be giving it to them.'

Star smiled. 'I suppose you could say that's the Sammy Nelson in you that's talking.'

CHAPTER 15

SCHEMERS

THERE WERE OTHERS WHO HAD THEIR EYES ON
the dramatic changes that were taking place in Glasgow,
people who never had seen, never would see their Glasgow
in a different light. Theirs was the way of the aggressor and
the brigand. They, rather than any particular area, had
given the city the label that the public relations men and
the planners thought they could erase as they set about the
annihilation of what had been the Gorbals.

Sammy Nelson viewed the new areas which the massive
redevelopment plan was creating as a great opportunity for
commercial enterprise, the thrust of his life. Others saw
them as new fields in which to spread their corruption and
depredation. Sammy saw the sprawling new council housing estates as a great chance to make a way of living from
which he would profit; others saw them as new scope for
ways of living from which they could plunder.

In the new order that was to be the Glasgow of the latter
part of the twentieth century, the decade of the Sixties was
to see the establishment of vast new dormitory suburbs on
the periphery of the Glasgow city boundary. These were to
be an attempt to answer the most hideous set of statistics
belonging to any city in Europe, provided, as they always
said, that you didn't include Naples in the list. Of course

there were lies, damned lies and statistics but no matter what you did with this collection of figures, there was nothing that could be done to demonstrate that when it came to housing conditions, Glasgow was an attractive place to have your home.

In the Gorbals, some ninety per cent of all housing stock had been deemed unfit for human habitation. These were not ancient structures, but had been shoddily built and shabbily maintained with no long-term view of how or if they would stand up to the vagaries of one of the most polluted atmospheres in the world, in conjunction with a climate which, at its best, had never been kind to anything that man had put up against it. The managers, known as factors, who worked for the absentee landlords were to make fortunes from them, but did so at a standard that bordered on the criminal.

About one-third of all the houses in the city consisted of just one bedroom. Nearly forty per cent had no bath. About a quarter had no toilet and an official report gave the view that 'deficiencies on this scale sound almost incredible in the 1960s'. They most certainly were.

The cry from the politicians had been '. . . houses . . . give them houses . . . houses at any price'. And that price was to include local authorities being sucked in by shyster builders; that price was also to give them crude, soulless barracks where the only thing that could be called attractive had been the architects' drawings. They had drawn images of affluent-looking people adorning the entrances to beautiful homes with well-tended gardens, with plants, trees and shrubs, all tastefully laid out. At the rear of the houses were trim lawns, just like the ones included in the sketches for other design projects, for hotels and public buildings – places which would have experienced and loving staff to look after them. But no one had challenged the architects as to how communities which had never known gardens, or ever expressed a particular desire for them, would look after the decorative spaces that had been so painstakingly drawn. Inevitably, the new gardens soon became shabby and overgrown patches and within a very short time the bold, brave new estates didn't look at all like the sketches and models the architects and planners had shown the politicians before building began.

They wanted houses and they got them. Nothing else. Even the name they were to give them was as basic as the featureless areas where they were to be built. They were called the schemes. And one of these schemes, a place the size of Perth, was so bereft of facilities it had neither a range of shops nor a pub and the number of police would have been stretched to maintain law and order in the smallest of villages.

However, the spiritual had been catered for in the plans and the men of the cloth were quick to move in with their buildings. Save their souls, they had thought, and all would be well. Shops and pubs and cinemas and dance halls and playing fields and the things that had made the life that they knew ... they would come with the millenium. Perhaps.

Fleets of vans were the first commercial enterprise to move in on the schemes, supplying the new householders with the basic commodities. There were mobile grocers, mobile fruit shops, mobile bakers and mobile ice cream stalls, with all the usual range of fripperies and delights previously available back in the old suburbs from the corner shops they knew as the 'Tallies'.

In the old order council regulations protected the shop-keepers' rights by apportioning trade and required that shops gain approval so that the customers' rights were also looked after. In the new order there was no such approval, no such protection. If one mobile shop was to tour a particular area at eleven o'clock, another would make sure he was there at ten-thirty and when another discovered that, he would be there at ten. It was the same with the butchers and the bakers and the ice cream men. When the rivalry became mayhem, 'friends' moved in to accompany the vans to make sure that other vans didn't take away their customers; and when the other vans became aware of this they too had to enlist 'friends'.

When the activities of these groups of 'friends' were brought to the attention of those who ruled the old suburbs they quickly extended their services to the schemes. A quick bout of what the papers called 'gang warfare in the schemes' was the sign that they had arrived. This series of incidents included the murder of two men, one kicked to death, the other hacked with a machete, and three found with a variety of serious injuries, one with broken arms and legs, another crippled for life after 'falling' from a third-storey window and another blinded by acid. The pickings were richer than they ever had been in the old parts of the city. The schemes offered some of the biggest captive markets imaginable; there were 60,000 inhabitants in one scheme alone. Among them were those who were to become victims of their new quarters.

In the past, people could pass the time of day in the busy thoroughfares near their homes, even stroll the short distance to the big stores in the city. Not any more. What shops there were in the schemes were for essentials. The variety and the character and the energy of the old high streets, with their vibrant life and activity, the calls of wayside barrowmen and wives, the patter of street corner worthies, the passing scene – that vital ingredient of life – had all been taken away. In their place people were given houses and from their houses all they could see were other houses; and surrounding them were green fields which made them feel like they were on an island and that they were marooned from the civilisation which had been theirs.

But there was a way to escape from their desolation, their isolation. The men who had brought the old ways to their new schemes were to provide them with that means of escape. They had dealt in the lucrative amphetamine market before, mainly to the young and gullible who were easy victims. But they still needed the 'pushers', the men who were their agents and representatives, canvassing for bigger markets from wider reserves. In the schemes the 'pushers' didn't have to push any longer. The new housing estates which had promised so much but were to offer so little were to provide a legion of frustrated women and men ready to surrender themselves to the prospect of a regular lift from the misery their life had become.

CHAPTER 16

SON OF TIGER

IT WAS 'SPARROW' OGILVIE THAT SAMMY
recognised when he went into the Kildonan Bar. The
Kildonan was one of a mere handful of the old Gorbals
pubs that hadn't been a victim of the demolishers' blitz-
krieg. Former residents would return there in search of old
mates or merely to recapture some of the flavour of the
suburb in which they had spent most of their lives.
Sammy's very first memory of it was back in the Twenties
when, on the rainy days that workmen would be sent home
from the building sites, little boys, the poorest ones of the
area, would gather just outside the pub at the steps to the
railway station in the hope that the men hadn't eaten their
packed lunches. They would beg, 'Any pieces . . . any
pieces, mister?' If they were successful they wouldn't go
hungry that night. But that was a long time ago, in another
world, and that part of it was best forgotten.

Sammy was doing his 'research', as he had told Star,
which meant he was exploring his idea that there was
money to be made in the schemes. So far he hadn't hit on
the appropriate one. It was the furthest thing from his
mind that the 'Sparrow' would be the key to that idea.

The 'Sparrow' was a typical wee Glasgow man of his
day, the kind of man who would have felt undressed to the

extent of embarrassment if you caught him not wearing his cap, his ever-present bunnet. A slender man in his mid-forties, he was sitting there at the bar beside some others who could have passed for brothers, all of them with their drinks before them, staring straight ahead, dream-like, as though in some state of suspended animation.

The very sight of the 'Sparrow' inspired a host of memories for Sammy. If you had asked how well Sammy knew him the reply would have been, 'I knew his faither'. And he would say that not meaning, as the phrase usually meant, that he thought any the less of the man, but merely because he actually had known his father, 'Tiger' Ogilvie, very well back in the days before the 'Sparrow' came on the scene.

No one knew him by any other name than 'Tiger' and only his parents could have told you that he had been christened Joseph. But it had been 'Tiger' since the days before he even went to school because, despite his lack of height, he was one of the most belligerent and cussed of individuals; one sight of you looking sideways at him and it was up with the fists. Maybe it had something to do with the Celtic character for he wasn't the only one like that. But he was one of the worst.

The 'Tiger' had been several years older than Sammy but they had boxed together in the St John's Boys Guild. 'Tiger' had been sent there in an effort to get some of the aggression knocked out of him, Sammy to learn enough to give a cuffing to the school bully. Father Fletcher and the coaches who ran the guild told 'Tiger' he should stick at the boxing for he was good enough to be a champion. Sure enough, in later years people were to point him out in the street and say that there was one who had touched the stars. Had it not been for the biased decision given against him in New York he would have been Scotland's first world champion. A few years later another little man from the neighbourhood called Benny Lynch had touched those same stars . . . and made them his very own.

'Tiger' had returned from New York minus the title, minus much of the prize money a crooked matchmaker had promised him and without the sight of one eye. At the age of twenty-eight, 'Tiger' would never work again. In the years to come, whenever you looked at the group of men who were a regular decoration on the corner of Cumberland Street and Florence Street, just by the Moy Bar in the days before it boasted its horrendous art-deco frontage, then one of them would have been 'Tiger' Ogilvie. 'Tiger', a corner boy for life with little other than his collection of diminished memories.

No one knew the characters of the Gorbals better than Sammy Nelson and when he looked at people, stories of their forebears and episodes and escapades in which they had been involved in the colourful old days would flood his mind, just as they had that day when he saw 'Sparrow' Ogilvie in the Kildonan. He often used to say: 'Imagine a "Sparrow" being the son of a "Tiger".' But it was true, for the man whose father had been 'Tiger' was the flipside of the coin, an inoffensive and chirpy little character with a cheery and friendly word for everyone.

'How's the old fellah? What'll you have?' asked Sammy, the two questions coming as one.

'Jesus Christ. Old Sammy Nelson,' exclaimed Ogilvie answering neither question. 'You're looking more like a bookie than ever, Sammy. Some tin flute, eh! Didnae get that in Jackson's.'

'No . . . West End Misfits,' came back Nelson, the eyes twinkling.

'Aye, that'll be right,' and in the same breath answering the question he obviously took to be the most important, 'a half will do me . . . and a half of special as well. The old man? A bit more doted. Stays with the sister out in the schemes. He's fine, though. Lost, but. Nae corner to stand at. Dying to talk to people and tell them about that time in Madison Square Garden. You know what he's like? That's all he remembers. Nothing else. Keeps asking the time . . . he forgets it as soon as you tell him, yet he can tell you it was Izzy Goldstein that was the referee the night he fought for the world title and that he could have tanked Benny Lynch . . . one eye and all.'

'How's work?' asked Sammy.

'Magic,' replied Ogilvie enthusiastically. 'Left Lorens the builders. Miserable bastards, they were. Minute late and they would clock you. Used to be a time when they were easy-going and you had good gaffers but it's a' this time and motion stuff now. You've to go hell for leather to make a wage. I was in the schemes with them and the women kept asking me to do wee odd jobs. And none of what you're thinking, Sammy Nelson! Though there was plenty of that as well for they're all bored out of their minds. Anyway, there's all sorts of things they were wanting doing so I thought there'd be a living in it and I couldn't have been more right. The first thing, they wanted their doors tarted up . . . you know, grills for the wee windows in them, extra locks and the like, and these new wee spy-hole things. I pick up about forty pounds a week and I don't break sweat. With Lorens it was twenty-five on a good week and that was knocking your pan in. And I don't pay tax. And I've got the dole money as well. And the wife's working. She pays tax, but. We go to Benidorm for the holidays. Ever been there, Sammy?'

The 'Sparrow' was in full flow and he never considered the prospect of an answer to the question.

'Now that's living, that Benidorm place. Heat, Sammy! Never known anything like it. Steak, egg and chips, Watney's draught and Johnny Walker Black Label at half the price and Ina sitting there wi' that new drink, Bacardi and Coke. That's all she drinks now. It's the travelling and a' that high life abroad that does it, like.'

'Wish I hadn't bought you that drink, "Sparrow". You could buy and sell me.'

'Aye, that'll be right.' They laughed as 'Sparrow' ordered a round.

'You were talking there about what they need for their new places in the schemes. What other kind of things are they looking for?'

'Sammy, they're at me for everything. Pelmets, extra locks on the doors, mortice locks, chains on their locks, and these spy-hole things. They're security mad. No' like the old days. Half of them are strangers to each other and they don't give a monkey's for one another. The old neighbourly thing seems to be out of the window. Some of them are a right wild bunch . . . well, you know a few of the places they came from. You know the joke about them keeping coal in the bath? It's true, Sammy. I've seen it.

'There's a street in one of the schemes and know what the bams did? They broke into the loft and demolished all the timber they could put their hands on . . . the joists, beams, cross-supports and the like. Know what for? For firewood, for Christ sake! The Corporation don't know yet but see when we get the first gales next winter, that roof'll end up in fuckin' Edinburgh.

'But don't get me wrong, they're no' all scruff like that. And I keep well away from the ones that are. If there's trouble on one side of the road, I'm on the other. Not like the old man. He'd go through a midden to get at a fight. I get all my orders from the hard-doing ones. They've a bit of pride in their new houses.'

'Are there many at your game?'

'No' that I can see. I cannae do half of the things they want.'

'How do you get the orders then?'

'Oh, they all know me in the scheme. I was in one of the maintenance squads when they first moved so it's no bother for me when I go round the doors. I don't do all the scheme. I can get a living just out of one wee bit of it. Every time I go to somebody's door they send me to a china who wants an order, and when I get there the next-door neighbour will be wanting this or that and then they'll come up wi' something that's all the rage and you cannae keep up wi' them. The latest thing is doorsteps. They all want marble doorsteps. There's flash for you, Sammy. Up ten storeys and wanting a fuckin' marble doorstep! They're no' really marble, but. It's a kind of terrazzo stuff. I don't do them. No' my trade. I make them nice wooden jobs instead which are right popular.'

'And you make forty pounds a week?'

'That's right. Not bad, eh!'

'But you work for it, getting the orders and making the stuff.'

'Doesnae hang on trees, Sammy.'

'How'd you fancy being my chief rep?'

'What do I know about the booze business?'

'Left that a long time ago, "Sparrow". My new line's home improvements. Aye, that's the name of the company. Star Home Improvements. We specialise in the kind of things you were talking about. We just haven't moved into the schemes yet, though I've been thinking about it. We could be doing with orders . . . lots and lots of orders. And I was thinking that if I'd a man like you to start in the schemes and then maybe get some others to join you, my company could start drumming up business in a really big way. What d'you think?'

'What kind of money are you talking about?'

'There'll be fifty notes a week at least. And you'll be collar and tie. No need to get your hands dirty again. You could put away the tools. Live like a toff, "Sparrow". Fancy it?'

'Aye, you might be on, Sammy. You might just be on. Fifty quid, you say. After tax?'

'Fifty quid in your hand. But you'll need to get me the

orders. Once we build up I'll have a team of salesmen going round and you can be their gaffer. Good future in it for you, "Sparrow". By the way, d'you know I've never known you as anything else but "Sparrow". What's your right name?'

'Francis. But I usually get Francie. That's all they know me as in the scheme.'

'I like "Sparrow" better,' Sammy joked. 'I'm only kidding. Francie it'll be. What're you having?'

CHAPTER 17

IN BUSINESS

SAMMY HAD BEEN RIGHT ABOUT THERE BEING good money to be made in the schemes. The venture he had founded on hearing about 'Sparrow' Ogilvie's one-man operation was to prove an outstanding success, his Star Home Improvements Company becoming the reality he had pictured. When he had told Ogilvie on the day they had met about his non-existent business, he had said he would contact him in a month's time, when he would be geared up to handle his orders from the schemes. And sure enough, with the help of Star, his former company manager Bert Steed and some others, he had found himself a joiners' yard and stocked it with all the necessary tools and equipment, purchased at a knock-down price in a bankruptcy sale. Because of the energy he had applied to his new collar-and-tie job, Francie Ogilvie got more orders than even he had ever thought possible.

Star hadn't shared Sammy's optimism at first and had quizzed him about the idea after he had told her all about his meeting with Ogilvie, going over the conversation they had together word for word.

'But why did you tell him that you had a business going when you haven't?' she had asked. 'That was telling fibs, Sammy.'

'No, Star. Don't say I was lying. For I wasn't really. You see the moment I told him that, well . . . then . . . that was the moment Star Home Improvements was born. As soon as he told me what he was doing, I knew right there and then that was what we should do. That was the very idea I'd been looking for. So that was it . . . there *was* a company, even though it was just in my mind.

'Another thing, I didn't want him to think I was pinching his idea. You don't tell people everything, you know. Gives them wrong ideas, wrong impressions. Best just telling some of them so much. Would've hated the wee "Sparrow" going about telling everyone he had given Sammy Nelson the idea that made him his second fortune.'

'Second furtune!' she had exclaimed loudly. 'God, Sammy, you don't even have a business yet and you're talking about a second fortune.'

'Don't worry, Star. I've got it all figured out. I went to see Bert Steed after leaving Ogilvie. He's working as a barman in a pub in Shawlands. Been back from England for a while, he tells me. Quite happy with life being an ordinary barman and keeping out of the road . . . you know! Anyway, bet you didn't know that Bert served his time as a joiner? I'd forgotten all about it because he worked for us for so long. But remember how it was always Bert who'd do any wee jobs that needed doing in the lounge bars? Anyway, I've asked him to be our gaffer . . . you know, look after our yard, supervise the men?'

'Our yard . . . what yard?'

'Got to get a yard, Star. This is going to be a big business. The proper stuff. Bert knows the trade, so he can run things.'

'So you're really going into this thing?'

'Bet your bottom dollar, Star. This is it.'

'You'll need an office staff, wages, men's time sheets, paying tax, National Health Insurance, processing orders, things like that.'

'Not at first. Got to creep before you crawl. I've talked it over with Bert. There's a team of tradesmen use his pub and he can get them working for us on a "homer" basis . . . when they finish their work they'll come to our yard and do a few hours. If he gets enough of them they can come on a rota basis.'

'Sounds a bit complicated.'

'Not really. Just needs organisation, that's all.'

'Why would they come on a "homer" basis, anyway?'

'Just to get us started, Star. None of that fuss with tax and insurance and all that carry on. Just bung them money in the hand for their two or three nights' work with us. The way things are at the moment they're all dying for the chance to earn an extra bob or two. There's auld gloomy Harold warning us times are going to be tough . . . did you see that one with the bins – who's he again? – aye, Jenkins, on TV the other night telling us how hard he's going to make it for us? How come it's always the Socialists that make it hard for us?'

'What happens if the factory or tax inspectors catch you?'

'Star, don't be so pessimistic. It'll just be for the first few months till we get on our feet then we'll be off and running . . . everything legitimate the way you like it. Anyway, the "homer" lot will just be doing the manufacturing work. We'll be getting a couple of full-time boys as well to do the actual jobs in the schemes, you know like locks on doors and that sort of thing? And I'll need your help as well, Star. We'll need to get a wee office going once I get the yard. It'll need a manageress. Can't do it without your brains, pet. It'll be better hours than you had when you ran our lounge bars and you'll be home every night for wee Jamesie coming back from school.'

Sammy Nelson was back at his old enthusiastic best, full of fervour and optimism about his project taking off and being a success. When he had finally finished outlining his

plans for the Star Home Improvements Company, Star
asked, 'What really made you go and see Bert Steed? Was
it because of this . . . or did you go and see him for another
reason?'

'What other reason?'

'Frankie Burns.'

'Well, I did want to know about that as well.'

'And what did he tell you?'

'Nothing much really. He spoke about why he'd gone to
England and how he'd thought that he'd be better out of
the way after Frankie had been killed . . . like he told you.'

'Anything else?'

'Not really.'

'Sammy Nelson! It's me . . . Star. Don't start telling me
only what you think I should know . . . like you did with
Mr Ogilvie. What else did he have to say?'

'I was going to tell you, Star. Bert discovered how Riley
knew that Burns was in town. It was a bent cop. It turns
out the police knew Frankie was around. They'd spotted
him coming off the train at Central Station. He was in
disguise but they clocked him. There's Special Branch men
there often, keeping a look-out for certain characters and
that kind of thing. But it wasn't the Special Branch man
that was bent. A rozzer in the office at their Headquarters
saw his report and it went from him to Riley.'

'How did Bert get to know about that?'

'Oh, there'd been a big stushie about it in the force. And
Bert's got good connections with them . . . two of his
cousins are cops. The story was the talk of the steamie with
the policemen. You see, the bent cop had apparently been
in some kind of cahoots with Riley, tipping him off about
raids and the like, information that he picked up in his job
at the office. He'd be selling it to Riley likely, though Bert
never said anything about that. Anyway, one of the last
papers he would have handled, apparently, was the Special
Branch man's report about Frankie.

'The cop had been under surveillance – that was how they knew he'd been in touch with Riley. It was enough to get him up on a disciplinary charge and get him the boot from the force but they'd nothing on him for a prosecution. Bert's cousin said the Fiscal just laughed when they asked for him to be charged and if the evidence would stand to nail Riley in some way for Burns' death.

'There was proof that they'd met but no proof of what they'd been talking about. The rozzer denied that he'd told Riley anything out of the police files. They questioned Riley as well when they found that out and he treated it as a big joke. He knew they'd nothing on him . . . and what d'you do with a man that's got about half-a-dozen witnesses for an alibi?'

CHAPTER 18

BIG BERNIE

IF THE SCHEMES WERE A GOLDEN OPPORTUN-
ity for Sammy Nelson to once again display his exceptional
enterprise, to Sonny Riley they were like being gifted a new
empire. He had never known such vast numbers in the one
place so ready to be manipulated. He had never known so
many so willing to be corrupted. He had never had them
so anxious to kiss the ring.

Sonny Riley took his looks from his mother, Bernadette,
who, as she told everyone, came from Donegal, Gweedore,
to be precise, and whether or not you had a minute to
spare, the story would continue. 'Ach, now wasn't it the
loveliest of places. We had a lovely wee house, all whitewash and thatch and wi' a fire that burned turf – that's
what ye call peat there – and the chickens running about
outside the door. Ach, now, weren't they the days!'

She had, in fact, come over on a cattle boat as a baby in
her mother's arms. Her father had been a labourer whom
she rarely saw because he was away most of the time
working on the dams. His brother, also a navvy, had told
them one night when he was drunk that the house they had
come from in Gweedore had an earth floor and only the
one room which they shared with a pig. But the chickens
and the whitewash was a nicer story . . .

Bernadette was a big woman now, weighing more than fifteen stone, and because of her difficulty in walking, or the difficulty she said she had in walking, she spent much of her time in bed surrounded by what she called 'my pals', engaged in their favourite pastimes – playing cards, drinking endless cups of tea, which the pals took turns at making, and gossiping. But when she was young Bernadette had been an attractive woman with a striking and strong face, characterised by its high and rounded cheekbones.

Having inherited her fine features, Sonny was a much more handsome man than ever his father, 'Snakey' Holden, had been. There was none of the 'burnt' look, that distinctive institutional appearance which came from the confines of long periods in prison, with the wariness and the suspicion that never left the eyes. Even his years in Peterhead, the 'university' of Scottish prisons, hadn't left their mark. Despite the innocent boyish appearance and the big bright blue eyes, he was a more ruthless man than anyone of his generation could remember.

His father had been vicious and vituperative but he had been content to confine his maliciousness to his immediate surroundings, to those who came within his shallow orbit or those to whom he bore a grudge, as he had Sammy Nelson and his family. Not so Sonny Riley. He experienced no greater satisfaction than seeing the terror he could engender and he luxuriated in the power it gave him. While others around him could spread their fear by their sheer physical presence, men with faces that awaited their first introduction to goodwill, Sonny Riley had to demonstrate his malevolence. When he did, such was the depravity of his associates, they would speak of him as if he were the Boy David reborn. In their ferocious, uncompassionate world, the only law was that of violence. He who could exercise it the most was the only maker of their laws. It was the way of all tyrants.

Riley had first taken an interest in the Castlehouse scheme when his widowed mother Bernadette had moved there with Gerry, the son she had borne by her second husband, Francis Riley, from whom Sonny had taken his surname. Bernadette had a variety of titles. To those in the street she was Mrs Riley, or if you wished to pretend you knew her a bit better it would be 'Sonny's mother'. To a select few, although they would never use the expression in front of her, she was 'Big Bernie', which, in terms of description, was being kind to a woman of her girth. The privileged ones who called her that among themselves were the close-knit coterie of women 'pals' who spent hours each day in her house sharing her way of life, doing her shopping or helping with the housework or the small-time money-lending in which she participated, as well as cooking the endless sandwiches of bacon, sausage or fried egg which seemed to be an almost permanent fixture of her right hand. When they spoke to her directly they would call her 'Bern'. To Sonny, the son around whom the entire world revolved, she was just plain 'Maw'.

With the money at Riley's disposal, Bernadette could have lived in a house anywhere in the city. But just as it was not his way, neither was it hers. Location was a low priority; the stratum from which they came was a high priority. When the neighbours and her other friends went to Castlehouse, that was where Bernadette said she would also go.

There was to be no other house in the scheme like it. They loved the expression 'no expense spared' and she had used it a lot when she had ordered the furnishings and the decor and the tradesmen to fit it out, never forgetting to mention to the workmen that it was her boy, 'my very own wee pride and joy' that was paying for all of it. She always added, in innocent menace, 'Of course, you'll know him? He's Sonny. Sonny Riley . . . you know?' And despite the surface smile and the impression that it was the proud mother who was speaking, the intent of those words was from a mind that paralleled that of the flesh and blood of whom she spoke. For she knew she didn't really need to ask the workmen if they knew who her son was. Like everyone else around, they knew that Bernadette Riley, mother of Sonny, had come to live in Castlehouse. Castlehouse was to be the worse for that.

Although it was strictly against the letting regulations to change the installations and interior fittings of houses built and owned by Glasgow Corporation, that rule was of no significance to the Rileys. There were no rules or laws in life other than what they decreed, and before she had moved from her old home in the Gorbals, tradesmen were hard at work for her in the new house she had been allotted in Castlehouse. Workmen had the kitchen and bathroom demolished, the new fittings ripped out and scrapped. In their place they installed the most expensive units that could be obtained in Glasgow. The new kitchen was imported from Germany. The bathroom came from Italy, with the walls finished in the finest of marble and the taps and fittings all gold-finished. In the lounge, which they called the living-room, a chandelier made up of 2,000 pieces of exquisitely cut tear-drop crystal hung, competing for domination of the little room along with a huge, ornate Tudor-styled electric fire, its basket filled with egg-sized chunks of coloured glass which glittered and sparkled in simulated flame effect. Housed inside an enormous Regency-styled cabinet was the biggest and most expensive television available in the Buchanan Street store where she had shopped, beside which was the latest in hi-fi players, a 'music centre' made of cheap wood-veneer board in a contemporary style that could only be described as offensive. That the Tudor clashed with the Regency and the offensive contemporary amidst a riot of colours which included a midnight blue ceiling and a pink shag-pile carpet was of little consequence. Neither did it matter that both chandelier and fire had to be extinguished in order to view the television screen. Nor that the vulgar lounge suite's black fur-fabric finish gave its huge settee all the appeal of a dead buffalo and that only one of its two armchairs would fit into the room because of their size.

Within a week of moving into her new home in Castle-house, the expensive German cooker was grease-spattered and stained by the old blackened and battered frying-pan which Bernadette refused to renew because 'my auld mother always said never use a new frying pan for they never taste the same'. The stench from the stale lard in it mixed with the smoke of hundreds of cigarettes consumed by the 'pals' had replicated the awful bluish fug which welcomed you to her old place in the Gorbals.

'Oh, aye,' said Bernadette on the first night she moved in with her fourteen-year-old son Gerry, 'it's right smash-ing, so it is.' Then she raised the living-room window, put a pillowcase across the sill, folded her arms on it and leaned out for a 'hing', which everyone in the old Glasgow knew was the only way to watch the world go by.

But even a 'hing' wasn't the same in the schemes, for there was no passing world any more. The scheme-dwellers would be in the streets when they went to their work in the morning and there again at night when they came home. But before and after these times, there was little to be seen. At night they were all in their little homes beside their televisions, or their blaring music centres. There was only movement in the streets when the mobile traders came along.

It was Bernadette who had first made Sonny aware of their numbers. 'Could hardly watch Bruce Forsyth at the Palladium the other night for them,' she had complained. 'See them and their musical chimes! If it's no' *Yankee Doodle Dandy* it's *The Teddy Bears' Picnic* or *The Skaters' Waltz*, and see that yin that plays *Colonel Bogey*! I'll bloody "Colonel Bogey" him the next time he turns it up as loud outside my window!' She wasn't fit enough now, but in her day Bernadette would have sorted out the tunesmith just as she had various traders in the Gorbals, her heavy message bag representing one of the most feared weapons in the district!

Her mood changed from menace to familial inquisitiveness. 'Are they giving you any work, Sonny?'

He looked over at her quizzically, but said nothing.

'The vans, Sonny. Are they giving you any work?'

'Work' was the word she used for what Sonny did. She never knew, or let on she knew, precisely what her beloved eldest son did, only that whatever it was, it made lots of money and kept her very happy. She knew, of course, he wasn't a joiner or a plumber or anything regular like that. It was just 'work'. She knew too that in the course of his 'work' there had to be long periods when he was sent away from home, to places like Barlinnie and Peterhead. But then, as she would tell the neighbours who would always nod and agree with her, for she was Sonny's mother, he was sent away to these places because 'they've got it in for my boy. Was a bit wild as a wee lad and they hold it against him. But my Sonny's far too good for them.' At that they would nod in agreement, even more enthusiastically than before.

'Aye, son,' she had said to the boy on whom she doted, 'I would hae thought there'd be a good bit of work for you among a' these boys that're coming round wi' their vans. I mean, we never knew anything like that before in the tenements, did we? All we had was Tony the ice-cream man with his wee pony and then his wee motor. Nothing like all these boys that're coming round now. They're doing everything, Sonny. My pals were just telling me the other night they're making a right fortune out of the schemes, so they are. Aye, they must be when you think of it, Sonny. They must be making a right good packet out of us ones here in the schemes. A right good fortune. My, but you're looking that well, Sonny. Your work must be agreeing wi' you . . . eh, son?'

CHAPTER 19

MOBILE MAYHEM

THE FOLLOWING DAY SONNY RILEY WENT OUT
with two of his closest cohorts, Mickey Kelly, a thin pasty-
faced man with a receding hairline that made him look
much older than his twenty-three years, and Pat Connors,
whom some of the kids would tease as 'Captain Birds Eye'
because of his similarity to the advertisement figure – but
only the ones who didn't have big brothers on whom he
could take out his spite and only when they knew there was
absolutely no chance of him ever catching them.

Bernadette hadn't been exaggerating. There were vans
everywhere. At some corners there were three, *Greensleeves*
competing with *Lili Marlene*, which was trying to outdo
Anchors Aweigh. The drivers competed for customers by
turning up the volume of their Harvin chimes machines so
that it sounded like the circus and the funfair had come to
town together. In one of the longer streets Sonny Riley
passed four of them, all with crowds of housewives and
children round them.

Connors said he had been told that van-men had been
bringing in their own chinas to look after them and had
already started carving up certain areas of exclusivity.
'They were saying in the Whistle yesterday there was a
barney between forty of them the other night, just to see

who was to look after the Crescent section. And they've got others going about kicking in their van doors to warn them off.'

'Is that right?' replied Sonny, with a smile that came over as a sneer. 'You know what you call that, don't you. Fuckin' lawlessness.' At that the sneer became a laugh and he repeated his jest. 'Aye, fuckin' lawlessness. That's what it is. And we'll need to put a fuckin' end to it . . . won't we?'

It didn't take long for Sonny Riley and his team to find all the work his mother had said they might get from the vans. The three men noted every vehicle that regularly used the scheme and the driver-owners were told that they could only enter the area in future if they paid an admission fee. The price of that fee would be based on their profits. One astonished driver queried how they would know what his profits were. 'Pal,' said Riley, using the word at its most menacing, 'we tell you what your profits are . . . Got the message?'

'And what happens if we can't make that much?'

'Then that's your hard luck.'

The fees were struck at ten pounds a week for the smallest of the vans, representing ten per cent of what they decreed a van of that size should be making in profits. Medium-sized vans, such as the fish-and-chip men and the ones with rolls and bakery goods, were to pay fifteen pounds and the biggest ones, the mobile stores which carried a full range of groceries, would have to pay a minimum of twenty.

Because they were the easiest of targets, the rebellion against the levies didn't last long. A first warning was slashed tyres. The second was a sledgehammer through the windscreen. There were no further warnings after that, and there was no set pattern to what recalcitrants received as punishment. Gino, the Italian chip man, discovered that, to his horror and ruination. He had parked his van for the evening, as he did every night, in the little square which was the big scheme's only focal point. There were some shops there, but all closed at five o'clock sharp – no one was courageous enough to be a lone sitting-target for the marauding gangs of teenagers whose night-time terror had added yet another dimension to the schemes that the planners hadn't thought about. There had been a small number of people waiting to buy late supper meals of fish and chips or one of the growing list of alternatives, again deep fried and again with chips, when the car had pulled up. Connors and Kelly got out. No one paid any attention to the two men as they levered off the lid of a gallon-can of white oil paint. As they walked towards the van, 'Birds Eye' Connors yelled at the waiting customers clustered round the van's serving hatch. Those who knew their Glasgow understood he meant business.

'Right, youse. Fuck off, the lot of you.'

It wasn't intended to inspire questions. The waiting group quickly dispersed, not even daring to look at the two men as they approached the van.

They entered Gino's mobile chip shop through the back door, Connors throwing open the sliding lid of the big frying tub and Kelly pouring in the contents of the gallon-can of paint. What happened after that was much more spectacular than they had expected. In fact, it took them by such surprise that they just managed to escape before the results of their deed enveloped them. When the cold, oily paint came into contact with the boiling fat, there was an enormous rumble, followed by a violent eruption, accompanied by a billowing cloud of blue-black smoke and noxious fumes which filled the van. The contents of the pan, a gruesome mess of oil, paint and lumps of sizzling sausages, fish, and black pudding, boiled over like a frenzied fountain. As the unfortunate Italian fled out the cabin-door, the hot oil cocktail was ignited by the stove and the fireball explosion blew him across the street.

The police arrived quickly on the scene, but no witnesses

could be traced, other than people who had rushed from their homes to rescue the Italian, and none of them, they said, had seen a thing. But the fish and chip van-men had got the message and the one who replaced Gino the following night and the others who were to do business in the Castlehouse scheme promptly paid their tribute to Riley from that night onwards.

Ferdi's, another Italian firm, which ran a fleet of small ice-cream vans that also sold soft drinks and cigarettes, were next to be subjected to Sonny Riley's enforcement methods. Ferdi had made it known that despite what had happened to Gino, he wouldn't be intimidated. He put the word around that each of his vans would be accompanied by teams of the toughest men obtainable until such times as they could travel unmolested. True to his word, he hired groups of men from certain towns in Lanarkshire whose reputation wasn't based on love and compassion.

Riley and his men discussed this development. Connors said that he would welcome the opportunity to sort out the intruders on his own. 'Five men in a car,' he said dismissively to Riley. 'Tell you what, they'll no' be back when they see the message I've got for them.'

'Tell us, then,' Riley had said.

'No, Sonny. I want to keep this one a wee surprise. It'll be in the papers.'

Just as he had intended, Connors waited for one of the vans on his own, sitting patiently in the vehicle which he had parked in Hawthorn Road, by the bus terminus. He had chosen that particular point because of the extra width of the road there: it was used by buses as an end-of-the-run turning point. The wide section of road allowed him to park his vehicle at right-angles to the pavement without interfering with the flow of traffic. For that reason too, one of Ferdi's vans parked there each night for about half an hour.

Connors looked over at the car which pulled up close

behind the ice-cream van and tried to ascertain whether there were four or five men inside it. It was merely an academic observation. Whatever the number, they were obviously the bodyguard squad, for the vehicle just sat there beside the van, with none of the men making to get out.

There were no buses at the terminus and the only people around were those standing by Ferdi's van. But they were quick to scatter, screaming and shouting in terror, when they saw Connors' vehicle, engine roaring in full thrust, racing across the road towards the car-load of men.

Connors was driving a bulldozer. Dressed in working overalls and boots, he had taken it from a worksite about a mile away earlier in the evening and had casually driven it to the bus terminus where he had waited. The first impact of the 'dozer's big blade on the side of the car stove in the doors and rocked it so violently it almost rolled over. It righted itself on four wheels again as he reversed the tracked vehicle in order to charge once more.

The man in the ice-cream van was so terrified as he looked on that in his agitation he had turned up the pitch of his musical chimes so *The Teddy Bears' Picnic* was playing at full blast. As they screeched out 'If you go down to the woods today . . . you're sure of a big surprise', the bulldozer crashed once more into the car, this time smashing it with such force it rolled over like a toy, two doors immediately crashing open. Four men leapt out to flee in panic.

The driver of the ice-cream van had run off too before Connors came charging at his vehicle. One hit was enough for it. The van was knocked into the air then landed on two wheels and toppled over in a crescendo of smashing glass. With the bonnet flying up and exposing the chimes' speakers, the *Teddy Bears' Picnic* could be heard even louder than before.

The picnic was the biggest and best the scheme had known, for until the cry 'Polis' went up, the van had been besieged by swarms of children attracted by the continuous loud music, which could be heard streets away. There it was, scattered all over the street waiting for them . . . boxes of spilled confectionery and cases of soft drinks and thousands of cigarettes, with no one to look after it all – which was the best surprise of the lot for this very special picnic. Castlehouse was having its very own *Whisky Galore*.

They came running with prams and shopping bags, plastic sacks and supermarket trolleys. As the children scrambled for their Mars bars and Flakes they were pushed out of the way by women grabbing at the cigarettes and bottles of ginger beer, and when the men arrived they began snatching the cigarettes from the children and the women, who screamed and hit out at them.

'I'm emptied,' shouted the driver, trying to be heard over the din of the unstoppable chimes.

'Can't hear you,' roared back the police sergeant.

'For Christ sake . . . I've been fuckin' done.'

'Aye,' said the sergeant, hearing him this time. 'And you'll get bloody-well done for breach of the peace unless you get that fuckin' music to shut up.'

Riley, Kelly and Connors had a great laugh that night in the Whistle as the story was retold.

'You want to have seen the bams jumping out of that car when I thumped it with the big blade the second time. One of them had on his Rangers scarf, daft bastard. Tell you something. There's none of those hun bastards in his team who can run like that. He's the kind Waddell needs to win them some games.'

When the next round was set up, Connors took a long slug of Carlsberg Special then poured the contents of a double vodka into the glass. 'I fancy that,' said Kelly admiringly. 'What d'you call it, Pat . . . electric soup?'

'No . . . a bulldozer.'

Their raucous laughter could be heard right round the pub.

CHAPTER 20

A MAN CALLED McDOUGALL

CASTLEHOUSE BELONGED TO SONNY RILEY. NO
van could enter the scheme unless it was known to him and
the members of his team. The team had deemed Castlehouse to be their territory, and they didn't have to broadcast the fact or take out advertisements in the newspapers.
Everyone knew. They knew about the paint in the chippie's
frier, they knew about the bulldozer . . . aye, they knew
about the bulldozer all right, for that story had become
legend and as happens with all legends it became so
exaggerated it hardly resembled the actual event.

The most repeated version was the one that said Connors
had pushed the bodyguards' car over on its side with one
charge of the bulldozer and then had run the big tracked
vehicle over and over the car until it ended up flatter than
a pancake . . . 'And I've a pal who saw it just afterwards
and he says that one of the men inside it hadn't escaped.
There was blood everywhere but there was no body for it
had been crushed to smithereens.' And there were even
wilder and more gory variations on the theme.

Despite these tales and the genuine stories of victims of
the vicious and ruthless way Riley ruled the scheme, there
were still those who refused to bend the knee. No matter
what, they would still bring their vans into Castlehouse. It

was a free country, after all, and there were the police to protect them. Of course, there were countries where everyone would succumb to people like Sonny Riley, but Scotland wasn't one of them. Hamie McDougall thought exactly like that.

Hamie lived in Castlehouse and knew the talk about Riley and his gang. Nevertheless, when he invested the money he left the Army with on the deposit for a medium-sized grocery van, he let it be known to anyone who suggested otherwise that no one would stop him from working in the district where he lived. Or any district for that matter. And he had good back-up for his bold and confident attitude.

Hamie had served with the Third Battalion of the Parachute Regiment in a variety of the campaigns which marked the death throes of the British Empire. In 1964 he was Mentioned in Despatches while fighting with the Paras in the Radfan, in one of those nasty little scuffles which nagged Britain in the troublesome post-war years and which were as memorable and as popular as recurring acne. The Radfan had been so completely forgotten about that McDougall would only mention it if someone asked him where he had served with the Army.

But the Radfan had a particular significance for his attitude to Sonny Riley. There had been a variety of reasons for the war in that part of Arabia, but one of them had been because a tribe called the Qutaibis forced anyone passing through their territory to pay them tribute. It so happened that the territory which they said belonged to them included the Dhala road, the principal route north for the pilgrims going to Mecca. A law had been passed forbidding them to charge the levy and because of that they had started shooting and killing travellers who refused to pay.

The night before McDougall had first been in action against the Qutaibis they had captured the commander and the radio operator of an SAS patrol, decapitated both men, then showed off their heads, stuck on long poles, around a variety of villages in the area. It was the way of the Qutaibis.

McDougall, a tall, red-haired man with a friendly smile, had reminded his wife Patricia about these Arabian tribesmen when she had expressed her fears about bringing his van into the district. 'For God's sake, Pat, you don't think I fought against those barbarous desperadoes out there just to chicken out on somebody like this Riley character. He's doing exactly what they did out in Arabia. It's crazy to even think that someone like him can get away with it here. For God's sake, this is Scotland. Things like that don't happen here. And this guy Riley certainly isn't going to scare off Hamie McDougall.'

Patricia had always admired her husband's courage but nevertheless tried to dissuade him from bringing his van into Castlehouse. 'Think of the children,' she had said, referring to their three young sons. But Hamie was adamant. 'I'm thinking of the children, all right. There's a good living to be made here with a van and there's no way this lot will make me move . . . nor will they get a penny out of me.'

Word had got to Mickey Kelly that a new van had been operating and, without informing Riley, he had briefed one of the local street groups – a 'gang', but not members of the Riley team – to take action. They often acted on the team's behalf if they wanted someone bullied or given a first-time frightener. It mattered not whether they were given a few stolen cigarettes or some amphetamines for their deeds, the mere fact they were doing proxy work for Sonny Riley was glory beyond reward. Anything on top of that was a bonus. 'Give him a fright,' Kelly had said. 'He's on his own so you won't have any problems and he won't be back once he gets the message. And make sure he knows you're doing it for Sonny.'

In the old Gorbals as well as in other parts of Glasgow, one of the recognisable faces was that of those loosely termed the street urchins. People would say they had an 'up-a-close face', which wasn't exactly appropriate, as most of the city's inhabitants at one time came from up a close. Yet it was a description that was understood. It applied to those who, from the earliest age – and in some cases that was as soon as they could walk – were shoved out of the door of their crumbling tenement homes with the words, 'Away and play'. And what they found out there in their world wasn't all play. It was about standing up for yourself; it was about push or be pushed; scratch or be scratched; kick or be kicked; take or have it taken. Naples had its children of the sun; Glasgow had its children of the streets.

Of course the parents were blamed for the negligent way they brought up their children but then the parents had been brought up the same way themselves. You could see the story in their faces. They weren't the handsome and nourished faces of the wealthy people who shared their city and whose parents knew about and could afford the good things of life. These faces had mouths which were tight and betrayed the rage and suspicion that seemed to be always in their hearts. There was little that was nice and gentle about their world.

Four of those who came from that world, boys of about eighteen, went that day to Hamie McDougall's van. He knew them in an instant. One of them had a stick which he wielded idiot-fashion, beating the side of Hamie's van rhythmically like it was a big drum.

'Hey, Jimmy,' one of them mouthed aggressively. 'You shouldnae be here, Jimmy. You could get yer face damaged for being here, Jimmy. This is Sonny's . . .'

He didn't get time to finish whatever it was he had in his mind. McDougall leapt from the van, grabbed the stick from the youth and drove it straight into his stomach as if it was a spear. As the youth doubled up in pain the stick crashed down on the back of his head. Astonished at the speed at which McDougall had reacted, the other three stood by and meekly watched until he turned round to the one who had been threatening him. 'Right, you . . . bastard.' As he went for him, the youth drew a long Bowie knife. It wasn't in his hands long. McDougall kicked it wildly into the air before swinging him round in a commando grip and choking the wind out of him with his heavy muscular forearm across his throat. The other two didn't wait to try their luck, scurrying quickly across the road to disappear into the entrance of a block of flats.

McDougall held the one he had winded tightly by the lapels of his denim jacket. 'If you or your fuckin' Sonny or any of your other chinas come near my van again, I'll fuckin' tear you apart . . . got the message, wee boy? Now pick up your pal here and fuck off.'

Kelly had screamed for mercy as Riley had beaten him up while Connors stood guard at the door of the gents in the Whistle. There was no greater sin in the way that Riley's twisted mind interpreted life than not to be told everything that was happening in the Castlehouse he thought of as his kingdom. It was bad enough that a man called McDougall, of whom he had never heard, had bucked his authority, but it was unthinkable for one of his men, one who was supposed to be among his most trusted lieutenants, not only to have failed in his bid to take action against the man but to have failed to inform him, Riley, as well. If word like that got about it could make it seem that Riley had gone soft or slack. They might even laugh at him. The mere thought of that incensed him like nothing else.

It wasn't a pretty scene inside the room at the rear of the Whistle. When the noise subsided and Connors had moved towards the door, Riley casually looked in the mirror, wiping clean a flick of Kelly's blood which had spotted his cheek. He then washed an ugly brass instrument which he had used to protect his knuckles while administering his beating, carefully combed his hair, straightened his tie and, without another look in Kelly's direction, said to Connors, 'This place fuckin' stinks. Have you got a drink set up?' Then they left.

Kelly lay unconscious in one of the cubicles where he had tried to be sick. It wasn't till they got him to hospital, where he was rushed to the intensive care unit, that he regained consciousness. There were no witnesses, of course, and Riley and Connors had long finished their drinks by the time the police arrived. There was no need for either of the two to have warned the manager or any of the other drinkers in the bar what to tell the police. They all knew.

'I saw him go to the toilets and there was a gang of boys in there at the time,' the bar manager told the police. 'Next thing you know we found him in that state. We heard them shout he was a poof. Seems he'd tried to interfere with one of them. But they didn't need to do that to him . . . did they? Terrible, so it is. These boys are getting wilder and wilder.'

There was a discussion about McDougall between Riley and Connors later that night. It was conducted in the usual terse fashion, profanities taking the place of emphasis, oaths replacing indications, obscenities substituting for decisions. But then, had there been anything resembling an exercising of the intellect in the conversation, Connors wouldn't have comprehended.

Riley was puzzled, if not perplexed, that there was someone like McDougall who actually lived in the area and thought that he could rebel against Riley's rule. Had it been someone from one of the other schemes chancing his luck, as it were, or someone from Lanarkshire who was ignorant not only of his dictat but of his prowess, then that might have been understandable. So, too, it would have been comprehensible if someone like Big Alex, the infamous one who ran the north of the city, had sent someone in to test the water on Riley's patch, or even to look for open confrontation with him. He wouldn't have objected to that. A good war with Big Alex might sort out a few things. But this man McDougall was none of these things. He was just a loner. A man from Riley's very own scheme, who must therefore know all about him and despite all that was standing up to him. So in Riley's interpretation of life, this man was an even bigger menace than any of the others. He had to be dealt with. Really dealt with.

CHAPTER 21

THE VISITOR FROM IRELAND

THEY HAD COMPLETED THE BIG MARCH, THE
civil rights one styled on successful marches in America by
the blacks in their widespread and determined bid for
equality. They had also experienced the first of their riots
and wasn't it terrible the scenes that they were showing
every night on television of soldiers and policemen coming
under attack with petrol bombs and rocks. Defence Asso-
ciations and Volunteers and Liberation Armies with their
various sections and rivalries were being formed and
mustered. They had even voted a woman with a lot of fire
in her heart called Bernadette Devlin, the People's Democ-
racy activist, to be a Member of Parliament in Westminster. The war was on again in Ireland.

Of course, people in Scotland knew all about it,
especially in the West of Scotland, and particularly in the
West's capital, Glasgow. For they knew all about Protestants in Glasgow and they knew all about Catholics too,
which was something the Anglicans of England could never
quite understand. They were both understood in Glasgow
because if you weren't one, you were the other.

Protestants who were working-class had their Glasgow
Rangers and their Orange Orders and they made no secret
that they were the bastions of the faith. Protestants who

would think of themselves as being above working-class had their selective golf clubs. Being upper-class chaps they didn't boast that their clubs were bastions too. But they were.

Whether you were vocal about it or not, invariably the heart would lie in one or the other of the religious camps. And just like the Bernadette who had become a Member of Parliament, Bernadette Riley, mother of Sonny, knew where her heart lay. The women who were her closest friends, the ones who among themselves called her Big Bernie, were all good Catholics. They followed the dramatic events unfolding in Northern Ireland as closely as they followed their glorious football team, Celtic. They saw both as victims of Protestant bigotry. And in the evenings, when the very closest of her pals were still there and the last of the bacon and sausage sandwiches had been eaten for the night and she had followed her first medicinal whisky with another and perhaps another together with her favourite screwtop bottle of Guinness, the patriot flames in Bernadette Riley would be rekindled. Even her accent would change as she talked about her beloved Donegal and the wee house, the one with the chickens round the door. There would be a little sing-song afterwards, with either Bernadette or one of the women kicking it off, more likely than not with *Danny Boy*.

'It was my very own mother who used to say,' said Bernadette one night, 'our songs were made for the pure and free . . . they shall never sound in slaveree.'

'Aye, well said, Bern. Never in slaveree.'

'That's right, Bern. We'll never gie intae them.'

'Oh, what bonny words your auld mother had.'

'Aye, she did that. She did that.'

Then came one of her own favourites, often *The Boys From Wexford*, but tonight it was *Kelly of Killanne*. 'More appropriate,' she said, 'for the time they're a' having over there.' And she rattled through the four long verses word perfect, the other women joining in with the rousing lines, 'Goodly news, goodly news do I bring youth of Forth, Goodly news shall you hear Bargy man; For the boys march at morn from the South to the North, Led by Kelly . . . the boy . . . from . . . Killanne.'

When she finished, there were loud shouts of encouragement for another song or at least another rendition, and the more emotional told her she had brought tears to their eyes.

When the singing was over, Bernadette said that they would need to be thinking about 'our friends across the water' and that they should be giving them some support. This brought nods of agreement from all. One said she had an uncle who lived in the Bogside in Derry. 'He's ma Mammy's brother Michael and the "B" Specials just walked up to him, hit him wi' a truncheon and arrested the poor man. Blood all over the place. And him wi' a bad heart as well. Terrible so it is.'

And three of them shook their heads together repeating the words 'Terrible . . . so it is.'

'Well, wait to youse hear the story I've to tell ye,' said Mary Connolly, a frail and thin little woman who weighed less than eight stone, who once lived in a room-and-kitchen house in Portugal Street and who, although it was hard to believe it possible of the wee soul, had given birth to eight children and brought them up in that very same house. 'We had a letter just yesterday from my sister Cathie. She married a Belfast man and they live in a place called the Falls.'

'I've heard o' it,' said one.

'Oh aye,' said another.

'Well, and youse have no' tae breathe a word o' this to any living soul, they've got a boy called Kevin and he's in a wee spot of bother.' At that point her voice changed to a barely audible whisper and the women had to lean towards her to make out what she was saying. 'Ye see, he's one of their Volunteers . . . that's what they call the boys who are in the . . .' At that point the whisper disappeared and without a trace of sound coming from her, she mouthed the words '. . . Irish Republican Army.'

'Is that so . . .?'

'Brave boy . . .'

'Good lad.'

The whisper returned. 'And Cathie, that's his mother like, wants us to look after him for a wee while. Ye see, they're wanting to arrest him for . . .' and the voice disappeared again as she once more said the words without sound, '. . . attacking a sojer.'

That brought another round of comments.

'Ah, God bless him, the boy.'

'Aye, we don't know the half o' it here.'

'They must be suffering terrible.'

'Aye, they sojers have it in for the Catholics.'

'I've seen it for masel on TV.'

'That's right, so have I. Terrible, so it is.'

'But mind,' Mary Connolly had her last word on the subject, 'that's just between you and me and these four walls.'

Bernadette came in at that. 'My auld grandfather Joe Docherty was in the IRA. Oh, the stories ma mother used to tell about him. It was in the days o' the Black and Tans and did he no' go and blow up two o' their armoured cars. Hated they were, they Black an' Tans. And the same man had fought for Britain in the First World War. In the trenches in France he was. And that's the thanks they got for it when they went hame tae Ireland . . . sending in they terrible Black and Tans after them.'

'Aye, right enough,' said one of the women.

'They've a lot to answer for.'

'Another wee drink for the road then, girls,' said Bernadette and they all nodded.

The mood and the other wee drink inspired another wee

song from their Bern. It came without the asking as she lustily burst forth: 'In Mountjoy jay . . . yell, one Monday morning . . .'

'Oh, is that no' lovely?'

'Aye . . . there's naebody can sing it like oor Bern.'

'High above the gallows tree . . . Kevin Barr . . . ree gave his young life . . .'

'For the cause of liber . . . tee . . .'

They didn't know the rest but rounded off the night by joining in with a repeat of the first verse, at the end of which they all applauded their Bern. There were kisses and hugs as they made to leave.

'Before you go, Mary,' said Bernadette, 'when's the boy coming over . . . your nephew? What's his name again?'

'It's Kevin. We're expecting him any day. Might even be tomorrow.'

A fortnight before he left for Scotland, Kevin Kavanagh, just eighteen, a student studying for an Arts degree at Queen's University in Belfast, had taken part in an attack on an Army foot patrol in the Falls Road. There had been six in the patrol and the one he had picked out, although he didn't know it at the time, was also an eighteen-year-old, only nine months in the Army and serving with an English regiment.

Just one bullet from Kavanagh's Kalashnikov AK-47 assault rifle was enough. There are not many who sustain only a wound when shot by a Kalashnikov. The fire-power is such that a bullet hit even on the arm or leg is too much for the central nervous system and is usually fatal. This English lad was one of the first soldiers killed in the new phase of the old conflict they knew as 'the Troubles'.

The attack took place in the Lower Falls, just where Dunville Park meets Grosvenor Road, that point being one of the easiest places from which to make an escape into the warren of back-to-back dry-closet Victorian terraces, the tiny dolls' houses they said were born to huddle and hate in the shadow of the long-silent mills that stood round them.

As soon as Kavanagh saw the soldier fall, he turned and sprinted with his rifle down Sorella Street, not much wider than a lane, then in through a friendly house in Abercorn Street where the door had been left ajar, out through the wide-open door at the back, over the small wall, in through the rear of another friendly house, out through the front, into Lincoln Street, where he handed over the rifle to the householder who had been waiting for it and who led him to the back of the house. Over one more wall and he was in yet another house, this time in Abyssinia Street, which meant he was already four streets away from the shooting. The chasing soldiers, still wondering where in the Grosvenor Road the man might be, had found themselves yet another Houdini killer.

He had taken the precaution not to return to his own house in nearby Leeson Street later that night. Just as well, for an RUC patrol escorted by soldiers in a one-ton Humber armoured troop carrier, the vehicle known as a 'Pig', called at Kavanagh's house. His student card had been found in the vicinity of the shooting and they wanted to question him about it. Kavanagh was already on their lists as a member of the new order which had developed as a breakaway from the official Irish Republican Army. They had already nicknamed them 'Provos' – the Provisional wing of the IRA.

Had they taken him in for questioning, the evidence against him in normal times would have been so tenuous no court would have listened to any charges brought against him. But these were changing days in Northern Ireland and under the new laws Kavanagh and his superiors knew he would have been detained, even tried and convicted. Because of that, he was ordered to leave the country. The following morning, with an Irish passport in the name of Seamus Rourke and a Dublin address which a computer check showed to be accurate, Kavanagh boarded the ferry at Larne for Cairnryan in Scotland. He was now an IRA man . . . on the run.

CHAPTER 22

SONNY'S NEW FRIEND

THEIR TRADE WAS TERROR YET THEY WERE from two different worlds. One thought of himself as the fearless freedom fighter, the other as the fighter to be feared. One was at university studying for a degree in the Arts, the other's schooling had been in the art of streetcraft. One saw himself as soldier for his nation, the other soldiered for his own salvation. Despite all that and more, Sonny Riley and Kevin Kavanagh, the man from Belfast, had struck up an immediate bond when they had been introduced at Bernadette Riley's house.

Because of his physical prowess and the fear he instilled in people, Riley, the introvert, would rather others speak to him than he to others. It was a rarity for him to shake anyone's hand, but then he inhabited a world where people rarely were introduced; newcomers in their midst would be accepted on the strength of the company which brought them along, there was no need for formal introduction. If someone did mention a name, the usual retort would be, 'Aye, we've met ... I've seen him around.' Any formal introduction would have forced the embarrassment of being an extrovert – having to shake hands, even smile and exchange some words. That was not their way. It certainly wasn't Sonny Riley's way.

He had made an exception for this man from Ireland when they were introduced that day, for Sonny had a curiosity about him that he had rarely shown for anyone else. His interest in Kavanagh had been aroused when his mother had whispered to him about the likelihood of his arrival. She told him that this was one of their top men 'over by' and she had also learned from Mary Connolly that the soldier at whom he had fired his rifle hadn't been the first. He had taken part in some of the big battles against the Protestants right from the start of the Troubles the previous year and was also one of their expert bombers.

'He's a right special one, this fellah,' said Bernadette.

Sonny had taken part in many a battle right enough, but the shooting and bombing bit, well, that was way beyond the kind of warfare that he knew about. Yet here was this young fellow, a mere stripling with his dark curly hair and studious face, and he had done all that his mother had claimed. Only eighteen as well . . . exactly half the age of Sonny Riley. This one was well worth a good talk with.

'Of course, it's this old Protestants and Catholics business,' Riley had said as an opening gambit the night they had sat together in the Whistle. He set down the pint of Guinness the lad had requested.

To his great surprise, the boy had replied that it wasn't really all about Protestants and Catholics and that the plot was thicker than that. 'The Protestants just represent part of the establishment which we're fighting against. Our present campaign grew out of the fight for civil rights. D'you know, those that rule where I live carve us out of jobs, out of houses, out of anything they think we shouldn't be getting? We're treated like the blacks in the southern states of America.

'My fight's to correct all that and for the day we have a federal Ireland, which will mean that after we beat the Brits we'll have to take them on in Dublin as well for there's as much establishment down there too, you know.

The Ireland I'm fighting for is one without any form of British control. It would have four provincial governments ruling the four ancient provinces . . . and there'd be no victimisation of the Protestants. We've a lot in common, you know. You scratch a Prod and it's just the same as scratching one of us Taigs . . . below the surface it's an Irishman that's there.'

It was all new stuff to Sonny Riley, but he was interested in what he was hearing; he even found it illuminating.

'An' how long d'you think the riots and the shootings and that are likely to go on for?'

'Maybe a year or two. Maybe another hundred years. Who knows? The thing is, Sonny . . . we've got to go on fighting. We can't just lie down to them. Too many have been too willing to do that for too long.'

Despite the youthful face, he was a big lad of nearly six feet and, thought Sonny, he could fairly sink the pints of Guinness which were being put in front of him.

'How did you learn about the guns and bombs and that kind of thing?'

'Oh, we've got schools out in the country. We go up in the mountains on training exercises and the like. It's just like being in the regular army. Well, we're regular soldiers, you know. The only difference between us and the Brits is that they've got uniforms and we don't. And we're for a far greater and more meaningful cause.

'D'you know they've brought these generals over to lead the campaign against us and they're just back from knocking the hell out of people in places like Aden, bombing villagers and doing the dirty work for some of those Arab rulers. And they think of us like we're a bunch of Arabs ourselves, that they can do what they like with us. Sonny, they've been trying to put us down since they made the terrible mistake of dividing the country and giving the Six Counties Home Rule in 1921.'

'What's the Six Counties again?' Sonny asked, getting more interested.

'Ulster is one of the four ancient provinces and as such has nine counties but when they split us up in 1921, they only included six of these nine counties in the new province they were to call Northern Ireland, or Ulster as everyone except us calls it.'

'I never realised that,' said Sonny, 'the whole thing's been a right carve up then, hasn't it?'

'Aye, Sonny. That's putting it mildly.'

'How long'll you have to stay here, then?'

'Goodness knows. I'm still a Volunteer though I'm away from the scene of the action. They might direct me to fight for them somewhere else. I just don't know at this stage. They'll get word to me somehow. Next week, after I've had a look around here and met all the relatives and that sort of thing, I'll see what I can do here. They're badly needing funds over by, as well as guns and ammunition. I'd like to see what can be done about that while I'm here.'

'Guns are a dodgy business here, Kevin. See as soon as you touch one here, the Busies are on your back. Word really gets around quick when you touch the shooters. That's how I've never anything to do with them.

'You mentioned funds, Kevin. So you're short of money, like?'

'Oh God, aye.'

'Well, you're in among friends here and it only needs the likes of me to whisper in the right ears and you'll see quite a few pennies coming your way. Tell me something. Are you handy wi' explosives . . . you know, making up bombs, say for a car . . . anything like that?'

'Oh aye. What's it you want to know?'

'Oh, nothing really. Well, it was just something I was thinking about . . . like. Would you consider doing a wee bombing job here?'

'Sonny, I'm a Volunteer. We only go for enemies – targets our officers designate for us.'

'Supposing I said this one was an enemy. Supposing I said this one had been in the Paras. And there's no need to tell you what the Paras've done in your country . . . is there? And supposing I was to say that if it wasn't for this one that I'm talking about, I could be raising a helluva lot of money which could be put to a decent use . . . like helping a' you boys over in Ireland? Would that make any difference?'

'Well, when you put it like that . . . there'd be a fair wee bit of wry rejoicing among all my mates in the Falls when they heard that the man who'd to go on the run had got himself a Brit Para in his spare time. Aye, they'd like that, Sonny. They'd like that a lot.'

'So you think you would, then?'

'Why not, if he's what you say he is. Just give me a wee bit of time to find my way about the place before you ask me to do anything.'

'Oh, there's no hurry, Kevin. This one doesn't look like going away. And, anyway, I want to give him another chance to think over what he's doing. He might just come to his senses and then we'll get round to making that wee bit extra which'll help your boys. But, then again, he probably won't.'

CHAPTER 23

McDOUGALL PROSPERS

SONNY RILEY HAD BEEN RIGHT WHEN HE HAD
told Kevin Kavanagh that the man he had in mind for 'the
wee bombing job' didn't look like going away. Every day
Hamie McDougall returned to Castlehouse with his grocery van and became one of the more popular of the traders
because of his easy-going and friendly disposition and his
way with the housewives. Hamie knew his customers all
right. He knew they liked a chat and a bit of interest shown
in them and their families. His van was also at its stances
much longer than the others who always seemed to be in a
hurry to move off to somewhere else where there might be
more money to be made.

The profits were good, so good that he had been able to
send his wife and the three boys on whom he doted off on
a holiday to Majorca, although he hadn't been able to
afford the time off himself to accompany them. When they
had returned he had been waiting for them with their first
car, a second-hand Austin Cambridge he had bought at
the Meat Market Car Auctions.

'And the next target I'm aiming for is a house of our
own,' he had told his wife Patricia the night they celebrated
the return of the family from holiday and the fact that they
had a car of their own.

'I don't believe it, Hamie,' she had said. 'A house of our own. After all those years in Army houses and then council houses and now the schemes. God, that'd be a dream. But can we really afford it?'

'I've got it all figured out and if things keep going the way they are with the van, we'll make it. No problem. I've even been over to Garrowhill looking at some of the ones there for sale. Good area, handy for a lot of the schemes and not too pricey. I saw one I'd love, with a good place at the side for parking the van and it was just over ten thousand.'

'Ten thousand pounds!' said Patricia, shocked. 'You must be joking, Hamie! How'd we ever afford anything like that?'

He explained that all they needed was a down-payment and that he had already been assured by a broker that he was a good bet for a mortgage. '"No problem," the man told me. I went to see a mortgage man up town and when I outlined my work and what I was making he said I was absolutely no problem. "Guys like you," he said, "are the ones we like. You're solid payers and good business for us in the future, because you always come back to increase your mortgages when you're earning more." As soon as he said that, then I thought, right, we'll get the car first and then save like mad for the house.'

She enquired about his work while they had been in Majorca. 'No more problems . . . you know, with those hoodlums who were worrying you?'

'No problems at all, love. They've chickened out, for they know they'll get more of what I gave them the last time if they come back. And I've got a pick-axe handle in the van just dying to crack open a couple of nuts.'

They were still laughing about that when the noise from the bedroom made both of them rise. It was the boys, playing a more boisterous game than usual. The room was messed up with pillows and bedclothes and they were warned that if they didn't behave and go to sleep, one of them would end up with a smacked bottom.

'It'll be wonderful for them,' Patricia said after they managed to settle them down. 'But it'll be wonderful for us too. The neighbours here are nice. They really are. I know there're some wild bits of the scheme, but I've got on well with them here. But . . .'

'I know what you mean, Pat. You just need to look at the state of the place. They never even attempted to finish it, did they? What's it they call it . . . landscaping? They never did much of that. Or did they do any? It was just houses, more houses and more houses. Remember the Maida Barracks I was in at Aldershot? God, they were a helluva lot nicer-looking than this. No wonder the kids go around vandalising everything. The authorities never cared for them when they designed this place and now the kids don't care.'

'It'll be the boys who'll benefit most by getting away from here, Hamie. They've been getting terribly wild recently. I caught young Hamish swearing one day before we went on holiday. And it was really foul stuff. That's not them, Hamie. And they'll just get worse. Oh that's marvellous news. A house of our own. What a dream! I do hope it all comes true.'

Hamie had been expecting more trouble from Riley's men. He had read all the signs and knew that something was happening, although he wasn't quite sure what. He had observed them in little groups at a distance, and had equated them with a reconnaissance platoon making observations of enemy forward positions, just as he had been trained to do and had actually done. Then he quickly admonished himself for giving them as much credit as an equation with soldiers. Hamie had nothing but respect for the military and for the soldierly behaviour of the professional British Army man. There was nothing soldierly, disciplined, courageous or tough about this lot. They were thugs and hooligans who were duplicating the same squalid lives of their wanton parents. When he read the reports of social workers and sociologists saying that these were people who were badly in need of help he would laugh to himself. And he would look at the hefty pick-axe handle always within reach and think . . . 'That's the help they need. That's the only help they know. Getting thumped. And that's the help they'll get if they come near this van.'

A stone hit the van one day as he had been parked at his usual stance in Castlehouse and he had seen two blokes run off. They weren't little boys doing the kind of thing some little boys did for fun in the neighbourhood. They were bigger than that, big enough to have the kind of intelligence to mean that it had been deliberate. Their idea of a warning shot.

Then another night, just after his last customer had left and he was putting up his shutter hatch, an airgun slug had pinged off a front mudguard. There was no one in sight this time and he debated whether there had been a motive or not. Taking a pot-shot like that didn't need a motive, for other van-men had told him they had had similar shots fired at them. Nevertheless, he was suspicious and saw it as part of the sinister pattern of scare tactics being deployed against him. He was right.

After Mickey Kelly had been unceremoniously humiliated and drummed out of the Riley team, Pat Connors had taken on a higher profile as Sonny Riley's deputy. He had only briefly discussed what they should do about the van-man McDougall. 'Oh, he's got something special coming to him,' was all that Sonny had replied, adding that until he got round to it, Connors could do what he wanted about him. The stone-throwing and the airgun shot had been from some of the youths Connors had told could win themselves some favours if they pestered McDougall's van.

The attacks grew in number and regularity to an extent that more than convinced McDougall they were organised and that it was Riley who was behind them. And it was spelled out to him when there was a repeat of the earlier incident when the four youths had tried to frighten him off. This time there were five of them, obviously high on drugs or alcohol by their maniacal shouts and whoops as they charged at his van with sticks, one of them brandishing a full-length sword.

'Sonnee . . . Sonnee,' they had taunted as they circled his van like a group of movie Red Indians. They were members of a gang who called themselves 'Young Young Cumbies', which was meant to indicate they were the descendants – and in fact, they may well have been – of one of the famous Glasgow gangs, the Cumbies.

'Sonnee's gonnie get you,' they jeered, together with other war-cries, like 'Cumbee . . . Cumbee' and 'Mental . . . Mental', the latter being the way they thought of themselves as rage overtook reason.

They were not to shout for long. McDougall came at them with even more speed than he had tackled the previous lot. And this time he was armed with the heavy hickory shaft. That came as a real surprise for the five as he rushed at them swinging it samurai-fashion, just as he had been taught in riot-control training in the Paras.

With the first flail of the stout stick he had smashed the shoulder of one of the youths. The next was the one with the sword. He felt the full force of it on his jaw and it took two of them to carry him off, the remaining two fleeing, shouting more taunts as they went, about Sonny Riley and how they would be back.

Riley gave that sneering smile of his to Connors when he reported what had happened. He would get him in his own fashion the next time.

'He needs a bulldozer this yin,' said Connors.

Riley shook his head, however. 'No . . . leave him. I've got something lined up for him. And it'll make your bulldozer look like a game of peever.'

CHAPTER 24

A STAR RETURNS

KEVIN KAVANAGH WAS ENJOYING HIS STAY IN
Glasgow. He had accompanied Sonny Riley to some of his
favourite haunts. Riley had taken him to the Gorbals, now
a hideous mess with most of the old slums gone and
replaced with gaunt tower blocks, one section getting so
much acclaim for its 'revolutionary design', it won its
architect a variety of prestigious awards. But then none of
the architects had to live there and share the inconvenience
of lifts that repeatedly broke down, or experience the first
of the damp which was already penetrating some of the
prefabricated concrete walls. The reason for the damp,
according to one story that was going about, was that one
of the builders had used plans he had for flats that had
been built in North Africa!

They had visited the favourite drinking haunts of Sonny
and his father before him, places like the Old Judge which
still remained, albeit standing on its own like some of the
other pubs, brick and plaster shoeboxes, the tenement
buildings which had once stood over them having been
demolished. They had gone, too, to the Brian Boru and the
Tara social clubs where the Irish community met and
where there was great talk in between the ballads and the
songs of the brave and the knave about 'your man from the

Falls'. Kavanagh was the first one they had met, a real live 'Freedom Fighter', as their weekly newspaper *An Phoblacht* called them. They would pump his hand, slap his back, tell him he was a 'brave man' and ask him, 'What was it like?'

Kavanagh meant a lot to their activities in raising funds 'to help with the cause'. This had become particularly active after the Battle of the Bogside and the jailing of their heroine Bernadette Devlin for her part in it. And they were still talking about the one that had followed that, the Battle of the Short Strand, in which a tiny Belfast enclave of 6,000 Catholics had been surrounded by 60,000 Protestants, and the Provisionals had taken to the streets with guns, to defend their people against the onslaught led by the newly reformed Ulster Volunteer Force. The war was on for real now.

The handsome young Irishman enjoyed the limelight he was getting from the Glasgow community. There was nothing like that in Belfast and this was a whole new and unexpected experience. It was also possible in Glasgow for a man like himself to relax without the fear of the midnight knock on the door. There wasn't much relaxing now in Belfast, particularly for those like Kavanagh whose names were in the computer and who headed the lists for the next round of internment.

He had almost got used to the unwholesome atmosphere that greeted you at the door of Bernadette Riley's house, but that day he had called there with Sonny he had to grit his teeth at the smell. It was just before midday. There had been a big group of Bernadette's pals with her the previous night and their 'wee party' had gone on till the small hours. He had never known air to be so hot, heavy and clammy. The overflowing ashtrays, two of them improvised from expensive Doulton soup plates, still hadn't been cleared, lending their own stale stench to the foul air now being fortified by the flow of thick, blue smoke drifting from the kitchen where two women were making the first of that day's fried sandwiches.

The door to Bernadette's room was open, as it always seemed to be, and in its usual semi-darkness, the blinds down and the curtains drawn, and lit by just one small light beside the bed in which she was propped up in her normal fashion, supported by a phalanx of ornately embroidered pillows, cradling a cup of tea as she waited for her cooked sandwich.

'Oh, I'm that pleased to see you boys,' she had said when the two had walked into the room. 'How're they treating you in Glasgow, Kevin?' She wanted to know all the places they had been and the people he had been meeting. She had been interested to know, too, all the details of the money that was being raised in the Irish clubs, of which she had once been a regular member.

'And how are the vans doing, Sonny? Are they giving you lots of work like you thought they might?'

'They're doing a right treat, Maw.'

'That's great, son. It really is. One of my pals was saying there's one been giving a bit of trouble. She saw him fighting with some of the boys from the scheme. He must've been annoying them, Sonny?'

'Aye . . . I heard about that. Bit of a troublemaker, I hear. Maybe he needs sorting out.'

'They tell me as well, Sonny, that there's lots of others coming into the scheme now. You know, these door-to-door salesmen. Making a fortune, they tell me. We'd one here the other day. A wee man, he was, and Jessie let him into the house. Know what he was on about, Sonny? Said he could get my house all done up. Tried to sell me a marble doorstep, so he did. He said they were doing a special offer on glass doors too. Says one would be good for my bedroom here, seeing as I always have it open. Would make the room look bigger. Right wee patter merchant! Aye, Sonny, they're a' into us in the schemes, trying to

make money out of us. Just as well we don't let them a'
away wi' it. My pals tell me this wee fellow got three orders
up our close alone. Must be making a right packet, so he
must. There's his card on the dresser over there, Sonny.
Maybe you know him?'

Sonny read the card and as he did he gave one of his
sneering laughs. 'Aye, Maw, I know them all right. I think
I'll maybe look them up. They cannae be allowed to go
about here making a fortune like that. Can they?'

'You're right, son. Shouldnae be allowed.'

He hadn't recognised the name that had been on the
card ... F. Ogilvie, sales manager. It was the name of
the company and of its managing director that had evoked
the forced laugh ... 'Star Home Improvements' and
'S. Nelson'.

CHAPTER 25

THE SPARROW IS GROUNDED

'SPARROW' OGILVIE, WHO ALWAYS INTRO-
duced himself 'Mr Francis Ogilvie, consultant manager of
the Star Company', had a way with his customers. He
could be described as a born salesman, but more likely that
birth had come after an American book he had read on the
subject. It had been called *Selling a Dream*.

In a sense, 'Sparrow' was living a dream. For all the
years he had worked, as he would say, 'with the tools', he
had dreamt about the day he might get a job where he
didn't have to work outside in all weathers, soaked and
frozen in the winter, exposed to what heat there might be
in the summer, and enduring the basic conditions that
represented life on the building sites. It was easier for those
with a better physique than his, but not the kind of life for
anyone so aptly called 'Sparrow'.

Now, thanks to Sammy Nelson's new venture, he had
achieved his ultimate ambition. He drove to work every
day in his little Morris Minor, wore a collar and tie and
never ever had to get his hands dirty. That was why when
he had got the job he had dedicated himself to being as
good a salesman as he possibly could. When someone had
suggested he read *Selling a Dream*, he immediately went into
the city to buy a copy. It was to be his bible in salesman-

ship, although he did graft on to what he was to learn from it a few ideas of his own, not least of them being his own innate sense of what they simply knew in Glasgow as 'the patter'.

Certainly not in the book was his own speciality – the 'ten per cent deal'. This he had devised on his own and it was yet another factor in increasing the amount of work he secured for the company. It worked this way. When he quoted a price for a job to a customer, it would be ten per cent more expensive than the actual price charged by the company. When the price was agreed with the customer, he would drop the hint that, as they had made such a good order, he would see what he could do about a cut. Then when they paid the agreed sum, he would hand them back ten per cent . . . the ten per cent he had added on in the first place. And he would always say, as he returned the money, 'Now, that's just between you and me, like.'

It worked like a dream and the customers were always so grateful at the trouble they thought this pleasant and harmless little salesman had gone to on their behalf. More important, they always contacted him again for more work, and he would use them to get names of friends and relatives who might like some work done too. Then, again very confidentially, he would add, 'You never know, I might just be able to arrange a cut for them as well, seeing it was you who recommended them. But I can't promise. Know what I mean?'

It had worked so well for the 'Sparrow', that it had taken him over a year and half before he had to move out of the Chapelhill scheme in search of new customers. That was when he had gone to Castlehouse, where he began to repeat his phenomenal sales success.

Sammy often had chats with him about his orders, trying to elicit what secrets there were to his prowess. He would tell Sammy some of his ploys, but not all of them. A salesman had to have his secrets.

'The first thing,' he would say, 'I never call at a house cold. That means, Sammy, when I knock on a door I've always got a name . . . and a wee message of some kind. You know, like I'll say, "Good morning. Was talking to Aggie Brown, your old pal from Baltic Street, and she says I was to tell you she's asking for you." Then I'm in quick with the reason why I was up at Aggie's house and it's never anything as corny as we were doing some jobs in her house or that I work for a home improvements company or the like. What I tell them is that the company was involved in arranging Aggie's new lifestyle and then I move on quickly to the gossip. But the gossip's only flannel for you've already planted the seed and they're dying for you to finish telling them that Aggie's daughter's expecting or Jeannie's boy's getting married so that they can ask you what you meant about Aggie's new lifestyle.

'Now, the moment they say that, you know you've got a new customer. It's like going fishing, Sammy. The hook goes in but you don't haul them to you right away. You've to play around a little, just to make sure. That's why when they ask about this new lifestyle thing, you act a bit reluctant about telling them. Try to give them another wee bit of gossip. Of course, by this time you're in the house, the bunnet's off and the kettle's on and they're asking you if you want a sandwich to go with the tea. And all the time they're getting more and more desperate to know about Aggie's new lifestyle. So then you explain that's the way Aggie has been thinking about life since we did a few jobs around her house.

'She said it to us herself after we'd finished the work. "It's like a new lifestyle I've got," were her very words. "So we think about it just the same." And when you get that far the only things they want to know are your prices and what you can do to their place.

'Sammy, the secret's selling them dreams. I tell them when they get that new terrazzo doorstep, "That's not just a doorstep you got yourself, missus, that's a whole new image."'

'A doorstep's an image?' queried Sammy.

'That's right, boss. A doorstep's an image. A set of new glass-panel doors is a dream. Doors, doorstep and a contemporary fireplace and they've got themselves a whole new lifestyle. I'm a dreams salesman, Sammy. I'm what the Yanks would call a hidden persuader. And I've never looked back since that book I read about it.'

However, he never mentioned his 'ten per cent deal' to Sammy. That was his very own little idea and hadn't come from any book. It was perfectly legitimate, of course, he would think to himself. If poets could have licence, then why couldn't salesmen?

It had been a similar such tale he had told Jessie, the woman who had opened the door to him when he had called at Bernadette Riley's, which was why he was the first salesman ever to gain entry to the house. When he looked around at the work that had already been done, he had concluded even he would be struggling to sell any new images to this woman, who had obviously had a small fortune spent on her home. 'This one's got images galore,' he had said to himself. Nevertheless he thought he should try something and because of the heavy, stale air in the house he asked Bernadette if she had ever considered what he called the new 'Norwegian airflow' system. 'They call it that because it'd make your house smell like a walk through a beautiful pine forest.' He never mentioned the words 'extractor fan', but because of her interest, he did say he would call back when he got some literature and prices. 'I think there just might be a special offer going on them,' he had added. It was then he had given her the card which she had later shown to Sonny.

Although he wasn't able to get a definite sale for Star Home Improvements at Bernadette's, 'Sparrow' Ogilvie had managed to secure the names of four of the women there and in subsequent calls to their houses signed up three of them for a variety of home improvement jobs or, as he told them, 'new lifestyle projects'.

Not long after his mother had shown him Francis Ogilvie's card Sonny Riley began regularly seeing Star Home Improvements vans, with their distinctive blue and silver livery, around the Castlehouse scheme. The sight of those vans had an effect on Riley. He hated that name ... Star. He knew it was used because that was the name of Sammy Nelson's niece, just as they had used it when they had owned the lounge bars. And he hated Sammy Nelson more than anyone else, for it had been him, he was told, who had killed his own father, Steven 'Snakey' Holden. That fact festered in Sonny Riley's mind. He had been positive too that they had sent Frankie Burns to get him ... that was why he had been particularly vicious when he, instead, had been the killer and the man from the Calton had died.

He thought they had gone from his life forever when he had been told that Sammy Nelson was living in the States and that Star had gone off somewhere 'with her Paki man'. But now they were back in his city once more and not only that, they were operating right under his nose in his very own Castlehouse. Making money out of *his* scheme! What the hell were they playing at even thinking about it? No one was going to make money out of Castlehouse unless sanctioned in some way by Sonny Riley. Castlehouse was his and he would show that to anyone who dared to think otherwise.

With the pressure being put on him by his mother, the only person in the world who could influence his ways, to help the cause in Ireland, more money than ever was needed. Therefore, absolutely no one would trade in his scheme without paying their dues. But even if it had not been for that, even if it had not been for the fact that traders paid him in order to operate, it was this name

Nelson again and this woman member of the family called Star. For that alone, something had to be done.

His pals had been right, of course, that night years ago when they had jokingly suggested to him as they drank in her bar that Riley 'fancied' Star Nelson. That was why he had turned on them so ferociously for their casual remark and no one had ever dared mention the subject again, in jest or otherwise. He would have loved a woman like Star Nelson. She represented class to him. Sonny Riley knew what class was all about. He knew it when he saw it but he also knew it was unattainable. He admired class and style, but so enmeshed was he in his own squalid world there was no way out. And that made him hate people like Star Nelson and Sammy Nelson all the more.

Like him, they had come from the Gorbals. But they had found the way out. They had got to the other side and now they had class and style. Sonny Riley knew he never would, and that was another reason why these people would have to be sorted out once and for all.

Three of the five who had surrounded Hamie McDougall's van went that night to get 'Sparrow' Ogilvie. Connors had told them who he was and what had to be done in the sort of language which they understood ... 'the wee skinny punter with the blazer and the fancy poof case. A hammerin' ... an' tell him no' tae come back tae Castlehouse.' It didn't take them long to find him, for Ogilvie had become a regular and distinctive sight around the streets of the big scheme, parking his car in one spot then walking to calls in the vicinity.

It may well have been that in their twisted minds there was a legitimacy in the command Connors had given them but they didn't need to do what they did to the fragile and harmless salesman. There seemed to be an unfathomable rage in their hearts; perhaps it was for being what they were, perhaps because of what they came from or because of the nowhere they were going to. Whatever it was, Francis Ogilvie was to suffer for it.

He was a little rabbit among three hyenas. Even against one of them the 'Sparrow' would have had no chance for, so unlike his father, the famous 'Tiger' Ogilvie, he was without guile or aggression or physical skill. He couldn't even have run from them.

A Detective Inspector described it in the papers the following morning as one of the most savage and vicious assaults he had come across 'in all my years in Glasgow'. He had added, 'I sincerely hope this doesn't turn out to be a murder inquiry that we're working on.'

The doctor at the hospital was reluctant, as they always seemed to be, to tell Sammy Nelson about the extent of Ogilvie's injuries. The look on his face had said, 'Is there any point in telling you, for you wouldn't understand, would you?', but his words had been different. They had been, 'You're not exactly a relative, Mr Nelson', in the plummy tone they used in many parts of Glasgow to make it clear exactly which part they came from.

Sammy was furious. This one was for the 'Listen, pal' message and that's what he got. 'You listen to me, pal,' said Sammy. 'What are you gonnie do . . . wait so that you can tell his poor bloody missus that his kidneys are ruptured, his brains are kicked in and he's got umpteen bones broken and he'll die the night . . . just because she's a relative? Is that what you're gonnie do? I'm Francis Ogilvie's best pal . . . I'm also his employer and more than that, I care about the wee man in there and that's why I want to know what the score is. All right?'

The doctor got the message all right and read the details from a clipboard he was carrying.

'Fine,' said Sammy, after he had finished. 'Now you can cut the medical patter and put it on the line for me. Is he going to make it?'

The doctor got that message too. 'His heart's strong, his lungs haven't been damaged, which augur well. He's in a very bad way otherwise and he's lost considerable blood. But he's in the best of care and I'm optimistic.'

It was three days before he recovered consciousness and Sammy was there, together with a policeman waiting for a statement. An arm and a leg were in traction and his face was badly discoloured, one side covered in heavy bandaging.

'How're you feeling, wee man?' Sammy said softly.

It took some time for the 'Sparrow' to focus on the world which he had departed from for more than seventy-two hours and there was only a hint of reaction to suggest that he had recognised Sammy's voice.

Sammy repeated the words again. 'How're you feeling, wee man? . . . You're going to be fine . . . The doctor says everything'll be all right.'

Sammy leaned closer to him to hear his faint reply. 'Aye . . . aye, Sammy.'

At that he fell asleep and a Sister asked the two men if they would leave for a while.

'What do you make of that then?' Nelson said to the policeman as they walked from the hospital. 'What kind of people do we have in this city of ours that do things like that? You know that wee man's nickname? "Sparrow". And that's what he is . . . a wee, chirpy, cheery bloke that wouldnae hurt a fly. A right wee sparrow. And then these animals get a hold of him. That wee man'll never be the same again. And I'll tell you something, if it was me that got hold of the ones that did it, none of them'd be the same again either. Let's hope you boys get them.'

It wasn't until one of the Star company vans had been attacked in Castlehouse, at a spot near where they had found 'Sparrow' Ogilvie, that the Riley connection emerged. One of the men in the van, terrified after the experience, had said that four youths who had surrounded them had, among other things, shouted threats that had included the name 'Sonny'.

Star and Sammy had discussed the connection between the attacks on 'Sparrow' and their van and Sonny Riley, and Star reminded Sammy of her talking on her return from Australia about 'the unfinished business with this man Riley'.

'I'd no plan then, I've no plan now. All I know is that something has to be done about this man. All right, I did a very wrong thing before when I paid for him to be killed and I'll never get over what happened to that poor man Frankie Burns as a result. That'll haunt me for the rest of my days. But a way must be found to do something about Riley. He must be got rid of . . . and please, Uncle Sammy, don't misunderstand that remark. I don't mean by any other form of disposal. I mean properly and legitimately.'

'Well, that leaves it up to the cops then, and they've got nothing on him or else they'd have nabbed him.'

'You mentioned once that there were six names who could give him an alibi for the night Frankie Burns was murdered?'

'That's right.'

'I never did ask, but how did you know that?'

'Big Alistair McDonald told me.'

'And he is?'

'He's a "dick". A detective sergeant. Works at the Central Division HQ with Tom Graham – you know, the Superintendent who was in charge of the Tallyman case years ago when they nailed Riley?'

'Yes, and the court found him not guilty. What's the possibility of getting the names?'

'You'll get nothing out of Graham. He's a Holy Wullie. Everything has to be by the book. Bugger wouldn't even let you buy him a drink in case it was said he was being got at.'

'How well do you know the sergeant?'

'Big Alistair? You know me, Star.'

'You knew his father?'

'That's right. His old man was stationed in the Lawmoor Street Police Office and I used to slip him a bottle of our whisky every week to turn his other eye, or maybe I should say turn his other nose, when we were getting brewed up. God, that's a long time ago now.'

'So you really did know his father. How well do you know Alistair?'

'You mean, do I know him well enough to ask him to get the names?'

'Yes.'

'Oh, I don't know. I think he's the bending type. But what good are the names to us? If the Busies can't get any joy out of them, how could anybody else? Remember these are all chinas of your man Riley. They'll be in his pocket in one way or another. No chance of any of them ratting on the bast . . . the basket.'

'Worth a try, though.'

'Aw, come on, Star. You just don't go knocking on the door of types like that. What would you say . . . "Excuse me, I'd like you to squeal on yer pal Sonny Riley and tell the cops that you really know where he was that night Frankie Burns was murdered"?'

'Sammy, I'm willing to try anything . . . legal . . . to get Riley. Would this sergeant fellow give you the names? Would you ask him? Would you do that for me?'

'Have I ever said no to you in my life?'

CHAPTER 26

HELP FROM A BLUE NOSE

SAMMY COULD HAVE RUNG AND MADE AN arrangement to see him, but he considered that would have appeared over-anxious. He did know where the man drank . . . Graham's at Glasgow Cross. The name of the bar was a good opening gambit when they met that evening after McDonald had finished work.

'Well, if it isn't *the* Sammy Nelson,' McDonald said when he recognised him in the bar. 'It's been a long, long time since I've seen you in here,' continued the big policeman, with the same gentle West Highland face of the man who used to be so grateful to Sammy for his weekly supply of whisky.

'Aye, I've been drinking in the other Graham's.'

'Never knew there was another one.'

'Aye, Graham's in Kearny . . . New Jersey.'

Sammy told him the long story of how he had gone off to the States for a spell and why it had been so long since he had seen him. McDonald was captivated by the account Sammy gave him of some of his experiences in the States, particularly by his adventures in New York. He listened intently, especially to the story about the Mafia and working with the New York City Police Department.

'Boy, wouldn't we love to operate like these guys. Would

be a lot easier to clean out a few of our hoods. And tell me, did the Mafia guys get jailed?'

'Aye . . . well, sort of. They got sentences. Five to ten years. They're on appeal now and apparently if you've got the loot and the right lawyer, that can go on for years. But it means they've got to be good boys or they'll be bagged for a real stiff one.'

'What a story. Sammy Nelson, a New York cop under-cover man. Make a good book.'

'Better movie,' countered Sammy. 'Sean Connery'd be perfect for the role.'

He changed the subject to speak about the crime scene in Glasgow.

'Oh, we've the usual psychopaths on the loose that we'd like to nail,' said McDonald.

'You mean ones like Sonny Riley?'

'That bastard. More lives than a bloody auld alley cat. D'you know . . . no, I'd better not say.'

'Come on, Alistair, it's Sammy Nelson you're talking to . . . knew your faither.'

'Aye, so you did. And he told me all about you, you old rascal. Oh well, anyway, they think Riley's into the IRA game now.'

Sammy could see that riled McDonald and he remem-bered his father's reputation as one of the staunchest Blue Noses in the Force. In an organisation like the Glasgow Police, that was saying something. The boy here's obviously the same, Sammy thought, and he decided to play on it.

'Is that right? Dirty Fenian bastard. Hanging's too good for that lot.'

'You're right, Sammy. Bloody traitors.'

'So what's he up to?'

'Special Branch are involved. They know he's into fund-raising but they think it could be worse. He might be into explosives as well. There's an Irishman been going about with him. They're watching him too, for they suspect he's on the run, but they're not lifting him yet till they can get good evidence on him.'

'Funny, here we are after all this time talking about Sonny Riley again. Last time we met we were talking about him.'

'You've a better memory than me, Sammy. When was that again?'

'When Frankie Burns got murdered . . . just before I left for the States.'

'Aye, I remember that day.'

'And you said at that time that you didn't lift Riley for it because he had six alibi witnesses.'

'Right. And not only that, we'd nothing else on him. Not one single bloody clue! But we know he did it. We'd a whisper from somebody. Nothing that would've meant anything in the Fiscal's Department though. No "evidence".'

'What about the six?'

'Their stories were identical. He was at a party in Lanarkshire with them and stayed the night.'

'Bet they were all Micks.'

'Well, that didn't take much figuring, Sammy.'

'Aye, and they'll be into this fund-raising game with him as well.'

'You're probably right.'

'Bastards, aren't they? Imagine that lot fund-raising. It'll be one to you, two to me, one to you, three to me.'

He could see McDonald's face get angrier.

'We're no' supposed to have any grudges like, but see these Fenians! I'd do anything to get them inside.'

'I don't blame you, Alistair. Messengers of the Pope, every one of them.'

The mere mention of the Holy Father's name made McDonald appear even more hostile. He's his father's boy all right, thought Sammy, and I've got him going.

'Aye, I'm not surprised about Riley being in with the IRA. They tell me he's never away from the chapel.'

'Is that right?'

'Aye.'

'Papish bastard.'

'The six names, Alistair. The alibi ones. D'you keep trying them? You know, to see if they've maybe changed their minds?'

'No. Too much on our plate. We know they won't change anyway.'

'Supposing a couple of them did?'

'Different story then. We'd be on to something with him.'

'What if somebody else, not the police, were to try them?'

'Like who?'

'Just say . . . somebody else. And supposing because of that somebody else, two or three of them changed their minds? Would that lead to you nailing Riley?'

'That's right, but I couldn't even think of a longer shot. What's your interest anyway, Sammy?'

'I'd like to see Riley in the same place as you.' Then he told him the story of 'Sparrow' Ogilvie. 'I've never seen anything as pathetic in all my life as that wee man lying up there in the infirmary. The people who do things like that should be shown no mercy. I'd string the bastards up, no messing.'

'The Superintendent's working on that case. He takes up anything serious that happens in Castlehouse on the basis that there's sure to be a connection with Riley. He's also building up a dossier on Riley's auld wife's moneylending racket.'

'Is she into that?'

'Aye, she gets Sonny's boys to thump the bad payers.'

'Probably sends her profits to the convent.'

That and the large whisky Sammy had just bought him stoked the fire a little more.

'Bastards . . . all of them,' said McDonald.

'What about a wee look at the names, then, Alistair?'

'Aye. Let me think about it.'

Sammy gave him a business card. 'Just pop them in the post, Alistair.'

'What's this, Sammy? Star Home Improvements? You were running pubs the last time we met.'

'All sold up. This is a better game. Don't have to mix with all the scruff you get in pubs.'

'You wouldn't by any chance do modern fireplaces?'

'One of our special lines.'

'The wife keeps talking about getting a new one.'

'Say no more, Alistair. I'll have a man call this week. This is just for you, like. Know what I mean?'

McDonald knew what he meant all right. The six names were in the next post.

CHAPTER 27

PRIVATE EYE ALFIE

BERT STEED HAD RECOMMENDED ALFIE. NOT
only had they been in the Army together but Alfie had also
been a close friend of Frankie Burns. They hadn't met since
their Army days but when Bert had gone to see him he had
been more than willing to take on the case. 'And he's a
good Gorbals boy,' Bert had told Star the day she had gone
to see him.

Alfie Rose was Jewish. His family were well-known
tailors and before the old Gorbals was destroyed they had
run a successful business in the Old Rutherglen Road.
Their home was in one of the roomy and spacious flats in
Abbotsford Place, the best of the old Gorbals' tenements.
Like most of the traditional Jewish community they had
prospered and moved to more southerly and affluent
suburbs, first of all to Crosshill and then up the social
ladder even further to Newlands, where Alfie now lived in
an eight-roomed stone villa.

The Rose Bureau of Investigation was an offshoot of the
Rose Collection Agency, a firm of debt collectors founded
by his father when small tailoring businesses had gone into
decline. Old man Rose had been born in Germany and
although he had come to Scotland as a child, he spoke
English with all the characteristics of someone casting for

a stage role as the archetypal Jew. His son Alfie, on the other hand, had an accent that was Gorbals Glasgow via the Scots Guards. It was Alfie's idea to diversify their collection company by incorporating a private detective agency.

Alfie spoke a lot about his two years' National Service, just as many Jews who served in the Forces did with great pride. Service in the British Army gave them an identity with their new country; it showed that when it came to the test, their loyalty was to their adopted homeland. And when Star had gone to see him, he spoke about Steed and Burns and how his time in the Forces had been two of the greatest years of his life.

Alfie Rose wouldn't have appeared in anything by Mickey Spillane. The suit was hand-cut and expensive and there were lots of gold bits showing – cuff-links, tie-pin, watch and two fillings in his teeth. His curly black hair was grey-tinted and the appearance was more company executive than private detective.

'It's mainly divorce work, you know,' he had explained to Star. 'We're not really into private detective work here like they are in the States, or even in London. So anything different and really challenging is welcome. Although these jobs do tend to be time-consuming and that does entail rather hefty accounts, if I can put it delicately to you, Mrs Jehan. From what Bert Steed outlined to me, this could certainly be time-consuming.'

'Neither time nor money is a consideration for what I have in mind,' Star replied. 'I want to get Sonny Riley where he belongs and that's in prison.'

'I'm with you there, Mrs Jehan. When Bert told me, I was immediately interested. All right, you're a client but what you're getting is an agent with a personal involvement, for Frankie and I were close buddies in the Army, you know. He was a great man to be with in the jungle.'

'I can imagine,' said Star.

'Okay, so we have six names and addresses here. My understanding is that all have been interviewed by the police and have given a statement to the effect that they were in the company of Sonny Riley throughout the night that Frankie was murdered and that they were even with him until well into the following day. Am I right so far?'

'That's the story.'

'So, what do you want of the six names?'

'Every single item of information you can get about each of them . . . their school, church, job, friends, habits, previous convictions, family background, everything.'

'A tall order. And if . . . no, I'll take that back, *when* I get the information, then what?'

'That I've still to figure. What I decide to do will depend on what information I get on them, so I must know every single thing there is to know about these six. A full dossier on each of them.'

He ran his eye down the six names. 'I know them all very well . . . the area where they stay, that is. Not the kind of place where people go to the ballet in the evening.'

'That's putting it mildly. I know that part of the world very well. I'd a chain of little shops once and one of them was there. It was forever getting broken into or vandalised in some way. I eventually sold up . . . it was more trouble than it was worth. But you never know, you may get a surprise. I always live in hope.'

'Mrs Jehan . . . I'm Jewish and our very life is based on that word. I'll begin work tomorrow on it . . . I'm more than willing to get you the information.'

As the Detective Sergeant had told Sammy Nelson, it was a long shot. But Star was more than willing to play the odds.

CHAPTER 28

EXPLOSIVE MATERIAL

KEVIN KAVANAGH, THE MAN ON THE RUN, HAD kept in touch with his bosses in Ireland, the men he addressed by their military titles, such as Officer Commanding and Adjutant. They had told him to stay where he was in Castlehouse, although it would be a good thing to spend some time in different houses in case he was being watched. They would contact him when necessary, through his aunt. Like the good soldier he was, he obeyed the commands to the word.

There was a new instruction in the letter he received that day as he had waited in his aunt's house for Sonny Riley to call. They had planned to go to a Celtic versus Aberdeen game at Parkhead and beforehand there was an arrangement to meet 'some of the boys' at one of their favourite pubs near the stadium.

'I'm looking forward to the match,' he had told Sonny when he arrived. 'Could be the last time I'll be seeing our grand old team in action for a while, though. I've to be off by the end of the month.'

'Back to Belfast?'

'No, I'm wanted in England.'

'England?' said Riley, surprised. 'What do they want you for there?'

Kevin smiled at Sonny's question. 'To be frank, Sonny, I haven't a clue.'

'But you don't just go off somewhere like that without knowing what's happening.'

'I'm afraid that's the way of it, Sonny. I know it's difficult to understand how we operate but let me explain it to you. One of the first things you learn when you become a soldier in the Republican Army is that you're there to obey, not to question. Because of the structure of the RA we're not like any other army. You just have to trust that the commands you're given are for our cause. We never question that trust . . . at least, this is certainly one soldier who'll never question it. So when I'm ordered to report to a particular house in Kilburn in London, the last thing I expect is to be told why I'm going there. All I know is they want me there for something they've planned, so I'll go. It might well be that I'll be there for months, maybe even years, before they're in touch again. This is going to be a long war and the boys are preparing for all sorts of campaigns.'

The use of the Army vocabulary made it seem all a big game to Sonny Riley. Of course he knew all about the IRA, or thought he did, but he never realised that they took themselves as seriously as this, talking as if it really was an army, that they really were soldiers. I mean, he was just Kevin Kavanagh, the likeable young student fellow that was a relative of one of his mother's pals and was good company in the pub and at Parkhead watching Celtic . . . but a serving soldier too?

It all mystified Riley. He knew about warfare but it was nothing like this. What Kavanagh had told him was about planning and preparation, thinking ahead, working out a campaign, as well as discipline and dedication. There was no similarity between that and the kind of warfare Riley knew. His warfare was mainly instant and consequences were something that happened to other people.

'When's that you go, then?' he asked.

'I've to be there by the first of next month ... about another fortnight.'

'So what about that job I mentioned, you know the Para – McDougall's the name – who's interfering with our fund-raising schemes?'

'Yes, I remember. You still want him taken care of?'

'Christ, aye. Fucker's a menace. Threatening our boys and still refusing to pay.'

'Well, there shouldn't be any problems. Just a case of getting the stuff together. Then I'll make it up.'

'You'll need ... what's it they use ... dynamite?'

'Aye, I'd love dynamite if you can get it, but there are substitutes that might be easier to get. You see, I don't know what things are like here, what's available and that.'

The subject fascinated Riley. Bombs! That was a different league from a kicking or using something that had a blade, which was the most complicated weapon he had ever used in his life. This was jungle man coming down from the tree to look at the shiny new gun of the explorer who had arrived in their midst.

'So if there's no dynamite what kind of stuff is it you use then, Kevin?' he asked with the curiosity of a little boy.

'It's a big subject, Sonny. I went to classes to learn what we needed to know and we used to have trials with the stuff. We had this wee cottage out in the wilds. It was way past the Barnesmore Gap up in the Blue Stack Mountains. God, it was a lonely spot. Sonny, you could have set off a fuckin' atom bomb up there and nobody would have known. But what great times we had! And we could experiment away as much as we liked. All that heard us were the birds and rabbits.'

But Sonny still wanted to know about the 'stuff', as Kavanagh kept calling it, and asked him once more.

'Basically, there's a variety of bombs but it's the filling that's the stuff that goes *BOOM*. Your big bang. The ones we were using before I came away were Commercial, Co-op and Anfo.'

Sonny smiled, and the customary sneer wasn't there. It was a little boy's giggle of curiosity and enthusiasm.

'Co-op . . . what we call the 'Co'? Do you need to have your number to get a supply?'

He thought this a great joke and laughed aloud. Kavanagh laughed too. 'No, you'll not get this stuff at the 'Co', Sonny. Co-op is the name of the stuff we use when we can't get the other two. It's the easiest to make up. You mix weed-killer, that's sodium chlorate, with nitro benzene. Anfo's a bit more complicated. We use fertiliser, the white pellet kind of thing the farmers scatter on their fields. The technical name for it's ammonium nitrate. This time you mix it with fuel oil, but you've to use a helluva lot of it to get the same effect as your Commercial or Co-op.'

'And the other one . . . what was it?'

'Commercial. We call it that because that's what it is . . . the stuff that's regularly used by the quarrymen and the like. The stuff we've been getting is made by Irish Industrial Explosives from down in the Twenty-six Counties. We don't get it direct from them, like, but it's easy enough to obtain from quarries. You can always get them to turn their backs while you get off with a load.'

'So you just get hold of this stuff and you've got a bomb?'

'That's just the start, Sonny. There's more to it than that. You need a detonator to ignite the stuff and then you need a device to set off the detonator. You just can't set it off yourself, you see, or else you go up with the thing. So you need what we call a TPU, that's a timing and power unit, to fire the detonator which explodes your bomb.'

'And where do you get them . . . the TPU things?'

'Make them yourself, mainly. Your TPU can be a time device or a trip one. Depends on the job. Do you want your man McDougall done in his car or in his mobile shop or what?'

'Makes no odds to me. We'll do some checks and see which is best.'

'Well, at any rate it'll be a vehicle so it won't be a time device. I'll use a form of trip one that he'll help set off himself.'

'That's clever. So what do you need altogether?'

'Wish I'd known about this before I came and I could have brought some things with me. A couple of Duponts would have been right handy.'

'What are they?'

'Detonators. American jobs. And they're right crackers.' He laughed at the use of the word. Riley saw the funny side of it too and laughed loudly with him.

'If I knew my way around here, Sonny, I could get all the things I need.'

'No problems,' reassured Riley. 'Just you tell me what you need and I'll get boys to do the shopping. Big Pat Connors is good at organising things like this.'

Connors did have the expertise and was able to arrange all of the items which Kavanagh had requested. He knew how to get good-quality explosive material . . . but he needed the help of the disgraced Mickey Kelly. He asked Riley if it would be all right to use him. Kelly had worked at a quarry site and still mixed with men who worked in them.

'Use the bastard,' Riley had said. 'It'll make him think he's back in the team again. That one's daft enough to think anything.'

Anxious to please, Kelly had volunteered to get all of the explosives when he had heard it was for Riley. And he did . . . some of the best high-grade ICI commercial explosive as well as half-a-dozen Dupont detonators.

Kavanagh had done some of the shopping himself, mainly for the various other little pieces from which he would formulate his bomb. He had experience at making his own TPUs and was able to rig one up from a dominoes box he found in his Aunt Mary's house, inside of which he put two 1.5v dry batteries and a modern clothes peg, the kind with the sprung ends, into which he inserted two brass drawing pins. These were the most vital part of the detonator. When the peg ends snapped together and the heads of the brass pins met, the circuit which fused the bomb would be complete. There were various ways of keeping the jaws of the peg apart until the time they were required to make contact. A dowel pin could be used, which would be withdrawn by the intended victim through simple actions like the opening of a door or a cupboard. Timing devices could also be used, but then you had to know the precise time you wanted your bomb to go off.

They had made checks on McDougall and it had been decided between Riley and Kavanagh that it was easiest to place a bomb in his car. In view of this, Kavanagh's TPU would consist of the clothes peg's jaws being held apart by a thin piece of fuse wire, the thinnest fuse wire he could obtain, strong enough to hold the clothes peg open providing there was no additional pressure. The moment there was pressure, like the shock of a small jolt, it would snap and the pin ends of the peg would meet.

It wasn't unknown, of course, for ends of the clothes peg to meet prior to any extra pressure being exerted. Did it not happen to his friend Cal Cullen when he was making up a bomb in the hut at the back of his house in Andersonstown? The biggest bit they found of him was a forearm with the tattoo SAOR ULADH, Free Ulster. That was how they knew it was him. There was the story too of Josie Grogan, walking like a hero, with a suitcase containing twenty pounds of Commercial to blow up the Grand Central Hotel in Royal Avenue. They never even found as much as a forearm. Josie had been vaporised by the enormous explosion.

They had learned from mistakes like that and Kavanagh knew that the way to prevent disastrous accidents en route to a target was to use a dowel pin as a safety catch, so the fuse wire would not take the strain of the opened clothes peg until the bomb had been placed and primed. In this case the bomb would be placed beneath McDougall's car. The moment he went over the first bump, even perhaps the movement of the car as he entered it, would put the required pressure on the fuse wire.

Riley had called several times at Mary Connolly's house in Castlehouse, ostensibly to see how her young nephew, his new friend from Ireland, was getting on, but mainly out of the consuming fascination he had for Kavanagh's bomb-making. Kavanagh had shown him how he had constructed the bomb which he was keeping zipped in his old duffle bag in the wardrobe.

'Don't you ever worry, Kevin . . . you know, that it might . . .?'

Kavanagh merely smiled at the suggestion. 'No chance,' he replied, explaining that the device wasn't primed and nothing could happen till that was done.

'Now here's something that's been puzzling me,' said Riley. 'How can you test a bomb . . . you know what I mean? How do you know you haven't got a dud because you cannae, you know, give it a wee trial run. Can you?'

'Easy,' Kavanagh had said. 'I've already tested this one . . . right here in my Aunt Mary's living-room.'

'For Christ's sake!'

'No problems, Sonny. All you do is put a bulb in place of the explosive. If it lights, then your stuff'll go up. It's your TPU that's the important fellow. If it's working, you'll get your bang all right. So what about your man McDougall? Is it still on . . . do you still want him to get this wee present?'

'Oh, it's still on, all right. The rest is up to you. You're the expert. Big Connors has checked out his movements. He keeps his car in the street outside his house and he leaves there every morning at about eight o'clock, drives to a yard in Dalmarnock where a few of them keep their mobile vans and then goes to the wholesalers before starting his rounds. Comes back at night around seven o'clock. Same routine every day, except a Sunday. And as far as I know his car sits there all night till the next morning about nine o'clock when he goes to his work again.'

'And the address?'

'Castlehouse Crescent, number 42. Garden like a midden outside.'

'And the car?'

'Austin Cambridge,' replied Riley, passing over a small piece of crumbled paper on which the registration number LYS 275E was scribbled.

'You couldn't miss it. Flashiest motor in the scheme. Only two or three years old. Cream, with a six-inch yellow stripe down each side. Polishes it every Sunday.'

'So this'll be a clean job then, Sonny?'

Riley laughed and repeated the words. 'Aye, a clean job. Clean right up in the fuckin' air.'

CHAPTER 29

ONE HELL OF A BOMB

THERE HAD NEVER BEEN AN EXPLOSION LIKE IT in Castlehouse. There hadn't been one like it anywhere in Glasgow since the air raids by the Germans in the early part of the Second World War, and that was thirty years ago.

It shook every house in Castlehouse Crescent, breaking many windows, and could be heard all over that part of Glasgow. It was Billy Henderson, a Corporation bus driver of 22 Castlehouse Crescent, who gave the best account in the reports which covered the front pages of all the morning papers, the one that was headed '*CARNAGE IN CASTLE-HOUSE*', which was probably the best summation of what had happened in the big housing scheme that night.

'Never heard anything like it since I was in Korea,' said bus driver Henderson. 'There was this blinding flash, then this enormous bang. Dear God, I really haven't known anything like it. And then it was just a mass of flames.'

The explosion had occurred just as the car passed Henderson's house, at the point where it had gone over a filled trench, dug across the road earlier that day by a gang of men from the Gas Board. They had put only a temporary filling in the trench as they were returning to do more work the following day. When the car's wheels went over the bump the car jolted and the pressure became too much on the slender fibre of fuse wire holding the jaws of the peg apart. They snapped shut, just as Kavanagh had said they would, and the bomb went off.

After the flash, the 'mass of flames' the bus driver had witnessed, an enormous fireball had gone up almost simultaneously with the roar of the explosion. Pieces of the vehicle that had been blown sky high then crashed back to the ground, clattering on the road and on the roofs of parked vehicles. A piece of bonnet landed on the roof of the three-storey tenement at number 16, a chrome bumper, twisted and bent, in the front garden of number 12, the shiny rim of a headlight cover further down the crescent at number 4, and a hub cap ended up in the opposite direction outside the house at number 44, rattling down the middle of the road then rolling further along the street like some child's toy, before spiralling slowly to a tinny halt.

Then, for a few seconds, there was an unreal and eerie silence before the screams and shouts of neighbours began as windows went up and men came running to see if there was anything they could do. But nothing could be done. What was left blazing in the middle of the road didn't even resemble a car. It was just a twisted, jagged, blackened mockery of something that had just minutes before been a stylish form of transport, and the pride of the family who owned it.

Hamie McDougall had come home as usual that night around eight o'clock. In fact, it was exactly ten past eight, as the men who had been watching as they sat in a parked car further along the road knew, for they had looked at their watches and smiled in the knowledge that they would not have to wait much longer. The driver, a big, well-built man, had turned round and nodded at the younger man in the front passenger seat. He picked up the duffel bag which had been sitting in his lap and walked the seventy-five yards down the street to the cream car with the yellow stripe. The driver heaved an enormous sigh of relief as the man with the bag got out of the car. Kevin Kavanagh was only away for a few minutes. When he returned to the car he said to Pat Connors, 'That's it. McDougall no more.' Then they drove away.

They had seen nothing from up in McDougall's house, or from any of the other houses, of the man in dark clothing who had walked briskly and silently carrying the small bag and who, when he got to the shiny cream Austin, had bent down to hang something on the long exhaust pipe just beneath the driver's seat. In the McDougall house on the first floor they had been too busy with the kind of things that normally happen in a happy household when father comes home from his work after a long day. The three boys were each vying for his attention, telling him what had happened that day at school and saying, 'Look at this, Dad', 'Look at my new book, Dad,' and 'What have you got for me, Dad?' knowing there would be the usual bag of sweets somewhere in his pockets.

'That was a rare smell coming from Peter's chippy van down at the terminus,' he had said to his wife. 'I had the window down when I passed and I got the full waft of it. I felt like those kids in the Bisto ad. Mmmm . . .' scrumptious.'

'That settles it, then,' Patricia had replied. 'I've nothing better than that for tea . . . how about fish suppers all round?'

'No . . . a sausage supper for me,' shouted one of the boys.

'I want a chicken one,' shouted another, and the third said he wanted special fish and fritters if they had them.

'Oh, fritters, Mammy . . . yes, I want fritters too,' said the others.

'Right . . . the lot of you,' said their mother. 'You're all coming with me while your Dad gets his wash and a chance to read the paper. You can make up your minds when you're at the van. Come on, get down to the car, quick as you can.'

Those were the last words he heard her say. The door of the house had closed and the noisy chattering and shouting of the running boys disappeared into the night.

Like everyone else he had heard the noise. He had been washing in the bathroom at the rear of the flats and it was two or three minutes before he went to the window, by which time he could see people running in the direction of the bright glow coming from further down the street.

'The poor, poor man,' an ambulance officer had said to Superintendent Tom Graham, kirk elder and legendary crusading crime-buster, when he had arrived on the scene, dressed as always, the shabby gaberdine raincoat hanging loose and unbelted, the battered soft hat, the ever-present briar dangling unlit from his mouth, a real character the TV men would one day invent. 'His whole family blown to bits. We didn't know till a neighbour told us, there'd been four of them in the car . . . his missus and their three wee boys. Never seen anything like it since the land mine hit Deanston Drive in Shawlands. I was on duty that night, you know.'

Graham merely nodded.

Alistair McDonald had been there with the Superintendent. 'What do you think, sir? Riley?'

'Aye, he'll be involved in some kind of way, except anything to do with the bomb. That needed expertise . . . skill . . . intelligence. That rules him out on all three counts. Putting a bomb together is beyond that one's mental capabilities. And that goes for all his chinas as well. Put that lot together and you still wouldn't have the brainpower to make a bomb. I wish they'd try; it'd blow up in their faces. Looks like we've got somebody new around. That Irishman Special Branch were watching! Better check with them if they're still on to him before we move in. Don't want to stand on their precious wee toes. You know the pull their gaffer's got. Other than that we'll need to wait till the explosives people get here and tell us what the hell caused this.'

Shortly after, just about the same time as the police mobile incident room was being parked nearby, a major from the Territorial Army unit at Yorkhill arrived in a plain black Ford car driven by an Army corporal.

'I've already been on the phone to HQ at Lisburn,' he said crisply, after asking for the policeman in charge and being introduced to Graham. 'We report all explosions like this these days. So I've given them what details I have. The RAOC wallahs say they're interested and want to have a look, so there're two ATOs from their EOD coming over. Much obliged, Superintendent, if nothing is swept up. These chaps like to see everything they can. Sorry I can't tell you their ETA but it should be ASAP. Goodnight, Super.' With that he left again.

Neither Graham nor McDonald had been in the Army. They hadn't understood much of what the major had said, except that somebody was obviously coming for a look. Hopefully it would be soon.

The ATOs from the EOD of the RAOC arrived just before midnight. One was a captain, the other a lieutenant. The initials meant they were Ammunition Technical Officers from the Royal Army Ordnance Corps 321 Explosives Ordnance Disposal (EOD) unit, stationed at Lisburn in Northern Ireland. The military authorities there had been concerned when word of the car bomb had reached them, thinking of a possible spread of the IRA's campaign to Scotland. Military Intelligence had been that this was not anticipated, but by the nature of the bomb it had been decided to make a quick check.

Superintendent Graham and Sergeant McDonald had returned about one o'clock in the morning as they wanted to speak to the two soldiers. Bombs like this were a new experience for both of them and they wanted to know as much as they could. The soldiers had put loose overalls over their civilian clothes and despite what little there had been left of the vehicle, they were able to reach some conclusions. The senior of the two men introduced himself as Captain Michael Bromley. He said that despite the state of what had once been an Austin Cambridge car, there were sufficient factors remaining to determine that the explosive used had been high-grade. 'The smell gives it away.' He also guessed that a TPU unit similar to ones which were currently being used in Belfast had been utilised to trigger the detonator.

What he didn't mention was the expertise on which their conclusions were based. Both would have been rated among the finest of explosives experts, having trained at the Royal Military College of Science, Shrivenham. In a very short period in Northern Ireland both had gained years of intense experience in practical work.

'Yes, it has all the hallmarks of a Belfast bomb. We would say that whoever did it was either from there or had been trained there. But I'm afraid it's up to others to draw whatever conclusions there might be from that. We've some samples here we'd like to take back for analysis, if it's all right by you, Superintendent?'

Graham nodded. 'Before you go, Captain,' he said. 'The explosion . . . I'm not up in these matters. What kind of force . . . or is that the right question to ask? I'm just curious to know what there is to know about it.'

'The explosion, Superintendent. Well, what I can tell you is that we assess V of D, F of I and Power.'

He noted the quizzical eyebrows of the policeman.

'I'm sorry to slip into jargon. It becomes a way of life, I'm afraid. I even give my wife an ETA for dinner. We use the terms V of D, F of I and Power when speaking about an explosion. These are our terms for Velocity of Detonation, and Field of Insensitivity. A good-quality explosive has a very high V of D, high Power and a high F of I. The material used in this bomb had all of these. In non-technical terms, however, all explosives, whether with high or low V of D and the rest, do terrible things to the body. Pressure waves enter the mouth, nostrils or any orifice, the lungs collapse and the body implodes. That's why limbs are torn from the trunk and flesh stripped from the bone. This all happens, mind you, in the merest fraction of a second. If anything can be said about the horrific way these poor victims went, it was that they wouldn't have known a thing. Their lives snuffed out,' he said.

'Let me tell you about something which happened in Belfast just last week. Three senior men of the Belfast Brigade of PIRA . . . my apologies, Superintendent . . . the Provisional Irish Republican Army, were on a mission to blow up a Security Forces base in the Ormeau Road. They got into a store just by the base and began priming their bombs. One of these must have touched something metallic and short-circuited. There was, as they put it, a "sympathetic explosion". In other words, the bombs blew up in their faces. Now, because of the nature of the explosion, that is, right in their very midst, we didn't know how many of them there were at first. One of them, you see, was blown through the heavy link chain fence surrounding the base with such force that he was literally . . . minced. Then we found pieces of another body, which meant there were two of them, but it wasn't until some time later we discovered a backbone on top of a high structure nearby and it was then we knew there had been a third man. Yes, Superintendent, a bomb explosion is a very horrible thing indeed. Very, very horrible.'

CHAPTER 30

MOURNING AND MERRIMENT

THE FUNERAL OF THE THREE McDOUGALL
children and their mother was one of the most moving ever
held in Glasgow. The story was of national importance and
even the BBC in London featured it prominently in
national news broadcasts on TV and radio, sending, as
they always did on such occasions, their own 'star' reporters from London to cover the story. Viewers were stunned
at the sight of the three small white coffins, two in one
hearse, another in the hearse carrying the larger coffin
containing their mother. The cameras lingered on the
mournful faces of the three children's classmates, many of
them weeping openly.

When Hamie McDougall, accompanied by his own
brother and sister, left his home in the big, black Austin
Princess hire car from the Wylie and Lochhead funeral
company, many in the street showed their respect in the
old and almost extinct Scottish tradition by pulling down
their blinds or drawing their curtains closed.

The story had been headline news for several days. One
of the most common lines taken by reporters was that the
police and the authorities were divided on whether or not
it was the outbreak of a sensational new gang war or the
spread of the IRA campaign to the UK mainland. They

concluded that the speculation of the IRA connection had been mainly conjecture, for though police did say off the record that the word from the Army in Lisburn was that it was a copybook provisional bomb, there were apparently no grounds for the theory that the IRA war had come to Scotland.

Nevertheless, many believed otherwise and there was considerable talk among several of the Ulster Defence Association and Ulster Volunteer Force cells which were burgeoning in Glasgow at the time, that they should move in on the Castlehouse estate 'and sort out these Fenian bastards'. The major problem in that proposed plan of action was that they didn't quite know who those Fenian bastards were, although they would have taken considerable satisfaction from indiscriminately targeting those suspected of what to them was a heinous enough crime . . . that of simply being a Roman Catholic.

Graham had given instructions that Kevin Kavanagh should be questioned. However, Kavanagh had pre-empted any moves in that direction by leaving his Aunt Mary's house two days before the bombing. There was no shortage of willing addresses where he could stay so he had stopped the first night at one house before moving on to yet another outside the area, where he had planned to spend his last few days before leaving for Kilburn.

Unaware of the outcome of their bombing, Riley, together with Connors, Kavanagh and some others, had celebrated at a party in a house in one of the four new multistorey blocks off Cumberland Street in the Gorbals. It wasn't specifically meant to mark the termination of someone who had been giving them problems in Castlehouse. Sonny's parties were held so frequently that the mere fact it was another weekend was cause enough for a celebration. Anyway, only the three men knew about the bombing.

Riley's parties were functions which many of his imme-

diate associates had grown to dread. They didn't expect to
be asked to every party but they would worry if they went
too long without an invitation, for that could be an
indication of their standing, or lack of it, with him. While
few of them really enjoyed Sonny's parties, they would be
just as afraid not to be there if asked, for that could have
its consequences too.

An even worse dilemma was the arrival of an unexpected
guest at a Riley party. Riley's nights of enjoyment had
been known to end in mayhem, in near murder, and on
one occasion in actual murder. Invariably he would display
the full spectrum of his bizarre and unpredictable personality, a revelation of character which was always signalled
by the disintegration of his smile into his hallmark sneer.
His mood would change rapidly as the night progressed
and the alcohol level within him rose, ranging from the
passive, but never pleasant, to the permissive, then per-
turbing before fringing on the psychopathic.

His drink tastes were simple, the traditional whisky and
water – 'and yer a fuckin' poof if you put lemonade in it' –
with cans of Export ale. There would always be a woman
close at hand and now that he was in his late thirties he
wanted them younger ... the way he remembered them
when he had first discovered their delights. And they were
always there for him.

He liked a few songs, of course, and most of the party-
goers could oblige. *Ob-La-Di Ob-La-Da, Do Wah Diddy
Diddy*. Marmalade and Kinks, Troggs and Monkees, Scaf-
fold and Animals and Equals and Dave Dee, Dozy, Beaky,
Mick and Tich. There was something about the new music
that made them sing and shout and smile and appear
happy. Even Riley joined in. And there were songs from
Engelbert and Tom, Dusty and Long John and Petula and
Sandie and Cliff, and they all cheered and clapped and
roared and whistled when Georgie sang his *Ballad of Bonnie
and Clyde*, some of the men rising to lend dramatics to the

words with imaginary Tommy-guns. When the ten 45s on the record stack had each slipped down the turntable spindle and been turned over to play their 'B' sides and replaced with another stack, it was time for the ballads. Some of them said you couldn't beat the old tunes and Sonny nodded at that for he was a traditionalist. He liked those favourites too. So on went the LPs of the old ones – Frank and Perry and Nat and Johnnie and Bing.

It was one of the best parties there had been for a long time. The more unpleasant aspects of Riley's kaleidoscopic character hadn't been revealed, not even when someone rendered a Jolson selection. And the solo singing was always the most tense part of the proceedings for it was often then that Riley's temper would flare, and he would turn on some unsuspecting singer, subjecting them to verbal humiliation and lashing out if anyone objected. Most of the other men would surround Sonny to demonstrate that they were on his side really and that they were only stopping the fight for the other fellow's protection. But the party that night in Cumberland Street ended without trouble. As Roy Orbison sang *It's Over*, Riley winked at big Connors and Kavanagh, both of them sitting with girls on their knees, and the three of them had joined in the last chorus: 'It's Over . . . It's Over . . . O – v – e – r'. They roared with raucous laughter when the tune finished and a Sonny Riley party that had never been so happy was over too.

About midday the following day there was a loud knock on the door of the house at which Sonny Riley had been staying in another part of the Gorbals. He had told the young girl lying naked beside him to ignore the knocks but they were repeated over and over and they could hear what sounded like the voice of the Irishman, Kavanagh, shouting Riley's name. Riley told the girl to answer the door and she got up and hurriedly put on her overcoat, a fabric imitation of something that somebody, somewhere had thought might resemble some kind of animal fur.

'Well, then, Sonny,' said Kavanagh, 'what d'you think?'

'About what?'

'Christ, haven't ye heard?'

Riley let the question go unanswered.

'The bomb last night.'

'Don't tell me it didn't go off.'

'It went off all right, Sonny. But McDougall wasn't in the car. It was his missus and his kids. Four of them altogether. Fuckin' police are everywhere. They were up at my aunt's at midnight – when we were at the party.'

'Where did you stay?'

'At Mickey Kelly's. When he got us the stuff, like, he said no one knew his address and I'd be safe there anytime.'

'Did you leave anything at your auntie's?'

'No, it's as clean as your proverbial whistle, Sonny. We were taught to clean everything up and move on. I'd done that a couple of nights ago, moved on to another house and now I'm at Kelly's.'

'And the bomb got his wife and weans?'

'Aye.'

'Fuck it. Busies will be every fuckin' place. They don't know this address so I'll be all right for a while and when they do catch up I'll give them a dozen names for alibi.'

That four innocents had died in the bungled attempt to get the former paratrooper didn't seem to concern him. His mind was racing through matters which were much more important, like the alibi, whether Kavanagh's old digs were 'clean' and what his next movements would be.

'I'm due in London next week so I'll just go down early,' said Kavanagh.

'They'll be watching the planes and trains.'

'Mickey Kelly is driving me down.'

'Doing his Sir fuckin' Galahad. Does he know the direction London is in?'

Kavanagh smiled.

Riley shook his head. 'Well, that's a right turn up, then.

What d'you call that, Kevin . . . a real Irish bomb? Go for one and you get four . . . and not one of them the right one.'

Kavanagh smarted at the innuendo but thought it best not to come back at Riley, although he felt he had to say something.

'Sonny, this is not the first time things like this have happened. We take the attitude that when innocent bystanders get hurt in any way, the fault is not of our making. We're only there because of the deeds and actions of a reactionary government that won't give us our freedom. Your man McDougall, you tell me, was part of that machine, impeding your people from collecting what they might for our cause. Therefore he was a legitimate target. And the fact that others died is the fault of those that cause people like me to be engaged in a military campaign. That responsibility lies fair and square at the feet of the British government. That's the way my command would see it and it's certainly the way I see it.'

He was pleased he had said that, for he wanted Riley to know how he felt about the mistaken deaths. But Riley wasn't impressed. 'Aye, fair enough, Kevin. You better be on your way, son.'

Kavanagh wasn't quite sure whether the use of the word 'son' was cynical or cordial. He wasn't waiting to find out.

'I'll be away then.'

'Aye, fine, Kevin. Drop us a card sometime.'

'Aye, Sonny. Might just do that.'

CHAPTER 31

ALFIE GOES TO WORK

FALLSIDE IN THE HEARTLAND OF LANARKSHIRE was not one of Scotland's beautiful places; and there weren't many beautiful people living there either. In Fallside, if your father wasn't a miner, he was in the steelworks. Fallside people worked in industries of dirt and dust, fire and flame and steam. They said in other places that where there was muck there was brass. There was lots of one in and around Fallside, but not an awful lot of the other.

Much of Scotland was about heather and hill, and the beautiful lochs and streams that they sang about. There weren't any songs about Fallside. The horizons there were spiked by tall chimneys which, if they didn't belch black smoke, puffed out white clouds of steam and noxious yellow vapours. Its mountains were the conical coal wastes they called 'bings', which festered the once pleasant landscape like a crop of unwanted boils. Fallside's sons and daughters lived in ranks of dreary, dun-coloured council houses where the stamp of life was the same drab equality of everyone else.

Private detective Alfie Rose's heart had slumped when his new client, Mrs Star Jehan or Nelson, had handed him the names of the six who had told the police that Sonny Riley had been with them at a party in one of their houses on the night Frankie Burns had been murdered.

'How the hell do you get anything out of Fallside?' he had thought to himself, though not expressing his pessimism to his new client. Alfie liked challenges, although had he been forewarned about this one he would have said that this was no mere challenge. This was Everest.

'Why oh why,' he had sighed, 'can't it just sometimes be as it is in the movies? The smart lightweight gaberdine hand-cut with the bulge under the left armpit – oh the comfort of that little automatic! – adjusting the sleek black shades as you ease behind the polished ebony wheel of the convertible with the white-walled tyres. Getting waylaid – or just plain laid! – by the occasional blonde or redhead with tits that scream "Touch me . . . feel me!" But no . . . there's nothing like that when you're a Glasgow private-eye! That's all about tailing balding, overweight, lusting middle-aged men with their one-night lovelies to hotels; waiting in the rain and freezing cold at the house of the wife of the executive who's down in London on business while she entertains her lover. Time them as they go in, time them as they come out, the lawyers always need bloody times. Why stay for the night when they could do the business in half an hour flat, with a brandy before and cigar afterwards? And there were those wearisome and endless statements from mothers and brothers and sisters and cousins and friends to substantiate the allegations if the divorce was to be on the grounds of cruelty. That was what being a private-eye in Glasgow was all about. And now it was to be Fallside! Oh well, some guys drive buses and others work on assembly lines. The money *is* good and maybe one day the California number'll come up.

'Now who the hell do I know in Fallside?' he had wondered. He kept his thick contact book closed, mentally running through the alphabet to see if a particular letter would spark off a name. None did. He opened up his loose-leaf book. There were plenty for Falkirk. Even one in historic wee Falkland. But Fallside! Nothing. He tried 'L' for Lanarkshire. Plenty under Airdrie and Blantyre and Bothwell and Cambuslang and Coatbridge and . . . bingo! Two for Fallside. John and Willie Tobin, 14 Clydeview Street, Fallside, and a phone number.

The case came back to him and he smiled. 'John and Willie Tobin . . . that's right. Why in hell didn't I think of them in the first place. The very people. Know everyone in Fallside and will help. Oh yes, they'll help all right for what I did for them.'

It had been a compensation case. The steel brokers' yard for which they worked flouted every safety rule in the book. The two brothers, big, able, fit men in their late thirties, had suffered serious leg injuries when a load of heavy steel pipes had rolled. They were weeks in traction and would never walk properly again. Despite that, they had lost out on their claim because the yard had said there was no proof that the company had disregarded safety procedures. But Alfie, together with an assistant, gained regular access to the yard by posing as workmen and had taken a series of photographs amply demonstrating that the firm had been grossly negligent. An action was raised in the Court of Session but on seeing the evidence the company had settled out of court. The Tobin brothers each received over £8,000 plus costs, which in Alfie's case had been hefty because of the time he had spent on the job.

They would be the very ones to help. 'Yeah, will they ever. And the family too. Oh God, yes . . . the family.' He remembered the celebration party the night the lawyers had done the deal in Edinburgh. It was the biggest event locally since VE-Day. Half the street had been there. Men with greyhound dogs kept coming in and out of the house and women appeared wearing curlers and slippers. The home-brew in pint glasses they got from the pub was poured straight from big five-gallon jars and was cloudy and had an awful apple taste, but, God, was it strong. They passed round hot sausage rolls without plates and there were people standing all over the front garden drinking and eating because there wasn't enough room inside. It had been a great night. But then that was Fallside.

The gold tie-pin and clip, the chunky chain bracelet on which he had his name inscribed and the expensive gold cufflinks went into his little jewellery box. The cheap, silver-plated ones came out. You had to dress the part in Fallside.

He had phoned first to check that they were still there. After all, with the kind of money he had helped them get they could have moved to a nice villa in Bothwell or Baillieston or Uddingston. But then they would have been away from Fallside, and John and Willie Tobin would have hated that. As he had thought, they were still there, still bachelors and still being looked after by their widowed mother, now in her seventies. They said they would be only too pleased to help an old pal like Alfie Rose. 'After all, if it wasnae for you, Alfie, we wouldn't be among the best doo and dug men in Lanarkshire.'

'How d'you mean?' Rose asked.

'Oh, it was the money you got us. We'd one of the finest lofts available built for our pigeons and we imported some of the best birds you can get anywhere . . . Belgian yins. And we bought some fine pedigree greyhounds . . . and they're doing right well. A' thanks to you, Alfie.'

Sure enough, it was a superb loft. 'It's got more than we've in the house,' John said proudly. 'Wish we'd the central heating our birds have!'

Alfie told them briefly about the job, was given their assurance that nothing would be said about why he was there and then showed them the list of six names.

'Well, you can forget about that one for a start,' said Willie Tobin, his brother John standing by his side and both of them dressed just as Alfie had remembered them, in a clash of drab browns and indeterminate blues, one with a jacket that had been part of a blue serge suit and trousers which had been part of a brown one. 'He snuffed it a year ago after walking in front of a red SMT bus going to Newmains. Drunk at the time, like.'

'And you can tick that one in the middle off as well,' said John. 'He's away for five years. Charged wi' murder, got off wi' manslaughter.'

Alfie, dispirited, asked, 'Are there any of them left?'

'Oh, aye. The other four are still about, but you'll need to be quick with these two . . . Bobby Watson and Danny Miles.'

'Are they going somewhere?'

'Aye, Barlinnie more than likely. It was in the *Gazette* the other day about them. Charged wi' something to do with cars . . . interfering wi' them or stealing . . . something like that. Remanded on bail and they'll be coming up before the Sheriff.'

'That leaves the two girls, then.'

'Oh, they two,' said Willie dismissively. 'Best place you'll find them is about the chapel.'

'What, are they nuns or something?'

'Naw, nothing like that. They were a right wild pair of bitches. Couple of wee tarts, you might as well say. Wore they wee miniskirt things up to their arses. You know the type? We used to call them "wee hairies". Then they must have seen the light for now they're never away from the chapel. Leading lights in the Altar Society.'

'What's that, Willie?'

'You know . . . it's the women that look after the chapel and that. Fix the flowers and see that it's kept clean. And they give a lot of time to the St Vincent De Paul. One of them's married wi' a family. I dinnae ken about the other one.'

Alfie Rose spent about a week in Fallside gathering what information he could about the four who were still living in the town. He knew there would be difficulties because

people in places like Fallside didn't take too fondly to
strangers, not strangers who are single men, dressed in nice
suits with neat collars and ties and who spoke with an
accent that wasn't from their part of Lanarkshire. People
like that were invariably snoopers: if they weren't from the
debt collecting agency they would be from the ministry
wanting to know if you were working and claiming social
security at the same time or how you could lift hundred-
weight bags off a coal lorry and take them to the top flat of
a tenement when you were on a invalidity pension? Tell
them nothing was the way.

But Alfie Rose knew all that. For much of that week he
looked out from under a greasy cap, wearing an old donkey
jacket and a pair of jeans that would never make the
fashion shops, and walking beside him a lean greyhound
dog with a wire muzzle over its mouth. In that guise he
could walk almost unnoticed into the Fallside Vaults where
he had been told the two men on the car charge were
regular drinkers. With a day and a half's growth and the
greyhound by his side, no one even looked up when Alfie
Rose strolled in. He was part of the normal pattern and the
only thing that was slightly not the norm was the face.
They assumed he was in Fallside from another part of the
county on dog business.

The barman had wanted to know, of course, when he
had asked for a whisky and a half. 'A whisky is a half,' he
answered gruffly.

'Ee, lad, I didn't know that,' he countered in an assumed
Yorkshire accent which he had perfected as a barrack room
caper when he was posted to Catterick on a six weeks
signals' course during National Service.

'Yer no' local then, like?' the barman continued.

'Nay . . . I'm up to see my old friends John and Willie
Dempsey . . . you'll know them? Grand lads. Aye, grand
lads, they are.'

Although the names had just been conjured up, the

barman nodded that he knew them but said he hadn't seen them for a while. 'And the dug?'

'Aye, looking after him for me brother. He races him down at Barnsley where I come from. He's away on a sort of holiday, if you know what I mean. Couldn't leave him behind. You know what it's like? Bleeding big pet, he is. Aren't ye Dash,' he added, fondling the animal.

When he left, the barman spread the word. Alfie Rose alias Mick Midgeley from Barnsley was, as they would say, in the club. He could come and go any time he liked.

The Tobins had described the two men he was looking for. 'You can't miss 'em. Watson's got frizzy red hair and Miles has one of these new-fashioned moustaches . . . ye know, the ones that drip aff the lip.' The descriptions had been spot on and they had been there that first day, standing nearby at the bar.

He had stood closer to the two men when he returned the following day, cracking a joke with the barman about a 'half' and a 'half' and then turning to the two men saying, 'Care to have a drink wi' me, lads? Ahm up on holiday, like.'

'Aye, we heard,' the one with the Mexican moustache replied, unsmiling.

'What'll you have then, lads?'

The acceptance of the two whiskies, albeit reluctantly, broke the ice and after a long talk about dogs he told them he would have loved a greyhound as good as this one for his own.

'It's me brother Arthur's, you see. They sent the lad down at the Assizes last week. Bleeding rozzers we have in North Yorkshire . . . I'm telling thee. They just picked on the lad and made up some story that he threatened to assault them and does the judge not send him down for six months! Mind you, he's got a bit of form, like. But for them to go making up stories like that! Your coppers up here

246

seem a much better lot. Was talking to one the other day
and he struck me as a right nice lad.'

'Don't you fuckin' kid yersel,' said the one who had so
hesitantly accepted the whisky. He was chatty enough now,
especially when he heard about the Yorkshireman's
brother. He went into his own spiel about the police.

'You think your brother's had it bad? See us two . . .
we're up before the Sheriff next week. And for fuck all.
They caught us tampering wi' a car and they've lumped
all sorts of other charges on us. And Ah'm gonnie tell you
something, mate. We know they havenae got the evidence
on us. It's a right put-up job. Couple of nasties in the Force
just wanted to get us because we've got a wee bit form as
well. Know what I mean?'

'Wouldn't trust coppers as far as I could throw one,'
said Rose. 'Any time we have trouble in't pits they always
gang up on't lads.'

He was definitely one of them, this one.

There were more whiskies exchanged and when it was
Alfie's turn he told the barman to make it doubles. 'So
what d'you think ye'll get, lads, when you're up before 't
beak?'

'The lawyer says six months at the most . . . aye, but it
would have been six years had the daft bastards been really
smart,' said the ginger one.

Alfie gave him a puzzled look. The one with the lip-drip
moustache gave him a cautionary one.

'Ach, he's aw' right,' said Ginger.

'Tell him if you want, then.'

'The joke is we've knocked off a hundred cars this year.'

'A hundred and ten,' corrected the moustache, all cau-
tion gone.

'Bit difficult to get rid of that lot?'

'Nae bother. We're in wi' a mob from your bit of the
world . . . Birmingham. Near you, in't it?'

'Aye, well . . .'

'This lot are right organised. They've bought an auld warehouse just off the London Road and we just drive the cars straight there after we nick 'em. It's cash on the nose from them, no messin'. They've got to know us, like. And we're in thick wi' them. Once this court case is out of the way we're really gonnie step up things here for them. Couldnae do otherwise with the money they pay . . . four hundred nicker for a Ford . . . got to have a new reggie, mind. And when they've got enough, they're on to a big transporter, each one tarped and then off to the South. And these daft bastards here nab us for just looking at a motor. Bloody terrible, so it is.'

Alfie let it ride at that without any questions and after they had finished the story he veered away from their self-incrimination lest they think twice about what they had said. 'D'ye know, that reminds me of a story about me brother, Arthur. Right wild lad is our Arthur. Anyways, he drives down in his old banger this night to Rotherham, gets himself into this big toff's house, Lord and Lady some'at, and he nicks all their silverware and a pile of jewellery worth a bleeding fortune. But the silly bugger goes and helps himself to some of His Grace's whisky. Drank nearly a bottle of the stuff then, pissed as a fart, tries to drive back to Barnsley. Makes it most of the way back but gets himself nicked and ends up in clink for t'night. Now when he's lying sleeping it off in a cell in Barnsley police station with his old Anglia parked outside, there's road blocks and all sorts of things all over the North Riding looking for His Lordship's treasure . . . and there it all is in the boot of Arthur's old car! In the morning they lets him leave without as much as havin' a look at his car. Coppers! Bloody thick as shit, the lot of them.'

CHAPTER 32

HEY JUDE!

IT WAS A RARE SIGHT FOR A CAR LIKE THAT TO be parked outside the Fallside Vaults. It was a hire Daimler limousine, the old carriage-style model used for funerals. In the back, behind the sectioned-off driver's front seat, there was room for six, three on the long, beige velour bench seat and opposite, with their backs to the driver, three on pull-down seats.

The driver, in a sombre charcoal suit, stiff collar and plain dark-grey tie, removed his chauffeur's peaked cap before walking from the car into the public house. He walked directly to the bar. The *Sporting Chronicle*s around the room were lowered and the men shuffling their dominoes or playing darts suddenly stopped. The Fallside Vaults had rarely known such silence.

The well-dressed stranger summoned the barman and asked, 'Mr Bobby Watson and Mr Danny Miles?'

It was the time of day the Tobins had told Alfie Rose that the two were always in the bar and there they were. The chauffeur repeated their names and the barman nodded in their direction. 'Mr Bobby Watson and Mr Danny Miles?'

'Is it the coupon?' asked the ginger one. Then he gave a nervous laugh, pretending he was enjoying his own joke.

'It'll be the lawyer,' said Miles. 'He cuts about wi' a chauffeur. So what's up anyway, pal?'

'Would you care to step outside, gents? I've someone in my car who would like a word with you.'

Watson and Miles looked at each other before Miles replied cockily, 'Aye, no problem.'

The chauffeur walked ahead, politely opened the wide rear door of the black limousine, then quickly entered the car first in order to pull down two of the fold-up seats. 'Mr Watson and Mr Miles, this is Mrs Jehan who wishes to speak with you.' Then he left to sit in the front of the car, closing the dividing window behind him.

The two men were bemused at the courtesies but nevertheless took the seats they had been shown and looked over at Star, sitting back relaxed, her trim legs crossed and one arm on the broad centre arm-rest of the wide seat.

'I'll be brief,' she said. 'My name is Mrs Star Jehan, although I'm also known by the name of Nelson. You don't know me but I know of you. Two years ago, both of you, together with four others from this town, lied to police in statements you made in order to substantiate an alibi for a Mr Sonny Riley. I want you to withdraw those statements and tell the police the truth of what happened the night that a man called Frankie Burns was murdered. That truth is that Sonny Riley committed the murder and because he'd previously been in your company at parties here in Fallside he asked you to lie on his behalf, which you both readily did.'

The men were dumbfounded at first and sat for some seconds gaping in wonderment at the audacity of this woman sitting opposite them and telling them what they should do.

Miles turned to Watson, 'Let's get to fuck out of this.'

'Sit where you fucking well are,' rasped Star angrily. 'I've got more to say.' Star opened the gold clip of the beige calf-leather handbag on her lap, took out a small audio-tape cassette and held it up in front of her. Watson and Miles looked puzzled as Star began speaking again.

'I've no desire to be sarcastic, but just in case you don't know, this is an audio-tape cassette. It's of great concern to you both. On this tape are your statements about how you're engaged in a nationwide car stealing racket.'

The puzzlement on the men's faces turned to shock.

'Every word you said the day before yesterday to the man from Yorkshire was recorded by a machine he had strapped to his body. It's all here on tape. Every single word. And, please, the pair of you, don't get any silly notions about trying to grab this out of my hand and running away like naughty little boys. This is just one of several copies I had made. Nor should you be getting any other ideas about me or my driver or this car. If I'm not back personally in Glasgow in one hour's time, the man you spoke to the other day will hand the original of this tape into the office of the Serious Crime Squad. Now are we perfectly clear about what is happening?'

They nodded sheepishly.

'There are two, and only two, courses which you can take in relation to this matter. One is that you accept what I say and confess to the police that you lied, for which you will at worst receive a minor sentence for interfering with the course of police duty or something similar. Or else, you can ignore my demand and suffer the consequences ... that is, being charged with the theft of one hundred cars or,' and at that she turned and looked directly at Miles, 'as you very accurately pointed out, Mr Miles, one hundred and ten cars, not forgetting your involvement with the men from Birmingham, who my contacts in the police tell me are involved in several murders as well as drug-running from Spain, all of which you will be implicated in through handling their money.'

'Don't listen to a fuckin' word, Bobby,' said Miles. 'She's fuckin' bluffing.'

'Oh really!' came back Star quickly. 'I did say you have your choice. Perhaps you'd like to hear the tape? I especially like the bit where you describe how you get the money from the men from Birmingham . . . what was it you said again . . . "cash in hand" . . . "no messing" . . . "we're in real thick with them"?

'And what was that other bit? Oh yes, how you're going to do even better for them when you get finished with this present court case. Yes, I think we got it all.'

Watson was the first to crack. 'How d'you know we'll get off light for lying to the cops?'

'Think about it. On one charge you're up for telling a lie . . . and, of course, as your lawyer will tell you, he'll plead that you were under duress from this notorious Glasgow gangster to do what you did. As opposed to that you're up for being part of one of the most wanted and ruthless gangs in Britain. Now if I were a really unscrupulous person, this tape would be delivered to the men looking after the warehouse off the London Road where you deliver the cars. Would be worth a small fortune to them . . . wouldn't it?'

'Have you fuckin' been there?' asked Miles angrily.

'Of course not. I leave things like that to my investigator.'

'How come you want Sonny Riley nailed?'

'Shall we just say . . . for personal reasons. But that aside, I'm not here for a debate. The deadline for that tape being delivered to the Serious Crime Squad was one hour from when we started speaking. There are just 50 minutes left. You'll have to act now . . . or else.'

They turned and stared at each other with a look of hopeless despondency. Watson bit his lip, Miles nervously fingered his moustache.

'What about the lassies . . . they lied as well?'

'I said I'm not here to debate.'

The men looked at each other again, then Miles turned quickly to Star. 'Take us to the polis.'

The big limousine dropped the two men at the police station in Hamilton where, before they hurried inside, Star warned them not to even think about any tricks as she had engaged a lawyer who would be making a call there later in the day. If he discovered that they had not made the requested statements, her investigator would go ahead with the delivery of the tape to the police.

The driver slid back the dividing window as the big car purred quietly away. He said, 'That was certainly some performance . . . I couldn't help but overhear.'

'Oh, please,' Star replied, 'you must forgive the language. I don't know what made me say that disgusting word. I detest swearing. But I just had to let them know this was really serious and it's the only word they seem to understand by way of emphasis. I feel like my mouth could do with a good wash-out.'

'That must be some tape you've got, then.'

Star smiled. 'It certainly is. It most certainly is. Would you care to hear it?'

'Love to.'

She reached beneath the seat and pulled out a case in which there was a portable tape-playing machine. 'The sound's not very good because it's the kind meant for dialogue . . . but I think you'll pick it up all right.'

She switched the machine on and began humming in tune with the music from the tape. It was The Beatles singing *Hey Jude*. 'Just love them,' said Star. 'They've brought back my faith in pop music.'

'You mean . . .?'

'That's right. We'd nothing on tape . . . except The Beatles, of course.'

CHAPTER 33

A DIFFERENT APPROACH

STAR HAD BEEN DELIGHTED WITH THE DOSSIER
of information Alfie Rose had obtained for her, even though
there were only details of the four who were still contact-
able. They laughed together as he told the story of how he
had gone about Fallside in donkey jacket and jeans.

'And you actually walked around with a greyhound!'

'Absolutely . . . and do you know something? I'm terrified of dogs. I go all goose pimples if even a wee bloody
chihuahua comes near me. To make me feel happy the
Tobins, who loaned me this dog, put a wire muzzle thing
round its mouth. Mrs Jehan . . . if you ever have any other
jobs for me, could you make it somewhere like Ayr or Largs
or St Andrews? Now there's a nice place.'

She had returned to see Rose the day after receiving the
dossier. 'I've been up half the night contemplating it but I
think I've something that'll work out,' she had said. Star
outlined her plan, an essential part of which was that she
had to thoroughly memorise the conversation between
Watson and Miles and Rose, the man they thought was
from Yorkshire.

Rose had frowned when he heard her plan, saying that
he was doubtful it would work in a place like Fallside but
at the same time he couldn't think of anything better. 'In

fact, I just can't think of any way at all for a person like yourself to go there and challenge men like these two.

'They're so untouchable in a place like Fallside. People like you and me are marked out as strangers as soon as we set foot in the place. Fallside people look like Fallside people and we don't. Perhaps your full frontal approach might work . . . I certainly hope so – you won't be doing it without considerable risk. Anything could happen. Wouldn't it be better if I was in attendance somewhere?'

Star insisted that this would not be necessary. Then she asked him to go through every word he could remember of the conversation in the public house the previous day.

'I'm quite optimistic,' she had said, 'for they would have read all about the case of the Glasgow councillor in the High Court recently. You'll remember it . . . the one who was getting people council houses for money. The police rigged a witness up with a machine to record everything that was said when the councillor was making a deal.'

The trial had made something of legal history in Scotland as the first time that evidence of that kind had been accepted in the High Court. 'I know our two men won't be the type to be too interested in the world news pages, but they'll know all about this case. At least,' she said holding up crossed fingers, 'I sincerely hope so.' Then she smiled to herself when she remembered her Uncle Sammy's story about how he had been similarly wired up by the police in New York in order to record the threats of the Mafia men. She realised, as Rose had said, that what she would be doing was chancey and that unlike her Sammy's episode, there would be no policemen waiting in the wings.

They had also gone over the names and the facts Rose had been able to obtain about the two girls. 'I've still to make up my mind about them,' Star had said, as she read over the names and details once again . . . Cathie Gallacher, neé Monaghan, aged twenty-four, housewife with one child, an active member of the Holy Cross Chapel in

Fallside, husband a self-employed painter and decorator ... Rachel Donaghue, aged twenty-six, single, bottling plant worker, friendly with Cathie Gallacher, both active in the chapel's Altar Society. Participate in work for the mentally handicapped and among the sick and poor of the parish.

'That's a real turn up for this pair, then,' Star had said. 'Hardly types like that who'd be at parties with the likes of Sonny Riley.'

'My information is that the single one, the girl Gallacher, was a bit of a wild one ... drinking, party-going, one previous conviction but only for a minor breach of the peace.'

'She doesn't sound all that wild.'

'No, not really. And that all stopped when she got involved in the chapel's activities. What are you going to do about them, then?'

'Put my thinking cap on again, I suppose ... and just hope there's an answer of some kind. Did you mention the name of their church? Oh yes, it's here. Holy Cross. Lovely. We're halfway there and I can't thank you enough, Mr Rose.'

'Alfie sounds a lot better.'

'You'll send me an account then?'

'I will. About the work I did for you, Mrs Jehan ... Star. It was my pleasure. That was quite a master stroke of yours yesterday. That was something different. And you're something different, Star. Perhaps we'll meet again?'

'Yes,' she smiled, 'perhaps. My thanks to you again ... Alfie.'

She had called the chapel to make an appointment and a woman she presumed was a nun answered the telephone. 'It's Father Damien you want to see,' she had said.

He was a tall man with the dark face of a Southern

Irishman but the accent was unmistakably Lanarkshire. 'Coatbrig,' he had said when Star had said she had been expecting someone with an Irish accent. 'Oh, we're not all from there,' he added with a warm smile, before suggesting she follow him to a small room at the rear of the chapel. 'A great wee place to have private chats,' he said as he indicated to a lounge chair in front of a desk. 'And how can I help you?'

'A lot I hope. Let me start, though, by saying that you must pardon me if I get my etiquette wrong in any way. I'm not Catholic and therefore not versed in such matters.'

'Please, Mrs Jehan, don't let matters like that inhibit you in any way.'

'Then I'll get right to the point. Do tell me, Father,' she began, 'what would be the likelihood of your intercession on my behalf with two members of your parish who committed a sin?'

'Goodness, that *is* a tall order. Well, for a start it would all depend on the sin. As you know there are all forms of sin. Wasn't it one of the poets who said that pleasure is a sin, and sometimes sin's a pleasure? We have to consider too that some sins, if not many sins, cause no great harm to others, while other sins do.'

'Would the nature of their sin matter to you if you were to consider some form of interceding?'

'Of course it would and it would also depend on whether or not harm was being done to others because of this sin. But you must tell me much more.'

'The nature of this particular sin was in essence a lie.'

'My dear, that is hardly something of my concern, unless I was listening to their confessions.'

'It may well be that you did hear their confessions.'

'If I did, then they would have been absolved of that sin.'

'But isn't the absolution only given if they make amends for the sin?'

'You are not in total ignorance of our Church, I see.'

She smiled in reply to the comment then continued. 'The essence of this sin, as I said, was a lie. Truth can be a very debatable subject, as you know. But in this case there's no debate. The story which they told, the lie, was a complete and utter fabrication. But it's not the lie which I've come to you about. It's the consequences. Because of what they said a man was not charged with a murder which he committed.'

'Mrs Jehan, priests like myself are not the policemen of the community.'

'I wouldn't expect you to be. And if it was merely for that man not being punished, then I wouldn't be sitting here with you today. Father, you must have read about that poor family who were wiped out by the car bomb in Castlehouse?'

'I most certainly did. A most dreadful affair indeed.'

'And that is why I am here today. The man who ordered that bombing was the man who was not charged for murder because two of your parishioners together with some others gave him an alibi. The two people concerned are both young women and they said he was with them in Fallside at a party, when in actual fact he was in Glasgow committing the gravest sin of all . . . taking another's life. Since then he has terrorised a whole community and is now involved in various forms of extortion in order to send money and explosives to Ireland. This man's sins, Father, most certainly affect an awful lot of people. And if the two I've come to you about were to recant the story they told the police about him, they could prevent others suffering.'

'This is a rather astounding story you tell me – a very disturbing story. A parish priest like myself has no rights, as it were, in such matters. His concern over any one of his flock who has told a lie or done something which might be considered evil is the harm it might do to others. In this case it appears harm has been done so I would have cause to speak to them. I would have to ask if they had confessed, and if they had then that is the subject finished, unless they tell me they want to speak to me about it. These are the sort of things I would have to establish first of all. One thing you haven't told me, Mrs Jehan. What's your involvement in all this and how did you get to know the names of these two women?'

'My involvement is that I had a connection with the man who was murdered. We did not know each other. It was just . . . a connection. And because of that I've gone to considerable trouble in an attempt to see that justice be done in his name. As for getting to know about the two women, there are some things I'm afraid I just can't tell you and this is one of them. But I can assure you the information is accurate, as you'll discover if you speak to them. Father, can you help?'

'Perhaps the answer to that is in the words of St John who said . . . "I will not leave you comfortless." '

Just two days later, in the evening, Star returned to the chapel in Fallside. She had received a call that afternoon from Father Damien to say that he had gone the previous night to speak to the girls and that they wanted to meet her. He had spoken to them separately, he had said, and their conversation had been in private, so he could not say what their reaction would be when they met her.

They were sitting waiting in the same room where Star had spoken to the priest, and after the briefest of introductions the priest looked at Star, smiled and said, 'I'll leave you ladies alone.'

The two girls looked concerned and Star broke the ice by speaking first. 'I'm pleased to see you here. The fact that you have taken the trouble to come and speak to me makes me most grateful indeed.'

'Missus,' interrupted the girl Donaghue, dressed in a brown swagger coat which had been the fashion two seasons previously and which was missing one of its enormous oval buttons, 'what kind of trouble is this gonnie get us into?'

'To be honest, I don't know the precise answer to that question except that it's up to you. But what I can tell you is that it's far, far better that you go to the police before the police come to you. Let me explain. Two of your friends, Bobby Watson and Danny Miles . . .'

'They're no' pals of ours, Missus. They're just boys we used to run about with,' Rachel Donaghue cut in.

'Whatever you say. Anyway, they went to the police earlier this week and made statements to the effect that they had told lies in order to give Sonny Riley an alibi. The police have six names of people who said he was at a party here in Fallside that night two years ago when Frankie Burns was murdered. Your names are on that list. They'll obviously be coming to interview you in light of the new evidence given by Watson and Miles.

'Also, you'll have read about the terrible bomb in Castlehouse. Well, this man Riley is implicated in that. If he'd been in jail where he belongs for the Burns murder this wouldn't have happened. But you two girls can help to put that right. Now, as I said, if the police come and interview you, it could result in serious charges against you. On the other hand, if you go to them and volunteer a statement it'll make all the difference. Should it come to you requiring legal help then I can arrange that . . . I've a relative who's a Queen's Counsel in Edinburgh. But more than likely there'll be no need for this as the Fiscal will require your help as witnesses and in return for that won't wish to pursue charges against you. But let me stress that time is very important and, as I said, for your own sake it's essential that you call on the police before they call on you.'

They sat in silence for nearly two minutes. The girl Gallacher, in a limp, pale-blue anorak, stained on one sleeve, nervously rolled the small ball of a handkerchief in her hands. 'You see, I've a wee wean.'

'Mrs Gallacher, there's no question of you or Rachel going to jail. And one guarantee of that is all the work both of you do for the church and the community.'

'Will you take us to the police station, Missus?' Rachel Donaghue asked.

'Now?' queried Star.

The girls looked at each other then looked back at Star. 'Aye . . . now.'

After showing the girls to her car, Star hurried back into the chapel to thank Father Damien. 'I don't know what you said to the girls, I didn't ask,' she said, 'but whatever it was it appears to have worked. They're coming with me to the police.'

The priest smiled. 'Obviously I can't divulge what was said between us but wasn't it also St John who said . . . "The truth shall make you free"?'

CHAPTER 34

THE PEGASUS MEN

THE TWO MEN SEATED IN THE BIG 3-LITRE
Rover opposite number 42 Castlehouse Crescent observed
Hamie McDougall closely as he drove up in an old Ford,
stopped and got out to walk smartly into the modern
tenement building. It already showed signs of abuse:
graffiti decorated either side of the entrance, one house was
empty with windows boarded up, and the front gardens
had never seen a spade or heard a mower.

'That's him all right,' said the dark, curly haired one.
The accent was Midlands.

The other man sounded unmistakably Ulster; 'Aye,' he
said, 'it's him all right. He's fit-looking. Walking smartly.
What'll we do?'

The Englishman looked at his watch. 'Wait. We'll give
him a quarter of an hour. Then we'll go up. Okay?'

'Aye, fine,' answered the Irishman. 'That'll give him
time. I don't know about you, but I'm not looking forward
to it.'

It was the first time McDougall had returned to his two-
bedroom home in Castlehouse since the funeral of his wife
and three children two weeks before. The Corporation's
housing department had been quick to effect repairs to the
building which had been damaged in the blast of the bomb

further down the street. The shattered windows had all been replaced although the raw and ugly gouges and the big scorch marks could still be seen in the tarmac and would remain there until the annual resurfacing of the street.

The door of his flat had been difficult to open because of the enormous pile of mail awaiting him. Many of the envelopes were unstamped and were obviously cards delivered by neighbours and residents of the scheme. He shook his head in amazement at the pile, picking a handful of the ones with stamps to look at their postmarks. It seemed they had come from everywhere, there were even several with the emu stamp of the Australian post and there were others from the United States. There were lots with the postmarks of English towns. He left them where they were and wandered through to the boys' bedroom.

It appeared strangely tidy. That was so unlike the boys, little rascals that they were. They used to say the floor was the best place for clothes for they could find them more easily there. 'And these silly coathangers . . . they're just for girls, Dad.' Where were all their toys, he wondered. He could see the toes of young Hamie's football boots peeping out from under his bed and his favourite Rangers scarf was there hanging on a hook behind the door together with the red, white and blue woollen cap which so many of the young fans wore. Nearby, on a wall covered with various pictures of team squads was young Hamie's favourite picture, the big autographed one of the young star John Greig which had come as a promotion with one of the morning papers. God, how that wee one loved his Rangers . . . he collected everything he could about them – programmes, especially souvenir ones, emblems and pennants, badges and rosettes, all obtained through some kind of barter operation which existed among his friends at school and in the street. He had all these things yet he had only been to see his idols, Rangers football team, once, back in the days before his dad had got the mobile shop and had to work on Saturday afternoons.

He had never known a young boy so excited as that day when they had walked together to the ground from the subway station nearby. They had arrived at the stadium early and he had wanted to wait outside for a while to watch the usual pre-match spectacle of various characters meeting up for their highlight of the week, but little Hamie had been anxious to get inside. Of course, he should have realised that none of what men like him saw outside in Edmiston Drive meant much when you were just seven years of age. What you could see inside was much more important. It was great in there because you could look around you at all those other fans taking their seats, while the ones over on the terracing were singing songs already, though the game hadn't even started. And, look, there was the very grass his team would be playing on when they came running out of the tunnel. Funny, Hamie had thought to himself that day, he had never been as excited as this when he was a young lad, but then he had never been taken to a Rangers match by his dad.

When they had got to their seats in the big Copland Road stand, young Hamie had tried to put his arm round his dad's shoulders, a little boy's way of saying thanks. Maybe they should have gone together more often; it had been a memorable day, not for the mere watching of Rangers or being at Ibrox, but for the rare empathy he had experienced with his son in his enjoyment of the spectacle. It was too late for that now.

From the boys' bedroom, Hamie had wandered through to the kitchen. That puzzled him too, for it certainly hadn't been as orderly and clean when he had left it with his sister and her husband to attend the funeral. He remembered the ghastly nightmare of the existence he went through for the two days prior to that most awful day, and the ordeal of the actual burials at the Linn Cemetery. How did he survive all that? The images still lingered, those of the scores of young schoolchildren all crying as the coffins passed, of the sombre and sad faces which looked straight at him in pity and compassion, and the . . .

The knocking at the door was like the sound you hear in a dream, real yet somehow unreal, near but strangely far away, and he waited for a while until it started again to make sure it wasn't just his imagination. He could hear a man's voice outside as he walked down the short passageway, and through the opaque glass of the door he could make out the outline of two figures. He swept aside more of the mail with his foot in order to open the door properly. When he did, the man with the familiar face standing there held out his hand to him and he took hold of it and began shaking it warmly. Unsmiling, the man said in measured tones, 'It's good to see you, Hamie.' After briefly clasping his hand the man put his two arms around him and pulled him towards him in a warm, brotherly embrace at which McDougall broke down and sobbed. The third man embraced the pair of them and they held tightly together as McDougall's shoulders heaved with deep sobs. Finally he stopped and pulled himself erect.

'That's it, lads . . . I'm okay now. It was the sight of you two. That really broke me up. That's what we were all about . . . wasn't it? Mates. You were always there by your mucker's side when he needed you. And, oh dear Christ, have I needed muckers. Come on inside.'

The three men had shared the very special and high form of friendship which exists among the parachute forces of the British Army. Stewart Campbell lived near Ballymena in Northern Ireland and Bob Thomas hailed from Birmingham, but the three had served together in a variety of locations during the five years they had spent with the 3rd Battalion of the Parachute Regiment.

Like McDougall, they were smart, well-preserved and ruggedly handsome men with that stamp which marked the courageous individualists who volunteered to be warriors, and who put their faith in a big nylon sheet opening above their heads to float them safely to earth. Men who did things like that were not of the ordinary breed, although nowadays life was quieter for them. Thomas had become a fitness fanatic and was now running his own string of gymnasiums in Birmingham, a chain named 'Pegasus' after the winged horse emblem of the Airborne regiments. Campbell ran his family's farm.

Of all the many great mates he had in the Paras, Campbell and Thomas had been the closest. They had been with McDougall the day he gained his Mentioned in Despatches award for outstanding bravery in the battle with the Qutaibis in Wadi Taym. When the sergeant and the corporal of their platoon had been wounded, McDougall had led the men up the steep slopes to the two ridges they had nicknamed Coca Cola and Pepsi Cola. Thomas and Campbell had covered McDougall as he had gone ahead on his own, taking out two vital enemy gun positions with gunfire and grenades. It was the stuff of Victoria Crosses or at the least of Military Medals, but the word was they already had their rations of medals. All there had been was that Mentioned in Despatches cluster which he could show on his Service Medal.

'You got beds for us, then?' Campbell asked.

'Aye . . . what . . . are you stopping?'

'Oh, we're stopping all right. We're here till we get them.'

Just then the doorbell went. It was Janet – he forgot her second name – the woman across the landing. She didn't say anything. She couldn't. The emotion overwhelmed her and the tears flooded her face. McDougall had always been awkward in such situations and didn't know what to say. It was the Irishman who noted his predicament and his cheerful Antrim accent helped. 'That's awfy nice of ye, Missus, coming over like that. Hamie here's gonnie be fine.

We're two old pals that have come to keep him company. To stop him from going astray, like.'

The woman had still not spoken but the comforting voice of Campbell calmed her and she was able to wipe away the tears with a large gents' handkerchief. Then she held up a key. 'It's yours. Mrs . . .' she couldn't complete the name. 'Mrs . . . left it with me. I've some tea and sandwiches ready. I'll bring them in.'

McDougall bit his bottom lip and shook his head when she turned to go back to her house. 'Aye, by Christ, this street might not look much. And Castlehouse doesnae look much. But see the hearts! They're something else, I'm telling you. You learn about people at times like this. Look at that stack of mail. Most of it's cards that they've been putting through the box from all over the scheme.'

The doorbell went again. This time there were three women, one in a pinafore over her skirt, the other two in jumpers and slacks. They were neighbours. One of them spoke, the other two wept. 'Just to let you know,' she said, 'that we'll keep an eye on your house and if there's anything you want just you say the word . . . and don't forget, mind. And Mr . . . we're helluva sorry. We really are.' The elegance was in their hearts, not in their ways.

Castlehouse had no pubs, so McDougall, Campbell and Thomas went by taxi to the Victoria, a fine old bar in Crosshill, on the south side of the city. Campbell and Thomas kept away from the subject as long as possible, transporting McDougall's mind back to the happy days in the regiment. The longer ago those days were the happier they seemed. Even the harshest moments were a laugh now.

'Remember Sarn't Cooke?' Thomas had said.

'Edinburgh bloke with a long head?'

'Aye ... gave him a right big head when he stood sideways. Proper swine he was.'

'Thought he was the reincarnation of the mad officer in *Beau Geste*, what was his name? Markov? Remember that time in Germany? A mid-summer's day in the nineties and he put us on punishment drill wearing full battle order and carrying rifles!'

'Yeah, and he was as frustrated as hell because nobody had cracked after an hour non-stop of it. Went into such a mad bleeding rage he almost burst.'

'What about that time in Aden when we went out to the souk up at Crater. Bob imagined that Arab bint was flashing her eyes at him over her veil ... the next thing you know her old man comes with his bloody big khunjar dagger drawn because he'd seen him eye her.'

'What about that riot in Aldershot?'

'In the Black Bull when half the bloody Durham Light Infantry tried to take on about thirty of us?'

'And the MPs had to fire live revolver rounds to stop it.'

The memories flowed and it was just what McDougall had needed. It wasn't till much later in the night that the subject of his family and the bomb came up. He told the two men the story of Riley and his various rackets in Castlehouse and other places. He had no proof, of course, but he was sure Riley had something to do with the bomb. Groups of Riley's thugs had tried various ways to warn him and his shop away from Castlehouse unless he paid them money.

'That bomb was obviously meant for me,' he said.

'Well, we'll take him out,' said Thomas.

'Listen, boys,' said McDougall, 'I appreciate your thoughts, but I don't want you two sticking your necks out on my behalf. I'd like to deal with this myself. And I mean that. It's a personal thing between me ... and them.'

'Absolutely no chance,' said Campbell. 'We can take

them out any way you want, Hamie. Bob here could do it with his hands, no problem, and I've brought a little friend along with me.'

'A shooter!'

'What else? And we're not leaving you, Hamie, till these people are sorted out.'

CHAPTER 35

NAMES IN AN ENVELOPE

IN ORDER TO REGAIN SOME OF THEIR LOST
sobriety, they had got out of the taxi some distance away
from Castlehouse Crescent so that they could walk some of
the way back to the house. None of them were drinking
men in the sense a drinking man was known in Glasgow.
But when they drank, as they often used to in the
3rd Battalion, they could take it with the best of them.
Thomas warned that he would still boot the other two out
of bed long before reveille in the morning for a five-mile
run before breakfast . . . 'Or else you don't have the right
to call yourself a real para.'

'There'll be no bloody runs tomorrow morning, Private
Thomas,' Campbell had said.

'Suit yourselves, lads. I've brought my running shoes.'

Then they broke into song, like they used to on such
occasions and, as they weren't football or party songs, no
one paid much attention to them as they walked the lonely
streets of Castlehouse. Perhaps it was just as well no one
listened; they were rough and coarse songs, songs that
insulted corporals and sergeants and Arabs and anybody
who wasn't one of them.

The lady from next door had obviously returned to do
some more tidying. The mail from behind the door had

been cleared away and was now neatly stacked in tidy piles on the family dining table. There was also a big bag of fresh rolls, a tub of margarine and a slab of Scottish cheddar cheese.

'See what I mean?' Hamie had said, slurring his words. 'Salt of the earth. That's what they are here . . . these people. Salt of the earth.'

'Aye, we've got guid folks like that o'er in Callybackey as well, Hamie,' said Campbell. 'Course, mind you, we're a' Scotch folk there as well. See yer Riley man, Hamie. Ye'll have to leave him to me. I mean, Hamie, this one has got to be mine.'

He repeated the name again, spitting the word out angrily . . . 'Riley. Agh! Fenian bastard. It'd mean a helluva lot more to me getting a Taig bastard like that than it would to you, Hamie. I mean, it's us that really know these people. They're fuckin' evil, the lot of them.'

Thomas cut in. 'Are you forgetting something, Stewie boy?'

'What's that now?'

'That I'm a bloody Roman Catholic.'

'So ye are, by Christ. But you're an acceptable one, Bob. You're not a fuckin' Irish one.'

'Oh, forget that Proddie and Pape stuff, Stewie. That's all I bloody well need at the moment.'

'Aye, right enough, Hamie. But I still hope I'm there when we get Riley.'

It was Thomas who, returning from the toilet, produced the small, brown, crumpled envelope. 'Looks like somebody couldn't afford a new one,' he said as he passed it over to McDougall.

The address was in pencil, written in uneven, crude strokes with the name spelled 'McDugald' followed by the word 'Urgent'. Inside was a lined piece of paper, roughly torn from a school jotter. There was a short list of names and addresses and at the top of the page the words: 'They were the ones.'

The first name was 'Sonny Riley', with his mother's address and two other addresses, with the words Monday to Wednesday, spelled as 'Wensday', after the first address and Thursday to Saturday after the second.

The next name was 'Pat Connors', with the address '126 Kingsway Crescent, Castlehouse'. Then there was 'Kevin Kavanagh, c/o Lenahan, 56 Kersdale Drive, Kilburn, London.' After his name was: 'Irishman – student – dark curly hair – tall – ', followed by a mark resembling an asterisk and the two words, 'the bomber'.

McDougall passed the paper over to Thomas who read it out aloud. 'Looks like you've got a special friend.'

'Looks like it,' McDougall replied.

After breakfast next morning they tried to put together what they could of the night before, recalling what pubs they had gone on to after leaving the Victoria.

'That was Pollokshaws Road,' said McDougall.

'Wherever it was I just remember they were some good old pubs. Sure it was like being at home in Ballymena.'

McDougall produced the sheet of paper with the three names and addresses. 'I don't think any of us could focus on much last night. Remember me getting that note through the door? It's a real gift, their names and addresses.'

'Tell us about them again,' said Thomas. 'I recall you reading the Riley one out. Who are the others?'

'One is a Pat Connors. I've heard of him, but I don't know him or what he looks like. Don't know Riley either, for that matter, apart from them shouting his name as a threat when they tried to bully me. I remember seeing his picture in the paper once. Got one of these supercilious smirks on his face.'

'I've got the very wee thing that'll remove that in a flash,' said Campbell.

McDougall drew him a severe look. 'Forget the gun, Stewart. I appreciate you're here, but no shooters. There are other ways.'

'As you say, Hamie.'

'What about the other one?' asked Thomas.

'Kavanagh. Kevin Kavanagh. He's the one they've scribbled "the bomber" next to. Don't know anything about him.'

'He's the one with the London address then?' said Campbell.

'Aye. Kilburn . . . that's the Irish quarter in London, isn't it?'

Thomas nodded before speaking. 'Wonder how he figures? D'you suppose they brought him all the way up from there to do the bomb?'

Campbell answered that with some more views on the Republican community in Northern Ireland. 'There'd be no need for that . . . we're crawling with the bastards over the water there. Learn to make up bombs before they can read, some of them.'

'Whoever's tipping you off seems to know . . . and wants something done,' said Thomas. 'I wonder why? Must have some kind of grudge.'

'Right,' answered McDougall.

'I mean, he's gone to the trouble of saying what nights Riley is at these addresses and even given that description of the Irishman. Well, whatever,' Thomas went on, 'it's London then, isn't it? What d'you say, Hamie?'

'Listen, boys, I've gone through all sorts of hell over this. At first there was the shock. Christ, I've never known anything like that. I mean, remember how upset we all were when we heard the Qutaibis had beheaded the SAS lads, the ones who were preparing our dropping zone? And that time we lost the lads in the platoon just after Bakri

Ridge? I mean, we were really cut up then but I'd never experienced shock before. Not even when my own father died. But what happened to Pat and the kids ... it ... it completely shattered me. It was like coming to a complete standstill. I couldn't think ... or react. There was just this terrible, gnawing numbness inside me.

'When I got over that, and after the funeral, the next stage came ... the anger and rage. I was consumed with hate and revenge. It's not a nice way to be and that subsided after I had a very long talk with the minister here and with my sister's minister down in Ayr. I was getting things in a bit more perspective by this time and they helped me to realise how wrong it was to be so filled with hate and to be seeking revenge. I had just wanted to kill, kill, kill. Every one of them ... and their families too. Anyone, anything connected to them I just wanted to destroy. But by beginning to understand what the ministers had spoken to me about I was able to come back to my normal senses again, thank goodness. Hate can be a terrible thing. Now I seem to have got over all that. I don't actually have hate in my heart for them any more.

'But I didn't go all the way with the ministers. Once I was able to rationalise it all, I did decide that, by Christ, they would have to pay. Oh yes, lads, they'll have to pay dearly for what they did to my Pat and my boys. I don't want them dead, though. That's too easy. I'll suffer for the rest of my days for what they did to me and there's no way I can turn my back on that. If the police get to them first, then I'll say ... fair enough. But I hope and pray I'm there before them for I want them to know what they did to me and I want them to suffer for it. I want them to remember for the rest of their miserable days on earth what they did to my family. They destroyed them. And they destroyed me. They'll pay for it.'

'We're with you, Hamie,' said Thomas. Campbell nodded. 'If we leave now we'll make it most of the way to

London. We'll stop off for the night some place with a good little pub and we'll be there sometime tomorrow. With a bit of luck we'll be meeting Mr Kavanagh tomorrow evening . . . when it's nice and dark. All right, boys?'

CHAPTER 36

REVENGE BITTERSWEET

AFTER HIRING A CAR ON A TWO-DAY LEASE from one of the cheap hire firms in Hendon, they had driven with the two cars to a garage in Golders Green, where they left Thomas's sleek Rover in a garage with a wired parking compound. The suburbs were near each other in that part of north London and when they had finished what they were going to do and picked up their car again, it would only take them minutes to be on the motorway for the north.

The hire car had been a precaution. As Thomas had put it, 'If there's any checking back, they'll come to a dead-end. My car won't be seen near Kilburn and if anyone does spot the other car, that line'll come to a dead end at the car hire firm. These little places don't care about your licence or anything so long as you bung them a whopping deposit . . . in cash.'

The address in Kersdale Drive, Kilburn, which had been left in the crumpled brown envelope at McDougall's house hadn't been hard to find. It was just round the corner from a pub called The Blarney Stone and was in one of those streets which had obviously been 'nice' at one time but was now part of an anonymous world of bedsits, rooms and flats where acquaintances last for minutes, neighbours for hours, friends for days. The once-elegant Victorian terrace houses had been sadly neglected by the rent speculators who now owned them. What did it matter how they looked? Those who came and went cared little and the owners, who could extract fortunes from such properties irrespective of how they appeared, cared even less.

Because of his accent, it was decided that Stewart Campbell should make the initial inquiries about Kavanagh. Although the accent was Protestant Ballymena, he could easily switch to Catholic Ballymurphy.

Gracious stone columns flanked the door at number 56 and Campbell winced at its strident purple paint. He bounded up the short flight of eight stairs and was about to knock when he saw the door was open. Inside the big hall was a table against a wall with a variety of mail, circulars and a pile of unread free newspapers. There was no one around and he had a quick flip through the mail, noting there was a letter addressed to C. Lenahan. Good, he had thought, at least he had come to the right place. Just then, a couple had come out of one of the rooms and at the same time a group of three young men had come in, but none of them had given him more than a casual look, except for one, who had smiled and nodded as though he had known him. Campbell smiled in return, remarking that it was turning out a nice day. One of the three then came back into the house asking, in an accent he took to be from Cork or somewhere thereabouts, if there was any mail for McCartney. Campbell answered in the negative and the man walked out again.

He checked if there was a board or a list indicating the names of residents but there was none. He then walked through to the rear of the hall where there was a short flight of stairs descending to a back hall, off which there were some rooms. To the left of the main part of the hall, brightly lit by huge skylight windows, there was a wide staircase leading up to the flats and rooms on the two upper floors of the big house. Most of the rooms he could see had small brass holders on the door frames in which there were cards with the names of the occupants. Some of the names had been scored out and replaced with other names and on a few of the doors there were no frames, just names on cards pinned to the door. Most of the names were of Irish origin.

In a small passageway at the rear of the first floor where there were only two rooms he saw a pale green card held to the door with a piece of sellotape, and the name . . . C. Lenahan. He was delighted at the discovery and stood quietly by the door trying to ascertain whether or not there was anyone in the room. It was difficult to tell for there were voices and so many other sounds coming from the other rooms. He thought he heard a noise from inside and stood still, almost without breathing, to check.

A loud voice from close by startled him. When he looked round a woman was standing there. She would be in her thirties, he reckoned, and was wearing a casual mix of jeans and a worn anorak. Her long black curly hair needed a brush as much as she needed some good dietary advice.

'Is it Charlie Lenahan you're looking for?' she inquired. The voice was West Belfast and in view of that he eliminated as best he could his own native accent.

'Aye . . . is he . . . ?'

'He's been away for over a week now,' she answered without waiting on the complete question. 'I think he's gone back, you know. D'ye want to leave a message? . . . if he comes back I can give it to him.'

'No . . . it's all right. You wouldn't know by any chance if Kevin's about?'

'The young fellow?'

'That's right. Tall and curly-haired.'

'Yes, I've seen him. But I don't know where he is. He'll probably be in at night.'

'Aye, right enough.' Campbell smiled at the woman then turned and walked out of the house.

'If I see them shall I say who called?'

'Just an old friend . . . I'll come back some time.'

Rather than have the car be seen sitting in the one spot for lengthy periods with the three of them sitting in it, they had taken turns, like military pickets, of an hour on and two hours off, keeping a look-out on the flat by casually walking up and down the street, while the car parked with the two 'off-duty' men sat elsewhere.

Just after six o'clock McDougall saw the young man. The description in the envelope couldn't have been more accurate. There had been lots of different people, mainly young, coming and going from the address but none had remotely looked like a tall young man with dark curly hair. This one did.

He was everything the note had said and dressed like a typical student in his jeans and cord blouse jacket. He was just a lad really. He would have been a mere child, McDougall thought, when he and his mates were fighting for their country. And when they were doing that this man would probably have been listening to those first tales, songs and poems of the struggle . . . the cause . . . the glorious fight for their lost freedom . . .. Was he really like that, he wondered? The force-fed nationalist? Or was he just a common criminal, a bomber for hire? Would he ever know?

About a quarter of an hour later the other two returned in the hire car and McDougall told them that someone resembling the description of Kavanagh had gone into the house and hadn't come out again.

'We'll park the car a couple of blocks away,' said Thomas, '. . . just in case.'

When they had done so, McDougall turned to address his two friends. 'Right, before we go,' he said, 'I want to get this clear . . . we're not taking him out. The first thing

I want to find out is . . . was it really him and was it Sonny Riley who ordered it? I don't care how we make him talk, but I want him to tell me these two things. Have we got that now?'

'Okay, 105,' replied Thomas using that common form of army identification, the last three digits of a soldier's regimental number.

McDougall looked surprised. 'You remember?'

'How could I forget? Your bloody kitbag with that number was right opposite my bed for years.'

They went over the detailed plans they had made of how they would enter Kavanagh's room and how they would go about making him talk.

'I'll bring the tool bag,' volunteered Campbell.

The letter that had been addressed to Lenahan on the table in the hall was gone. Campbell suggested that Kavanagh would probably have taken it.

'I'll lead the way,' he said, turning up the wide staircase to the first floor and then indicating with a nod the direction of a door at the rear of the short passageway. The stairwell was filled with noise from the flats, mainly TVs but someone was hitting the high decibels with heavy metal rock music too.

'Reminds me of when the shows come to Ballymena,' Campbell joked as he bent down to unzip the plastic hold-all he was carrying, extracting a heavy joiner's hammer and a wooden mallet with a broad head, together with a strip of torn white sheeting and some rope. He distributed the items between the other two, keeping the hammer for himself. He then went forward to the door and gave it four soft knocks. As they waited for a reply, they looked around the passageway, noting that there was no light coming from under the only other door. They could see light, however, coming from the flat outside which they stood and there was also a TV or radio playing loudly. When Campbell knocked again the volume was turned down sharply and a voice from inside answered casually, 'Aye, who is it?'

'It's Gerry Hannigan,' said Campbell in an assumed West Belfast accent.

'And who do you want?'

'Charlie.'

'Charlie who?'

'Lenahan.'

'He doesn't live here.'

The eyes of the three men met, puzzled at the response from whoever was behind the door. Why was he saying there was no Charlie Lenahan?

Campbell came back quickly again. 'I'm just a delivery man and was told to bring this stuff here for C. Lenahan.'

'Hold on,' said the voice.

There was a fumbling with the two locks of the door, the last making a loud click as it unlocked. At the very split second the door began to open the three men burst into the room, instantly overwhelming the tall young man with such speed and surprise he didn't even have the chance to yell out. After they had quickly gagged him they tied his legs tightly together and bound his upper arms to his chest, leaving his lower arms with some freedom of movement.

Thomas walked over to the TV. *Steptoe and Son* was on and he turned up the sound, which contained loud bursts of spasmodic laughter. They switched off the bright bulb that lit the room, so that the only light remaining was the dancing blue glow of the black and white television screen. They left him lying like that on the floor while they systemically searched the room. There was one letter with a Belfast postmark and addressed to K. Kavanagh, c/o Lenahan. In the pocket of his jacket they found another letter addressed to him, c/o Connolly, in Castlehouse, Glasgow. 'He's yer man, all right,' said Campbell.

McDougall kneeled on the floor beside him and grabbed his hair with both hands. He spoke directly to his face.

'Right, just nod or shake your head to answer yes or no to my questions. Sonny Riley got you to do the bombing in Castlehouse?'

His head didn't move. Then suddenly and violently it jerked forward, his eyes dilating wildly as the noise of a loud crack filled the room.

'Well, that's three of them gone,' said Thomas, holding the heavy wooden mallet he had used to smash the fingers of Kavanagh's right hand.

'Did Sonny Riley get you to do the Castlehouse bombing?' asked McDougall once more, holding him tightly by the hair. Kavanagh kept his head still, his fear-filled eyes staring straight ahead before visibly bulging as the loud noise of the mallet crashed home once more. The mallet hammered home twice more on the same hand, the noise being drowned out by howls of the studio audience at the antics of the two TV comedians cavorting in their junkyard.

'If you even pretend you've passed out, Kavanagh, you'll get a lot worse done to you,' said McDougall, at the sight of the bound man closing his eyes for longer periods than a normal blink.

Thomas got up from where he had been kneeling, on the right side of Kavanagh, and went round to his left where, as before, Campbell was holding his hand on a thick cutting board that had been lying beside the sink in the room.

'I want to know . . . was it Riley? Sonny Riley? Did he get you to do the bombing?'

Defiantly, his head remained still, neither in acceptance nor denial of McDougall's questions. This time there were two loud cracks, one quickly after another, the full force of the mallet wielded by Thomas being followed by that of the heavy joiner's hammer on the fingers of Kavanagh's left hand.

His head began to move in a nodding fashion and as

soon as it did the two heavy tools smashed down once more, the bones of every left-hand finger, as were those of his right hand, fragmented, the knuckles pulverised. Thomas and Campbell then got up and removed Kavanagh's tennis shoes and socks and Thomas looked down at him saying, 'Right . . . now it's for your feet.'

'Hold it a minute,' said McDougall as Kavanagh nodded his head more visibly. Kneeling astride the Irishman and holding him by the hair once more, McDougall said, as he untied the gag, 'Okay, Kavanagh. Spell it out to me. You did the bombing for Riley?'

His head nodded.

'What did Pat Connors do?'

'The car. He drove the car.'

'How much did Riley pay you?'

He shook his head.

'What do you mean you don't know?'

'Nothing. No money.'

'You went from here to Glasgow to do a bombing for nothing?'

Kavanagh shook his head with some difficulty and in a faint voice said, 'From Belfast.'

'Are you in the Republican Army?' cut in Campbell.

The head was still again.

'Get that fuckin' board beneath his feet,' rasped Campbell.

The head nodded slowly.

'You filthy, Fenian bastard,' said Campbell, raising the hammer once more.

McDougall restrained him. 'That's it. I know all I want to know and he's had all the punishment I want him to get. Let's go.'

'You're going no fuckin' place,' came a voice as someone came into the room and closed the door behind him.

'Who are you?' snapped Thomas.

'The Lenahan you guessed wrongly was Charlie Lenahan. The name's Cathal and get your man untied,' he said, flicking his gun in the direction of Kavanagh, now lapsing into unconsciousness.

The two shots that rang out just then were in such quick succession they could have been as one. Thomas, still holding the mallet, quickly seized his chance, flailed it down on the arm of the man who had fired the first of the shots, who stumbled forward, the gun falling from his hand and sliding across the floor to be grabbed by McDougall. Thomas raised and swung the mallet once more, this time with a loud crack on the back of Cathal Lenahan's head.

'What happened to Stewie?' shouted Thomas, as McDougall leaned over him.

'Oh no,' he gasped as McDougall turned him over. 'Must have been that first shot . . . right in the forehead. Oh, Jesus . . . blown the poor bugger's bloody brains away. Lenahan saw him pull his gun but got his shot in first. Bloody hell. Right. Let's get the other one gagged again and make tracks . . . fast.'

'What about Stewie?' said McDougall.

'Stewie's gone, Hamie. Gone. You're into action again. This is the battlefield. No time for the dead. Let's go.'

They opened the door cautiously. Obviously no one had heard the shots. The hall was still full of the cacophony of loud noises, someone from somewhere above now playing an amplified guitar.

'Don't run,' said McDougall as they stepped out into the short passageway. 'We'll just walk normally.'

'Hold it,' said Thomas. 'Keep a lookout here for a second. I forgot to get the hammers and stuff.' He turned and dashed back into the room.

From where he stood, McDougall could plainly hear the two muffled shots coming from the room. A door opened somewhere and a voice shouted, 'What the bloody hell's going on . . . who's got the crackers?'

It seemed an eternity before a figure appeared at the

door of the room. Thomas was carrying the plastic hold-all.

McDougall gave him a stern look but said nothing.

'Let's go,' said Thomas. 'No looking back.'

The two men, in a deliberate but unhurried pace, walked down the stairs and out of the building. Nothing was said between them till they returned the hire car and retrieved the Rover. It was only then, as they drove north, that McDougall spoke. 'Did you need to do that, Bob?'

'Yes. Events had overtaken us. What was the alternative . . . leave Stewie there with a couple of live Republicans? The Lenahan one would probably have died anyway. I didn't realise it, but Stewie's shot had hit him . . . in the guts. But now like his pal he's a dead man . . . and you know what they say about dead men, Hamie!'

CHAPTER 37

STEWIE'S SECRET

THERE HAD ONLY BEEN A SMALL, TWO-COLUMN story on the front page of the late editions of the following morning's newspapers which McDougall and Thomas bought as they drove into Glasgow. The *Daily Record* was headed 'London Mystery Shooting – three men dead'. It went on to say that three men, thought to be Irish, had been found in a bedsit flat in Kilburn, London, and that Special Branch officers were investigating links with terrorists operating from Northern Ireland. By the evening, however, it was one of the main items on the TV news and in the following morning's papers there were fuller accounts of the shooting, this time providing details of the men's names and ages.

The stories of the shootings varied as they were all based on speculation. However, the better informed had used inside information from Scotland Yard and the papers' own staff correspondents in Belfast. One of these stories read:

Campbell had gone from Belfast to London with two other Protestant paramilitaries in order to get Lenahan, a senior officer in the Belfast Brigade of the Provisional Wing of the IRA. Lenahan had fled from Belfast because he was wanted by the Royal Ulster Constabulary for his part in bombings and the killing of two leading members of the Ulster Volunteer Force. It was also thought he was forming London cells for the IRA in preparation for a future bombing campaign in the capital. Kavanagh was also on the run and the three Protestant extremists had been tipped off about their London hideout and had gone there to kill them. However, Campbell had been shot dead in the quick exchange of bullets in the small room and the other two men had quickly fled. Special Branch men were still carrying out extensive inquiries in relation to the two gangs. It is thought that the two Protestant killers who escaped are still in hiding among sympathisers in England.

'Quite a story, eh?' remarked Thomas as they read the pile of papers they had brought to McDougall's house.

'Is it ever,' smiled McDougall. 'So glad they're concentrating on all those Protestant sympathisers in England.'

'Imagine an RC like me hiding among that lot!' joked Thomas.

However, next day the sensation broke. Most of the newspapers had the story, but two of the tabloids carried it at its fullest, together with an extensive picture portfolio. The stories were based on what one of them headlined *'THE SECRET LIFE OF KILLER CAMPBELL'*.

Stewart Campbell was a respected farmer from Ballymena by day. But at nights and weekends he had another life . . . as a senior officer in the outlawed Ulster Volunteer Force. Because of his extensive experience as a soldier in the Parachute Regiment, who had seen active service in Southern Arabia and in Borneo, Campbell had been enlisted by the UVF in order to train newly formed battalions in Belfast. He gave the Protestant volunteers training in counter-terrorist warfare as well as in the specialist tactics and infiltration techniques used by men of the Special Air Service with whom he had also served on detachment while with the 3rd Battalion of the Parachute Regiment. Because of his huge success in training the UVF volunteers, Campbell had risen to be one of the Force's most senior men.

That, it appeared, was the accurate part of the story. It then strayed into the speculative, with a long and detailed description of how Campbell had organised the secret mission and had travelled to London together with the other two UVF men in order to assassinate Lenahan.

Campbell organised the mission along classic SAS lines. After entering the IRA men's hideout in London, they held them captive for some hours during which time they tortured the younger of the two men in order to obtain information about other IRA men thought to be in the capital. There is now considerable panic in the IRA about just how much Kavanagh revealed before being shot in the head. There will also be a shake-up of their command in Belfast in order to find out who informed the UVF of the two men's whereabouts.

The story went on to give details of Lenahan's background and of how he had escaped two years previously from Crumlin Road Prison where he was being held on charges of murder and attempted murder. Kavanagh was now known also to be wanted for questioning in relation to the killing of a young British soldier.

Pictures accompanying the long article included some of Campbell on his farm at Cullybackey, his wedding day snaps, his first red beret picture, taken on the day of the graduation parade at Aldershot when he had been presented with his paratrooper's 'jump' wings, and another of him wearing an Arab kaffiyeh head-dress while returning from patrol in the Radfan mountains.

'Bloody hell,' said Thomas, 'look who's right there with him . . . us two!'

'Good God,' McDougall exclaimed. 'So it is . . . just as well we had on the kaffiyehs. You can't make out our faces. But what a story about Stewie. Did you know anything about this UVF stuff, Bob?'

'Come on, Hamie. D'you think he'd tell a Mick like me? He did say to me once that things were getting really rough over there and it was back to the old frontier days for Ulstermen. "And Bob," he said, "when it comes to the bit, people like me have got to stand up and be counted." But he never went into any details.'

'Well he certainly stood up all right . . . and was counted. What a bloody character, and us two not knowing. Thank God he went the way he did, though. At first I thought how bloody awful . . . poor Stewie, ending up as some anonymous bloke turning up dead in a dreary London bedsit. But now he'll be a folk hero among his own people in Northern Ireland for what he did.'

'Did you notice,' said Thomas, 'that right through all these stories, they've obviously got nothing on Stewie's two pals?'

'That's right.'

'They apparently haven't a bloody clue who they're looking for. Nothing about them looking for a particular car or anything like that. Nothing about descriptions of the two who were thought to be involved.'

'Yes . . . that's the good news,' said Hamie. 'The only good news. I'm really hurt at losing Stewie. He died through wanting to help me. When it happened I thought, oh God, this whole thing is going wrong. I'd hate anything else like that to happen, Bob. In fact, it just can't happen. If only he hadn't brought that damned gun.'

'If only he hadn't brought that damned gun, Hamie, bloody Lenahan would have got us two.'

'I guess you're right.'

'Listen, don't have any more worries about this. I've come to do a job and want to see it through with you. Connors next?'

'No. Let's forget him. He can have his miserable life, whatever it is. It's Sonny Riley I want.'

CHAPTER 38

THE DECOY GAME

IN ANOTHER AREA OF GLASGOW, ANOTHER MAN was as vitally interested in the various newspaper reports on the deaths of the three Irishmen in London. He lived in a part of the Govanhill district where there was a small enclave of corporation tenements called 'the slum clearance'. The description had been another of the city council's housing gaffes. It was an expression used in the Twenties and Thirties to describe the homes built specially for people whose houses in the old slums had been demolished. The name was to become a stigma for decades after. Instead of living in a slum, they lived in a slum clearance but it meant the same. It became just one of the many labels marking caste in the city. You could be classified because of your speech; that was the greatest giveaway of all. If it wasn't that, it would be your address. If a particular area had some slum clearance houses, that was a further means of classification.

In one such house the man who found so much to interest him in the Kavanagh killing now lived. For just like Hamie McDougall, the man in that house was out for revenge from what he had suffered at the hands of Sonny Riley. He was Mickey Kelly, and that was why he had delivered the crumpled brown envelope to Hamie McDougall's house.

When he read about what had happened in London two nights previously, Kelly could hardly contain himself with the joy and excitement he felt. It meant that McDougall had accepted the names he had given as targets. He hoped it would be the turn of Connors and Riley next. How he wished to see them both hurt. Riley for the horrific beating he had given him in the toilet of the Whistle, a beating from which he had never recovered and never would – the doctors had told him his kidneys were so badly damaged they would cause him pain for the rest of his days. And Connors for being a liar and cheat in duping him into acquiring explosives and detonators for Kavanagh. Then he had read about the McDougall car bomb. He had suffered constant nightmares ever since. That woman and her young children would still be alive had it not been for his involvement.

He had to get his revenge on Riley and Connors but even had he been well he knew he was no match for people like that. Besides, he would never have had the courage to even try. He had even fled from his flat in Castlehouse for fear of Riley, which was why he was now living in his married sister's slum clearance house in Govanhill. His only hope of getting any kind of revenge was by doing it in some anonymous fashion through a third party. McDougall was ideal. The story he read in the papers that morning was Mickey Kelly's first indication that his plan was working.

Later that week McDougall and Thomas returned to the flat in Castlehouse to find another brown envelope behind the door, similarly re-used and crumpled.

'Look at this,' said McDougall, opening it and extracting a sheet of paper, torn from a school jotter, as before. Scribbled at the top in bold letters were the words: 'RILEY'S FLITTED'. There were then two further addresses, both care of other names, one in the Gorbals, the other in Baltic Street in Brig'ton. The note indicated the days he was likely to be at them and the names of two pubs in which he would be drinking; the Old Judge was written after the Gorbals address and the Blue Lagoon lounge bar after the Brig'ton one.

'So that's why we haven't spotted him at the other two addresses,' said Thomas. 'Well, your friend, whoever he is, certainly has been a big help. What'll we do about these new places where he's living?'

'Try them and carry on as planned, I suppose,' said McDougall. 'I must confess I haven't a better idea.'

They had formulated a plan of action against Riley when they returned from London. Thomas had broached the subject of firearms again, remembering McDougall's taboo on them when Campbell had mentioned he had brought a gun.

'You see, Hamie,' he had said, to McDougall's great surprise, 'I've brought along some ironmongery myself . . . "just-in-case" stuff, you might say. Know what I mean?'

He had shown him the slim wooden box slipped unobtrusively beneath the heavy rubber mat covering the boot of the Rover. He unlocked the box to reveal two guns, one a small Austrian military weapon, a Steyr 5.56 rifle, a model with a dual role as rifle or sub-machine gun.

'I remember that bloody thing,' said McDougall. 'It's one of the neatest little rifles I've seen. You took it from that tribesman you picked off the day after the Bakri Ridge job.'

'Your memory serves you well, Hamie.'

'But how the hell . . . ?'

'Did I get it back to Blighty? Easy. Just watch.'

He gave the gun a half-turn and the eight lugs holding it rigidly together parted. The small rifle was now in two neat sections.

'The bloke at Customs said, "What the bloody hell is this?" I laughed in his face, telling him it was one of those cheap "repro" jobs they sold in the souk at Aden and I was taking it home for my boys. It's just a bleeding toy, I said. And blimey does he not turn out to be an old Para, so he just gives me the nod and I was in with it. Very handy little number to have.'

The other weapon was a sawn-off shotgun, its wooden butt replaced with a short metal holder.

'What d'you do with that? Shoot deer at close range?'

Thomas smiled. 'It wasn't all beer and skittles setting up my health clubs, you know. We have our problems down in Brum too. There were these West Indians, boxers like. One of them was a British champ and he started opening up some gyms at the same time I was getting my Pegasus chain off the ground. They weren't nearly in the same class as mine, but his boys thought I shouldn't be in the business and started cutting up a little rough. I had to get myself this little friendly persuader here and, Hamie, it saved the day . . . let them know I wasn't to be mucked around.'

McDougall had been against the use of guns, but was finally persuaded by Thomas that they were faced with a much tougher proposition in getting Riley than they had been with Kavanagh, despite its complications.

'Just one blast aimed at his legs from a fair distance, Hamie, and he'll suffer all right. If I use small bird shot at about six yards he'll have so much metal in him you'll be able to pick him up with a magnet. Remember the Tin Man in *The Wizard of Oz*? Well, he'd run Riley out of the park the way he'll walk after this. It's everything you want, Hamie – clean, effective, has the "suffer" factor and, maybe most important, if any of his pals are around they won't be all that hot in coming near when they hear my little friend here go bang-bang.'

Reluctantly, McDougall had agreed to the use of the gun. All they had to do now was find Riley.

'What night is it?' Thomas inquired. 'Thursday. And where does our fine friend reckon he'll be?'

McDougall read from the piece of paper. 'Thursday and Fridays, the Blue Lagoon, Baltic Street. He lives there as well, which is a bit of a surprise . . . that's real Blue Nose country.' He explained the significance of the area in terms of it being the home of the Brig'ton Billy Boys, probably one of the most famous ever of Glasgow gangs, whose anthem was still sung by Rangers football supporters, particularly if they were playing against arch-rivals Celtic. 'Maybe it's part of his plan . . . you know, no better place to hide than among the enemy? I don't suppose the cops would go there, if they were looking for him, would they?' said Thomas.

'No, I guess not. Anyway, it's Thursday. Shall we check this "Blue Lagoon" tonight?'

Evening closing hours for public houses had been extended from nine-thirty to ten o'clock, a reluctant condescension from authorities so mistrustful of drink and their fellow Scots that for most of the century they had imposed rigid controls on where, when, who with and how they should drink. But the optimists said there were signs that the day of liberalisation of this form of enjoyment and social intercourse was on the horizon. Until that day dawned they were given an extra half-hour.

McDougall took Thomas to the Mitchell Library where they went over old newspaper files on the sensational Tallyman trial in which Riley had been a central figure. 'I've only seen him once since then. One day in the scheme, Castlehouse, and he hasn't changed much. The same boy's face, the same stupid sneer.'

Flipping through various other books in the Glasgow Room of the big library, Thomas went back to the pictures of Riley over and over again in order to build up a complete image of the man in his mind. He stared long and hard at the various photographs. 'I'd hate to take the wrong guy's legs off,' he joked to McDougall.

'Will it be . . . ?'

'Hamie, don't tell me you're worrying that my friendly

little persuader will really take his legs off. That was only a
turn of phrase. You said you wanted him to suffer. Well,
I'll make sure of that all right. We'll leave him most of his
legs.' He looked at Hamie and smiled. He studied the
pictures then said he had Riley totally fixed. 'Almost know
him as if he was my brother. You're right about him being
"different" though. You wouldn't miss that face in a hurry.'

And he didn't that night. He recognised Riley immediately he spotted him leaving the little Blue Lagoon lounge
bar with a group of his associates. McDougall and Thomas,
both dressed in raincoats and wearing caps, stood on the
pavement opposite the pub, facing each other in the
manner two acquaintances might on a casual meeting in
the street, their voices slightly raised as they exchanged
niceties: 'How's Malky?. . . Haven't seen you for ages . . .
Where've you been? . . . Where're you working?'
McDougall had his back to the bar while Thomas
observed. In the middle of their chat he whispered, 'I can
see the bastard. He's with an ugly blonde. Face like a bat.
But flashing her knees and a long, sexy pair of pins.'

There was the usual noisy mêlée of a Glasgow public
house flushing out its customers at closing time, the
farewells measured by the amount drunk, with two men,
part of a group, at that inebriated stage where they wanted
to show everyone they would square up to each other, but
hoping that their friends would quickly pull them apart.

Riley and his blonde were with a group of about ten,
most of them, apart from Riley, with carry-out bags for the
something, somewhere to which they were obviously
headed. After they had turned the corner into Springfield
Road nearby, Thomas said, 'Well, it wouldn't have been
too easy tonight, would it?'

'No, not with that mob with him.'

'But we'll wait. There'll be a night when he fits into the
plan.'

'You never know. We might be lucky tomorrow night.'

'I wouldn't worry, Hamie. We've plenty of time to do this right and we'll wait till exactly the right moment.'

According to the note they had received, Riley would be back at the Blue Lagoon the following night, and then at the Old Judge for two nights. They had been present every night, Thomas armed each time with the short shotgun he carried inside his coat, hopeful for conditions that suited their plan. But on each occasion Riley had been accompanied by groups of people, usually six to about a dozen, and had gone off in various directions with them.

Exactly a week after the night they had first seen him coming out of the Blue Lagoon lounge they observed him again. They were sitting in a cheap hired car rented by the day from a company called The Rental Man, one of the many car firms which proliferated around the Barrows and Meat Market area of the East End, most of which, it appeared, only traded in the tired and the dejected. The Rental Man's fleet of hire cars consisted of any of the old bangers for sale in his used-car lot. No form of document or identity was required when hiring a car from The Rental Man, who in turn never concerned himself about the likelihood of someone not returning with a hire. He charged a twenty-five-pound deposit on each vehicle and his customers always came back for their money, which was usually more than they would have got had they tried to sell the car. But his cars suited the two men: they knew they could not be traced.

'How about that?' Thomas had joked as he toyed with the play in the column gear change of the old Hillman Minx they had hired for three pounds a day. 'You've got as much chance of winning the pools as finding the bloody gear with this thing. Did you notice the wing mirror? I went to adjust it and the bloody thing fell through the . . .'

'Hold it, Bob . . .' cut in McDougall.

They had parked the car near a little playpark along from the Blue Lagoon in Baltic Street in the hope that

Riley would pass on his way to the address at which the note said he was staying, further along the street.

'Don't look up, Bob,' said McDougall, 'but I can see him. And I don't want him to think we're paying any attention. He's with a blonde. She fits the description of the one the other night.'

'He's not into taste, is he?'

'See what you meant about the legs, though. Christ, Bob, this could be it.'

Thomas continued to look in another direction, while barraging McDougall with questions. 'Any of the mob with him?'

'No, there's no one else. Just him and her and they're heading in the direction of the house up the street.'

'The plan?'

'Looks like it, mate. The plan.'

There was a long glove compartment under the dashboard of the Minx and Thomas leaned forward to retrieve the short shotgun which was lying there.

'Keep looking away,' McDougall cautioned again.

'Where's he now?' Thomas wanted to know.

'Almost diagonally across from the car. He hasn't even glanced in our direction.'

'Good. Then I'll get out and take up my position.'

'Okay. I'll give it a few seconds yet before I get out.'

Their plan was simple. They would waylay Riley as he walked along the street. Thomas, with the gun, would wait on the opposite side of the street and McDougall would entice Riley to part from the woman so that she would escape the shotgun blast. McDougall would walk behind Riley at a measured distance and when the moment was right he would get Riley to turn in his tracks to come back towards him. As he did so, he would pass by Thomas, waiting on the other side of the road with the shotgun. There was nothing original about their ploy. It was a basic decoy trick with no complications.

When Riley passed their car, walking on the other side of the street, Thomas slipped the gun beneath the old gaberdine raincoat he was wearing, holding it with one hand through the slit pocket of the coat. He then casually walked along the street in the same direction as Riley, but a few yards behind him and keeping to the opposite side.

McDougall was now also out of the car, and had crossed the street to walk between forty and fifty yards behind Riley and the woman. After a long, red sandstone tenement, the houses gave way to a series of old factory buildings. Somewhere in this stretch they intended to make the attack. There were no houses and no tell-tale eyes in this section of Baltic Street.

McDougall hadn't felt excitement like this since the last time he had stood near the exit of the big plane from which they used to jump, particularly at that point in the operation when he hooked on the static lines which opened the parachute and a slim umbilical of webbing became his destiny. The tension always rose in those moments and would continue to do so till he had exited and heard the loud clap of the big chute opening. It was just like that now, he thought, as he gulped a few quick breaths of air to help slow down his racing pulse.

About thirty yards on and they would be into that portion of the street with the old factories. Thoughts flitted through his mind. 'It won't be long now, Riley,' he was saying to himself. 'Oh, if only I could make you suffer like I have . . . but I can't, can I?' There was no suffering like that. The anger within him welled the more he thought about it. 'Is this all we're going to do to him? Take his legs away? Why don't we do away with him, as Bob suggested? Yes, that's what we should be doing. But we're not . . . because I said we shouldn't. What was I thinking of? This man hasn't the right to live. But it's too late now . . . isn't it? He's almost there.'

Just fifteen more yards. His mind raced again. 'Look at

the swagger of him. Bet the face has the stupid sneer too. And the woman! Cheap and nasty little floosie. We should give it to her as well.'

A few more yards and that would be it. He could see Thomas stopping and positioning himself on the other side of the road waiting on Riley to turn and come back towards McDougall.

Remember what the despatcher used to shout in the planes: 'Red light on ... stand by. Green light on ... jump!'

Riley was at the spot. The green light was on. There was no one else in the street and McDougall stopped and shouted.

'Riley!'

He did not turn round. McDougall let him take a few more paces before shouting again.

'Riley ... Sonny Riley. You're a bastard, Riley.'

Riley and the woman stopped, then turned. It had worked. He would take up the challenge now, all right.

'Aye you, Riley,' taunted McDougall. 'Your old mother's a fucking whore, Riley.'

He couldn't make out what Riley said for he was about fifty yards away but there were words as he left the woman where she stood and started advancing on this lunatic, whoever, whatever he was, who would even dare to utter such words.

'Come on, Sonny,' McDougall shouted again. 'What's keeping you? You frightened or something?'

Thomas waited for the right moment to make his move. He would cross the road towards the advancing Riley and as he came into a range of six to eight yards he would fire his shots. His coat was unbuttoned and his right hand groped along the top of the barrel to the point where it was joined to the metal handle that replaced the wooden butt. He pushed the small safety catch to the off position but would wait for a few more seconds before taking the gun from out of his coat and cocking it. There was a lamp-post which Riley would soon pass and he was using it as a marker. When he reached it he would advance. Six yards to go. Five. Three . . .

Just then three big cars came roaring into view, the one in the middle skidding wildly as it came to a halt with the other two in a screech of brakes and tyres and doors flying open right at the very lamp-post Thomas had been moving towards. Both he and McDougall stood rooted to the spot as, from one of the opened car doors, a man in a navy-blue suit barked orders at the uniformed men who surrounded Riley before quickly bundling him towards and then into one of the cars. As soon as the door snapped shut behind him, the three vehicles raced off again with the same fury as they had arrived.

None of the police had paid any attention to Riley's two stalkers and Thomas had quickly changed his mind about extracting the shotgun. When the three cars disappeared into the night along the street in the direction of Brig'ton Cross and the city, there were just the three left standing there . . . Thomas on one side of the street, McDougall on the other and, further along, the woman. It was the noise of the woman's high heel shoes clicking on the concrete pavement that broke the silence as she turned round and hurried off in the direction in which she had been walking with Riley just seconds before.

McDougall looked over at Thomas who was staring at him.

Thomas spoke first. 'Bloody hell, Hamie. Bloody, bloody, bloody hell. I've never felt so frustrated in all my bloody life.'

He brought out the shotgun, held it into the air and fired off both barrels.

McDougall was shaking his head in disbelief. 'How could they do that to us? It was perfect. It was working like a dream. Everything was just as we figured. And he had fallen for it. He never even noticed you. It was the perfect decoy and . . .'

'Do you realise,' said Thomas, 'had they been half a minute later we'd all have been in the nick? Two minutes later they'd have had a legless Riley lying there and we'd have been off. It had to be at that precise moment, Hamie. Bloody hell, I don't know whether to weep or cry.'

'I've got a better idea.'

'What?'

'Let's go and get pissed.'

CHAPTER 39

ARRESTING DAYS

BALTIC STREET WASN'T THE ONLY PLACE TO experience sudden and dramatic visits by the police that night. It had only been one part of a combined operation in the city, planned in the police headquarters near Glasgow Cross earlier that day.

When two taxis pulled up at an address in Castlehouse and a party of men and women got out, the doors of two unmarked cars immediately swung open and a number of plainclothes policemen rushed at the biggest of the men, who swung the heavy bag of bottles and cans he was carrying, knocking unconscious the nearest of the officers. There was a fierce fist-fight between the police and the other men, the women joining in as well, before a van-load of uniformed reinforcements with drawn truncheons drove up and Pat Connors, Sonny Riley's chief henchman, was handcuffed and led away.

It was a much more sedate scene in the small enclave of 'slum clearance' houses in Govanhill when police knocked at the door of the house occupied by Mrs Ina Fagan. She was the sister of Mickey Kelly and although he was shocked at their presence, he went quietly when told why he was being arrested.

*

When the two Fallside men, Watson and Miles, and the two women, Cathie Gallacher and Rachel Donaghue, had gone to the police and confessed that they had told lies in order to give Riley an alibi for the night Frankie Burns had been murdered, the police had taken a keen new interest in the case. The confessions on their own hadn't significantly raised the hopes of the police. But what had were the events which followed the appearance of a brief newspaper story relating to the case.

The local freelance newspaper correspondent in Fallside had been tipped off by his police contact about the confessions of the two men and the women. The story, which appeared in all of the national newspapers after he filed his information, read to the effect that new moves were expected in the unsolved murder of the former Scots Guardsman and Military Medal holder Frankie Burns. An unnamed police detective was quoted as saying that the information they had now received gave them a definite line to follow and could prove vital for their next line of inquiries.

Few read the story with more satisfaction than Mickey Kelly. He hadn't thought of it before, but now was his big chance to *really* square with Sonny Riley. For Kelly had been there in the Gorbals the night they had got Burns. A gang of six, led by Riley and Connors, with Kelly as lackey, had gone after him. Those were the sort of odds they thought appropriate when tackling a man of Burns's reputation. He had put up an incredible fight when he had been ambushed just as he was about to shoot Riley, but had been no match against the six. When it was over and they had run off, Riley had passed the knife he had used to Kelly, with the command, 'Get rid of it!'

Although the weapon was never seen again, Kelly had kept it in the same blood-stained rag in which he had wrapped it that night before tying it up in a neat little parcel of newspaper and string and hiding it in a cupboard. It had been among the few possessions in the suitcase he

had carried on the day he moved to his sister's house.
When he read the story that morning about the new
inquiries into Burns's death, he left his sister's house and,
with the aid of the stick he now used to help him walk,
made his way to the newsagent's in the row of shops at
Aikenhead Road in Polmadie where he bought a big brown
envelope. From there he went to the Post Office nearby,
took the unwrapped knife, the newsprint round it now
yellowing, from his inside pocket and put it in the envelope
together with a note, in the same laboured printing he had
used in the ones he had sent to McDougall. It said, 'This
is the blade Riley used to plunge Frankie Burns.' Then he
posted it to the man to whom he knew it meant most:
Superintendent Tom Graham of the CID. The effort of
walking the short distance to and from the shops was so
much for him that when he returned to his sister's house
he collapsed on to the sofa in her living-room. But despite
the exhaustion and the pain, there was the immense
satisfaction of knowing he would be getting some revenge
for the beating he had taken from Riley and from which he
still suffered.

The prints on the knife together with the traces of
Frankie Burns's blood gave the police the hard evidence to
arrest Riley all right. But what Kelly had overlooked was
that he too had fingerprints on record and there were
several of his there also. Hence the police also visited his
house as part of their operation.

The swoop on Connors had been based on information
given by the four from Fallside. They all said that the alibi
for Riley had been arranged through him. Connors had
originally come from Fallside and the four told the police
they had only met Riley on one occasion, at a party in the
Lanarkshire town, as a friend of Connors.

The trial of Sonny Riley didn't recreate the drama of the
Tallyman trial. There was nothing sensational in what,
after all, was just another gang murder. The majority of

cases which came before the High Court when it sat in
Glasgow were of that nature, sad and dreary litanies of the
pathetic and primitive lives which the Glasgow gangsters
lived. However, there was slightly more interest than usual
in this case because of the involvement of the notorious
Riley and because the victim had been a Scots Guardsman
who had been decorated with the Military Medal.

The Crown had a watertight case to present on Riley
and Connors. Most of it was founded on evidence supplied
by Mickey Kelly in return for which no charges were to be
made against him. The most horrific part was when Kelly
testified that he had seen Riley mutilate Burns's face after
the former soldier had collapsed and was obviously dying.
He said too that he had seen Connors put a knife in Burns.

Riley, who had the famous and flamboyant Nicholas
Fotheringay as his Queen's Counsel, made much play on
the reputation of Frankie Burns. A variety of witnesses
were produced who told the court that Burns had acted as
a bodyguard to Rachman-type slum landlords in the
Gorbals, that he had boasted to them of the murders he
had committed both in London and in Glasgow, that he
was known to be an associate of the men referred to as
'The Twins', that on several occasions in public houses
and other places in Glasgow he had shown off the gun
which he sometimes carried, and that he had been heard
to say threatening things about Sonny Riley and how he
would 'get him' one day.

But there was no answer to the strong case put up by the
Crown, not the least of it being the production of the actual
murder weapon bearing both Riley's prints and Burns's
blood and the damning eye-witness evidence of Mickey
Kelly who, while he may have been one of the accomplices
on the night they had gone for Burns, testified he had taken
no part in the actual assault on the man but had seen the
roles played by Connors and Riley.

It took the jury just over an hour to return a verdict of

guilty on the charges against the two men. In his short speech before sentencing him, the Judge, Lord Kintyre, said that it was obvious from Riley's record that he was one of the most vicious and violent men ever to come before the Court and that Glasgow would be a much safer place without his presence for a long period.

Throughout the speech, Riley had looked around the court in complete indifference to the Judge's remarks, nodding and smiling to those he recognised. When the sentence of life imprisonment with a recommendation that he serve at least fifteen years was passed, he laughed sneeringly at Lord Kintyre, saying sarcastically, 'Thanks, pal.' He then looked over at Kelly, menacingly drawing his forefinger across his throat, before being quickly hustled from the court by uniformed police. His behaviour in the dock was as hackneyed and predictable as that of the accused in so many previous trials heard in the High Court. It was somehow expected of them to act thus: to demonstrate their defiance; to flaunt their contempt for the normal rules of society; to show that they had no respect for anything other than their own order.

The threats Riley had made to Mickey Kelly for giving evidence against him were never to be carried out. Nothing would have been easier for Riley, even from within the confines of his cell in Peterhead Prison, sited on a lonely headland in the north-east of Scotland, than to have had one of his supporters carry out some form of retribution on the partly disabled informer. Even had he decreed that Kelly be killed, it would have been done willingly and without question. But it was by cunning that they and their ilk survived and Kelly was not short of that.

Despite telling the police everything he knew about the murder of Frankie Burns, he had said nothing about the tragic bombing of the McDougall family in Castlehouse. Although he had obtained the explosives used by the Irishman Kavanagh for his devastating car bomb, he knew he would have got another deal from the Lord Advocate's office in return for the information he could have given them. But he had other plans for this vital knowledge.

Riley's mother Bernadette was to read the details when she visited her son in Barlinnie Prison in Glasgow, where he was being held prior to his transfer north to the long-term institution at Peterhead. They had been written by Kelly on a sheet from the same old school jotter and delivered to her personally with the request that she read them to Sonny on her next visit. The note said: 'Call your team off, Sonny. Remember it was me who got you the stuff for McDougall's car. Remember it was me that gave it to big Pat. Remember it was wi' me that Kavanagh stayed the night he left his auntie's. He tell't me everything. Anybody comes near me Sonny and the cops will get a letter I've left wi' a lawyer. Yer old china, M. K.'

Mickey Kelly had just bought himself one of the best safety passes in the city.

CHAPTER 40

CELEBRATIONS AND MEDITATIONS

THEY DIDN'T RING THE CHURCH BELLS ON THE night Sonny Riley was arrested in Baltic Street, Brig'ton. But they might have for the relief and satisfaction it brought to so many.

Just as they had intended, McDougall and Thomas had gone out and celebrated in a memorable pub crawl. They started at the Victoria and, in honour of Campbell, they went round those very same bars along Pollokshaws Road that had reminded him of some of his own drinking places back in Ballymena.

'Do you realise, Bob,' McDougall said, 'it was exactly a fortnight ago tonight that the three of us were in here? Poor Stewie! Who would ever have thought it was to end this way for him?'

Thomas was more philosophical. 'Oh, I don't know, Hamie. The game he was into over in Ireland, anything could've happened. It could have been a lot worse in some ways. If he hadn't got it in London he could've got himself in real trouble over there, maybe taken a few more lives himself, maybe ended up in jail for the rest of his days like so many of them. He was right in the thick end of it, you know. Maybe fate did him something of a favour that night in Kilburn.'

'You could be right.'

'So what're you going to do, Hamie? Stay on in Castle-house and get your shop going again?'

'No way. I've got it up for sale and I'll get a good price for it, 'specially now that Riley is out of the way. Guys will be flocking into the scheme at the news he's been nicked. But it's not for me. I'm selling up and going out to join the brother in Kearny.'

'Where's that?'

'New Jersey. It's a small town just outside New York. Full of Scots. The brother, Donnie, went there about seven years ago. He's in the building trade and has done real well. You should see the photos of the house he's got. I took out papers about a couple of years ago although I hadn't told the family. It was Pat and the boys I was thinking about. Far better opportunities for them out there. I should be hearing about my visa soon, then I'm off. What about yourself, Bob?'

'Back to business. The Pegasus Clubs are doing well. But we must keep in touch, Hamie.'

'You bet. You bloody well bet we will. Come over and see me in New York.'

'That's for sure. Let's drink to it.'

Life was not the same for Bernadette Riley after her son was sentenced to life imprisonment. She lost a small fortune in her money-lending operations through bad debts. With Sonny out of the way, debtors knew there would be no retribution if they were late in paying or even opted not to pay. The word quickly went round that none of Sonny's henchmen were willing to do his mother's enforcement work and her house suddenly emptied of the regular callers with their small bundles of repayment money with interest at four shillings in the pound, doubling up every week the debt was unpaid. With the loss of the considerable profits she was making from that source and the lack of the cash her son had been supplying her with every week, no further monies were handed over 'for the boys'. They mumbled that their cause had lost a patriot.

Most of the people she spoke of as her friends dropped away too. There was no kudos any longer in boasting that they were 'pals' of the mother of Sonny Riley, a position which had given them considerable social cachet in the Gorbals and then Castlehouse. Sonny Riley didn't matter any more in these places. Only Mary Connolly and another two women were regular callers and the constant rounds of tea with sandwich fries were soon to become a thing of the past.

As Hamie McDougall had predicted, the mobile shop men returned unfettered to Castlehouse and for a considerable period to come they were to enjoy relative freedom from the predators who coveted them as an easy source of money. They knew that would not be the way of it forever, for those who understood Glasgow appreciated that, in one fashion or another, a new Sonny Riley would emerge.

In view of their vital evidence at the trial of Riley and Connors, Watson and Miles, and Cathie Gallacher and Rachel Donaghue were given suspended sentences on the charge of conspiring to give the police false information. The two men, however, were sentenced to three months' imprisonment on charges of car theft and attempting to steal a car.

The biggest celebration of all over the jailing of Sonny Riley should have been at the home of Star and Sammy Nelson, but his removal from society was something of an anticlimax for them.

'It's a bit like getting an old carbuncle or some other kind of sore removed,' Sammy had said. 'You don't go dancing in the streets for that. Yet, when you think of it, they had one hell of an effect on the lives of the Nelsons. It's 1970 now and it was 1927, just after you were born, that Snakey Holden, Sonny Riley's old father, killed Jamesie, my brother and your Dad. Then they got old Mickie Doyle, the man that used to make the whisky when we had the little distillery going, and Rab Blair, a lovely man and one of my old pals. Then my dear wife, your Aunt Peggy, took a nervous breakdown because of Holden and died. And there was that Pakistani fellow who was a pal of your husband, then Frankie Burns. My God, when you think of it, that family, first a Holden then a Riley, have haunted us in one way or another for more than forty years! And now no more. But they've caused too much sadness in our lives for us to celebrate. Far too much sadness, Star.'

There were tears in his eyes and he sat there quite still. It was the first time Star could recall seeing him so upset and to spare him any embarrassment, she quietly left the room.

Some minutes later she returned. 'You were right, Sammy,' she said, 'about not celebrating. As you said, there's been too much sadness.'

Then there was a loud pop as she thumbed off the cork from a bottle of Moët. 'But there's no harm in us having a little champagne supper . . . is there?'

CHAPTER 41

MEMORIES

THE MOVE BACK TO POLLOKSHIELDS WAS A great triumph in the life of Sammy Nelson. He had scraped and clawed his way out of the Gorbals as a young man and despite his advancing years he had said he was capable of doing it all over again when, near to bankruptcy, he had left for America, and he had done it. He had got back on his feet and returned with even greater determination to win back the lifestyle to which he had become accustomed, in Pollokshields, the best address in Glasgow.

When he had shared Star's small house in Govanhill, the area adjacent to the Gorbals in which he and his first wife Peggy had lived before the war, he had found his beloved niece as determined as himself to return to the way of life they had once known. They were fighters; they had experienced being down, but had never contemplated being out.

After Sammy had established his home improvements company, Star had leapt at the opportunity to contribute her enterprise and energy to the company. She had profited considerably as a businesswoman from her previous dealings in competition with Glasgow's Asian traders and from what she had learned during her time in the East, living and working among one of the world's most astute trading communities. It had been Star who had bypassed the Scottish firm supplying them with the terrazzo doorsteps for customers in the schemes to deal direct with the importer in England and after that to import the material herself from its source in Italy. She had done the same when they needed bulk orders of glass after stimulating the new fashion of glass panels in interior doors, once more importing direct from England and West Germany. It was the same with all the other commodities they handled, and all the time they were lowering their prices to a level with which others found it impossible to compete. They were also increasing their profits.

It was a simple story, she had often said to her Uncle Sammy, and it was the oldest of stories in the trading world . . . keep out the middlemen. 'Why should others jump on your back for a share of your and your customers' money?' was the theme she had preached so often when they were formulating business plans.

Sammy had tried to buy his old home, Sammar, but had been unsuccessful. The new owners weren't selling so he had bought another similar villa near his former place. 'Oh, well,' as he had said to Star on completing the deal, 'we've got the second best house in the scheme.'

'Scheme!' chided Star jokingly.

'Aye, you're right, they wouldn't like Pollokshields being called a scheme,' he had laughed in return.

With the struggles in re-establishing themselves over and the other clouds removed from their lives, Sammy would often muse to himself about the future for Star and Jamesie. He thought of the boy as his own grandson and fussed over him like he was a son, supervising his enrolment at Hutchesons Grammar, where he had sent his own son, John. From time to time, without the slightest effort in the art of subtlety, he would come straight out with his thoughts to Star, saying things like, 'You'll need to be getting yourself another man.' When she dismissed him for his suggestions, he would counter, 'It's young Jamesie I'm thinking about. Boys need a father . . . not an old, doting grandfather like me. You don't want the boy growing up wild . . . do you?'

'Maybe I'll meet some rich farmer's son . . . how'd that suit you?' Star surprisingly replied one day to Sammy when he mentioned the subject in his usual direct fashion.

The remark took him aback. 'What d'you mean . . . some rich farmer's son? Where would you meet a farmer's son?'

She knew she had him puzzled and toyed with him. 'Oh, so darling uncle is surprised. Well, well, well.'

'Is there something I don't know?'

'There may be.'

'For God's sake, lassie, tell me . . .'

'Oh dear, it's a shame to tease you. There's nothing that you don't know, except that I'm going away for a few days to see the Camerons down at Kirkconnel. I'd a letter from Mrs Cameron and they're dying to see young James. Ages since we've had a break, and James should learn something about life in the country.'

'Which ones were the Camerons again?'

'The people whose farm I lived on when I was evacuated during the war. I was what they called their "vac".'

Sammy's tone took another turn. 'Oh, I remember that carry-on all right . . . and that sojer that came looking for you.'

'Don't go saying any more about that,' she came back quickly.

He knew instantly by her tone to say nothing further. 'Aye. Best letting that fly stick to the wall. Where's it again . . . Kirkconnel?'

'That's right . . . Kirkconnel, in Dumfriesshire.'

Star was in her early forties now but looked a much younger woman, retaining her shapely figure, her attractive features taking on a refined appearance as she aged gracefully. Thinking now about the trip to Kirkconnel, she remembered her childhood days in Dumfriesshire; how dramatically they had ended when new owners took over the estate, its farms and the magnificent Lydeburn House. The Camerons quit their tenancy in favour of a smallholding near the village of Kirkconnel. They had invited her to move with them to the smaller place, but she had chosen the alternative course of returning to live with her mother in the Gorbals. After what had happened with Andrew and Robbie Fordyce that night at Lydeburn House, she could not have chosen otherwise.

The estate had been owned by Andrew and Robbie's parents, Colonel Mitchell Fordyce and his wife Jane. They were one of the most respected families in the county, their roots in the district going back centuries. In their day they had even entertained royalty. Every county had its legion of Fordyces, those diehard believers in the principle that everyone had their place in life, and that their own place was in the upper echelon of the Establishment, with the tenant farmers, their horsemen and shepherds beneath them, in the village the shopkeepers, and beneath everyone the miners. As long as everyone stayed in their allotted place, life would proceed happily. Colonel Fordyce was nonetheless a kindly man, a vigorous worker on behalf of the community, the first to support a good cause and often as not to be nominated its chairman. His wife, whom they nicknamed 'Lady Jane', was as kindly disposed as her husband and would join in the many activities of the area in the role of an attentive and caring neighbour.

Star had been injured in the attack on her, and Wull Andrews, the Camerons' worker, had run all the way from the high moorland farm to fetch the doctor from Kirkconnel. He, in turn, had insisted that the police be called. The humiliation of it all had been too much for the colonel, who committed suicide.

Not long afterwards, the twins had volunteered for the

Army, were posted to the HLI and served as officers in Germany. Robbie was killed in the last three days of the war. At the conclusion of hostilities, Andrew, then a captain, signed as a regular officer. Before being stationed in Palestine he had come to offer what remorse he could to Star. He missed seeing her, however, and told the long tale of the rape to Star's mother, Isa, the first she had known of it. When Sammy heard of it he had been enraged and swore to kill Andrew. Apart from a letter eloquently expressing his contrition, Star had heard nothing of Andrew Fordyce since.

That most traumatic of times in her life, as well as the fond and pleasant memories of life at Glenmulloch, was on Star's mind as she drove down to Kirkconnel that weekend with her son James. Wullie Cameron was waiting by the smallholding road-end, his best shepherd's crook, the one with the carved head of a thistle, in hand. Both he and his wife Anne were overjoyed at seeing Star again, for in the years she had lived at Glenmulloch they had come to think of her as a member of their family. Their own only child, also a girl, had died of meningitis as an infant.

'God, ye cannae hide money, Star,' Wullie Cameron said as she stepped from the neat BMW saloon. 'The city must be doing you well, lass. I never thought I'd see the day when our "vac" would be driving about in something like this . . . and looking like she does. That's a fine looking boy you've got with you there, Star. Guid pair of shoulders on him. Would be handy about the farm.'

'Oh, you've never changed a bit, Wullie. Always looking at people's build and thinking how good they'd be at working. You don't need muscle anymore now though. . . everything's mechanised, isn't it?'

They reminisced together late into the night about the old days and life as it had been up on Glenmulloch, where there had been a Cameron family for seven generations. Star asked Wullie if he missed his old home. 'Guid God, no' now, lass. I'm too old for the herding and all that needs doing up there. They might have all their machinery now, but they cannae afford workers and the man who runs Glenmulloch does everything by himself. Anyway, when I'm working about my wee place here I can still look up and see it away up there on the hillside and that gives me a lot of satisfaction. And when it comes the time, I'll have a good view of Glenmulloch from that plot in the graveyard just up the road that's specially reserved for a' us Camerons – they thocht, ye see, that it was aye a guid idea to keep an eye on the young yins.'

'Oh, tuts now, Wullie, what kind of talk is that you're giving Star? You make an awfy lot o' things up. Don't you listen to him, Star. He's just a havering auld thing at times.'

Star told them some of the things she wanted to do when she was there, including taking young James for walks up the old Lime Road, a track that went by the old colliery and up through Samsiston and Neviston farms to Glenmulloch. 'I want to show him what it's like guddling for trout in the burns. And the birds are nesting just now. I want to show him that too. There's so much for a young lad in the country.'

'Will you be coming to the kirk with us in the morn?' asked Anne Cameron, white-haired now and stooped.

'Do you know, I never thought about that. I'm like the majority of Protestants, I suppose. I'd like to think I'm a good Christian, I certainly try to be but never seem somehow to get round to going to church.'

'You used to always go with me,' said Anne Cameron.

'Oh, I remember. Little St Conal's, just as you enter the village. When you were speaking to the minister I'd be going round reading all the old gravestones. There's the one for the railway poet – what was his name? – yes, Alexander Anderson. Another for the shepherd who the stone says died because he had been buried beneath the snow with his flock. And I remember seeing the Glenmul-loch one, though I didn't realise it was facing our hill. There I go . . . calling it "our" hill as though I still lived up there!'

'Oh, aye, lass, I think like me there's still a part of you living up there,' said Wullie.

'I suppose I could come,' Star replied. 'It'll be another "first" for young James here. He's never been . . . at least not with me. There's been a couple of times with the school.'

'Oh my God, Star, is that no' something terrible,' gasped Anne Cameron. 'A boy of that age and he's never set foot in a kirk! Star, you should be ashamed of yourself.'

She held her hands up in disbelief when Star explained that had her life taken the course that it had been following when he was born, James would have in all probability been a Muslim.

'I take it Reverend Archie McMath has retired? He was getting on.'

'Oh, aye. Long since. It's Mr Fordyce we have now.'

Anne Cameron could see the quizzical look on Star's face. 'Yes, Star. Mr Fordyce. The Reverend Andrew Fordyce.'

CHAPTER 42

A TIME FOR FORGIVENESS?

THE LITTLE BOY WAS FASCINATED WITH HIS first visit to a cemetery. He was chattering excitedly about the wording and the ancient scroll on the gravestones, and asking endless questions of the elderly couple he called Aunt Annie and Uncle Willie.

They had all emerged together from the little country church and after mixing with a variety of groups and renewing old acquaintances, Star had been introduced to the minister, Reverend Andrew Fordyce. The older couple left them talking together while they accompanied the boy.

There was still a soldierly air about the man who had once been a regular officer with the Highland Light Infantry. He stood erect, occasionally running his hand through his long and dark, wavy hair and looking intently at the woman who had figured in his life in a more dramatic fashion than any other person. Yet, it had been such a fleeting episode. She was a woman he didn't know; merely a passing encounter that had inspired a momentary deed.

'Before I say anything, Star . . . did you ever get my letter?' When she said she had, he replied that made him pleased. 'I say that before I even inquire about your thoughts. I just wanted to know that you knew what mine were at the time I wrote that letter. They haven't altered since, apart from the fact that my contrition has never diminished. I suppose you got a surprise when you heard I was the minister here?'

'How did you know I'd be told?'

'Well, you better than most are aware of how a shepherd knows his flock. I know mine like I would my family and when Annie Cameron said you were coming down for a few days I knew she'd tell you who the minister was. I've obviously been concerned about what your reaction might be. At least you did come to the service . . . knowing. I suppose that says something – I wouldn't have been surprised had you not been here today. But I'm so glad that you are.'

'Why?'

The directness of her quick response surprised him. It was not the kind of reply he would have expected . . . one that demanded an answer. But then he didn't know what to expect of this woman.

'Well, obviously it has haunted me all these years . . . what you thought after the letter and if you'd ever even considered, dare I say it, forgiveness.'

'I'd be an unusual person if I hadn't considered it . . . or else one with a heart of stone.'

'Even a heart of the softest flesh would be pardoned for not finding room for forgiveness in such circumstances.'

'Oh, I think there has been room all right, Mr Fordyce . . .'

'Andrew . . . please.'

'As you will . . . Andrew. But having the room for forgiveness and expressing it are two very different things. I mean, I hope you didn't think that if and when we ever met again I'd say something like, well, it's been a long time, Andrew, but all is forgiven. It'd be a rather pat thing to say . . . would it not? How many years is it?'

Her forthrightness startled him and he was glad she had

followed a question which would have been difficult to answer with one to which there was an easy reply.

'Twenty-two years, Star. That's when I came to see you in the Gorbals.'

'Yes, and it was six years before that . . .'

Their eyes met, then he averted her gaze, looking down before returning to the subject to which she had obviously given much thought.

'I didn't mean, Star, for you to say all is forgiven, or even anything like that. More important to me is that you know how I feel . . . how I felt when I wrote the letter. Forgiving, I know, doesn't just come with the words. It begins with understanding.'

'And how does it end?'

'With more understanding, I suppose.'

'And not the expression of a simple two-word sentence . . . I forgive?'

'No . . . not necessarily.'

'Or not at all?'

'I think it would need to come in some form but not necessarily those two words. Burns described it as "the torturing, gnawing consciousness of guilt" and when you've experienced it like I have for more than a quarter of a century then it takes a lot more, Star, than just two words to absolve it. But one does seek it. It says in the Psalms, "Blessed is he whose transgression is forgiven, whose sin is covered." I may be a minister of the Church of Scotland, but because of my folly as a youth I have never felt blessed.'

'Then I feel for you . . . I do.'

There was much to this lady, he thought. The challenge she had given him in their short conversation was more than a surprise. The memory of the night he and his brother wantonly tried to ravage her was only a blur; it was the realisation that had left the raw scars. But there were other memories of this girl with the unusual name. There were the times he had watched her at work in the fields near Lydeburn; a fetching young woman, he had thought then, albeit that she was a mere girl in her teens. Sometimes she was the shepherdess with dogs running at her commands, her long, dark red hair flowing in the wind; at other times the servant, carrying the big picnic basket to the fields for the workers' tea breaks. There had been a sensuality about her, even at such a distance. She was bright too. When you had the background of a Perthshire boarding school and your home was such a splendid fine place as Lydeburn, you did not expect a Gorbals girl to confront you with such flair of conception and reasoning as she had done today. It was a curse, he knew, that people conceived such impressions but it was a fact of life that they did. It was time to change the subject.

'Mother still speaks of you.'

'Oh, she's keeping well then?'

'She's in her mid-seventies now, but hale and hearty and very alert.'

'Yes, I'll always remember the conversation we had together . . . before I left to return to Glasgow. Tell me, has she absolved you? Has she ever come out and said, "All is forgiven, son"?'

There was a direct look with the question and he thought there were still more depths to this woman than he first imagined.

'You put it very bluntly, Star. But in the context of everything it's a fair question, I must admit. And to be honest, I've never really thought of it as pointedly as that. She does forgive me. I know that. But she's never said as much. I know she understands that the person who was Andrew Fordyce then is not the Andrew Fordyce that lives today.'

'But we all change . . .'

'Star, the furthest thing from my mind is to try and seek excuses . . . to plead that it was because of something that had nothing to do with me. I could have soothed my

323

conscience a long time ago by convincing myself of that. I could even have ended up believing it. Instead, I faced up to the fact that there was no excuse.'

'Was becoming a minister anything to do with you seeking solace?'

He smiled. 'If that was the case, I'd be a real sham of a minister. No, I became a minister because that was the way of my mind. Robbie's death started it. As I tried to explain in my letter, I seemed to inherit his whole psyche after he was killed. It was as though he'd taken possession of my soul. And when I went to Palestine the reappraisals which he was having about his own future continued with me. We'd a terrible job to do in Palestine ... to keep Muslim away from Jew and Jew from Muslim. And there we were, in the Holy Lands, keeping the peace ... with our guns. There had to be another way, I thought, and then one day while on the slopes of Mount Sinai, at the very spot where they said Moses had received the Law from God, I vowed I'd dedicate the rest of my life to being a man of peace. And I did.'

'And a man of understanding, Andrew?'

'Yes ... and a man of understanding.'

'Then you'll understand my feelings.'

'I do ... very much. But I'd be happier if you appreciated mine.'

'Were you expressing them today in your service?'

'You listened intently.'

'I don't miss much.'

'I didn't mean them to be too direct, as it were. Only appropriate. And were they?'

'Yes. I liked your reading.'

'Did you think it appropriate?'

She paused at that, not answering immediately. 'Yes, Andrew. Perhaps you could say it was ... appropriate.' She paused again before adding, 'And welcome.'

He had read from the Ecclesiastes, the chapter based on

the theme of there being an appropriate time for everything. 'To everything there is a season, and a time to every
purpose under the heaven.' He had said it with much
feeling and she had overheard some of the congregation
remarking on it when they had gathered outside the church
after the service.

He was saying how pleased he was that she had enjoyed
the service when the Camerons returned with young James.
Star held out her hand, saying, 'Pleased to have met you
again, Andrew. Annie here is always saying you never
know what a day brings. It's certainly been a surprising
one for me.'

'And a revealing one for me,' he replied. 'I hope you and
young James can attend my services again.'

She gave him a warm smile but said nothing further.

The previous evening, after the shock revelation about
Andrew Fordyce being the local minister, Star and Annie
Cameron had sat by the fire talking. Wullie had been to
Mac's Bar and had gone to bed early, slightly tipsy. 'That's
a life in the hills for you,' Annie Cameron had said. 'He's
never had a pub near him in his life and now there's one
just a mile or so down the road and he loves nothing better
than a pint or two.'

Star was eager to know about the reaction locally when
Andrew Fordyce had returned to the district. 'It caused
quite a rumpus in this village, I can tell you,' said Annie
Cameron. 'When the Reverend McMath intimated he was
going to retire, we advertised in the usual fashion, under
"Pulpit Supply" in the *Standard* and in that paper from
Glasgow all the farmers buy. We'd a good number of
applications and a committee was set up at the kirk to
discuss them. And, of course, the name Fordyce leapt right
out of the hat. Wullie was on the committee and he says
he's never seen such scenes among elders of a kirk. Some
were saying they'd never have the man in their kirk, and
others that we're supposed to be about Christianity and

here was a boy from our very midst, who came from one of our best families and wanted to come back and be among us, and here they were rejecting him. Oh, the debate went on for a good few weeks. People fell out over it and there was lots of bad feeling. But we won the day.'

'You and Wullie were in favour, then?'

'Goodness, aye, lass. How could we have been otherwise? He was volunteering to come into the lions' den, as it were. The man must have had some courage to do that. Fortunately good sense prevailed and we let him be our minister. Well, we had to, didn't we? You can't live in the past. It's only Christian to forgive and forget, after all.

'Now, everyone's saying that they'd been for him right from the start, because he's turned out to be one of the finest we've ever had. He gets round his parish all right. Never fails with the sick or them that's in need of comfort. Nothing high and mighty about him. The miners were all for him as well, and more so now; he fights for all their causes and he's never off the back of the MP and others about getting more jobs for the district. Oh, we chose the right one all right, Star.'

'And what about Mrs Fordyce?'

'Of course, aye, you'll not know about that. Lovely lassie. A Sanquhar girl. She died having their first bairn. And the wean was lost as well.'

Star had lay awake for hours that night, first of all reliving yet again, just as she had relived it so many times before, the day she had been attacked by the two Fordyce boys, the day that stood out more than any other in her entire life. It was always on instant recall, always fresh, always vivid; oh yes, horrendously vivid. And when the memory was rekindled it was always accompanied with feelings of fear and anger. Always. Somehow she had never thought about forgiveness. But should she? Would perhaps another feeling dispel that horrible blot, that ugly stain, that was always there when she thought of the past? She was now in a new phase of her life, one where the terrible threat of Sonny Riley had been dispensed with and all the struggles of the past few years seemed to have been overcome. The future had never looked so promising. Why then should this one foul memory linger on as it did? Perhaps there really was a time to cast away stones . . . a time to love. If the memory of that day was always to be as bitter as it was, should it not be that all thoughts of it could in some way be dissolved? It was fear and anger on which that day thrived, therefore might it not wither and die with feelings of forgiveness and love? Of course it would, she thought; just why had she taken so long to come to such a painfully obvious conclusion? It had to be the way . . . hadn't it? Forgiveness. And love too?

CHAPTER 43

AULD LANG SYNE

CLANEY AND ALEX MITCHELL HAD COME HOME
on one of the charter flights which left New York and
Newark airports mainly carrying members of the various
Scottish clubs in Kearny. Other flights were also winging
their way from Toronto in Canada for the same reason –
within the next week was the biggest event in the Scottish
calendar, Hogmanay. And as part of the great annual
celebration there was also the most important fixture on
the national sporting calendar, the Rangers and Celtic
football match.

No matter how much they loved their homes in the New
World, no matter the prosperity which life there had
brought them, no matter the new friendships they had
made or that their children were as American as the Sons
and Daughters of the Revolution, there were always those
moments when, in solitude, they would think emotionally
of the place that really meant home to them. And there
was no time the emotions flowed stronger than at the
approaching New Year. It was then that Mother Glasgow
would beckon most of all.

In anticipation of those special moments the celebrations
had already begun on the charter flight from Newark, New
Jersey, to Prestwick, near Glasgow, which would give this
plane-load of exiled Scots a week or so in their homeland.

'How long is it then, Alex?' Claney had asked Mitchell on the flight.

'Over thirteen years now. Autumn 1957, and everything I know about the place was what was happening at the time when I left. I've never bothered to get the papers sent or anything like that. Tell you who was my favourite singer when I left . . . Nancy Whisky! Remember her . . . the Queen of Skiffle? A great turn. We'd a holiday that year to the Isle of Man. We flew there and back from Prestwick and it cost six quid. Then just before I left we went to every show we could, thinking, well, that's it, sort of stuff. Didn't know when or even if we'd ever see them again. And we saw Ma Logan at the Metropole. They tell me it got burned down? Great wee place. Remember the smashing shows they used to have with a real waterfall and the singers jumping about in the heather? Jimmy Logan was with Stanley Baxter and David Hughes in *Five Past Eight* at the Alhambra, and there was Lita Roza belting it out at the Empire. And I went to see my last game . . . the League Cup final at Hampden Park. More than 100,000 there and I should have stayed at home. D'you remember the score? Rangers got tanked rotten by Celtic . . . seven – one. Bet the Tims are still singing about it . . .'

'You'll be dying to see your old place?'

Mitchell shrugged nonchalantly. 'My old place has gone. We lived up in the Rotten Row, Townhead. A throughgaun' close.'

'God. Remember them!' said Claney. 'Cumberland Lane in the Gorbals was like that. Now that was the real ancient Gorbals. Bloody terrible as well. It was like hiding one row of houses behind another.'

'Aye, and to get to your row of houses you'd to go through somebody's close in the main street.'

'D'you know, they couldn't even get a hearse to the ones in Cumberland Lane? There was one pend but it was too narrow. They couldn't even turn the hearse round. They'd to unhitch the horses and then push the hearse up the lane to get near a house where there was a body. That was when I was a boy, like.'

'Primitive, wasn't it! Anyway, our old place is all away now. I don't know how I'll take to it all. When I left Glasgow it was like leaving an old house that you were finished with. You went out, shut the door and that was it. All you care about for the rest of your life is the new place . . . and that's what Kearny is for me. The "bells" will be good though, and then the game on the Saturday. Great!'

'Aye, I'm looking forward to that more than anything,' said Claney enthusiastically. 'I'm not a big fan . . . I don't take all this Rangers-Celtic stuff seriously. Like you and Sammy, I like to see the Rangers winning but you couldn't call me a Blue Nose . . . you know, going about chanting about Catholics and the like?'

'I know. They're mad . . . the bigot bams. Thank Christ they forgot all about that when they came to Kearny,' said Mitchell.

'Oh, aye. We're best without it in Kearny. See me, I just treat the game as a big laugh. See some of the characters that go to it – absolutely magic! I was at one with Sammy once. He's good value at them. I like his patter. I spoke to him the other night on the phone. He sounds his old self again. Bounced right back. That home improvements business he started up went like a bomb, he says, and he's worth a packet again, though he didn't exactly say that. You know Sammy. But you can tell. You can't hide money, as they say. All his troubles seem to be behind him now, specially since he got the Riley man fixed up. God, that was some caper. I'm looking forward to seeing him again. Great old bugger.'

'How old'll he be now, Claney?'

'Believe it or not he's nearly seventy. No. I'll take that back. Sounds better when you say he's in his sixties.'

'Why's that?'

''Cause he's the same age as me!'

CHAPTER 44

THE GATHERING

IT'S ENACTED IN THE NAME OF FOOTBALL. BUT the passion it arouses has little to do with sport; it's that brand of passion only divided religion can generate, displaying as it does a hatred between the two camps of followers the depth of which cannot be matched in any other aspect of Scottish life. Some say that if every man entering the park was issued with a rifle, the result would be like the Somme revisited.

Sammy, Claney and Mitchell's affiliation with Rangers could be equated with that relationship which so many Protestants have with their church. They don't participate in its services, but it's always there when required. The three friends could be called supporters, but it was years since any of them had been to a game. Today, they had met by arrangement for their first drink, in a little pub just off Brig'ton Cross, that particular landmark having sort of Dome on the Rock significance to legions of Rangers supporters.

It was before midday and the bars had only been open for about half an hour. There were loud shouts as each turned up, the mid-Atlantic tones of the two visitors disintegrating to a mere trace in the excitement of their home-coming. They shouted old greetings to each other and to others who recognised their well-known faces.

'How's it gaun', auld yin?' was the welcome they had given Sammy when he had arrived just after eleven-thirty. 'And cop the coat,' Claney added, stroking the elegant, neat-fitting blue nap with its velvet collar. 'That's something else, Sammy. Bet that cost you more than a ton. Where'd you get it?'

'You know me, boys, I don't like to boast . . . but seeing you ask, it cost a ton and a bit and I got it in Paisley's. Nothing but the best.'

'You wouldn't cop me wearing a coat like that to Ibrox,' said Mitchell. 'Last time I remember being there it was dungarees you would have needed . . . and a pair of fisherman's wellies to get into the toilets. Bet it hasn't changed.'

'Tell you what, boys,' came back Sammy. 'You could be doing with a couple of coats like this. It's bloody freezing out there.'

They ordered doubles to start with, on the grounds that because of the cold they needed that wee bit extra whisky. 'Just to get the fires started,' as Sammy said.

They spoke about the prospect of the game and how the teams had been faring. 'You'd be the last one of us at an Old Firm game?' said Mitchell to Sammy.

'Aye, that could be right,' he replied with a roguish smile. 'A wee fellow called Alan Morton was doing all the scoring. Do you know if Waddell's picked him for the team today?'

They laughed heartily – the Rangers' legend had last played for the club in 1933.

'Where're you staying?' Sammy asked Mitchell.

'Got a sister in the schemes. You want to have heard the neighbours last night . . . they all ended up hammering into each other. And that was them celebrating the New Year! God Almighty!'

'Aye, an' that was just his sister and her pals,' jibed Claney, and they roared with laughter and set up another round of doubles.

'I couldnae afford to live here again,' said Mitchell. 'Whisky was thirty-seven and a tanner when I left and now you're paying two pounds ten bob for it. It's twenty-five bob for a dozen cans of lager and four bob for twenty ciggies. Daylight robbery! Another thing . . . See the size of a bottle of whisky here! The Yanks wouldn't entertain them that size. They'd treat them like miniatures. I wouldnae dream of buying anything smaller than a litre bottle . . . and I usually get half a gallon!'

'Ah, but you don't get *Z-Cars* and *Steptoe and Son* on the telly. See what you're missing!'

'But we get Perry Como and Dinah Shore, and see *The Untouchables*! Would run *Z-Cars* right out the park any day. And your drink's still daylight robbery.'

'It was that bastard with the pipe and the Gannex that started it,' maintained Sammy. 'Prices have never been as bad. Ted Heath's going to be a better Prime Minister.'

'He was at the Playhouse with his band the last time I went to the dancing there,' cut in Claney, and they laughed even louder.

The floodgates of the best of their memory-lane recollections were opened. Each in turn contributed the name of a different band that had been their favourite all those years ago. 'Oscar Rabin' . . . 'Geraldo' . . . 'Jack Parnell' . . . 'Billy Ternent' . . . 'Joe Loss'.

Then it was the places they danced.

'You couldnae beat the Denny Palais . . .'

'Away ye go, the Plaza had a' the class . . .'

'The Albert was for the real dancers like me . . .'

'Don't tell me you went there . . . one of the patent dance pumps-in-a-brown-poke-under-the-arm brigade?'

'That was me and proud of it.'

'It was the West End Ballroom for the real lumbers . . .'

'Christ, even Frankenstein could get a lumber there. The Locarno was a lot better place. Better talent.'

'Were you there the night of the riot with the Yanks . . .?'

'Aye. It was every Friday.'

'I thought it was every fuckin' night . . .!'

'Did you ever lumber big Onga . . .?'

'Big Onga the darkie . . .?'

'Who didnae . . .?'

'I didnae . . . that's how I never had to go to Black Street . . .'

'Ah, but you don't remember the Parlour . . .'

'Oh, Christ, Sammy, you're going way back to the Dark Ages . . .'

'Better than the darkie ages . . .!'

'Ah, but I remember the one we called the Tripe in Tradeston . . . the room was that wee they had to stick the band up on a shelf . . .'

'What about the old Coffin up past the Gushetfaulds . . . they used to take the razors off them at the door and they could collect them when they left again. See the Wild West! Fuckin' Disneyland compared to Glasgow back in the Thirties . . .'

'Hey, barman . . . another round.'

'What's this fuckin' "barman" stuff?' joked Sammy. 'See the look he gave you! They don't like being called "barman" here. Did you think you were back in Kearny talking to Big Hamish? Great character, so he is. How's he getting on anyway?'

'Runs a bar in New York now . . .'

'Christ, I'd like to hear him recite some of his book of facts at the Bowery Belle . . .'

Just as Sammy said that, an explosion of musicians stormed into the little pub, some with accordions, some with flutes and one with a big bass drum, carrying the name of the band painted in bright blue: 'Sandy Row True Blues'. The boys from Ulster had arrived, about thirty of them, dressed to a man with their red, white and blue Rangers scarves and caps.

'Oh, Christ,' shouted Sammy, barely audible above the din of the music, the singing and the loud voices. 'Here come the bad boys from Belfast. See this lot! They'd make Fullerton's Billy Boys sound like Tims. Look at them, bare arms and it's fuckin' freezing outside. That's to show their King Billy and Red Hand tattoos. They think they've come home when they come over here. But they're good boys . . . a right laugh, so they are.' Then he shouted a welcome to them, 'How's it gaun', boys?'

There were other shouts of encouragement from around the bar and the pub's regulars as well as Sammy thrust brimming pint glasses into the men's hands. The pub suddenly became a party.

Mitchell turned to shout to Sammy, 'You're showing your true colours now, you old Blue Nose bastard.' Then the three of them joined in the lusty singing that had started up.

> *Then fight . . . and don't surr . . . enn . . . der . . .*
> *But come when duty calls . . .*
> *With heart in hand and sword and shield . . .*
> *We'll guard old Derry's walls . . .*

A great cheer rang out from everyone in the pub, one small section adding their one one-word chorus of 'Die . . . die . . . die!'

'Christ, but you've got to see the funny side of it all,' laughed Sammy. The three men were smiling broadly. 'Can you imagine the look on his face,' said Claney, 'if some punter walked in wearing a green and white scarf?'

'There's nobody *that* mental,' said Sammy.

They had just finished their third round of doubles and chasers when Claney shook his head and turned to Sammy. 'Don't know about you, auld yin, but I'll need to go for a walk. My head's spinning and I want to be fit for a good bevvy during the game.'

'Aye, so do I,' said Sammy.

'Fancy a walk up town? Might do some shopping.'

'Good idea,' said Sammy.

'I want to go and see some chinas,' said Mitchell. 'Where'll we meet?'

Sammy had the reply in an instant. 'The Clachan . . . Paisley Road West . . . two o'clock . . . a bevvy and a carry-oot. . .'

The musicians struck up again and everyone in the bar took up the song. It was the one they knew and loved best of all.

> *It is old and it is beautiful,*
> *Its colours they are fine . . .*

The three friends turned to each other and joined in to finish the song.

> *My father wore it as a youth,*
> *In bygone days of yore,*
> *And it's on The Twelfth . . . I love to wear,*
> *The Sash my father wore.*

Jostling their way to the door, they cheered and shouted and stamped their feet as the great cry went up – 'Come away the 'Gers!'

CHAPTER 45

INTO VALHALLA

IT WAS THEIR ARENA OF SUBLIME JOY AND
happiness, their amphitheatre of supreme affection, a sub-
stitute for the kind of place to which religious zealots would
go to touch and kiss and revere. At times it was also the
abode of the arch-enemy who looked upon it as the bastion
of bigotry. Ibrox Stadium in Glasgow could be all things to
all men.

They arrived there more than half an hour before the
three o'clock kick-off, having met at The Clachan for more
drinks, and bought their carry-outs for the game. As they
were early, Sammy had suggested that instead of going
straight into the big bowl they should go round to the main
door entrance of the impressive red-brick stadium in
Edmiston Drive.

'What for?' inquired Claney.

'Well, you two are over to see everything you can, so you
might as well come round and see some of the characters,'
said Sammy. 'They're ten a penny there. All the camel-
hair brigade. Might see somebody you know.'

'You mean, somebody *you* know?'

'Well, what's the odds? We've plenty time.'

The camel-hair mob, as Sammy called them, were the
Flash Harrys who had made the grade in life. There was

no shortage of second-hand car dealers, scrap-yard mer-
chants, bookmakers, those who said they did 'this-and-
that' as well of those with faces that blatantly said, 'Ask no
questions' among them. They each had one thing in
common. Money. The newest of new money. Every man of
them would have an up-a-close background but had hit the
magic seam in one way or another. When you were of their
mould there was no finer place in all the world to show you
had made it than outside the hallowed doors of the
cherished Ibrox Stadium. That small stretch of roadway
where they would congregate outside its main door was
their very own Hall of Fame. Sammy Nelson would have
been a nobleman among them, for few had made more
than him, but it wasn't his style to show it. He preferred to
look at the others showing it.

They were there aplenty for this day of days, milling
around, some standing in little groups, others on their own,
looking for that bit of recognition they worshipped more
than anything but their money could buy. Perhaps one of
the well-known byline sports writers or one of the new
breed of sports commentators they called 'stars' because
they appeared on television would pass and give them a
nod. They liked that. Or maybe a smile from one of the
star ex-players. They liked that even better. Or the chance
that one of the directors, the real powerhouse people of
Rangers, the bluest of all the Blue Noses, would stop for a
word.

'It's never changed, has it, boys?' said Sammy.

'Aye, you're right,' nodded Claney. 'You'd think they'd
all come straight from McLaren's or Carswell's, the
outfitters.'

'Do they hire out their camel-hair coats?' joked Mitchell.
'I just cannae get away with them wearing gear like that to
come to Ibrox!'

'Ah, but it's nice where they go,' said Sammy. 'John, the
man himself, asked me to a game one time and I sat with

him in the members' section of the stand in there. Real toffs' stuff, so it is. You get a wee bevvy before the game, tea in china cups, a City Bakeries fern cake at half-time and the waitresses are in black with wee lace aprons. All very sedate and pan-loaf. Till they take their seats out on the stand. Christ, you should hear the ham sandwich! We were playing Motherwell that day and losing two–one. You should have heard them! I thought they were bad on the terracing till I got an ear-load of this lot. I mean, I've heard the real hate stuff but this lot were for exterminating them. Every player in the Motherwell side was cursed upside down for being a Fenian bastard. Motherwell . . . for Christ sake! Most of their boys were Proddies at the time but that didn't matter. Because they were duffing the 'Gers they were called all the Papish fuckers under the sun. And the worst of the lot were these dandy bastards here with their sheepskin and camel-hair coats, flashing the new identity bracelets they're all wearing. That's their mentality. Somebody says it's the style to stick your name on a bit of gold and wrap it round your wrist and these daft bastards fall over each other to fork up a hundred nicker a time for it.'

'It's what you call an identity crisis,' quipped Claney, then, nudging Sammy, 'Hey, take a look at who's at the door. Wee Erchie McWilliams.'

'Christ, so it is. Look at the state of him. That's a fuckin' officer's coat he's wearing . . . the wee cunt was a private in the Pioneer Corps. Can hardly write his name and the last time I was talking to him he was trying to be a' toffee-nosed, telling me about the problem he has parking his Merc. Not his car, mind you. His Merc. They've got to tell you what they're driving.'

'Maybe he's hoping to get a nod from the manager when he goes in?'

'Wee bastard'll be lucky to get a nod from the doorman.'

'Who's that big one with the rolled umbrella and the bowler?'

'He writes for the papers,' said Sammy. 'I was introduced to him up in the tea-room that day I was in the members' section. They call him Willie. And they say it that polite way. No' Wullie. Willie. I had a few words with him. Lives in the Kelvin Court and talks like it. After he went away John was telling me that any time the 'Gers lose he goes away in the huff. Goes straight back to his office and doesn't speak to a soul. They say he doesnae even talk to his editor. Yet look at him. The old school tie, better dressed than the Duke of Argyll but pure Hun at heart.' Then he laughed. 'Just as well we're all good boys!'

'Right,' said Claney. 'This bag of booze is knackering my arms. C'mon, let's get round to the terracing and get a place.'

'Aye, and see the real people,' said Mitchell.

The real people were standing, just as they had done since football had begun in Scotland a hundred years before. Nothing needed to change; the fans came in their thousands the way it was. There were more than 70,000 of them that day. Conditions may have been primitive, but you did as you were told in Scotland, and if the football establishment said this was to be the way of it, then so be it. They were the masters of their sport and they were not to be argued with.

The three men headed for the area of the stadium known officially as the East End. But no one who wore the red, white and blue colours of Rangers ever called it by that name. To them it was the Rangers End, just as the opposite West End was known as the Celtic End.

They entered the ground by climbing up the steep stairway marked number 13 and when they reached the highest point they could see the entire stadium.

'Say what you like about it, boys,' said Sammy, as they

stood for a minute to take in the scene, 'but there's a sight
for you. It's like being gathered round the Black Stone.'

'What black stone?'

'The one in Mecca that a' the Arabs go to every year.
Saw it on a TV documentary a couple of nights ago. It was
just like this, only they were all wearing sheets.'

He was right about it being a sight. Despite everything,
the freezing weather, the cramped conditions, the abysmal
lack of facilities, the big stadium with a 70,000 crowd on a
Rangers and Celtic day was indeed quite a spectacle. The
mid-winter light was already dimming and the powerful
floodlights were on, shedding a flattering brilliance over
the big arena.

Across the park, the green and white of the Celtic
supporters' scarves and flags merged to give the high
terracing a greenish hue, diffused every now and then as
another cloud of blue cigarette smoke wafted up as though
exhaled in unison. Before them, in the sweep of the steep
terrace, were their own fans, barely one without some
identifying badge of blue, whether a rosette, a cap, or a
scarf, and sprinkled among them the would-be hardest of
hard men, wearing only a blue T-shirt or short-sleeved
team jersey.

The three friends followed the usual routine of finding a
place to stand by walking down one of the passageways of
the steep terrace until there appeared to be a gap big
enough for them to push their way in. There was never any
room near kick-off time at such a game. You merely
followed the routine of pushing, heaving and shoving until
the crowd around you compressed some more and you won
yourself the one square foot of territory deemed sufficient
for a spectator.

'I'm glad we brought that extra bevvy,' said Claney as
he passed round the half bottles of whisky and cans of beer.
'You need something on a day like this to warm you up.

Bloody freezing, so it is. You'd think they'd turn the heating on.'

'They haven't paid their electric bills,' wisecracked Mitchell.

'Aw, come on, boys ... are you not soaking up the atmosphere?' Sammy pleaded.

'Is that what you call it?' replied Claney. 'Some bastard nearly peed in my shoes there. How's that for atmosphere?'

'Och, it would have warmed up your feet for you, Claney,' laughed Sammy.

The pipe band brought some cheer to the crowd as everyone settled into their places on the packed terracing. But the fans knew better than to expect anything that smacked of razzmatazz. This wasn't showbusiness. This was Scottish socccr. So they improvised. The Celtic fans teased with their Irish and Catholic songs and flaunted the flag that infuriated, the tricolour of the Irish Republic, bringing out the worst in the Rangers fans, who responded with insults about the Pope, priests and anything that smacked of Catholicism.

The fans around Sammy and his mates were chanting 'If you hate the fuckin' Pope ... clap your hands' to the tune of *Coming Round the Mountain*. It made Claney laugh.

'You're right, Sammy. You've definitely got to see the funny side of it. Imagine taking this lot seriously!'

The fan standing swaying beside him, who had obviously spent much more time in the pub that morning than they had, turned to Claney and said, 'They're bastards.'

'Who?'

'Them o'er there,' he replied, nodding in the direction of the Celtic fans on the opposite terracing. 'They're the bastards that are bastards. And d'you know what? They huvnae won a Ne'erday game here for half a century. And they're gonnie get fuckin' tanked the day. Come away the 'Gers. You fuckin' beauties. Here ... huv a drink.'

They jumped in the air as the blue-shirted team came

running out. 'Keep the fuckin' heid, boys,' Sammy shouted to some younger fans. They laughed good-naturedly in response, one of them joking to his pals, 'Hey youse, mind these auld pensioners here, boys,' but they were more interested in shouting about what was happening on the field.

'There's big Derek. Come on, Derek. Gie it tae them, Derek.'

Big Derek was their new hero. Just seventeen, tall and handsome, he had headed the goal that had won the vital match against Celtic in the League Cup final. In terms of heroes, they didn't come much better than that.

'Stick it on them like you did in the Cup,' they shouted and the mention of the Cup had them singing to the tune of *Coming Round the Mountain* again:

> *There is no holy water in the Cup,*
> *There is no holy water in the Cup,*
> *There is no holy water, no fuckin' holy water,*
> *There is no holy water in the Cup.*

They ended it with their favourite chant of all. 'Fuck the Pope!'

The sub-freezing temperatures of the previous few days had transformed the playing surface; the normally soft and pliable turf where the players could exercise their footballing art and display their spectacular sliding tackles, was concrete-hard and bumpy. It was so firm it rejected the grip of studded soccer boots and they had to don rubber-soled trainers instead. Heavy tackles were out, as falling on that ground in these conditions would mean serious injury. Nevertheless, when the referee blew his whistle for half-time, the fans seemed happy enough. There had been no goals, but each set of supporters took the attitude that while they might not be winning, the great thing was . . . they weren't losing.

Alex Mitchell struggled out from where they were standing to get some hot pies from the catering stall at the top of the terracing. There was the usual chaotic scramble around the stall in order to get served and the game was just about to resume by the time he returned. The pies were almost cold.

'You'd have thought they'd have given us at least one goal after us coming 3,000 miles,' Claney said.

'Give us some goals!' exclaimed Mitchell. 'More like it, you'd think they'd give us some fuckin' seats. This is primitive standing here like bloody sardines. Prehistoric, so it is. When're they gonnie learn here? See over by, at the American football! Spot on, so it is. All right, it takes you about five years to get used to the game. Play one minute, stop for two and all that kind of stuff. But you eventually get the hang of it. And see the way they treat you! Different class. I go with the family. Meet the mates from work outside the ballpark before the game, bring the portable barbecues and have a big nosh up and a couple of bottles of wine while the kids play with each other. Then it's inside for pre-match entertainment. Everybody gets a decent seat and guys come round all the time with coke, popcorn and hot dogs. And I'm talking about *hot* dogs . . . no' bloody freezing pies. Spoil you rotten over there. An announcer even comes on and welcomes you to the park. That's right, they actually welcome you. Not like here. Know something? I think they'd rather we weren't here. The punters are just a fucking nuisance to that mob up there that runs this game. What do they give them? I'll tell you . . . SFA. That's what you get here. Sweet Fuck All. Just look at the state of this fuckin' place . . . guys peein' in their beer cans or down the back of your leg. Prehistoric, Sammy. That's what it is. Prehistoric.'

'But the patter's good, Alex,' replied Sammy, and Mitchell's growing anger instantly subdued.

'Well, maybe they'll give us a goal in the second half.'

Two supporters beside him heard the remark.

'Don't you worry, son,' one said. 'We're gonnie tank these Fenian bastards over there. Look at them. Wi' their fuckin' IRA flags up. See that. That gets my fuckin' dander up.' And to prove that it had he let out a bellow of a roar. 'Fuckin' Fenian Papish bastards.'

'See me,' said his pal. 'I widnae let the bastards into our ground. Fuckin' animals the lot of them. Here, boys . . .'

He turned and proffered a full whisky bottle. They were fellow fans, after all, companions of a cause, brothers of a bond, people who had no time for 'these people' across the park.

A thin mist-fog was descending in the airless night, mixing with the cumulus of tobacco smoke, even more dense now than at the beginning of the game. The second half had started and there were no more conversations, just the shouts directed at players, encouragement for the ones in blue, discouragement laced with invective and abuse for the ones in green. At the very least, they were all bastards, and that went for the referee and the linesmen too. The legitimacy of a decision was never questioned. If it was for their team it was just. If it was against them it was wrong. Unquestionably wrong.

An honest arbiter would have said Celtic were the better team on the day. Although they had not proved the issue by scoring a goal, they made most scoring chances and looked the likelier winners. Little Jimmy Johnstone was coping with the unplayable surface better than most and providing his team with some great opportunities. But when neither team had scored with only a handful of minutes left, thousands were turning their backs on the big day out, heading for the exits. There was only one thing worse than a half-time cold pie and that was a goalless draw.

Sammy and his friends considered leaving, but Alex Mitchell, surprisingly, voted for staying.

'Thought you'd be dying to get away,' said Sammy.

'Not on your Nelly. I want to remember just how pitiful this whole scene is, so I'm gonnie suffer the full ninety minutes.'

A strange and eerie silence descended on the Rangers side of the field in that eighty-ninth minute of the game, while from the opposite side of the ground a roar went up like an echo coming from nowhere. Their colours were hoisted too, scarves held aloft in outstretched hands tinting the entire terracing green. Celtic had scored.

The Rangers fans gritted their teeth as the songs came at them, the words bawled with the greatest of fervour.

> *Oh! Oh! Oh!*
> *We don't care what the Rangers say,*
> *What the hell do we care!*
> *For we only know that there's going to be a show,*
> *And the Glasgow Celtic will be there.*

That was it. With just one minute left of official playing time they turned with the others to leave.

'Right, boys,' said Alex. 'It was seven–one the last time for me. But one–nothing's just as bad. Come on . . . let's go. Who scored anyway?'

'Jinky Johnstone . . . he deserved it.'

'For Christ sake, Claney. You'll get us lynched.'

The three men merged with thousands of others from the huge sweep of the East End of the big stadium, traversing slowly along the slope to one of the passageways, then ascending the side of the bowl to a broad summit corridor leading to the head of the steep stairway down to ground level.

'It's straight from here back to Brig'ton,' said Sammy. 'Dying for a pint. Need something to take away the rotten taste of they pies.'

'Aye,' added Alex Mitchell, 'and that rotten whisky that guy gave us. I think they must have made it themselves.'

'Terrible what some people get up to . . . isn't it . . .'

They were never to hear all of Sammy's joke, they just caught the smile on his face as the shout went up, followed by the eruption of the loudest cheer of the day. It was a goal. The best of goals. The best of the very best of goals. A Rangers goal. A goal that meant they hadn't lost after all. They hadn't won either but it was more important that they were not defeated. Their Saturday had been rescued. The completion of their New Year celebrations could have real meaning now. A goal! A magnificent Rangers goal. The most dramatic of goals. A goal from Colin Stein that lifted their game from the realm of sport to that of high drama, coming as it did in the very final seconds of the last minute of the game. It was the stuff of Grand Opera.

Wild cheering and dancing, the jumps and kisses of joy, shook the Rangers End. But there was no turning back for the three men or any of the hundreds around them who would have loved to be part of it: they were by now engulfed in the one-way flow of exiting fans channelling into the corridor on the rim of the high terracing which led directly to Stairway 13.

Emptied of fans and seen from afar, the steep stairway could easily be mistaken for one of the new dry ski-slopes, such was its dramatic descent from the top of the high banking of the stadium's spectator terracing. Stairway 13 was the route by which they had entered and the principal entry/exit point for the fans who went to the Rangers End terrace of the stadium. It was a viciously short and steep decline, 100 feet in length, going down in a gradient of about two and a half to one. It was well-known to the fans. When there was a big crowd, like there was that day, the flow of people was such that no one had any control over movement. There was no deviating from the direction dictated by the concrete channel of the summit corridor along which the tightly packed crowd was flushed. They were a river of humans, churned in the rapids, waiting to be cascaded out of the stadium.

The pressure grew alarmingly as they approached the place where they would be funnelled on to the steep descent. Cries went up as fans in front realised they could no longer even struggle or push or shove others out of the way. Their arms were being straitjacketed to their sides. The mass was fused into a single force.

They said afterwards that it wasn't so much the disaster that had been waiting to occur as the catastrophe that *had to* occur. The single reason why it happened, they never discovered. The lad on top of the shoulders of his companion could have fallen, the one waving his jacket might have stumbled, or it could have been the fans who tried to turn and go back up the stairs when they heard the shout of 'goal'. Thereafter hundreds of people avalanched down the stairs en masse.

When the police and rescue workers moved in to clear the human mountain, they were confronted by a gruesome sight. In the middle of the heap of dead, dying and seriously injured there were ranks of fans standing silent and still, with faces twisted and hideously discoloured. Their bulging eyes stared ahead but saw nothing. They were all dead.

CHAPTER 46

OH SAMMY!

STAR WAS CONCERNED WHEN SHE HEARD THE news on the radio just after tea-time that evening. There had been an accident at the New Year game between Rangers and Celtic at Ibrox Stadium. A spectator had died and others were injured. Not long after that there was a newsflash saying there had been two deaths and many injured at the game and that there would be fuller details in subsequent bulletins. Later, in the main news, the announcer said gravely that reports were coming in of a 'major accident' at Ibrox. It was feared there had been 'a considerable number' of deaths. He went on to say that the death toll could be in excess of thirty and that hundreds had been injured.

Just after the second report she had tried phoning the police for information but all the lines were engaged. The moment she replaced the telephone it had rung. It was Bert Steed.

'Sammy was saying last week he was thinking of going to the game with Claney and Alex Mitchell. Did he go?'

'Oh, Bert, I'm out of my mind sitting here waiting on him to call. Yes, he went with the others to the game. He left early. They were going to make a day of it. He didn't know when he'd be back and I wasn't to worry about food or anything for him. After hearing the news I was sure he'd call to let me know everything was all right. If he wasn't involved he must have heard about the accident. Oh, Bert, you don't think . . .?'

He assured her that there would be thousands there and that Sammy's chances of being caught up in it would be minimal. The news reports had been sketchy about details of the accident. They speculated about the likelihood of some kind of crowd disturbance or the possibility that one of the stands might have collapsed.

It was nine o'clock when Steed phoned again.

'Star . . . I know you'd have phoned if you'd heard. No news I take it?'

'Not a word, Bert. I'll have to go to the police. This wait is killing me.'

'Give me ten minutes. I'll pick you up and we'll go together.'

They were directed to the Stipendiary Magistrate's Court building near Glasgow Cross where, they were told, there would be details of all the dead and injured. Neither had experienced anything like it. Together with others who feared for friends and relatives, they took their place in the public gallery of the courtroom while from the bench, in the place where the gowned magistrate would normally sit, a plain-clothes police officer was methodically reading aloud lists that had been compiled, giving as much detail as possible of the dead and injured who still awaited identification.

Star held Steed's arm tightly as they sat and listened to what seemed an unending roll of victims' descriptions.

'Injured. Male . . . youth of about seventeen years . . . fair hair . . . brown casual jacket . . . blue Rangers scarf . . . tattoo of a rose and the word "Mother" on the left forearm.'

There was a commotion in the middle of the room as a woman and some other relatives got up, one of the men shouting loudly, 'Aye. Aye . . . that's our boy.' And they were led away.

'Dead. Middle-aged male . . . six foot . . . heavily built . . . dark moustache . . . small scar on left of forehead . . . signet ring with initials BRC . . .'

There were some quiet whispers but no response from any in the gallery and the policeman on the bench moved on to the next victim.

'Dead. Youth . . . five foot eight inches . . . age between fourteen and sixteen years . . . dark, curly hair . . . jeans and navy blue sweater . . . keyring with the word Rothesay . . .'

'Oh Christ . . . oh Christ . . .' a woman sobbed. The policeman continued reading.

'. . . Small thistle tattoo on right upper arm and the words "Scotland Forever".'

The sobbing woman gave a loud, piercing scream, and shouted again and again, 'It's my Billy . . . my Billy . . . oh, no, my wee boy Billy.'

Two women police officers quickly moved in to help her from the court. The man on the bench read on.

'Dead . . . young male . . . twenty to twenty-five years . . . medium build, five foot seven inches . . . jeans, Scotland team jersey, Rangers scarf, woollen cap and navy anorak with the Scotland team badge and the number 105 in bold lettering on the inside pocket.'

'That's his,' said a middle-aged woman, sitting with two men. 'It's my Jim's. That's my Jim's jacket.'

Her senses didn't want to come to grips with the reality. All she could do was say over and over again as they led her out that the jacket belonged to her son.

The man on the bench went on to the next on his list.

'Dead . . . elderly male . . .'

Star stiffened where she sat, grasping Steed's arm in a steely grip.

'. . . Grey hair, plain grey suit, grey pullover, blue nap coat . . .'

'Oh, Bert . . . no . . . tell him to stop . . .'

'. . . Velvet collar on the coat with the label Paisley's.'

While a policewoman comforted Star, Steed went forward to the big table in front of the bench where a clerk handed him a slip of paper on which there were some details and the number '55'. He also said that a car would take them the short distance to the City Mortuary.

The small red-brick building beside the High Court building had never known such a crowd. Hundreds were gathered outside the door, awaiting the return of relatives and friends who had been admitted to identify sons or fathers or brothers. There were harrowing cries as grim-faced men and women came out of the building with the news that they had recognised loved ones.

Star insisted on accompanying Steed into the building, but once inside, Steed prevailed on her to stay in the little chapel area, crowded with other women who were waiting, while he was led away by a uniformed policeman.

An attendant took the slip of paper and explained, 'He's with the overflow in the post-mortem room.'

Bert was visibly affected as he entered the big room to see the anonymous, white-shrouded bundles, more than a dozen of them, lying on the floor. 'Over here,' beckoned the attendant, bending over a particular corpse before throwing back the sheet to expose the white, naked body.

Steed stared for about a minute before responding to the policeman who had accompanied him. The experience had profoundly shocked him. It was the whiteness of the corpse, so white it seemed almost translucent, as though it wasn't of flesh at all but of some strange synthetic covering stretched tightly over an assembly of bones that had once been a man, contrasting so vividly with the face which, when the life had been squeezed from its body, had contorted and discoloured with ugly crimson, scarlet and purple blotches.

He took one last look, nodded at the attendant and the covering sheet was replaced once more. It was too much for Bert Steed. When he returned to the small chapel he broke down and wept in Star's arms.

'Oh Star . . . Star. It wasn't him, Star. It wasn't Sammy. It was Claney.'

CHAPTER 47

ALIVE AND WELL

THEY TRACED SAMMY IN THE EARLY HOURS OF
the morning, after returning to the Stipendiary Magistrate's Court and enduring the agony of listening to fresh
lists of dead and injured. One of these new lists provided a
description which tallied with Sammy's. He had been
admitted to the Southern General Hospital. There was no
word of Alex Mitchell.

The Southern General was the nearest infirmary and
many had gone straight there in search of friends and
relatives who had not returned home. Every now and then,
a survivor, his wounds attended to, would be discharged
into the milling crowd outside, to be hugged, welcomed
and fussed over by relieved relatives as they helped him
away. Listening to the accents, it struck Star that this was
not just a Glasgow disaster. There were lots of Fifers – you
could always pick out their sing-song speech. There were
others from Edinburgh and Ayrshire. It was a night that
affected all of Scotland.

As they approached the small room where they had been
told Sammy would be, an elegantly dressed woman in an
expensive fur-collared Burberry came out looking obviously
distressed. A duty nurse confirmed that they had come to

the right room but insisted they wait for the Sister before going in.

There were four patients in the room. The Sister led them to a bed in the far corner by a window. The first sight of Sammy gave Star a shock and Bert put an arm round her.

'He looks terrible,' she whispered.

There was an oxygen tank on a trolley next to his bed but it was his colour, a greyish, unnatural pallor, which shocked Star. The sight of him lying there under the crinkled plastic sheet of the oxygen tent was a surreal experience. It seemed impossible to tell whether he was alive or dead.

In fact Sammy Nelson was presumed dead when first extricated from the horrific mound near the bottom of Ibrox's Stairway 13. But a paramedic had noted a flicker of life and Sammy was rushed to hospital.

After some time a harassed doctor, a young man in his early twenties, appeared. He spoke with the Sister first of all, then asked Star about her relationship to Sammy. He looked at the clipboard and said, 'He's an elderly man, but very fit. He is suffering from the effects of crushing but apart from that, little else. There are no bones broken and at this point we haven't ascertained internal injuries. We've been helping him through with an increased oxygen supply. He's being closely monitored and the good news is that there's been no deterioration in his condition since admission. He's in the best place . . . and I'm optimistic. Really, there's very little else I can say. We'll have a much clearer picture by tomorrow.'

He hurried away. Star and Bert returned to have another look at Sammy.

'It's his colour I don't like,' said Star. 'But still, when you consider what he must have been through . . .'

Sammy, together with his friends Claney and Alex Mitchell, had been engulfed in the human snowball that had rolled down Stairway 13. Mitchell had been pulled out first. Although they didn't know it, he was in a neighbouring ward with a broken arm.

Bert and Star decided there was nothing further they could do and that they would go home and meet again in the morning. But just as they were leaving the big hospital Star heard a man's voice call her name. It had a familiar ring, although she couldn't place it at first. It was Andrew Fordyce, the minister from Kirkconnel. He looked tired and strained and although he was more than surprised at seeing Star, he did not say so and instead inquired with obvious concern if she had a friend or relative who had been injured. He was sorry to hear her news.

'And who do you have that's here?'

'Some young lads from the village. I've found three of them so far – alive and well, thank God. But there's one lad we've still to find.'

'Were you in Glasgow or did you travel up specially?'

'Oh no, I came up as soon as I heard. There're always lads from the village at the game and I had to come to see how they were. I feel as responsible as anyone for them. But irrespective of that, seeing the impact of this terrible tragedy, I'd have come whether or not we'd local boys at the game. People like me have our uses at times like this, as I've found out tonight . . . I do hope your uncle recovers soon. You're very fond of him, Star.'

'More than you'd realise. I never knew my father and Sammy has been one to me all these years.'

'He's the one you mentioned to me, Star . . . the one who wanted to see me about . . . about something . . . all those years ago?'

'That's right. That was the same Sammy.'

'He must love you very much to have wanted to do what he intended.'

'Yes, Andrew. That's the kind of man he is.'

Star and Bert Steed returned to the infirmary the following day for the afternoon visiting hour. They walked together along the same corridors from the main door and eventually reached the room where they had seen Sammy. A Sister and some nurses were obviously busy in the ward. They knocked at the door of the small room and went in.

'Oh my God, Bert . . . he's not here.' The bed which Sammy had occupied the previous night was empty and neatly made up. Star quickly checked the other three patients, then turned and ran towards the Sister. 'Mr Nelson?' she asked anxiously. 'Mr Sammy Nelson? Where is he . . . please?'

The Sister smiled. 'Oh, we had a bit of a reorganisation this morning. Mr Nelson is in here now . . . at the top of the ward.'

'How is he, Sister?'

'You were here last night?'

'That's right.'

'Well, I think you'll get a surprise. Second last bed on the left at the top of the ward.'

As they approached the bed Star recognised the same well-dressed woman who had looked so worried and upset as she left the smaller room the previous night. She was holding Sammy's hand and laughing. It was a completely different Sammy Nelson from the frail man in the oxygen tent they had left the night before. He was sitting up, wearing a laundered pyjama jacket. His hair had been combed and he was looking remarkably fresh and fit.

'I don't believe it,' said Star, dabbing away a tear after she had been kissed by Sammy. 'What a difference! It's just amazing. I was so depressed after seeing you last night.'

'I know,' said the woman in an accent that suggested West End old money. When Star turned to her she introduced herself as Mrs Dalziel, quickly adding, 'It's Dorothy.' Then they both looked at Sammy again. Star asked him for details of his remarkable recovery.

'The doctor told me all about it this morning,' he explained. 'You see, I was in an oxygen tent only last night.'

'Yes, we know,' Star cut in.

'But apparently I came to in the early hours. Then they found nothing wrong with me. I just had the stuffing knocked out of me and apart from my chest being all bruised, I'm fine.' He flashed a roguish smile. 'Star, you'd better put a bet on for me today. With this kind of luck, I'm on for anything.'

They asked if he had heard about the others and he said he had been told about Claney. Alex Mitchell had visited him earlier in the day before being discharged, his broken arm being his only injury.

'Claney was so happy about everything yesterday. We'd gone up town to do some shopping and he insisted on going to Paisley's 'cause he wanted a coat like mine . . . you know that blue nap one with the velvet collar? Well, he got the last one in the shop. Said he'd be the talk of Kearny when he got back wearing it.'

'That explains why we thought *you* were dead.' Star told him the story of the description they had been given, which had included the coat among the clothing.

'You know, even after I regained consciousness in here I'd no idea what I'd been through,' said Sammy. 'The papers this morning made it real. Don't ask me how I survived, Star. All I can recall is the shouting, pushing and shoving, then I remember going head over heels . . . and nothing after that. Don't know how they got me out, who got me out, how I got here . . . nothing. I remember wakening up. I couldn't figure out where I was till a lovely wee nurse told me there'd been a terrible accident and I should get some sleep. I just did as she said, turned over and had a good night's sleep. Then another lovely wee lassie came in this morning and helped me to shave and get all scrubbed up. But poor Claney. Everything was

358

going so well for him over by in Kearny. They're going to get a helluva shock when they hear the news.'

He stared straight ahead. Dorothy turned to Star.

'You must be wondering why I'm here. Sammy and I have become friends. You see, we're near neighbours. You'll know my house, of course – Sammar.'

'*Our* Sammar?'

'That's right. We bought it when Sammy here left for the United States. My late husband just adored the place.'

'What she's not telling you,' interrupted Sammy, in his best done-it-all, South Side accent, 'is that I saw her clipping some roses one day in her garden and said, "Missus – d'you know it was me that planted them?" And she says, "Oh, were you the gardener?"'

Dorothy closed her eyes in mock embarrassment, then laughed and playfully slapped his arm.

It was Sammy who first saw the minister approach his bed. 'Good afternoon, Reverend.'

Star looked round quickly and, smiling warmly, said, 'Oh, it's you, Andrew.'

Sammy was surprised Star knew the minister but before he could say anything she quickly introduced him as a friend from Kirkconnel where she had once lived. Andrew Fordyce told them that the fans from Kirkconnel were safe and had all been accounted for. Then they spoke about the terrible tragedy of the night before, Sammy going over his story of how by some miracle he had emerged from the middle of that horrendous pile of dead and dying. He told him too about the death of Claney, his close friend, and how he would have to do something about organising his funeral. 'He's got no relatives here, you see . . . his wife Sadie, his two kids and the grandchildren, they're all in America.'

'I'd like to help if I may,' replied Andrew Fordyce. 'It's much easier for someone with my job . . .'

CHAPTER 48

CLANEY

IT WAS A WEEK OF GREAT SADNESS IN SCOTLAND as the dead were returned to their home communities for burial. There had been a special mass at St Andrew's Roman Catholic Cathedral in Glasgow, and the composition of its congregation was to make it a unique occasion for a Catholic church in Scotland. The photographers vied with one another for the shots every reader would want to see in their papers the following morning . . . those of the star Rangers players with their coach Jock Wallace, manager Willie Waddell and chairman John Lawrence all standing together inside a Catholic chapel.

It should have been taken for granted, of course, but it wasn't. When it was Protestant versus Roman Catholic in Glasgow and the West of Scotland, nothing was taken for granted. Even the national newspaper had said in its leader column that 'years ago this would have been unthinkable' and that 'regrettably there are still among us many who cannot wholly forget their prejudices' – comments that were in the best tradition of understatement.

Because of the fact that the majority of the victims were boys and teenagers and that star footballers and varied dignitaries were among the mourners, many of the funerals were witnessed by huge crowds. But the funeral of Jimmy

McLean, the man everyone knew as Claney, was limited to a small coterie of his nearest and dearest life-long friends. Some, like Sammy Nelson, had known him since he was a young man in the days just after the First World War.

Andrew Fordyce, the minister, kept his word about giving what help he could for Claney's funeral and made most of the necessary arrangements. He went to Pollok-shields to visit Sammy, who had been released from the Southern General Hospital two days after the disaster. As he would be conducting the funeral service, he said he wanted to know something of Claney's background.

'I'll tell you something about Claney,' Sammy said. 'Do you know anything about the military life?'

'Yes . . . a bit. I was in the war with the HLI.' After a pause he added with a smile as he pulled at his minister's collar, 'And I most definitely wasn't wearing one of these.'

'Well then, you'll know something about what Claney went through. He did one of the bravest things you could imagine during the war. He was a deserter. I know that doesn't sound right. What's it you say . . . a contradiction in terms? You see, Reverend, Claney never ran away from anything in his life. And that's how brave he must have been when he made that decision to be a deserter.'

He told the minister how Claney had been a Sapper with the Royal Engineers, engaged in mine-clearing operations prior to the big British offensive in the North African desert. 'He only spoke about it once and I'm probably the only one who knew the full story.

'They'd go out at night – it was always night 'cause they were under enemy fire as well as having to walk across the minefields. A platoon of about twenty men, all of them mates, would go out each night and they'd be allotted a particular section to clear. In the morning, when they went back to camp, there'd be a roll call. It was only then you learned which of your mates had been killed. When they were sweeping in the minefields, every now and then they'd hear a bang. That was one of their mates getting blown to pieces. They'd been operating like that for weeks. Then one evening when they were having the roll call before going out on a sweep Claney looked around at the men in the platoon. The realisation of it all struck home to him. Not one of his original mates was left in that platoon. They'd all been killed. It shattered him when he thought about it 'cause the logic of it all was that it *had* to be his turn next. He thought he was going to crack up right there and then unless he did something. And that something was deserting.

'He'd done his bit, Mr Fordyce. More than his bit. It must have taken real guts for him to take the decision he did . . . and to do it where he did, right there in North Africa. Just think about it, getting from North Africa to here in wartime without being discovered! But Claney did it. I won't go into all the details, but believe me that's some story on its own . . .

'The Military Police came hunting for him in the Gorbals all during the rest of the war and for years he was on the run. He couldn't have an identity card, ration books, clothing coupons or employment cards. He had nothing. He couldn't even stay with his family for fear of the police. He was strictly on his own. But, trust Claney, he made out. He used to make and sell coal briquettes. Collected the dust from the big coal rea in the Gorbals. A pal in the building trade used to bring him home wee bags of cement every night and he'd set up his wee briquette factory in the back courts of houses around the Gorbals. One week it'd be in Thistle Street, another Florence Street, then Lawmoor Street . . . always on the move. But that was Claney in business and making himself a living. He used to sell sticks as well as briquettes. Did they have stick men where you came from?'

Fordyce shook his head.

'Well, the stick men sold wee bundles of chopped wood,

neatly tied with string, to be used as kindlers. They went round the doors selling to housewives. He used to get the wood for nothing, cadging it at joiners' yards or using old boxes. Claney was the original survivor.

'He was still on the run from the military when he came to work for me. I was in a variety of, eh, enterprises you might call them, and I'd never have been successful if I hadn't had a right-hand man like Claney. We'd quite a few adventures, I can tell you, but I think they'd be best kept out of whatever you're going to say at the funeral . . .!

'I'll tell you something, Reverend. Not many came out of the same mould as Claney. I certainly don't know any that're left. He knew the Gorbals back then, forty years ago, when things were really tough. Aye, "great days", "happy days" you hear some of the old yins saying when they have a crack about those times. But there was little great or happy about them, Mr Fordyce. The only great and happy things were the people themselves . . . the rest was surviving. You'd to be something special to survive the hardships and escape from them. People laugh and think you're kidding when you tell them things like that now-adays, but that's the way it was. We were a sort of fodder for the upper classes . . . the pennies and shillings we paid as rents for sub-standard houses made their fortunes. And when they wanted a war, they just had to say the word and off we went with never a question of whether it was right or wrong. We were useful: we were always there, there were plenty of us and we were cheap. You've to understand all these things to understand what kind of person Claney was.

'And, do you know, despite the kind of background he had, there was no bigotry in him? When I was in the hospital I was thinking how sad it was for Claney to go like that because one of the last things he'd have heard in life was all these men standing around him shouting the vilest abuse across the park. Claney couldn't take that. He told me that's why he enjoyed Kearny so much . . . that's the place in the States where he was living. Just as well he didn't take it too seriously. If he had he wouldn't be going to his grave the happy man he was. Do you think that lets you know a wee bit about our Claney, Reverend?'

'Yes . . . I think I know and appreciate what Claney was about now. As you say, a brave man. A very brave man. I'm so sorry I didn't have the privilege which you had of sharing his friendship. That's obviously been a most satisfying experience in your life.'

'You put that nicely, Reverend.'

CHAPTER 49

CONFESSIONS

THE SUBJECT OF DOROTHY DALZIEL, THE NEW
woman in Sammy's life, wasn't raised until after Claney's
funeral. Star teased him. 'That was a bit of a surprise, you
old rascal, when Mrs Dalziel turned up the hospital. So
how long have you been keeping her a secret from me?'

Sammy smiled at the suggestion. 'She's not a secret. At
least, she wasn't meant to be a secret. I just thought there
was no point in mentioning her if it wasn't going to be
serious.'

'What do you mean, serious?'

'You know fine well what I mean . . . now it's you that's
being the rascal.'

'Well, that still doesn't answer the question. Is it
serious?'

'Well, we didn't know . . . did we? That's why I never
said anything to you. No point in me telling you about
every woman that I meet.'

'So you meet women fairly regularly?'

'More than you'd imagine, you teasing wee besom.
Talking to me like my old mother. Anyway, the Ibrox
business certainly let us know just how we felt about each
other. As soon as she heard about it she went straight to
the Southern General, thinking I might be there, which

turned out to be right. I suppose you'd call it a classic example of woman's intuition.'

'Yes, we saw her that night. She really looked upset. She seems a very nice person. When's the wedding?'

'Trust you! Trust women! A couple just get to know each other and the first thing they're asking is . . . when's the wedding? Star, we haven't even discussed anything like that. Mr Dalziel died of a coronary just a few months ago and two of their children are quite young. She says it'd upset them terribly if another man was introduced to the house so soon. And I can accept that. The truth is, Dorothy's a friend. I appeared in a time of need, I suppose, and for one reason or another we seem to enjoy each other's company. But that's the end of the story . . . so far. Who knows what the future holds? Anyway, I know you hate it when I raise the subject, but what about yourself? I keep telling you, that boy needs a father.'

Normally that line of conversation would end there, but for a change Star had something she wanted to say. 'Sammy, I've been meaning to tell you, but I've been fearful of what you might say . . . or even do.'

'Tell me, love.'

'It's about Andrew . . . Andrew Fordyce, the minister.'

Sammy took hold of her hand. 'Star, dear. I know everything.'

She looked up at him in great surprise. 'How . . . who told you?'

'The boy did himself. We'd a long talk yesterday about Claney and when we'd finished he said there was something he wanted to tell me. What a shock I got – I never for a second connected the Reverend Fordyce with the young soldier I'd been out to kill. He told me the whole story, going right back to the very beginning . . . the night he and his brother . . . his father committing suicide . . . about the time he had come to see you in the Gorbals.

'Fate could so easily have taken another course, Star.

Remember? Andrew was to have met you coming out of your work in the clothing factory and if he hadn't had that emergency recall to his regiment for the Berlin Air Lift it'd have been me he'd have met ... and I was carrying a Mauser pistol.'

'I'll never forget that night, Sammy. It was the very first time I met you ... Goodness, I didn't even realise I had an Uncle Sammy, and almost immediately you tell me you've been out trying to kill Andrew Fordyce. I couldn't believe that you wanted to kill somebody for someone you hadn't even met.'

'And I said I'd gone to do it because you were family. Gorbals family. My brother's very own lassie. Touch one of us Nelsons and you touch us all. That's why I'd gone for him ... but you know all that. Anyway, Andrew told me everything, and that took some guts. I hold nothing against the boy now. In fact, I've got nothing but admiration for him. Claney would be right proud if he knew it was someone like that who'd be conducting the service at his funeral.'

'So it won't shock you to know that I've been invited to Kirkconnel next weekend. Andrew has asked me down to meet his mother ... we haven't seen each other since ...'

'Aye, I know. He told me that as well.'

'And ...?'

Sammy smiled. 'Oh my God, lassie, do you think I'm blind or something? Don't you think I saw the look on your face that day he came over to my bed in the Southern General? That's only the second time I've ever seen you like that. But you're not going to get me asking about the wedding, like a woman ... you'll tell me the minute you know!'

He kissed her on the cheek and held her to him in a warm embrace.